SUCH SWEET SORROW

Catrin Collier

CENTURY

Published by Century Books in 1996

3 5 7 9 10 8 6 4 2

© Catrin Collier 1996

First published in the United Kingdom by

Century Books
Random House UK Limited
20 Vauxhall Bridge Road, London, SW1V 2SA

Random House Australia (Pty) Limited
20 Alfred Street, Milsons Point, Sydney,
New South Wales 2061, Australia

Random House New Zealand Limited
18 Poland Road, Glenfield
Auckland 10, New Zealand

Random House South Africa (Pty) Limited
PO Box 337, Bergvlei, South Africa

Random House UK Limited Reg. No. 954009
A CIP catalogue record for this book
is available from the British Library

Papers used by Random House UK Limited are natural, recyclable
products made from wood grown in sustainable forests.
The manufacturing processes conform to the environmental
regulations of the country of origin.

ISBN 0 7126 7508 6

Typeset by Pure Tech India Ltd, Pondicherry
Printed and bound in Great Britain by
Mackays of Chatham plc, Chatham, Kent

For the Welsh Guards who suffered heavy casualties while fighting the rearguard at Dunkirk; and for Sergeant Edgar Carter, RASC, who returned to spend so many happy years with his beloved Peggy.

Acknowledgements

I would like to thank all those people who have so generously shared their memories with me during the year I spent writing and re-searching this account of Pontypridd during the war.

Mr Romeo Basini of Treorchy who first told me about the intern-ment of the Italians during the Second World War and the sinking of the *Arandora Star*.

My parents Glyn and Gerda Jones, my husband John, and my children, Ralph, Sophie and Ross for their love and support, and for giving me the time to write this book.

Margaret Bloomfield for her friendship and help in ways too numerous to mention.

As always, I also owe a great debt of gratitude to Mrs Lindsay Morris and the staff of Pontypridd Library, especially the archivist, Mrs Penny Pugh, and Mr Brian Davies and the staff of Pontypridd Historical Centre for their unstinting professional assistance.

Beth Humphries for the superb professional job she always does in copy-editing my manuscripts.

And above all my editor Mary Loring for all her suggestions and being there whenever I needed to talk, and my agent Michael Thomas for his help and encouragement.

And while gratefully acknowledging the assistance of everyone I would like to stress that any errors are entirely mine.

Thank you.

Catrin Collier
Swansea, July 1995

Chapter One

'D^AMN and . . .'

'Less of your language, William Powell.' Fumbling blindly for the wall to her left, Tina Ronconi braced herself and stooped to help William from the pavement. It wasn't easy. A fine drizzle obscured what little light they might have hoped for from the moon. She couldn't see anything other than the pale glimmer of the white handkerchief she'd pinned to the lapel of her coat, and the even fainter, intermittent white line painted on to the kerb.

'That's my leg you've got hold of, not my arm,' he complained irritably.

'Why are you upside down?'

'Because some dull clot put their ashbin out for innocent people to fall over,' came the muffled reply.

'Stop fooling around.'

'I am not fooling around. I'm trying to stop the bin from rolling down the hill and waking half the Graig. What a stupid place to put it.'

'Outside the front door ready for the ashman?' Tina suggested mildly.

'They should have waited until morning. Don't they know how dark it is in a blackout?' As he managed to right the bin, the lid escaped his clutches and rolled noisily, clattering over the pavement into the road. A sash window slammed open behind them.

'When you've *quite* finished having a party out there, some people are trying to sleep!'

'And others could walk home in peace if idiots didn't set booby traps on the pavements for them to trip over.'

'Is that you, William Powell?'

'Mrs Roberts!' William switched to his charm-laden, market sales-patter voice. 'You sound lovely in the dark. If Mr Roberts isn't around I'll serenade you. Would you like something romantic or patriotic?'

'I'll serenade your backside in a minute, boy.'

I

'Sorry, Mr Roberts, didn't know you were home.'

'And where else would I be at this hour of the night?'

'You made me promise never to tell.'

'Why you . . .'

Another window crashed open further down the street. William grabbed Tina's hand and hauled her up the hill before the argument escalated.

'This is hopeless,' Tina cried as William led them into a lamp-post. She stopped for a moment, straining her eyes into the darkness in the hope of recognising a familiar shadow in the gloom. 'I'll bring a torch tomorrow.'

'Dai Station will only yell at you to switch it off the minute he sees it, even if you point it at your feet and wrap the regulation two sheets of tissue paper around the lens. If you ask me the ARP wardens in Ponty are training to join the Nazis. Haven't you noticed how they're all growing moustaches and practising the goose step? It's a ploy to encourage boys to volunteer. You can't beat up the ARPs, lads, but we'll give you a crack at the next-best thing.'

'You'd better not let Dai Station hear you saying that.'

'Why not? It may give him the inspiration he needs to join up and do some real fighting instead of reporting little old ladies for showing chinks of light when they put the cat out at night.' Blocking her path he drew her towards him. 'Mind you,' he reached out, feeling for her face with his fingertips. 'The blackout has some advantages.'

'Not here, Will.' She ducked under his arm as he bent his head to hers.

'As it's blacker than a coal hole everywhere, what's the difference between here and there?' he grumbled as she caught his hands in hers, tucked her arm into his, and forced him to carry on walking up the hill towards her home in Danycoedcae Road.

'A lot. It won't take Tony long to close the café. He and Diana will be right behind us.'

'As they can't see any more than we can, they won't know the difference between us and a pair of tomcats.'

'Perhaps we ought to walk in the middle of the road,' she suggested after hitting her ankle painfully on a raised doorstep.

'You want to get knocked down by a car?'

'We'd hear it.'

'Not necessarily before it clouted us. Ouch!' He reeled into her, almost knocking her off her feet.

'What was that?'

'Another ashbin jumped out and attacked me.'

'Not much further,' she consoled.

'What's the point in getting there when you won't even give me a goodnight kiss to make up for all this suffering.'

'You're not suffering any more than I am.'

'But I will be. You live further up the hill than me. I could have turned up Graig Avenue by the vicarage. Instead here I am, risking life and limb, not to mention the walk back down Iltyd Street . . .'

'Have you had your registration papers?' she interrupted sharply as they turned the corner. She'd waited for an opportune moment to ask him the question all evening, but despite the atmosphere of pessimism, the war and the blackout, the café she helped her older brother Tony to run had been busier than usual. Tony and her younger brother Angelo who worked in the kitchen hadn't been able to dispense with her services for a moment. But even if she could have stolen a few minutes away from the counter and till, William hadn't left the table where he'd played cards with a crowd of boys from the Graig until closing time.

'They came yesterday morning.'

Neither the casual tone of his disembodied voice nor the light squeeze he gave the fingers she'd tucked into the crook of his elbow fooled her. 'And?'

'There's no "and" about it. I don't think the army is into accepting excuses like, "I'm otherwise engaged for the duration." '

'You can go back down the pit. Everyone says they'll soon be making mining a protected occupation.'

'For good reason. It's worse than a battlefield down there.'

'More men get killed on a battlefield than down the pit,' she retorted tartly, shivering at the thought of him leaving Pontypridd – and her – possibly for ever.

'I'll take my chances on a battlefield any day.'

'You can't mean that?'

For once he dropped his baiting, bantering tone. 'I've never told anyone this before, but I wasn't that sorry when the pits closed. Living on bread, scrape and charity seemed a small price to pay for being able to breathe fresh air and walk around in daylight. That's why I jumped at the chance of working for Charlie when he offered me a job, and why I'll carry on working in his shop, no matter how much they up the money in the pits.'

'But going into the army will mean leaving the shop.'

'That can't be helped.'

'But Charlie will never manage without you . . .'

He laughed briefly. 'The way prices are being controlled and

3

rationing is beginning to affect profits, half of the shopkeepers in town will be forced to lay off staff. No matter how philanthropic they'd like to be, no businessman can afford to pay an assistant to stand behind a counter when there's nothing to sell.'

'I know what you mean. Tony registered our three cafés with the council weeks ago, but we still haven't been told how much food we're going to be allocated, and Papa says they're soon going to have to ration everything, not just bacon, ham, butter and sugar.'

'Let's forget the war for five minutes and talk about us.' He halted at the white cross her father had painted on the wall outside his house.

'How can there be an us, if you're going away?'

He wrapped his arms around her, burying his face in her beret and hair. The cooking aromas of the café vied with the clean, fresh fragrances of soap and eau-de-Cologne. He had met Tina on their first day in Maesycoed Infants school, and announced to his mother that evening that he intended to marry her. But it was only now, when they were closer to being separated than Tina knew, that he realised just how much he did love her.

'The last thing that's going to be needed in this war are butchers,' he began awkwardly, trying to pave the way for what he had to tell her. 'The kind that joint animals, anyway,' he continued drily.

'So what are you going to do?' Her heart was hammering so violently she wondered that he couldn't hear it. She already suspected the answer to her question. She'd overheard her brothers whispering early that morning and noticed that her father's copy of the *Western Mail* was missing from his chair. The same copy she'd seen the advertisement in.

WELSH GUARDS

VOLUNTEERS REQUIRED NOW FOR THE WELSH GUARDS. AGE 20–35. HEIGHT 5FT. 9INS OR OVER.

MEN CAN PRESENT THEMSELVES FOR ENLISTMENT AT ALL RECRUITING CENTRES. ENQUIRIES WILL BE ANSWERED AT ALL POLICE STATIONS.

MEN REGISTERED TO BE CALLED UP UNDER NATIONAL SERVICE, BUT NOT ALREADY CALLED, MAY ENLIST NOW IN THE WELSH GUARDS.

ENLISTMENT ON NORMAL ENGAGEMENT OR FOR THE DURATION OF THE WAR.

It was the phrase MEN REGISTERED TO BE CALLED UP UNDER NATIONAL SERVICE, BUT NOT ALREADY CALLED that had caught her eye. William's cousin Eddie had written home about his life in the Guards, not exactly in glowing terms, but with an obvious pride in his successful

4

completion of an arduous training course that had equipped him to do a dangerous, necessary and vital job – in France. She'd seen the look in William's eye as he'd passed Eddie's letters around the café. He and Eddie were close, and good friends of both her brothers, and joining the Guards was probably the only way the boys would be able to guarantee that they'd be allowed to serve together.

'Well seeing as how I've got to go some time soon anyway – '

'You've joined up, haven't you?' she broke in, unable to bear the suspense a moment longer.

'We decided it would be better to join the Welsh Guards together than wait until they called us and run the risk of being split up and sent God knows where among the English.'

Her mouth went dry. The darkness that swirled around her was suddenly tinged with red. None of her suspicions had prepared her for this terrible certainty.

'You did it today? Not just you, but Tony and Angelo as well?' Resentment boiled inside her, not just over William's defection, but Tony's and Angelo's. Just who did they think was going to run the cafés now?

'Yes,' he answered quietly.

'That's why you all went out together this morning?'

He bent his head and kissed her forehead. Because of the darkness she couldn't tell whether he'd meant to kiss her there, or on her lips. 'It makes sense, love.'

'No it doesn't. It doesn't make sense for any of you to go.'

'It's not as though we want to . . .'

'Oh yes, you do,' she contradicted bitterly. 'You might say you don't, but just look at the lot of you! You haven't a brain between you! You can't even wait for them to come and get you, you have to volunteer. What do you think war is? A picnic in France with continental girls fawning all over you? Soldiers get shot. They die!'

'I know what war is. My father got killed in the last one, remember?'

'Then you've less reason to go than anyone. Your family has paid the price once; don't break your mother's heart a second time. Please, Will, stay and work in the pit,' she begged, refusing to accept that it was already too late for him to change his mind. 'They'll win this war whether you go or not.'

'None of us are stupid enough to believe that we're important in the scheme of things, but we've no choice. Can't you see that? All of us are going to be called up – this month – next month – it's only a matter of time. And as we've got to go, we prefer to go together.'

'So it's better to get killed in crowds? Is that what you're saying?'

'No, but having a mate around can make a difference. My father joined up with half the men from the Graig. When he died Bob Roberts from Danygraig Street was with him.'

'And you want Eddie, Tony and Angelo to hold your hand when you get killed?'

'I've no intention of getting killed.'

'I bet every soldier who's ever marched away has said that.'

'Eddie says the biggest danger in France is being hit on the head by a leaflet dropped from a German plane. As soon as we've done our training we'll be sent to join him, and just the threat of a trained force stationed across the German border will be enough to make Hitler back down. You'll see.' He'd read a similar sentiment in a newspaper, and although he didn't really believe it, he repeated it in the hope that it would deflect Tina's anger. He loved her, but he was very wary of her one and only shortcoming – the infamous and explosive Ronconi temper.

'Then go. The lot of you – but don't come crying to me when you get killed!' Blinded by tears as well as darkness, she turned abruptly on her heel and felt for the gap in the wall that marked the step that led to her front door.

'Tina, please . . .'

'Don't Tina me!'

He put his arm around her shoulders and dragged her back into the shelter of the wall. 'I would have had to go sooner or later, you know that.'

'But not now,' she cried.

'My going won't make any difference to us. You know I love you.'

'No I don't.'

'I'm telling you now.'

For the first time she was glad of the darkness. He'd always been far too adept at reading the expressions on her face. 'How am I supposed to know you love me when you've never told me?'

'I assumed you knew.'

'Assumed! I thought you were just passing time with me, like that Vera Collins.'

'It's always been serious between you and me,' he broke in indignantly. Vera Collins was a married woman he'd had a brief affair with, an incident he'd long since relegated to ancient history, but unfortunately one Tina never failed to resurrect every time they argued.

'Ssh!' Locking her hands around his neck, she stood on tiptoe and kissed his cheek. He crushed her against him with a fervour that belied

6

the separation to come. Almost as though he could hold on to her by simply clasping her as tight, and for as long as humanly possible. But the embrace, far from reassuring, only served to remind Tina that he would soon be gone.

Summoning all her strength, she thrust him away. 'When will you have to go?'

'I'm not sure. Next week, perhaps the week after.'

'You didn't think to ask?'

'The recruiting officer couldn't tell us. You will wait for me?'

'You expect me to wait around for years . . .'

'It won't take years.'

'Don't tell me you're one of those fools who believe the war will be over by Christmas?'

'Not Christmas, but by then we'll have pushed out over the French border and have Jerry on the run.'

'That's not what Papa thinks. He knows someone who travelled through Germany last summer. He told us that the Germans have built up a huge war machine. That their army is already trained, and they have factories working flat out producing arms. What do we have? Gas masks, rationing and sandbags? We're not going to beat anyone with those.'

'Whose side is this friend of your father's on?'

'Ours, of course.'

'Italian or Welsh?'

'The Italians are neutral.'

'Non-combative,' William corrected, recalling the stance Mussolini had taken when the Germans and Russians marched into Poland.

'What's the matter with you? Tony and Angelo joined up alongside you, didn't they?'

'They're Welsh.'

'And Italian,' she countered. 'We're both, and proud of it.'

'There's no reason why you shouldn't be. I wasn't accusing you of anything.'

'I didn't say you were,' she capitulated, ashamed of her touchiness. 'How many others are going with you?'

'Glan Richards from next door, Charlie . . .'

'Russian Charlie?' Tina was shocked. William's boss who had an unpronounceable name had been christened Charlie by a market wag when he'd opened a stall in Pontypridd. He hadn't been married a year, and she couldn't see his wife, Alma, being very happy at the thought of losing her husband before they'd even celebrated their first wedding anniversary.

7

'He said now he's married Alma, he's more Welsh than anything else, and if Wales is fighting a war then so is he.'

'Against his own kind?'

'We're not fighting the Russians.'

'They marched into Poland like the Germans, didn't they? I'm surprised that the recruiting office let Charlie join up.'

'They haven't yet,' William answered evasively not wanting to get sidetracked into discussing the hard time Charlie had been given by the senior officer.

'And your Uncle Evan?'

'The pit manager's already warned him that they won't let him go. Experienced miners are worth their weight in gold now that war's been declared. You still haven't answered my question,' he reminded her, deliberately drawing the conversation back to personal matters.

'You want me to sit at home and wait for you, while you go to France and have a whale of a time with French girls who don't know any better than to throw themselves at Welsh boys?'

'I had hoped we could choose an engagement ring before I go.'

William's matter-of-fact assumption that she would fit in with his plans kindled a blaze of conflicting emotions Tina could barely understand, let alone control. He'd been around as long as she could remember. He was tall, dark and far too good-looking for her peace of mind, with a wicked sense of humour that drove her to distraction, simply because most of the time she found it impossible to tell whether he was clowning or serious. But loving him hadn't blinded her to his shortcomings. He had an eye for other women. Vera Collins's son's black curly hair and dark eyes was proof enough of that, but fortunately for William, Vera's husband was either the forgiving or the stupid sort.

It had been hard enough to overlook William's philandering until now, when they had only been boy and girlfriend – if only he hadn't been going away – if she could have kept him in Pontypridd where she could watch him – if he hadn't already had at least one affair: there were simply too many 'ifs' in the equation. 'I don't want to get engaged to a man who may never come back,' she answered forcefully.

'You won't be, because I will be back.' He folded his arms around her once more. 'I can't remember a time when I didn't love you. All you have to do is turn your enormous, dark eyes on me to get anything you want that's mine to give. And you love me, Tina, almost as much as I love you. We're made for one another.' He caressed the back of her neck with his hands, curling the soft tendrils of hair around

8

his fingers. 'Do you remember the fight I had with Tony when I told him we were going to elope?'

'As we were six years old at the time I don't think we'd have got very far.'

'We would now.' He slid his hands down to her waist.

'Then let's elope, now. Tonight,' she suggested impulsively. 'I have some money, we could go to Gretna Green.'

'And if I get a letter from the army tomorrow?'

'You won't be here to receive it.'

'They'll come after me and charge me with desertion.'

'How can they do that, when you haven't been there to desert?'

'We'll get married the minute the war is over.'

'I could have grey hair by then.'

'No war can last that long.'

'It's not just the war. There's Mama and Papa. They've never liked the idea of you and me. If the war hadn't broken out Papa would have carried out his threat and sent me to Italy to marry a nice, Catholic, Italian boy.' She made it sound like a fate worse than death.

'They accepted your brother Ronnie marrying my cousin Maud, and she's Baptist and Welsh.'

'And they got married in an Anglican church and Papa wouldn't even go to the wedding. Sometimes I think it's just as well Ronnie carried Maud off to Italy the day after. Papa's hopelessly old-fashioned, he really does want all of us to marry Italians.'

'He's not having much luck in that department, is he?' William commented, thinking of Tina's elder sister Laura who was married to one of the local doctors, Trevor Lewis. 'You're not going to try and make up for his disappointment in Ronnie and Laura by marrying an Italian, are you?' he asked anxiously, wondering if there was a café-owning rival for Tina's hand that he was unaware of.

'No, but I don't want to get engaged to someone I might not see for ten years either.'

'A minute ago you wanted to elope.'

'A minute ago I wasn't thinking straight. The least you could have done was tell me you were going to join the Guards before you did.'

'I might have if I'd thought you'd be reasonable about it,' he asserted, furious with her for ignoring his offer to buy her an engagement ring.

'Reasonable – '

'Why do all Italians have such foul tempers?'

'You're the one who's shouting!'

Temper rising, William lifted his hat from his head and shook the raindrops from it. The only sound in the street was her quick breathing and the quiet patter of rain.

'Goodnight, Will.'

Turning sharply, he seized her and kissed her the way he'd wanted to all evening. Kissing and holding was as far as he'd ever gone with Tina, although there had been long walks around the deserted paths of Shoni's pond last summer when he'd burned to do a whole lot more, and would have, if she hadn't slapped his face.

'We could get married before you go?' she faltered when he finally released her. She had a sudden, dreadful, terribly real premonition that he would never come back. That this was all the time they were ever going to have. She loved him, would always love him, and wanted to prove it to him before he left, even if it meant spending the rest of her life a widow.

'No,' he answered swiftly.

'Why not?'

'Because I love you.'

'If you really loved me, you'd marry me. It would make everything more permanent, more settled than if we were engaged. We'd have something more than just the end of the war to look forward to.'

He searched his mind for words that would explain his feelings. How he'd been overwhelmed by trying to assume the responsibilities of the man of the house at four years of age. How he'd been forced to stand by and watch his mother struggle, not only to make ends meet and feed and clothe him and his sister, Diana, but also bear the loneliness that had settled like a blight, clouding her life after the arrival of the telegram that had brought the news of his father's death. He had seen the sadness and wistful yearning in his mother's smile whenever she had looked at his father's photograph, watched her sob her heart out on the anniversaries: his father's birthday – their wedding anniversary – the date of his death – Armistice day . . . He had slunk into the house more times than he could count with torn trousers and bruised knuckles from fighting boys who had repeated the rumours about his mother and any and every man she stopped to talk to; even – God forbid – his Uncle Evan who'd never had any thought in his head other than practical ones of how to help his brother's widow and children. He loved Tina far too much to risk putting her through anything like that.

'How can you love me and not want to marry me?' Her voice shattered the silence, reminding him that he hadn't voiced a single thought.

'I don't want you left alone.'

'I'd be just as alone when you leave, whether we marry or not.'

'But you wouldn't be left with a wedding ring and possibly a baby. You'd be free to look for another man.'

'And the thought of me with another man makes you happy?'

'Of course not, but . . .'

The door opened behind them and there was a swish of blackout curtains being dragged aside. 'Tina, you going to be out there all night?'

'No, Papa.'

'Time you were in bed, girl.'

'Evening, Mr Ronconi,' William called out.

A loud sniff was followed by the door slamming.

'We'll talk tomorrow.' Tina kissed him one last time before turning and feeling her way up the steps.

'I do love you, I really do,' he repeated despondently as she closed the door softly behind her.

'How come Angelo signed up for the Guards with you and Will?' Diana Powell asked Tony Ronconi as he checked the locks on the back door of the café. 'I thought they were advertising for men between the ages of twenty and thirty-five?'

'They are, but they decided to make an exception in Angelo's case.'

'Exception! He's only seventeen. He lied about his age, didn't he?'

'Lie is a strong word.'

'Does your father know?'

'No, but he will when I get home.'

'And if he won't let Angelo go?'

'Papa's no fool. He knows Angelo will have to go some time, and better he goes with me and Will to look after him than later by himself.'

'I'm not sure you two can look after yourselves, let alone Angelo.'

'We'll be fine.' He walked behind the counter and opened the door that led to the kitchen. 'I've locked the back door, Angelo. I'll lock the front on my way out.'

'Your turn to sleep here tomorrow,' Angelo shouted above the clatter of pans.

'As if I could forget it. Just make sure you're up by five to serve the early-shift tram crews.'

'Have I missed yet?'

'There's always a first time.' Tony followed Diana behind the curtain he'd hung in front of the door to comply with blackout regulations. 'Don't open the door for a moment,' he ordered, tussling with the folds of cloth in an attempt to reach her.

'I have to get home, work tomorrow.' She slipped through his restraining arms and darted out into the rain.

He closed the door behind him, turning the key in the lock before posting it back through the letterbox. His pulse was pounding, and his hands were damp from more than the rain. Although he would have walked barefoot over hot coals rather than admit it to his brother, or William, or Glan Richards, who assumed from the stories he'd spun of his exploits with women that he was far more experienced than he actually was, he was terrified at the thought of going to war and getting killed without ever having known what it was to sleep with a woman. And as he'd been 'courting' William's sister, Diana, since the summer, she was the obvious choice. Even if she exacted marriage as her price for bestowing the privilege.

The more he considered the idea of marriage, the more attractive it became. Diana was uncommonly, head-turningly pretty, in a brown, curly-haired, dark-eyed way that wasn't unlike the Italian ideal of beauty. She had a sweet nature and, unlike his sisters, an even temperament. He could quite happily spend the rest of his life with her, especially if it meant being able to sleep with her before he went away.

'You wouldn't be able to run away from me if we were married,' he blurted out suddenly, as he caught up with her under the railway bridge that marked the beginning of the Graig hill.

'Married!'

'Why not?' he broke in quickly. 'We've being going out for a while.' He put his arm around her waist. 'I'd like to stake a claim in case some other man decides to snap you up while I'm away.'

'I haven't even thought about it. I don't know what to say.'

'Try yes. We can get a ring, apply for a special licence, and marry before I go, or we could get engaged now and married when I get embarkation leave. The recruiting officer promised us that we'd have a break after our six weeks' training.'

'Do you want to marry me, or do you just want a wife before you go away?' she asked perceptively. It was the most tactful, if obtuse way she could think of phrasing a difficult question.

'There's no one else I want to marry. Come on Di, are you going to say yes, or no?'

'I don't know,' she answered hesitantly. 'I love you Tony, you know that. . . .' All she could think of was her secret. A corrosive, destructive secret she'd managed to keep hidden from most of the people who mattered, like her mother, Will, and Tony. But her boss,

Wyn Rees and Tony's sister Laura and her doctor husband, Trevor, knew about it. If she married Tony, would Laura tell him?

'Then that's settled. We'll see Father O'Donnelly tomorrow.'

'Father O'Donnelly? I'm Baptist.'

'Papa won't let me marry outside of the Catholic Church. You don't mind converting, do you?'

'No, but . . .'

'If you take instruction and work hard you should be ready by the time I finish my training.'

Diana's head was spinning. Tony's words echoed, alien and incomprehensible through the shrouding darkness. She couldn't think of anything except her secret. It wouldn't be fair to keep it from Tony, but once she told him, would he still want her? 'You're sleeping in the café tomorrow night?' She'd spoken in a whisper, but he understood her – perfectly.

'Yes.'

'If I stay with you for a while, will you walk me home afterwards?'

A lump rose in his throat. He hadn't expected this. Not from a decent girl like Diana. 'Are you sure you want to stay?'

She clung to his arm. 'Yes.'

'Then I'll tell Papa we're getting married.'

'No, please. Not until after tomorrow.'

'Then we'll tell everyone the day after tomorrow. We'll buy the ring then. This isn't just about . . . about you staying on at the café,' he stammered in embarrassment. 'I want to marry you.'

'I know, Tony,' she echoed, hoping and praying he'd still feel the same way about her and marriage – after tomorrow night.

As the radio concert of Tchaikovsky's sixth symphony drew to a close, Alma Raschenko looked up from her knitting at her husband, who was sitting in an easy chair across the hearth from her.

'You haven't told me how it went in the recruiting office.' By nature, Charlie was a silent uncommunicative man, and it had taken Alma months to become accustomed to his ways, and to understand that the silences between them didn't necessarily mean that he was unhappy, troubled, angry, or that he loved her any the less. But there was a considerable difference between his silences and the full-blown argument that had flared between them last night when he had told her of his intention to join the Welsh Guards. Feeling betrayed, abandoned and resentful, she hadn't exchanged a word with him above the absolutely essential since he had returned to the shop with William Powell early that afternoon.

A frown creased his forehead as his white-blond hair fell low over his eyes. 'It went as I expected it to.' He folded the newspaper he'd been reading.

'They signed you up along with the boys?'

'They signed up the boys. They didn't want an alien.'

She tensed the muscles in her face, forcing them to remain rigid. They didn't want him! She suppressed the instinct to fling herself into his arms and cover his face with kisses. That meant he'd stay with her, here in Pontypridd, and continue to run his shop for the duration. Of course the war would make a difference, especially to their profits, but she'd been poor before and survived the experience. Poverty held no terrors for her in comparison to Charlie's absence.

He left his chair and walked to the window that looked out over Taff Street.

'The blackout,' she warned as he laid his hand on the curtain.

'I forgot.'

Sticking her needles into the wool, she left it on the chair and joined him. 'Feodor,' she murmured. He liked to hear the sound of his Russian name, and she was the only one who used it. The rest of Pontypridd, even old friends like Evan Powell and his nephew William who worked for them, called him Charlie, as she had quite deliberately done since their argument last night. 'Don't let this alien business upset you. People aren't boycotting the shop, trade is as good as it ever was. Everyone in the town thinks of you as one of us – '

'But I'm not one of you,' he burst in harshly. 'I am one of the same breed who marched into Poland.'

'No,' she countered firmly. 'You're my husband. You took on my nationality when you married me. This is your home now.'

'A home I cannot leave between ten-thirty at night and six in the morning.' He walked away from the window and went to the fire, kicking down the coals with the heel of his boot.

'What difference does that make?' she asked practically. 'We're up too early to go out late at night'

'Before this, I could have if I'd wanted to,' he retorted testily. 'This country gets more like Russia every day.'

'Only because we're at war.' She picked up her knitting and stowed it in the brass slipper box next to her chair. He had told her a little – a very little – of his past in Russia: just enough for her to guess at what he had suffered there. She knew that he had lost everything to the Communist regime. Home, family, wife and unborn child, and her greatest fear since he'd told her of his wife's existence was that one day he'd go back to try to find her. The remote possibility had loomed a

14

more likely spectre since the outbreak of war. Her geography was shaky, but she knew that Britain was separated from France by the English Channel, and there was no strip of water to divide France from Russia. But when she had tried to confide her fears to Feodor last night, he had laughed and tried to tell her just how great a distance separated France from Russia. She hadn't wanted to listen. The continent was the continent, and her husband had another wife there, and if that wife was alive she would undoubtedly want him back. Because anyone who had known and lived with Charlie simply couldn't help loving him.

'You tried, darling,' she consoled, trying not to allow her relief to show. 'If they don't want you, there's nothing you can do about it.'

There was an abstracted look in his eyes. 'They didn't say they didn't want me, only that they wanted to interview me again. In Cardiff, on Monday.'

'But why?'

'They wouldn't say.'

'Is it something to do with Russia invading Poland along with Germany? Could they be secret allies?'

'I don't know.'

'Everyone is saying that it's better for the Poles to be living under the red flag of Communism than under the heel of the jackboot.'

For the first time in two days a glimmer of a smile crossed his face. 'Who's been telling you that?'

'Evan.'

'Ah, the Red Miners' brigade.' He wrapped a heavily muscled arm around her waist. 'They ought to be careful what they ask for. If they are ever forced to live under the red flag, they'll discover the reality of Communism is very different from the ideology.' He looked down at her. 'I'm sorry, I shouldn't have been angry with you yesterday. But joining the Guards is important to me.'

'Because you feel the need to be more Welsh than the Welsh?'

'You understand me so well. I'm sorry I can't be a better husband.'

'You're a perfect husband, which is why I don't want to lose you.'

'You won't.'

'I might if you join the army.'

'I have too much to live for to get in the way of any bullets.'

'Feodor . . .'

'Enough talk, let's go to bed.' He hooked the guard in front of the fire and opened the door. She glanced around the living room before she switched off the light. She had a great deal to be grateful for. Feodor had spared no expense on the flat above the shop. The living room was comfortable and carpeted, and there was even a tiled bathroom with hot water on tap, fed from the range in the kitchen. Her mother, who was frail and blind, lived with them and Charlie had taken special care with her room, furnishing it with padded, upholstered furniture so she wouldn't hurt herself even if she did get the odd knock, taking it for granted that his wife's mother was a part of their small family, never once complaining about her presence or about having to shoulder the responsibility of another mouth to feed.

She was happy, and not only because life was comfortable for her and her mother for the first time in their lives. Charlie's shop, the flat and their high standard of living were only the trimmings. She could survive without them. But Charlie was the bedrock of her existence, and she would sooner not live at all than without him.

As she lay awake in the blacked-out bedroom, her hand resting on Charlie's chest, monitoring the quiet, measured beat of his heart, she was struck by a paralysing, panic attack. It carried the same spine-chilling dread as the fear of death she'd experienced as a child, when she'd first discovered that she too was mortal and would one day lie in a grave like her father. She simply couldn't, and didn't want to, imagine a life where Charlie wouldn't sleep beside her each and every night.

'The war won't last for ever. If they let me go, I'll be back.'

She recovered enough to tighten her hold on him, but her blood continued to run cold at the thought of the interview on Monday. An interview conducted by men who didn't know – or care – what Charlie meant to her.

'I promise you, Alma, no matter what, if they let me go, I'll be back.'

As he moved towards her, kissed her lips, her hair, her breasts, she tried to immerse herself in the sweet familiarity of his lovemaking and quell the logic that led her to question the value of such a promise from any man who actually wanted to go to war.

Chapter Two

'SOMETIMES I feel as though I spend my whole life grubbing about in the dark,' William complained to Diana as they left their uncle's house in Graig Avenue to go to work.

'The army will change all that. You'll be living under canvas, answering bugle calls come rain or shine, drilling from dawn to dusk, and then, while you tend to your blistered feet after lights out, you'll no doubt start moaning that you never see the stars.'

He knew from the tone of her voice that she was annoyed with him. 'I did tell you that I was thinking of joining up.'

'Thinking is one thing, doing quite another. You could have mentioned that you were going to the recruiting office yesterday morning.'

'We sort of decided on the spur of the moment.'

'No doubt late the night before after a few pints. And when you sobered up, none of you were brave enough to risk looking foolish in front of the others. Some soldiers you'll make,' she sneered.

'It wasn't like that,' William remonstrated, irritated because she'd guessed too close to the truth for comfort.

'Well, as Mam used to say, what's done is done. There's no use in crying over spilt milk, or in your case signed papers. Just you take care of yourself, that's all.' She clutched William's arm as she stumbled over a stone in the unmade road. She and her brother had fought like cat and dog since cradle days, but they had learned to depend on one another, all the more since their mother had been sentenced to ten years' hard labour for receiving and selling stolen goods.

'I will.' He cleared his throat awkwardly. 'And seeing as how you're whining that I didn't tell you about going to the recruiting office, I suppose you'd better know that I'm thinking of asking Tina to get engaged.'

'To you?'

'Of course to me . . .' his voice tailed as he realised she was baiting him.

'Have you asked her?'

17

'Last night.'

'And what did she say?'

'That she'd rather get married.'

'Can't say I blame her. An engagement's neither one thing nor the other. But then Tony's asked me to marry him.' She dropped the information casually, preparing him for an announcement that she hoped Tony would make tomorrow.

A sleepless night spent reading old nursing textbooks that had belonged to her cousin Bethan had given her a newfound confidence, and that coupled with Tony's proposal had convinced her that feeling the way they did about one another was enough to make anything possible.

'You? You're a baby. You're only . . .'

'Eighteen, and old enough to know my own mind.'

'What did you tell him?'

'That I'd think about it.'

'As you're under twenty-one you'll need Mam's or Uncle Evan's permission, and I'll do all I can to persuade them not to give it,' he asserted pompously, wondering if his mother's permission would count because she was a prisoner.

'Mam married Dad when she was eighteen. She won't stand in my way.'

'That was different. Dad had a job. He was steadier than Tony'll ever be, and he wasn't about to go off to war.'

'He volunteered when war broke out.'

'And he didn't come back, which is all the more reason for you not to marry Tony now. Do you want to be left with a pathetic widow's pension and a couple of kids like Mam was?'

'I wouldn't mind if I had what Mam and Dad had first,' she hit back defiantly.

'What do you know about what they had? You weren't even born when he was killed.'

'I know plenty. Mam used to talk to me about him. They loved one another very much.'

'So now you're an expert on love!'

'More of one than you, by the look of it.'

'Diana, this isn't a joking matter.'

'Who's joking? We've planned it all very carefully. Tony wants us to get engaged now, so I can take instruction while he's training, that way we can get married on his embarkation leave.'

'You're turning Catholic?'

'Don't sound so shocked. Turning Catholic won't transform me into a saint.'

'A saint! You're a tenth-rate Baptist, and I don't doubt you'll make a tenth-rate Catholic.'

'This coming from the most religious man on the Graig.'

'Has Tony told his father and mother about you? Because if he hasn't, I warn you now, they're not going to like the idea. They gave Trevor Lewis a hard time when he married Laura and they played hell with Ronnie when he wanted to marry Maud . . .'

'And they're going to be overjoyed at the thought of you marrying Tina?'

'I told you, nothing's settled. She hasn't given me an answer – yet.'

'And I haven't given Tony an answer – yet,' she echoed, crossing her fingers behind her back.

'Bloody women. You're all the same. Can't make up your mind what dress to wear, let alone what man to marry.'

'Language!'

'Women are enough to drive a man to drink, let alone swearing.'

'That's because men never grow up. All you're good for is starting stupid wars.'

'Two minutes ago you wanted to marry a man.'

'I said I was thinking about it.' Tossing her head high she walked ahead of him, only to trip over a cat that squealed and scratched her legs, tearing a hole in her stocking.

'Damn!'

'Now who's swearing?' When she didn't answer him, he tried coaxing her out of her temper. 'Come on Di, you could say something.'

'Like what?'

'How about, "I hope it works out for you and Tina." '

'After what you've just said about my marrying Tony. No fear. Besides, I'm thinking of Tina. She's a good friend, I'm not at all sure she deserves a half-baked twit like you.'

'I am not half-baked.'

'No? Only a half-baked twit would play around with Vera Collins.'

'Isn't anyone around here ever going to forget that?'

'. . . And then to go and join the Guards without saying a word.'

'Like Tony?'

'Sometimes he can be half-baked too.'

She paused outside the sweet shop she managed for Wyn Rees. As Wyn's father also owned the sweet shop next to the New Theatre, the family was considered well off by Pontypridd standards. Well off would have been enough to set them apart on its own, but as Wyn was also saddled with the reputation of being 'a queer' he was treated as an outcast by most of the males in the town, William included.

'Boss is in early.' William nodded to the shadow of a van parked outside the shop.

'Oh no, I must be late.'

'See you tonight, sis.' William carried on swiftly down the hill, crashing into another pedestrian in his eagerness to escape a possible meeting with Diana's boss.

Diana negotiated the blackout curtain to find Wyn piling boxes from the shop floor into the back storeroom.

'It's an offence to hoard sweets, even for a retailer,' she smiled.

'I'm checking stock levels against the ration cards that have been registered with us.'

'Are you going to be able to keep the two shops going?' she asked, her heart skipping a beat at the thought of losing her job. For all the talk of a shortage of manpower and the conscription of men, there was still an unemployment problem in Pontypridd. And well-paid jobs, like working for a considerate boss like Wyn Rees, were scarcer than diamond tiaras in the valleys.

'To tell you the truth I don't know.' He heaved the last of the boxes into place. 'I came here early so I could talk to you. You're a first-class worker, Diana.'

'You didn't come in early just to tell me that.' She unpinned her hat and carried it together with her coat into the back room.

'I couldn't have managed these last couple of years without you. You've kept this shop going, you've never complained, not even when I've asked you to man the theatre shop late at night after you've put in a full day here. You've always been there ready to take over when Dad's been too much for my sister to manage by herself . . .'

'Are you trying to tell me that you're closing this shop?'

He stood up and leaned against the counter. 'I don't want to, but I can't keep both shops going at the new, reduced stock levels now that sugar rationing's begun to hit trade,' he confessed.

She sank down on the chair in front of the counter. 'How much notice are you giving me?'

'None at the moment. But the way things are it can only be a matter of time. Diana, I'm sorry, I'll do all I can to keep you on, you know that, but I can't guarantee you'll be here six months from now.'

'I'm sorry. You're trying to be fair with me, and I'm behaving like a spoilt brat. It's just that this is the best job I've ever had. I can't imagine working anywhere else.'

'We might all be working somewhere else, whether we want to or not, by the time this war is finished.'

'You've had your registration papers?'

'Yesterday.'

'Will and the two Ronconi boys have joined the Welsh Guards.'

'If it wasn't for Dad and my sister, Myrtle, I'd have been tempted to do the same thing.'

'How is your father?' she asked, remembering her manners.

'Dr Evans told us he'll not see summer out this year, but then he said the same thing this time last year. And when I look at Dad lying in bed with Myrtle fluttering around him, wearing herself out, I think he'll outlast me and my sister. I wish I could do more to help her. She never has a moment to herself.'

'It must be quite a strain.' Diana felt sorry for Wyn's spinster sister. Ten years older than Wyn, and undeniably plain, she had sacrificed whatever life she might have had to care for her father and brother when her mother had died. 'If there's anything I can do to help either of you, you know where to come.'

'Thanks, Diana. And as soon as I make a definite decision on the future of the shops, I'll let you know what's happening. If they can be kept open I can't think of anyone else I'd rather entrust the running to, than you. But with all the men going away I've a feeling there may be jobs on offer at a higher rate than I can pay, and I don't want you to miss out. So if you get a chance of anything better . . .'

'Than this?' she laughed. 'I'll see a flying pig first.' Wyn had upped her wages from twelve and six to a pound a week since she'd started working for him. There weren't many other shop assistants in Ponty-pridd earning that kind of money.

'I've got work to do. We'll talk again soon.' He was reluctant to leave. Diana was the only one, apart from his sister, he confided in, and the one person he counted on as a disinterested friend. Desperate to keep that friendship, he was concerned about imposing on her good nature. 'Perhaps we could meet for tea in the New Inn on Sunday? I've heard that they're still serving cakes there.'

'I'd like to, but I'm not sure what I'll be doing.' Wyn knew her secret; and she had a great deal more than just her job to be grateful to him for. He had proved himself a true friend when she had been most in need of one, and that had led to her seeing the man behind the 'fairy' and 'queer' gibes. To her, he was an essentially good, kind man, and boss, and it bothered her that William and her cousins had joined the rest of the men in the town in shunning and ridiculing him. She'd even quarrelled with William over Wyn, telling him in no uncertain terms that she was old enough to choose her own friends, and meet with whom she pleased.

'I'll see you some time.'

'It's just that −' the secret he was a party to brought a flush of colour to her cheeks − 'Tony Ronconi's asked me to marry him.'

'And you're going to?'

'I don't know. I'll have to tell him everything.' She forced herself to look into Wyn's eyes. 'Everything,' she reiterated, 'about me and that night. Then it will be up to him.'

'He'd be a fool to turn you down, Diana.'

'You don't think it will make any difference?'

'Not to someone who loves you.'

'Thank you for that, and for being there whenever I've needed help. If I do get engaged to Tony I hope you'll come to the party?' It was suddenly important to her that Wyn approve of her choice of husband.

'I'd like to, and congratulations.'

'Congratulations are a little premature. He only asked me last night, and I haven't told anyone apart from you, and William. Tony isn't even going to tell his family until tomorrow, so you will keep it quiet, won't you?'

'Of course. And thanks for telling me. I won't feel so bad about having to close the shop if you marry Tony. You'll be needed in the cafés. Particularly after the boys have left.'

'I'll balance the books and bring them down to the New Theatre shop at seven.'

'See you.'

Wyn closed the door behind him and walked to the van he'd bought only a year ago. It had seemed a good investment then, because in addition to the two sweet shops he'd set up a small wholesale confectionery round, supplying some of the cafés in Ponty-pridd and the Rhondda that were run by people who had neither the time nor the transport to visit the wholesalers themselves. But now, when he faced being called into the army, and his father was too ill to leave his bed for more than an hour at a time, he looked on it as a millstone. Myrtle would never be able to nurse his father and run the businesses. Something would have to go. The war had brought every-thing tumbling down around his ears, as well as honing a keener edge on his fraught relationship with his father.

He slammed the doors shut on the back of the van and checked the cardboard hoods on the lights. It still wanted a full hour to daylight, and if hadn't been for the coat of white paint he'd given the running boards and bumper he doubted he'd have found the door to the driver's side.

He climbed inside and hunched over the wheel. He had a difficult round ahead of him and he'd never felt less like facing people. If only everyone, including and especially his father, would accept him for what he was. But then, it wasn't only his father. It was the so-called family friends who were forever calling into the house on the pretext of enquiring after his father's health and his sister's well-being so they could whisper scandal and innuendo into his father's ears, telling him that they had seen his son around town with this or that man, or boy. Even their wives added to his problems with their sly hints and endless questions.

'Isn't it time you married, Wyn? A wife would take some of the load off poor Myrtle's shoulders. It's *very* hard on her, you know, having to look after you and your father the way he is. Do tell, is there a young lady you're hiding from us? But then there must be, a tall, good-looking, strapping young fellow like you.' Nudge nudge, wink wink.

Tall, good-looking and living a lifestyle that could bring him a jail sentence if he approached the wrong man or was seen showing affection to one of his men friends in a private or public place. Which was why his relationships rarely lasted more than a week or two. It was simply too dangerous to risk anything approaching permanency lest the police notice and start following them. Some of the older constables, like Diana's Uncle Huw Davies, were prone to turning a blind eye to discreet behaviour, but not the younger, keener ones. And then there had been the ultimatum from his father last night, which still burned, raw and painful in his mind.

'You and Myrtle can stop pussyfooting around me, boy. I know I haven't long to go. But I'm giving you fair warning. I'm not stupid. I know what you are, and you're to put a stop to it right now. Do you hear me? Either you find yourself a girl and get married, or you lose the businesses. Because as sure as God made little apples, I won't leave you the shops, the van or a penny piece until you change your ways. I won't have mine or Myrtle's name held up to mockery in this town a moment longer because of your filthy, unnatural habits.'

It wasn't the first time his father had tried to lay down the law about the way he lived, and he didn't doubt for a minute that his father was serious. But then, perhaps that was the best way things could work out for all of them. Myrtle would get the businesses and Diana to run them if he could keep her on that long. He would go into the army, and if this show was anything like the last one he'd get killed. And with his death everyone's problems would be solved, especially his father's. He'd have a heroic son he could be proud of for the first time in his life. The more he thought about the idea, and remembered his closest friend, and lover, who had gassed himself after being caught with a vicar in the park toilets, the more the solution appealed to him.

Tony Ronconi left the café after the midday rush and walked up High Street to Rees's sweet shop. Relieved to find it empty apart from Diana, he produced a card that had circles of various sizes punched along its length. 'Find your ring size,' he ordered as he pushed it over the counter.

Diana's eyes sparkled as she slipped the third finger of her left hand through the first hole.

'I thought I'd go into the jeweller's and see what they had.'

'You've told your parents?'

'Not yet. It might be better if we bought the ring first and present them with a *fait accompli*. It worked for Ronnie.'

'It did?' she asked sceptically.

'I'm over twenty-one,' he said airily with a certain amount of bravado.

'It's important for us to get your father and mother's blessing.'

'If it will make you feel better I'll tell them tonight.'

'Wait until tomorrow.' She realised that the ring card and his promise to tell his parents was his way of assuring her that whatever happened between them that night was a prelude to marriage.

'But why?'

'Please, humour me,' she smiled nervously. 'And if you still want to, we'll get engaged on Sunday.'

'If I want to? Wild horses couldn't stop me.' He glanced over his shoulder to make sure no one had sneaked into the shop while they'd been talking. As it was empty he leaned over the counter and kissed her. 'We'll have a party in the restaurant.'

'What about the café?'

'Angelo can run it.'

'On his own?'

'I have.' There was an indignant tone in his voice that reminded her so much of his oldest brother Ronnie, she began to laugh.

'What's so funny?'

'You. I can see that I'm going to have to put my foot down from the outset. If I don't, you're likely to start trying to boss me around the way you do your brothers and sisters.'

'They're annoying, you're not.'

'Tina's my best friend.'

'Say that again and you'll go down in my estimation.' He looked down at the ring card. She'd pushed her finger through the middle hole. 'If you're sure that's your right size I'll get one.'

'I'd prefer to choose my own.'

'Trust me.'

'I already do,' she whispered, handing back the card as the door opened and a crowd of small children flooded into the shop.

William stared despondently at the teeming rain as he carried empty trays from the counter into the kitchen at the back of Charlie's shop and stacked them next to the sink ready for washing. He usually looked forward to Thursday. It was half-day, the only day in the week he could count on getting off work early in the afternoon. Since the cinemas had reopened, he and Tina had taken to spending every Thursday afternoon curled up next to one another in the back row, arms and legs entwined as they watched the film, stealing kisses when the newsreels showed lines of goose-stepping Germans, Hitler meeting Mussolini, the crews of the *Exeter* and *Ajax* being cheered by London crowds, or the British Expeditionary Force landing in France.

He wasn't even sure whether Tina was angry with him after last night. They had parted so quickly, he hadn't had time to ask her if she'd meet him. He didn't even know if she had the afternoon off from the café. And because he wasn't certain how much time he had left before he'd be sent his travelling orders, he wanted to take her somewhere more special than the back row of the Palladium or the Park cinema. He racked his brains trying to think of a place where they could be alone. If it had been summer, he could have taken her to Shoni's pond, or the park. He might even have suggested it now, cold as it was, if this miserable downpour showed any signs of letting up.

'You look as though you've found sixpence and lost a shilling, William,' Alma commented as she carried another empty tray out of the shop for him to wash.

'That's just about how I feel.'

'You're sorry you joined up?'

'It's not that. It's the weather. I'd like to go out this afternoon but there's nowhere to go.'

'How about the pictures? *It Happened One Night* is on in the Palladium. Charlie's taking me.'

He wondered again if it was worth risking rebuff and asking Tina to go with him. Perhaps if he went to the café and found her there, she'd talk to him.

'If you want to go now, I can finish up here,' Alma offered generously.

'You mean that?'

'It'll only take me as long as it will take Charlie to set up the market stall ready for the morning. As you'll have no choice about putting in a full day there, make the most of the time you've got now. Go on, off with you.' She glanced at his grubby apron and overall. 'And if you're seeing Tina, you'd better use our bathroom for a wash and brush-up. Only don't pinch too much of Charlie's cologne. He notices when it goes down too quickly.'

'You're a gem.' He untied his apron and kissed her on the cheek.

'Don't let Charlie catch you doing that. Not with your reputation,' she shouted as he took the stairs two at a time.

Ten minutes later, hair slicked back with a fingerful of Charlie's pomade and smelling of a cologne that was too astringent for his taste, he hared out of the shop and down Taff Street. He felt even more confused as he went over the conversation he'd had with Tina the night before. Why would any girl want to get married but not engaged? It simply didn't make sense. No sense at all.

'You've finished early, even for a Thursday,' Gina, Tina's younger sister greeted him as he walked into the café.

'The boss gave me time off for good behaviour. Tina around?'

'In the kitchen. Angelo's been burning toast, so she offered to show him how to make it.'

'Is it safe to go in there?'

'When is it ever safe to go near Tina?' Tony shouted from the back room where he was clearing dirty plates.

William lifted the counter flap and pushed the swing door to the kitchen. Tina wasn't showing Angelo anything. She was sitting immersed in a women's magazine at the preparation table, a cup of tea and a doughnut in front of her.

'I wondered if you'd like to go the pictures? Alma said they're showing *It Happened One Night* in the Palladium.'

'Seen it,' she answered briefly.

'I thought we could talk. We didn't really settle anything last night.'

She looked at him over the rim of her cup, her eyes dark, reflective pools that gave no insight into her thoughts. 'No, we didn't, did we?'

'Tina . . .' he looked over to the corner next to the back door. Angelo was sitting on a stool, smoking a filched cigarette and smirking at every word they were saying.

'Tell you what, why don't we go to Cardiff?'

'Cardiff!'

'There's a film on in the Capitol that I want to see. We can talk on the bus.'

'All right,' he agreed hastily, afraid to object in case she changed her mind. 'Cardiff it is. Do you want to go home and change first?'

'I'm not good enough for you and Cardiff?' She was wearing a new, dark blue woollen dress that clung to her curves and highlighted a bluish tint in her black hair.

'You're good enough to go anywhere,' he complimented, managing to forget Angelo's presence for a moment. 'Will Tony be able to spare you?'

'After what he and Angelo did yesterday they have no choice. You should have heard Papa last night. Heaven only knows how we're going to run the cafés without them. Useless as they are,' she shouted, making sure that Angelo could hear her, 'they do represent two extra pairs of hands.' She picked up her teacup. 'Give me five minutes to drink this and brush my hair and I'll be with you.'

'I'll wait for you in the café.'

'Tea?' Tony asked as William lifted the flap and pulled a stool close to the counter.

'Yes please.' William debated whether to mention Diana's revelation and decided against it. He had enough problems of his own without delving into his sister's and Tony's affairs. Besides, Diana might see sense yet and tell Tony she was too young to get married. 'Tina said it would be all right for me to take her to Cardiff.'

'She did, did she?'

'Is it?' He pulled out a packet of cigarettes and offered Tony one.

'I suppose so.'

'You in the dog-house over yesterday?' William eyed him carefully, wondering if Tony was being offhand because Tina had told him that he had asked her to marry him.

'Papa shouted a lot, but then he always does when we do anything that upsets his neat, orderly world. Sometimes I think he'd prefer it if we were made of dough so he could mould us how he wants, and then stand us in a row ready to do his bidding.'

'It won't be easy for the girls to run this place without you and Angelo.'

'Don't you start. What about you?'

'Neither Uncle Evan nor Diana were over the moon at the thought of me in uniform, but then it's my life.'

'That's what Angelo and I tried to tell Papa last night,' Tony commiserated. 'We couldn't even talk to Mama. All she did was cry, in between threatening to go down the recruiting office and tell whoever's in charge that Angelo's only seventeen.'

'Will she?' William asked, worried because he had vouched for Angelo's age.

'She changed her mind after Angelo pointed out that if she did, he'd only have to go later without us.'

'Happy families.'

'Sometimes I think it would have been easier to have been born an orphan.'

'It's not as though we'll be away that long.'

'Didn't you read the *Observer* this week? Article there reckons the war will last three years.'

'Three years!' William tried to imagine three years away from Pontypridd, three long years without Tina. He couldn't. It stretched before him, an unimaginable time span.

'Of course it may not last quite that long.' Tony didn't sound at all convincing.

'You beginning to wish that you hadn't joined up?'

'Are you?' Tony answered flatly, turning the question on him.

'No,' William asserted too insistently. 'Besides, what's done is done.'

'I wish I had a pound for every time I've heard that today. Is Charlie sorry he went with us?'

'You know Charlie, he never says a word about anything important.'

'You think they'll take him after that second interview next week?'

'I don't know.' William's attention focused on Tina who had finally emerged from the kitchen. She was wearing her best coat and hat, had put on pink lipstick, dabbed powder on her nose, and he could smell the 'essence of violets' scent she was wearing from where he was sitting. Surely she wouldn't have gone to all that trouble if she intended to turn down his offer of an engagement ring.

It was cold and wet waiting for the Cardiff bus on Broadway. William tried to huddle under Tina's umbrella but even that turned into further cause for argument. When he angled it to suit his six-foot-three frame, the wind and rain blew under the cover and soaked Tina's hat and hair, and if she put it at a comfortable level for herself, the spokes stuck into his chin or eyes. Both of them were glad when the bus finally came.

'Upstairs, front seat?' He ran up the narrow metal staircase ahead of her so she couldn't accuse him of trying to look up her skirt, and he remembered to stand back so she could take her favourite inside seat. 'You thought any more about last night?' he asked as he dug into his pocket for money to pay the conductor.

'Yes.'

'Do you want to get engaged?' he whispered, afraid of being overheard by the other passengers.

'I told you I want to marry you.'

'That's not what I asked.'

'If you don't want to marry me, you don't have to,' she snapped tartly.

'It's not that I don't want to. It's just that I could be away for years.'

'At last, a man who's finally prepared to admit that this war is going to last longer than six months.'

'No one knows how long it's going to last,' he retorted irritably.

'If I'm prepared to marry you and wait as long as it takes for you to come home, you should be grateful, and not insist on a stupid engagement. A half-measure that's neither one thing nor the other.'

'You been talking to Diana?'

'No, why?'

'Nothing. It's just that I'd rather you were free while you waited.'

'Because of what happened to your father?'

'Yes.' There was a pathetic look on his face that tore at her heartstrings. She simply couldn't bring herself to compound his misery a moment longer.

'We shouldn't be spending what little time we have left quarrelling,' she declared, finally capitulating and hooking her arm into his.

He knew then that Tony hadn't said a word to Tina about marrying Diana. If he had, she would have brought it up and used it as yet one more argument in favour of a hastily arranged wedding. 'Do you want to get a ring in Cardiff? An engagement ring,' he added so there could be no mistake.

'If that's all you're prepared to give me, I suppose it will have to do,' she murmured, mischief and love glowing in her eyes.

He would have kissed her if they'd been alone. As it was, he had to content himself with squeezing her hand. Not for the first time that day he wondered what on earth had possessed him to join the Guards. Then he remembered Tony's assertion that as they'd have to go anyway, it was better to be first in line so they could pick out the cushiest numbers for themselves before the rush.

He hoped Tony was right. Because suddenly nothing seemed worth leaving Pontypridd and Tina for. Especially war.

Chapter Three

'I THOUGHT they'd never leave.' Tony rammed the bolt home below the lock on the café door. He glanced at Diana, who was standing nervously in front of the counter stacking dirty cups on to a tray. He walked across to her and took a cup from her hand. 'I'll see to all this after I take you home.'

'There's so many . . .'

'They can wait.' He stroked the side of her face gently with his fingertips while staring intently into her eyes. 'You are sure you want this?'

She swallowed hard, her secret clouding her mind like a toxic mist, poisoning her every thought and move. She would never be able to bring herself to get engaged to, much less marry, Tony without telling him the truth. And she couldn't think of a better time to begin than now, after she went upstairs with him. 'I'm sure,' she murmured.

'I'll go up first and pull the blackout curtains. There's no electric light, so you'll have to bring the candle from the kitchen.'

Diana walked behind the counter and into the kitchen. She found what she was looking for on the windowsill: a stub of candle glued by a puddle of wax to a cracked saucer. Lifting it down, she took the box of matches from next to the stove and opened it, snapping three in half before she finally succeeded in lighting the wick. Switching off all the downstairs lights she carried the candle to the foot of the stairs. She sat on the bottom step, shivering, trying to keep a grip on herself while waiting for Tony to call her. It was peculiar how even the most commonplace objects could be transformed by candlelight. The wavering flame lengthened shadows, animating them into threatening, malevolent shapes that reminded her of the ghastly ghoul and ghost stories William had spun to frighten her when they'd been children. She was aware of a heightening of sensitivity, as though her body was preparing her for disaster – or an experience she would treasure for the rest of her life. Which would it be?

Willing optimism to win, she looked around, consciously absorbing the scene, storing it for some future date when Tony would be away and this moment would be no more than a bitter-sweet memory. Setting the candle on the stair next to her she hugged her knees and tried to picture the rooms they'd share when he came home on leave. It would have to be rooms. There was no way she'd be able to afford, or justify renting a whole house, not when he'd be away most of the time, but then it would give them an opportunity to save for a home of their own.

'I've blacked out the bedroom, it's safe to come up.'

She turned her head, Tony was standing at the top of the stairs looking down at her.

'Are you all right?'

'I was miles away.'

'If you want to change your mind, I don't mind waiting until after we're married.' Half of him wanted her to walk up the stairs, the other half – an uncharacteristically doubtful, nervous half – wished she'd insist on leaving for home right now.

She shook her head. 'No, I don't want to wait.' Picking up the candle she turned and slowly mounted the stairs.

'You sure this is the ring you want?' William patted the box he was carrying in his coat pocket.

'It's exactly the ring I want,' Tina assured him for the twentieth time since they'd bought it. Small, old-fashioned, its simple gold band was set with a single green stone that the pawnbroker had assured them was an emerald, but after William had handed over the money he'd drawn out of the bank for the purpose, he'd begun to wonder. He had been prepared to pay double the amount the pawnbroker had asked, for a brand new engagement ring, but the moment Tina had seen that particular ring in the broker's window she had fallen in love with it, and unable to resist her excitement he had bought it for her.

'I knew it was the one the minute I saw it. Haven't you ever looked at something and realised right away that it was meant to be yours?'

'Yes.' He took her hand into his, pulled off her glove and kissed her cold fingers.

'I'd still have preferred a wedding ring.'

'And I'll buy you one, the minute the war is over.'

'You'll write?'

'Every chance I get, and I'll be back on leave.'

'Promises, promises, but as it looks as though that's all I'm going to get, I suppose they will have to do.' She leaned her head on his shoulder. He looked up, just able to make out the blackened outline of the roofs of the end houses in the terrace, and the stripped branches of the wizened bushes at the side of the road that led up to Penycoed-cae. They turned the corner and walked to her door, their footsteps dragging as they drew closer to the white cross that glimmered faintly in the blackout.

'Will,' she stopped and led him across the road out of hearing distance of the houses. 'Before you go away, wouldn't you like to spend more time with me?'

'All I can.'

'You know what I mean.' Although her face was veiled by darkness, she lowered her head.

'I know what you mean,' he whispered.

'There must be somewhere we can go . . .'

'We'll talk about it some other time,' he broke in quickly.

'We may not have much time left.'

'We haven't. Any minute now your father will open that door and call you in.'

'That's not what I meant.'

'I know.' He kissed her slowly, and thoroughly, sending scalding shock waves of passion through both their bodies. 'I'll come up tomorrow straight from work and talk to your father. Don't give him any warning. If he's going to be difficult, I'd rather he was difficult with me than you.'

She turned and walked across the road. She was prepared to give William everything before he left and she couldn't understand his reluctance to take advantage of her willingness. She'd even devised a plan. All they'd have to do was take a bus into Cardiff, book into a guesthouse early in the evening and leave before the last bus back to Pontypridd.

She turned at the door and looked back. She couldn't see William, but she could hear his steps as he stumbled over the rough sliver of hillside that separated Danycoedcae Road from Iltyd Street. She reached out and felt for the key in the door. There had been times, especially on long walks last summer, when she'd had to fight to stop him taking advantage of her, but then that had been before he'd told her he loved her. Of course! Why hadn't it occurred to her before? All she had to do was inveigle him into a situation where they wouldn't be disturbed, and she'd soon change his mind about everything – including marriage.

William didn't turn right towards his uncle's house at the bottom of Iltyd Street, but left, towards the Graig Hotel. Officially it was closed; unofficially the back door would be open as it had been every night

32

since war had been declared, so right-minded Welsh patriots and ARPs could drink toasts to the success of Britain and her Allies.

He felt peculiar. Unsettled and restless, unnerved by Tina's hints about spending time together. He loved her but there were some things he found difficult to talk about, especially to the woman he loved and intended to marry – eventually. How could he begin to explain to Tina about the other women he'd had sex with? How he longed for their lovemaking to be unique and very special. A magical, mystical, beautiful experience, as different from the quick fumblings and gropings he'd shared with Vera Collins, who'd used him as a brief diversion from her husband, as a long soak in a real bath was from a quick wash in a bucket in the back yard. He wanted there to be much, much more between him and Tina than embarrassing, hurried copulation in a shed or grubby borrowed room.

When he imagined their wedding night, it was set against an idyllic background, like the honeymoon suites in Hollywood films, complete with roses, champagne, soft music and the ultimate luxury: all the time in the world.

The problem was how to explain to Tina that their first time should be perfect? Something worth waiting for. Knowing Tina, if he tried she'd laugh at him for being a stupid romantic, which he undoubtedly was. But then how could she know that although he'd managed to hold his own with the Veras of this world, he was absolutely terrified of turning his initial experience with the virgin he loved into a complete and utter disaster.

'You sure you won't get into trouble for being late?' Tony asked nervously, moistening his lips with his tongue as he faced Diana across the single bed in the spartan bedroom above the café.

'No, I told Uncle Evan that you'd have to lock up the café before you brought me home. He said he didn't mind as long as I wasn't out alone late at night in the blackout.'

'You don't think he guessed?'

'Why should he? You've brought me home late before.' She placed the saucer that held the candle on the seat of a rickety wooden chair next to the bed.

'I suppose I have.' He looked at the bed, then the rest of the room. For the first time he saw it through a stranger's eyes. Shabby, grimy and devoid of anything remotely resembling comfort let alone luxury. A depressing place to celebrate love and begin a new life. The inadequate light of the candle could not conceal the condensation stains on the peeling wallpaper. Neither could his hastily applied

33

cologne nor Diana's scent mask the cold, stale, musty smell of damp. 'I'm sorry about the surroundings,' he apologised. 'None of the girls has ever slept here, and I never realised how dismal it is until now.'

She tried to smile at him but the muscles froze in her face. Lean, thin and very dark, he looked almost satanic in the flickering shadows. 'Is there another room, or is this where you sleep when you stay overnight?' she asked nervously, looking from the narrow bed to the bare floorboards, their corners powdered with dust and fluff balls.

'There's another room but we use it to store stock. Ronnie was the one who actually put the bed in here.' He walked to the window to check the blackout curtains; not that they needed it, he'd been meticulous in closing them, but he could no longer look her in the eye. 'He used to sleep here when he and Papa quarrelled.'

'Over Maud?'

He turned around. 'I think there were even more quarrels between Ronnie and Papa before Maud came on the scene than there were afterwards.'

'It's funny.'

'What?' he asked anxiously, still half dreading – half hoping – that she'd change her mind.

'My cousin Maud marrying your brother, and now me here. Maud and I were closer than most sisters before she went away.'

'Which only goes to show that Ronnie and I have the same good taste in Powell women.' He took a step towards her and she shrank instinctively away from him.

'You know I'd never do anything to hurt you.' He reached out and touched her hair. She shuddered as though he'd burnt her. 'You're freezing.' He wrapped his arms around her. 'You are sure . . .'

'I'm sure, Tony,' she interrupted forcefully.

'Then perhaps it's time you got under the bedclothes.'

Turning her back on him, she pulled her jumper over her head. She looked around: the only place to put it was the chair next to the bed, and she'd used that for the candle.

'Here, I'll take the candle.' He held out his hand. She handed him the saucer and he lowered it to the floor on his side of the bed. The light flickered and dimmed as the flame scuttered in a draught, casting the room in shadows that hung between them, as thick, heavy and apparently tangible as black lace curtains.

'I'll turn my back if you like.'

'Thank you.' She slipped her blouse buttons from their loops. Sick with fear and apprehension she undressed quickly, removing her skirt, blouse, stockings and bust shaper, but leaving her long petticoat and bloomers. She pulled back the bedclothes and slid beneath the sheets; they were icy, clammy and cold to the touch. She lay there trembling, facing the door as she listened to Tony moving around the room behind her. She started at the loud thud of his shoes as he threw them on to the bare boards. There was a click as he unbuttoned his braces. A soft hiss of linen whispered in the air as he removed his shirt, escalating the tense atmosphere. The ring of metal hitting metal told her he was unfastening the buckle on his trouser belt. A sudden weight depressed the mattress behind her as he sat on the bed.

'You really are cold.' He laid his hand on her back as he crawled in beside her. Gripping her shoulders he pulled her close until the front of his thighs nestled against the back of hers. She steeled herself to accept the touch of his body, long, lean and hard muscled against hers, while fighting a sour tide of nausea that threatened to rise from the pit of her stomach as he stretched his naked legs over hers.

'You all right, Diana?'

She nodded, unable to answer him.

'I love you.' He turned her gently, rolling her over until she faced him. The warmth of his hands flamed through the thin silk of her petticoat, searing, scorching and repugnant. She closed her eyes tightly as he kissed her hair, her cheeks, her lips, gritting her teeth and tensing herself as he embraced her entire body with his own.

She stretched out her hands and gripped the sides of the bed as he slipped the straps of her petticoat from her shoulders. He undressed her slowly, carefully, kissing and fondling each breast in turn as he uncovered them. She concentrated every fibre of her being in an attempt to close out what he was doing to her, but awareness came, harsh and unwelcome as his passion heightened and all pretence of tenderness fled.

Lost in consuming, uncontrollable desire, Diana, the person with her own capacity for pain and pleasure was forgotten, as lust propelled Tony singlemindedly towards his own climax. His indifference was neither deliberate nor calculated, but Diana was conscious of it. It was as though she'd been transformed into a vessel whose sole purpose was the gratification of his pleasure; and when he'd finally done with her, she leaned over, pulled the chamber-pot from beneath the bed and was quietly and thoroughly sick.

Shame and guilt ridden, he sat alongside her, cradling her forehead in his hands. 'Diana, I'm sorry. So terribly, dreadfully sorry. Did I hurt you?'

'No. It's not anything you did. It's me.' Pulling the topmost blanket from the bed she wrapped it around her shoulders. Sitting hunched,

35

on the edge of the bed, she buried her face in the folds of cloth that covered her knees.

'It's not you . . .' he faltered. 'Everyone says the first time is difficult for a woman. I shouldn't have rushed you . . . I should have – '

'It's not my first time,' she confessed starkly. The words were finally out in the open between them. Relief washed over her. She'd said it. She'd finally said it! Tony knew. She didn't have to conceal her secret from him any longer.

'Not the first? I don't understand. Who . . .'

She heard the anger in his voice and flinched as though he'd struck her. 'I should have told you before.'

'Did you love him?' he demanded.

'I hated him. I'll always hate him.'

'Then why?'

'He raped me.'

'Raped! Who?'

She raised her head and forced herself to look at him. Light shone dimly upwards from the floor, casting amber shadows in the hollows of his cheeks and eyes. 'It happened when I worked for him.'

He knew it couldn't be Wyn, and she'd only worked for one other man in Pontypridd. 'Ben Springer. I'll kill the bastard!'

'Someone beat him up shortly afterwards. They made sure that Ben wouldn't be able to do what he did to me, to any other girl.'

'William?'

'No. William never knew. You won't tell him?' she pleaded anxiously.

He shook his head, he couldn't trust himself to answer her. All his life he'd dreamed of a sweet virginal bride. Now he couldn't even bring himself to look at her. Just thinking about what had happened between them left a bitter taste in his mouth.

'I'm sorry, I had no right to do this without telling you first. It's just that I thought you'd realise before . . . before it happened.' Words tumbled out one after another in an erratic flow. 'And then it would be easier for us to talk about it. But it isn't, is it? If anything, it's worse.' She waited for him to say something – to touch her. When he didn't, she clutched the blanket to her chest, picked up her clothes from the chair and carried them downstairs to the washroom off the kitchen.

She dressed hurriedly in the dark and waited until she was fully clothed before flicking the light switch. Only then did she dare look in the mirror. Her face was pale, bloodless; her eyes dark, her hair ruffled. Taking a comb from her bag she tugged it mechanically through her curls, slipped on her coat and went to the front door. She looked back at the stairs, but Tony hadn't followed her. She slammed the door, pressing her weight against it to make sure the lock had latched, before turning towards the white tiled railway tunnel that marked the beginning of the Graig hill.

Tony sat in the bed for a long time after Diana left. He'd heard her go into the washroom, heard her open the front door and knew he ought to call down to her to wait for him to walk up the hill with her, but he couldn't bring himself to go near her. How could he face her, knowing what he did about her now? And to think he'd actually considered marrying her.

He recalled Ben Springer's obscenely fat body and clenched his fists. If the man had been in the room with him, he could have quite cheerfully pummelled him into jam and strangled what was left. Then he remembered the rumours that had circulated Pontypridd after Ben had been attacked. Stories to the effect that a doctor had been forced to remove the remains of Ben's testicles after they'd been subjected to a thorough kicking. He'd asked his brother-in-law, Trevor Lewis about Ben's injuries at the time, but Trevor had tersely reminded him that no doctor could discuss private matters involving a patient.

But if William hadn't attacked Ben, who had? He swung his legs out of the bed and reached for his clothes, all excitement at his first sexual experience fading to a dull, embarrassing and humiliating ache. Someone had done the right thing in hurting Ben, but he wasn't surprised that whoever the hero was, he hadn't waited around to claim Diana as a prize, because whatever else, she certainly wasn't fit to be the wife of any decent man, not now. Not after an experience like that.

Diana walked slowly up the hill, stopping every time she heard a footstep ring out into the darkness. Reason told her it wouldn't be Tony's, but reason didn't prevent her from hoping. It was only when she reached the halfway point and followed the broken white line past the entrance to Factory Lane that she started to think through the full implications of what had happened. It was then she realised that even if Tony had run after her, there was nothing she could say or do to undo the damage to their relationship. The look in his eyes after she had told him that she had been raped had been condemnatory and final. He would never, never, smile at her again as he had done when she'd climbed the stairs to the bedroom. Not tonight, not tomorrow, not ever again. Any love he had felt for her had died the moment she'd told him he wasn't the first man to touch her. And even if it hadn't, it wouldn't make any difference. How could it, when she'd been repelled and sickened by his touch? Why was the filthy act even called 'making love' when it involved so much pain and degradation for a woman? Were there any women who actually enjoyed it? Would she have been any different if Tony really had been the first?

There was no point in even thinking about it, not when tonight's experience had only served to confirm her suspicions that she'd be repulsed by the touch of any and every man. Ben Springer had marked her as irretrievably as if he'd branded her. She was not only soiled goods, she was damaged. She loved Tony with all her heart and soul, as much as she was capable of loving any man, yet loving him was not enough. She hadn't been able to bear his nakedness near her own. Kisses exchanged in the comparative safety of a public place, like the street after dark, had been endurable. But only because there was no risk of anything more intimate happening.

After what Ben and Tony had done, no other man would want her, which was probably just as well now she'd found out she couldn't be a wife in every sense of the word. Poor Tony! She'd hurt him so much, simply by falling in love with him. He deserved better than her. Hopefully when he left Pontypridd he'd be able to put her and this dreadful night behind him. But where did that leave her? What did she have to look forward to? A spinsterish old age, a dried-up aunt-hood to William's and her cousins' children.

She stared down at the white line on the kerb wishing she had the courage to end it. There was no point in living any longer. She had hurt the one man she loved, brought shame on her family by allowing Ben Springer to do what he had to her. She wasn't even a proper woman. Women made men happy, including the ones who could be bought in station yard, and she couldn't even offer her man that much.

'Diana or Will?' Evan Powell opened the kitchen door as Diana stepped into the passage, barely giving her time to pull the blackout curtain.

She dried her tears in the thick, heavy material Evan's common-law wife, Phyllis, had bought to shroud the doors and windows, and called back, 'It's Diana.'

'You all right?' he asked, picking up on the tremor in her voice.

'Fine.'

'You don't sound it.'

'I'm just cold, it's freezing outside.'

'Is Will with you?'

'No, he went into Cardiff with Tina.'

'You didn't walk up the hill by yourself in the blackout?'

'Tony brought me home,' she lied quickly.

'You look half frozen. Come into the kitchen and get warm.'

'I'd rather go straight to bed if you don't mind, Uncle Evan. I'm tired, and Friday's always a long day.'

'Have a cup of tea first.'

'No, really.'

'Come on.'

Her uncle wasn't usually so persistent. She straightened her skirt as she walked down the stone-flagged passage, wondering if her uncle and Phyllis would guess what had happened to her. But then why should they? No one had guessed what Ben Springer had done to her, and she had been in much more of a state then. Evan was holding the door open. Heat laden with wholesome cooking smells blasted towards her, warm and comforting, and there sitting in an easy chair next to the hearth, was a small, thin woman with a careworn face, who looked smaller, older and more shrunken than she had done behind the distancing barrier of prison screens.

The glossy, curly hair Diana remembered so well was dry and wiry; more grey than black when viewed close-up. The hands that had been soft and cared for were gnarled and scarred by deep cuts. But it was still her mother.

'Mam!' Diana flew across the kitchen. 'I thought you had years more to do.' She hugged her mother, unable to stop the flood of tears she'd held in check since she'd left Tony.

'Time off for good behaviour,' Megan replied in a hoarse, cracked voice. 'Come on now, girl, don't cry.'

'Why didn't you tell me Mam was coming home?' Diana demanded of her uncle.

'Because I didn't want any fuss,' Megan answered for him. 'There've been so many conflicting reports going around the prison since the war started: first that they were thinking of releasing people from sentences that didn't involve violence, then they weren't. I didn't know whether I had grounds for hope or not until last night when I found that I was going to be one of the lucky ones.'

'I can't believe you're actually here.' Diana was holding on to her mother as though she was afraid she'd disappear at any moment.

'Stand back and let me take a good look at you. It's a real treat to see people without bars between me and them.' Megan looked Diana up and down. 'You've grown up,' she declared, stifling a sharp pang of regret that she hadn't been around to witness the event.

'Will's going to be so surprised when he finds you here.'

'So I gather,' Megan said acidly. 'I hear he's joined the Welsh Guards.'

'With Glan next door and the Ronconi boys.'

'I thought he'd have more sense after what happened to your father.'

'This war will be a very different affair to the last one, Megan.' Evan's attempt at reassurance failed miserably.

'It's a war,' Megan asserted flatly, 'and that means boys will get killed.'

'Not ours.'

'Let's pray you're right.' She turned back to Diana, taking her hands into hers. 'Come on then, tell me what you've been doing, without a warder listening in on us for once?'

Diana looked down at the skin on her mother's fingers: it felt as though she were holding twigs covered in sandpaper.

'Tea first.' Phyllis poured out two cups and pushed one towards Diana, and one towards Megan.

'As it looks as though these two are settling in for a night's gossip, I think we'd better go to bed and leave them to it, love.' Evan put his arm around Phyllis's shoulders.

'Please don't go on my account, Evan,' Megan pleaded. 'You're making me feel as though I'm throwing you out of your own kitchen.'

'I've work in the morning and young Brian will be up early to keep Phyllis busy. We'll talk tomorrow night.' Evan led Phyllis towards the door. 'But I'd like to say, welcome home, Megan. It's good to have you back.'

'I'll only stay as long as it takes me to get my own home together again, Evan.'

'Your home is here, with your children and us,' he contradicted firmly. He'd only recognised Megan when he had walked in after work because of her resemblance to her mother. Her weight had practically halved in prison, and the harsh treatment had aged her twenty years. He'd always been fond of Megan, and after his brother's death he had found it easy to transfer the affection he'd felt for his brother to his brother's family.

'We'll see, but in the meantime thank you for looking after Will and Diana for me.'

'Didn't they tell you, they've been looking after me,' he winked as he followed Phyllis through the door and up the stairs.

'Are you really all right, Mam?' Diana asked as she moved her chair closer to her mother's.

'Just a bit giddy, that's all. It's been a big day. I still can't believe I'm

40

sitting here, in Uncle Evan's back kitchen and not behind a mesh screen in prison. It's so good to be able to touch you after all this time.'

'Isn't it?' Diana leaned forward and impulsively hugged and kissed her mother.

'Get on with you.' Megan pushed her daughter away because she was dangerously close to tears. 'I've a lot to catch up on, so it seems. Elizabeth leaving Evan, and Phyllis moving in. I never thought he'd find the courage to live openly with her, although I suspected that something was going on there for years.'

'Isn't it marvellous? They're so happy together.'

'God knows Evan deserves as much happiness as he can get after suffering Elizabeth's wifely ministrations for over twenty years. And speaking of husbands and wives, he tells me you and Will are both courting strong,' she added artfully.

'I think Will was hoping to buy Tina a ring this afternoon.' Diana tried to deflect her mother's interest from her affairs to her brother's.

'It's serious between them, then?'

'I think so.'

'Then why in hell did the fool go and join up?' Megan spooned sugar into the tea Phyllis had poured. 'You think they'll get married?'

'I don't know, what with the war and everything – '

'Damned war!' Megan cursed angrily.

'One good thing has come out of it.'

'It has?'

'You're home.'

'And all the boys have gone or are going. Evan told me Eddie's been in the Guards for months. Signed up a couple of days after marrying Jenny Griffiths. Something happen there I should know about?'

'None of us knows what really happened between Eddie and Jenny, other than he seemed to want to get out of Pontypridd in a hurry. But Will and the Ronconi boys signed up in the Guards because of Eddie. They're hoping to be able to serve with him.'

'And Haydn's in ENSA.' Megan switched the conversation to Evan's oldest son. 'Singing for his country and married. I noticed that Evan couldn't stop talking about her, as opposed to his other daughter-in-law.'

'Jane's a sweet little thing, you'll like her.'

'An orphan, Phyllis said.'

'She might be an orphan, but she's got enough gumption in her to stand up to Haydn.'

'Good. Apart from Evan, the men in this family always have had too much of their own way.'

41

'I can't see Tina letting Will get away with anything.'

'And Maud's still well and happy in Italy, and Bethan . . .' Megan began, referring to Evan's eldest daughter who'd married the local doctor.

'. . . has the most beautiful baby girl you've ever seen,' Diana interrupted excitedly. 'Just wait until you see Andrew. He's the most besotted father in Ponty.'

'I can imagine. I'm glad it's worked out for those two. And Charlie's married to Alma Moore. I don't think any of us saw that coming.'

'She's good for him, and he's been marvellous to Will and Eddie.'

'That just about covers everyone except you.' Megan turned her dark, perceptive eyes on her daughter. 'Aren't you going to tell me anything about yourself?'

'I'm happy. Wyn Rees is a wonderful boss – '

'So work's fine. What about your free time?' Megan interrupted.

'That's fine too.'

'Really? What's this I hear about you and Tony Ronconi?'

'We've been seeing one another, but I told him tonight I don't want to get engaged or married. Not now he's joined up.'

'You don't love him?'

'He's going away. No one knows what's going to happen, everything's so unsettled.'

'You're not prepared to wait for him?'

'It seems silly to get married to a man I might not see for years.'

Megan might have spent the last few years physically separated from her daughter, but she knew her, and knew her well. 'So you quarrelled with Tony tonight?'

Before Diana had time to answer, the front door closed and William came whistling down the passage. He opened the door and stood rooted in the doorway. 'Mam! How on earth did you get here?'

Megan rose unsteadily to her feet, and for the first time Diana realised just how frail her mother had become.

William dropped his hat on to the table and scooped Megan into his arms.

'I had no idea you'd filled out so much.' Megan began to cry, seeing a mirror image of her long-dead husband in her son, even down to the fate that was leading him to war.

'Don't cry, Mam,' William consoled clumsily, knowing exactly what his mother was thinking. 'You can't keep a bad penny from turning up. I'll be back,' he promised recklessly. 'I promise you, Mam, unlike Dad, I'll be back.'

Chapter Four

WILLIAM reached out for the alarm clock that was shrilling and rattling in the biscuit tin next to his bed. He squinted through one eye as he silenced it; it was no use, he couldn't see his hand in front of his face, let alone the clock. The blackout curtains with which Phyllis had covered every inch of window in the house cut out even the faintest glimmer of light but . . . as the alarm had only just sounded there was no harm in stealing *five* more minutes.

Pulling the bedclothes over his head, he snuggled into the pillow and closed his eyes. Friday morning! It wasn't as bad as the outdoor market mornings of Wednesday and Saturday when the population of every surrounding valley poured into Pontypridd, but the butcher's stall he ran for Charlie in the indoor market still had to be opened. He didn't like Friday's customers as much as his Saturday regulars. The only people who could afford to patronise the market twenty-four hours ahead of the Saturday-night knockdown bargain auction, when the remaining perishable goods were sold off by the traders for whatever they could get, were the crache. And serving the crache meant being careful. No calling any woman 'love' or man 'mate', not that there'd be many men shopping. It would be 'sir' and 'madam' and bowing and scraping, and he'd have to man the stall by himself because the shop would command all of Charlie and Alma's time and attention. He'd be lucky if one of them would be able to spare ten minutes to bring across his midday dinner of meat-filled baps and tea.

He hadn't realised how much he'd miss Eddie, especially in the shop, until after his cousin had gone. Butchering was hard, physical work, but when he had asked Charlie in the recruiting office how he expected Alma to manage both businesses without them, the Russian had muttered something about giving the market stallholder notice. Surely Charlie didn't expect Alma to keep the shop going by herself with no help at all? Just humping the bins of kidneys, liver, tripe and offal Charlie had taken to buying from the slaughterhouse since meat rationing had been enforced, would be too much for her. And that was without the cooking, pressing and slicing.

Perhaps it might be as well if the army did turn Charlie down. It wasn't as though he was desperately needed. There were enough single blokes to fight the war without dragging in the married men. But then how could he really regard himself as single, when there was Tina to consider?

'Letter for you, Will,' Evan shouted up the stairs.

Clutching his pyjamas close to his shivering body, William slid out of bed, hopping in a mockery of an Indian war dance as his bare feet hit the freezing linoleum. He opened his door, grateful for the warmth of the strip of jute carpeting on the landing and stairs.

'It's Ministry of War.' Evan handed it over.

The door to the downstairs front room that had remained empty since Haydn had left, opened, and Megan stood in the doorway, wearing the old brown dressing gown William remembered from his childhood. He glanced at her as he slit the top of the envelope with his thumb.

'Well?' Megan demanded tensely.

'They want me to report to training camp on Monday.'

'This coming Monday?'

William nodded, avoiding his mother's eye. 'As I've only two working days left, I'd better let Charlie know before I set up the stall. He's either going to have to find someone to take it over, or give it up before next Wednesday.'

'Something wrong, Will?'

Diana was standing on the stairs already dressed for work, her hair neatly waved, a touch of lipstick heightening the colour of her mouth.

'Monday,' he answered briefly. 'The Ronconi boys will probably be going the same time.' He kissed his mother's crinkled cheek. 'We'll have a couple of days together, Mam.'

'Yes.' She tried to smile at him before returning to her room, but the smile didn't touch the frost blighting her eyes.

William climbed back up the stairs. Three days! So much to do in such a short space of time. Tina had wanted an engagement party; it would have to be held on Sunday, or left until his embarkation leave. Seven weeks from now he could be facing the German guns on the French borders, but before then he'd have to face something far worse – Tina's father.

He bundled his clothes under his arm and carried them down to the wash-house. Suddenly the familiar routine was filled with poignancy. He sensed his whole world closing in around him. Ahead loomed another. A strange, alien environment full of foreboding and menace. Would he have killed his first man two months from now?

He pushed open the door to the kitchen, appreciating the warmth that flowed towards him. Phyllis was cutting bread on the table and his uncle was heaping small coal on the fire to bank down the flames.

'The good thing is, they're not giving you any time to change your mind,' Evan commented, sensing something of the unease William was feeling.

'Probably afraid to in case I do a runner.'

'Best not try that, boy. I haven't heard that they're shooting deserters yet, like they did in the last one, but I've no doubt they'll start if they think they're losing too many.'

'Salt fish and bread and butter?' Phyllis asked as she went to the frying pan to turn the fish over.

'Not this morning, thanks. I haven't time if I'm going to tell Charlie I'm leaving before I open up the stall.'

'You're not going to be any use to your customers or Charlie on an empty stomach,' Evan warned, 'and Charlie's entitled to his last two days' work out of you.'

'Small piece then, please, Phyllis.' William glanced at the clock as he walked into the wash-house. Five o'clock. The stall should be opened at six, and it would take him an extra quarter of an hour on top of the usual half to walk down the hill and give Charlie the news.

Tomorrow he would work on the stall from six in the morning to seven at night. It could be worse. The council had cut the town's traders' opening hours at the beginning of the war. Before, he'd been lucky to finish before eleven on a Saturday. The only time he'd really have to say goodbye to Tina was Sunday, and he wanted to spend some time with his mother.

'Watch you pull the curtain over the door before you go out the back,' Phyllis shouted as he pressed down the latch.

'I have, but you think Dai Station would have better things to do than creep along back lanes watching people go to their ty bachs. This warden business has given every dirty old man in Ponty an excuse to turn peeping Tom.'

Phyllis carried on cutting and buttering bread as Diana walked in, Megan following soon after. The morning rush in the house was eased by the tradition of the women washing and dressing in their bedrooms, the men in the wash-house.

'What can I do?' Megan asked.

'Sit down and have breakfast,' Phyllis suggested shyly.

'No fear. I've never been waited on hand and foot in my life, and I've no intention of turning into idle crache now. If I'm going to live here, I'll pull my weight.'

'You will, soon as we've got this lot off to work,' Phyllis promised,

45

conscious that as Evan's sister-in-law, Megan had more right to be in Evan's house than she did.

The door banged open and William, washed, shaved and dressed in record time, walked into the kitchen as Diana walked out.

'Problems?' Phyllis whispered as she glanced after Diana.

'Probably upset at the thought of Tony getting a letter.' William picked up a piece of bread from his plate, pushed the slice of fish Phyllis had dished out on top, folded it over and crammed it into his mouth. 'You'd better get used to long faces,' he mumbled after swallowing the first mouthful. 'Ponty will soon be filled with girls mourning the loss of the handsomest man in town.'

'Girls?' Megan repeated. 'I thought you were as good as engaged to Tina?'

'That doesn't mean that the others can't view male perfection and dream.'

'Sit down to eat, boy.'

'I will now.' He dropped his bulging sandwich on to his plate, stood behind the table and bent his knees, lowering his head so he could see his face in the mirror set over the fireplace. Buttoning on his collar, he pulled his tie around his neck.

'Here, let me.' Megan had to reach up to knot it.

'My little mother.' He patted her on the head.

'Less of that. You're not too old to have the back of my hand across your backside.'

'Really?' He picked his mother up with one hand, almost dropping her when he realised how thin she was beneath her oversized winter-weight skirt and pullover.

'Bye, Mam.' Diana returned to the kitchen and picked up her bag.

'Not without breakfast,' Phyllis pleaded.

'Wyn's coming up this morning to go through the ration books again. He always orders breakfast for both of us to be brought over from the café across the road.'

'I'll buy something in town as well, if you don't mind, Phyllis.' William abandoned the remains of his fish.

'If you haven't time to eat here, you won't have time to eat in town,' Phyllis protested.

'I'll pick up a pie and eat it as I go. Bye Mam, see you tonight.' William bent his head and kissed his mother before diving into the wash-house to scrub his teeth with salt.

'Do me a favour?' Phyllis asked as she followed him out of the wash-house and down the passage.

'For you, anything!'

46

'Phone Bethan from Charlie's to let her know your mam is home.'

'Will do,' he replied absently.

'Try to remember. You've a lot on your mind.'

'None of it comes before Mam,' he called back as he ran down the steps.

'You didn't expect to go so soon, did you?' Diana asked William as he caught up with her.

'No.'

'Mam's not saying much, but she's taken it hard. You should have written to tell her you were thinking of joining up,' she reproached him.

'I was going to. I never thought they'd release her so early.'

'Just as well they did. If they hadn't, she wouldn't have had a chance to see you before you go.'

'Leave off, Di,' he snapped, guilt making him irritable.

'Admit it,' she pressed. 'You never gave a thought as to how she'd take to seeing you in uniform.'

'So, tell me what I can do about it now?' he demanded testily.

'You can make an effort to be more thoughtful in future.'

'A guardsman's mother's allowance isn't up to a wife's, but it's better than nothing and I'll send Mam more when I can.'

'It's not money she needs. I can keep her on what I earn.' She tried to forget Wyn's warning about the shop closing.

'Don't shut me out, Di. I know I won't be here, but I'd still like to contribute my bit.'

'You will,' she retorted acidly. 'I know Mam. She won't be able to stop worrying about you.'

'For pity's sake, I feel guilty enough as it is without you rubbing it in.'

'I know,' she capitulated, ashamed of herself for taking her misery over Tony's rejection out on her brother.

'Then stop harping on.'

'Write, Will,' she pleaded. 'Every chance you get.'

'I promise,' he murmured.

'See that you do. Food, rest and a quiet life without worrying about you for once, might make a difference.'

'I hope so. Every time I look at her I get the urge to kill the bastards in that jail.'

'Talk like that isn't going to help Mam.'

'But punching a few warders might make me feel better.'

'Just as regular letters from you will make Mam feel better. What about Tina?' she asked, changing the subject because it was too painful to dwell on her mother's frail state of health.

'Bought her an engagement ring yesterday.'

'I told Mam you might,' she smiled. 'You talked to her father yet?'

'Tonight.'

'Expecting the same kind of trouble he gave Trevor Lewis when he married Laura, and Ronnie when he wanted to marry our Maud?' She couldn't help wondering how the senior Ronconis would have taken the news if there had been two, not one engagement planned.

'Possibly,' he answered evasively. 'What about you and Tony?'

'There is no Tony and me. I broke off with him last night,' she revealed flatly.

'But why? I thought . . .'

'We decided with the war and everything it wasn't going to work out for us.'

'Are you sure? Look, what I said yesterday about you and Tony being too young, well, maybe I was being a bit hard. You don't have to get married, you could get engaged like Tina and me . . .'

'I don't want to talk about it.'

'Look, I know Dad died in the last war, but everyone says it's going to be different this time. There are so many other fronts, and at the moment the boats and planes are bearing the brunt of the action. And I think they'll go on doing so. The soldiers won't get the hammering they did in the trenches in 1916.'

'Why? Because General Powell says so?'

'Diana, talk to Tony again, or let me – '

'No! Absolutely not. I forbid you to say a word to Tony, or anyone. This is my business not yours.'

'But you're miserable. I can see it.'

'I don't want to talk about it. Not now, or ever. Got to go, Wyn's in ahead of me again.'

William couldn't stop thinking about Tony and Diana as he carried on walking down the hill. All summer it had been Tina and him, Tony and Diana. They'd spent a lot of time together, mainly in the café because Tony and Tina hadn't been able to leave it for any length of time, but when they had managed to get away, they'd gone for walks in the park, or over Shoni's, and once they'd even managed a trip to the pictures. The thought of Tony and Diana's relationship ending cast a blight over his engagement to Tina.

He paused on the Tumble. Despite Diana's edict and the urgent need to see Charlie, he turned his steps towards the café. After fighting his way through the blackout curtain, he found Tony pouring out a trayful of teas for a tram crew. He waited until Tony had taken them through to the back room before tackling him, and when he did he saw the same miserable expression on his friend's face that his sister had been wearing.

'Did you get your orders?'

'Angelo brought the letter down with him. I sent him over the station to check the timetable. There's a train leaving just after seven on Monday morning that will get us to the camp on time.'

'I didn't think it would be so soon.'

'It can't come quick enough for me.'

'About you and Diana . . .' William began awkwardly.

'She asked you to come here?'

'No, but she told me it was over between you two.'

'Did she say why?'

'She said neither of you wanted to wait for the other, but that's a load of rubbish. You're as keen on her as I am on Tina. I know it's none of my business, but I – '

'You're right, Will, it is none of your business,' Tony broke in brusquely. 'Stay out of it.'

'That's what Diana said. But don't you see, it is my business? She's my sister, you're my friend . . .'

'And we're entitled to our privacy.'

'I'm sorry.' William was taken aback by the vehemence in Tony's voice.

'Do me a favour?'

'Name it.'

'If you value our friendship don't bring this up again.'

'Diana would kill me if she knew I'd brought it up this once. You won't tell her?'

Tony shook his head. The only consolation he had was that it was going to be a lot easier to put William's confidences out of his mind, than Diana's.

'So you see I'll only be able to work today and tomorrow.'

'Thanks for stopping by to tell me.' Charlie picked up a tray of sliced, pressed ox-tongue and slid it beneath the counter.

William wondered what it would take to raise an eyebrow on his boss's calm, implacable face. Perhaps Charlie would show some reaction if he announced the Germans had parachuted into Ponty park? He was almost tempted to try.

'Monday morning?' Alma chipped in. 'They didn't give you much time to pack.'

'I thought I'd get more.'

Alma looked at Charlie. 'You'll have to give up the market stall.'

'I'll telephone Cardiff when we finish this.'

'Can I telephone Bethan please, Alma?' William pulled a handful of change out of his pocket.

'Of course. Nothing wrong, is there?'

'No, it's just that my mother came home yesterday.'

'Your mother!' Both Charlie and Alma smiled. Megan had been Charlie's landlady before she'd lost her house along with her freedom, and Megan had been one of the few people in Pontypridd who'd had a kind word for everyone. That in itself had been enough to endear her to Alma. 'Is she well?'

'I've seen her looking better.'

'Would it be all right for us to call in this evening to see her?'

'You know Uncle Evan, open house where you two are concerned.'

'Tell him we'll be up as soon as we finish here.'

In the event it was Andrew, not Bethan, who came to the telephone. William passed on the message, left the shop and walked through the indoor fruit market to the butcher's market. Tonight his mother, Charlie, Alma, his uncle and Phyllis would enjoy a nice social evening. He wished he could join them instead of facing Mr Ronconi. What possible defence could he put up if Tina's short, fat, elderly father tried to throw him out of the Ronconi house?

'I hear you're going to be my fiancé-in-law?' Trevor Lewis grinned as he approached William's stall.

'Who told you?'

'Tina, she's been calling in on Laura on her way to work for the last month. I think she's hoping to find a niece or nephew there one morning.'

'No luck?'

'If he or she doesn't appear soon I might have to admit Laura to a lunatic asylum. But it can't be much longer, that's why I'm doing the shopping.' He studied the trays of offal, scrag ends of lamb, belly pork and tripe that covered three-quarters of the stall. The better cuts were furthest from the edge, zealously guarded by William who knew how few people could afford not only the money but the coupons to buy them, and how many might be tempted to slip a choice steak or chop into a bag of sheep's brains.

'What can I do you for?'

'Better make it something even I can cook, in case junior does decide to move.'

'I've got some sausages off the coupon.'

'What's in them?'

'Do you really want to know?'

'No. But tell me,' Trevor smiled maliciously, 'you renting a suit of armour to protect yourself against Papa Ronconi's wrath, or just wearing a tin ARP hat?'

'He's really that bad?' William cut a string of sausages in half and pushed them on to the scale.

'It took six months to recover from the hiding he gave me.'

'It's not a joking matter. What can I do if he refuses to give us his permission?'

'You'll live. Ronnie, Maud, Laura and I did.'

'The question is will I live engaged to Tina, or not?' William muttered as he wrapped the sausages.

A market day had never dragged so long for William. It didn't make any difference that tomorrow was going to be his last for the duration, whatever 'the duration' was going to be. Every few minutes he found himself studying the crowds flocking around the stalls, wondering if he'd ever see this customer, or that one – or even work on the market – again. He kept watching the door, wishing Tina would appear so he could tell her how sorry he was that they had so little time left. She finally turned up at six o'clock, her face flushed, her hair and clothes adorned by a sprinkling of raindrops.

'You're soaking you silly girl,' he scolded. 'Where's your coat and umbrella?'

'In the café.'

'They're not doing any good there.'

'I had to see you. Any chance of you finishing early?'

He eyed the stock on the counter. 'I might if I start knocking the odd penny a pound off what's left. Why?'

'I told Papa you wanted to see him.'

'You did what?'

'I thought he might be nicer to you if he had some time to get used to the idea of you being in our house.'

'And what did he say?'

'You know Papa.'

'Only by reputation, and something tells me I might not get to know him any better.'

'Mama's invited you to tea.'

'I'll have to call in home on the way.'

'You don't have to change.'

'My mother's home.'

'I thought she had years left to serve.' Tina lowered her voice, realising Megan's sentence wasn't the sort of thing she should be discussing in public.

'Looks like they're emptying the jails to make room for Old Nasty and his Nazis. You got to get back to the café?'

'I told Tony he'll have to manage without me for the rest of the evening. You heard about him and Diana? He's as touchy as a winkle that's lost its shell about it.'

'So I've heard.' He lifted the flap set in the counter. 'How about giving me a hand? Sooner we sell this lot and I drop the takings off to Charlie, the sooner we can go.'

William hardly said a word to Tina as they walked up the hill. Deciding to get engaged was one thing; asking Mr Ronconi for his daughter's hand, quite another. He wasn't *that* afraid of the man, but he'd seen him lose his temper with Angelo in the High Street café, and he'd rather Mr Ronconi's rage was directed at someone else's head.

'Penny for them?' Tina hugged his arm.

'They're not worth a farthing. Come and see my mother.' He led her around the corner and up Graig Avenue.

'Does she know about us?'

'All that Diana knows. How much have you told your father?'

'That you're out to seduce me.'

'Tina . . .'

She ran up the steps to his uncle's door, opened it, and dived through the blackout curtain. William caught up with her in the folds.

'It's like being smothered by a nun's skirts,' he whispered as he stole a kiss.

'And what would you know about a nun's skirts?'

'They're the same as any other woman's only bigger.'

She lashed out trying to hit him, accidentally swinging the curtain wide. The cry of 'Put that bloody light out' resounded from the street below.

'Careful,' William said as he switched off the hall light, 'we don't want to have to sell the ring to pay a twenty-five-bob fine.'

'Any more talk about nun's underwear and there won't be an engagement.'

'Skirts, not underwear. You didn't really tell your father I was out to seduce you, did you?'

'I didn't have to, he suspected it all along.'

'Someone should enlighten him on the differences between Welsh and Italian boys' intentions. Ours are strictly honourable.' Scooping the vast folds of the blackout curtain into his arms he finally managed to shut the door.

'What if your mother doesn't like me?'

'Unlike your father, my mother likes everyone.'

'What's that supposed to mean?'

'I've been talking to Trevor.'

'Papa gave him a rough time over Laura, but then she was the first one of us to get married. I think Papa just doesn't like the idea of any of us growing up.'

'Ronnie was heading for thirty when he married.'

'But Maud was only sixteen, and it wasn't long after Trevor and Laura. There hadn't been enough time for Papa to calm down.'

'Trevor's a doctor. Compared to him, what prospects have I got to offer? Not even a steady job after Monday.'

'Charlie will keep your job open for you.'

'Charlie might not be able to keep the shop open for himself if rationing gets any worse,' he prophesied gloomily. He helped her off with her coat, shouting, 'It's only me,' before leading her to the back kitchen.

It was warm, bright and cheerful after the damp, dark hill. Megan was sitting in Evan's chair, Bethan at the table beside her nursing her baby. Phyllis was bustling around making tea and, judging by the splashes coming from the wash-house, Even was bathing after his shift down the pit. There was no sign of Diana.

'It's good to see you, Tina. Come and sit down,' Megan said as soon as the initial greetings were over.

'You'll have a cup of tea and something to eat, Tina?' Phyllis offered.

'I could murder a cup of tea, but we'd better not eat.' She glanced slyly at William. 'I promised my mother we'd have tea in our house.'

'No doubt your father's got me down for the first course.'

'Sliced, battered and fried,' Tina agreed. 'It's good to see you home, Mrs Powell.'

'It's good to be home. What's this I hear about you and my Will?'

'It'll come to nothing if her father doesn't like me.' William crouched beside Bethan and poked his finger into the shawl-wrapped bundle on her lap.

'This isn't the great confident William Powell I used to know.' Bethan pulled back the shawl to reveal a tiny, scrunched face and a mop of reddish brown hair partially hidden beneath a bonnet.

'You know what he did to Trevor, and he threw Ronnie out of the house.'

'Trevor was still alive the last time I looked, and so's Ronnie and Maud,' Bethan reassured him.

'I suppose I'd better wash and change. Sackcloth and ashes do?' he asked Tina.

'You sure you know what you're doing?' Bethan asked Tina after William had disappeared through the wash-house door.

'I think there's possibilities for improvement there,' she said with mock gravity. 'Mind you, I'll be careful to keep him on a tight rein.'

'I'm glad you've decided to wait until the war's over before getting married, love.' Megan reached over and took the baby from Bethan.

'That's William's doing, not mine,' Tina confessed. 'I'd marry him tomorrow.'

'If you do, you'll avoid all the rows people usually have in the first year of married life,' Bethan said practically.

'How's my granddaughter?' Evan asked as he walked in, his face scrubbed pink.

'Angelic, but then what do you expect with the mother she's got.' The front door opened and closed.

'Diana?' Evan asked.

'No,' Megan replied, a small frown creasing her forehead. 'She sent a message up with Roberto Ronconi to say she's stocktaking for Wyn and she'll be home late.'

'My brother's really upset that it's over between them,' Tina contributed clumsily.

'It could be just a lover's tiff,' Bethan said kindly.

'I don't think so.' Megan lifted the baby on to her shoulder and rubbed her back. 'But then Tony and Diana are very young.'

'And they haven't been courting anywhere near as long as Will and I.'

'They didn't start in infants' school, if that's what you mean,' Megan laughed.

The doors to the wash-house and passage opened simultaneously and Andrew walked in the same time as a spruced-up William. Bethan looked at her husband and William sensed the whole room lighting up. Registering the look on Andrew's face he suffered an uncharacteristic pang of envy. It must be absolutely marvellous to look into someone else's eyes and know their thoughts, as Andrew and Bethan so clearly did. He wondered when, if ever, that kind of intimacy would develop between him and Tina.

'Hello, beautiful.' Andrew walked over to Megan and planted a kiss on his daughter's cheek.

'See what I mean?' Bethan complained to Megan. 'All the books younger sisters, Theresa, Stephania and Maria, and all of them were staring at William with critical, dark eyes.

'Only a stupid man would moon over a girl like you,' twelve-year-old Alfredo declared flatly.

Wyn Rees waited until the main film had run for ten minutes after the interval before closing his confectionery booth in the New Theatre. He checked the money in the till, separating the takings from the float which would be returned to the cash drawer the following morning. Bagging the coins into two canvas bags he pocketed them, then scanned his depleted shelves. His stock was running pitifully low. Two more nights at this rate of sale and he'd have nothing left, and no means of replacing it. Life was so unfair. It had been a struggle to keep the business ticking over during the depression, then, just as the pits had reopened putting money back into the miners' pockets and increasing trade levels, the war had to break, bringing a rationing that threatened to bankrupt him if he didn't diversify into something else – and soon.

The question was, what to sell that wasn't rationed? It was a problem that was beginning to preoccupy not only him, but every trader in Pontypridd. He glanced at the half-empty boxes that were left. He may as well go up to the shop in High Street now, and check on what remained rather than leave it until the morning.

After locking the kiosk he walked around the corner to the Old Tram Road where he had parked his van. Was there really any point in shuttling stock between the two shops? Perhaps it would be as well to wait until one or the other ran out, and close that one first. Then, with only one shop to run, there was nothing to stop him handing it over to Diana's care and joining up. The thought was an attractive one. Life with his increasingly cantankerous father and put-upon sister was no picnic, and he'd have the dubious consolation of doing something for his country if he was in the army. But he had the niggling feeling that army life would be even worse than civilian for a man like him.

Straining his eyes into the darkness, he drove the short distance to High Street. Why did night always bring memories of his friend who had gassed himself? Was death like this, a conscious darkness? Or did suicides writhe in a specially constructed, torturous hell reserved for self-murderers as the officiating minister at the funeral had assured the mourners? He didn't want to believe it. His friend had encountered enough of a hell on earth from his unforgiving father and the people

warn wives not to exclude their husbands from the family circle when the baby arrives. But this husband of mine totally ignores me in favour of Rachel.'

'You've got to admit, she's far less demanding than you,' Andrew grinned. 'It's good to see you home, Megan. Sorry I didn't have time to come in this morning.'

'Bethan said you had ward rounds.'

'And an endless queue of patients. This war has flushed out every hypochondriac in town, not to mention doting mothers who clog up the surgery asking how ill their sons have to be to avoid the call-up.'

'You can't blame them for wanting to hang on to what they've got,' Megan said softly. 'Not after last time. It cost Pontypridd dear.'

'That depends on whether they're worth hanging on to. Some of the darlings I saw this morning are liabilities, even for their mothers.' He turned to William: 'You're dressed like a dog's dinner.'

'William's braving Papa Ronconi to ask for Tina's hand,' Bethan announced.

'Can I shake your hand while it's still dangling from the end of your wrist?'

'Very funny.'

'Hope you get off lighter than Trevor, but then you've picked a good time. I think Papa Ronconi might be in a good mood now there's imminent prospect of a grandchild.

'Laura's in labour?' Bethan asked eagerly.

'Not exactly.'

'First time I've heard of a woman being "not exactly" in labour,' Megan observed.

'Trevor is planning on taking her for a bumpy ride in his car up Graigwen Hill to Llanwonno and back. He asked if you'd be around if he needed a midwife.'

'Of course I will.'

'Tea, Andrew?' Phyllis asked.

'Have I got time?' He looked at Bethan.

'All the time in the world, but if Trevor telephones to say they need me when we get home, it means you're going to have to take over your daughter.'

'Any time.' He tickled Rachel's toes. 'Yes please, Phyllis, now that no one wants me to do anything for five minutes, tea would be wonderful.' He sank down on the chair opposite Megan. 'You don't have to worry about the boys, they'll be all right,' he said, reading the look on her face.

'I wish I had your confidence.'

'Don't forget they've got Eddie waiting in the regiment to look after them, and,' he rubbed his jaw thoughtfully, 'no Nazi in his right mind will go near that one.'

Everyone burst out laughing. Eddie had knocked out Andrew when he'd been courting Bethan.

'More tea?' Phyllis asked Tina and William.

'No, thank you,' Tina answered. 'It's time we were on our way.'

'You'll let us know what happens?' Bethan asked.

'If I live,' William replied as he and Tina went out.

Constable Huw Davies plodded slowly up the Graig hill. The standard, police-issue blackout torch dangled unlit in his hand. He'd been walking the beat in Pontypridd for close on twenty-five years, and knew every lamp-post, every pothole and every loose paving slab.

As he drew alongside the shops in High Street he checked the windows for small yellow lines that might signal an infringement of lighting regulations. He liked to do the rounds ahead of the duty ARP wardens; they thought nothing of reporting the tiniest ray escaping from a scratch in the line of black paint most of the householders had edged their panes with, whereas he found a warning was generally more than enough to black out a house whose occupants would be hard pressed to find the twenty-two shilling plus fine the magistrates invariably imposed. As he reached the first shop he tested the lock. He had found the tobacconist's door open once, and two wide boys from Treforest hiding under the counter. He was kind-hearted, but not gullible, and the cock and bull story they had told him about searching for a lost cat had hastened their appearance before the town magistrate.

Satisfied that everything was sound and secure he went whistling on his way.

Diana heard her uncle's whistle and drew comfort from the familiar sound. She was curled into a corner behind the counter of the sweet shop, her back to the shelves, an untouched pastie from Ronconi's in front of her. She looked down at the book in her hand and turned the page. She hadn't a clue what the book was about or even why she was going through the motions of pretending to read it. She couldn't remember a single word on the page she'd flipped over, but hiding away was better than facing people, even kind, well-meaning ones like her mother and brother. How could she even begin to explain to them that her life was over? That she'd forfeited all right to happiness and a normal life; that she'd brought nothing but shame down on to the head of everyone who'd ever loved her.

Chapter Five

WILLIAM'S nerves were stretched to breaking point by the t and Tina had negotiated the short cut between Iltyd Stre Danycoedcae Road. He tripped over the kerb as he left the ground for the street, and, in putting his hands out to save his clo managed to ingrain his palms with gravel and coat his fingers thick, sticky mud.

'Just practising my grovelling,' he said as Tina accidentally wall into him.

'From my point of view I'd rather you did it in the light.'

He hauled himself to his feet, only just resisting the temptation t wipe his hands on his trousers. 'I suppose you'll expect me to wash before I shake your father's hand?'

'It might be an idea.' Now that they were drawing close to her house, he could detect traces of nervousness in her voice that matched his own. He hung back, holding his hands stiffly away from his clothes as she opened her front door. He tried to remember what Eddie had said about his most fearsome boxing opponents: 'They're only men. Like us they put their vests on over their heads, haul their trousers over their bums and unbutton their braces to go to the ty bach.' Crude but effective.

'Are you going to stand there all night?' Tina's voice was muffled by the inevitable blackout.

'You'd better switch off the passage light and hold back the curtain, I don't want to get it dirty.'

'I haven't switched the light on. It's us – Tina and William,' she shouted. 'William's coming through to the back, he fell over and needs to wash his hands.'

'Now they'll think I'm clumsy as well as stupid.'

'No one thinks you're stupid,' she retorted irritably as she closed the door.

'Yes we do,' came a disembodied chorus of voices.

Tina switched on the light. Sitting on the stairs were her two youngest brothers, Alfredo and Roberto, in front of them her three

of Pontypridd without burning after death. If there was a God, and sometimes he wondered, wherever his lover was, he'd be at peace.

He pulled up outside the shop in High Street, left the van, and unlocked the door. To his amazement, light flooded out when he pushed back the curtain.

'Diana?' he called out uncertainly as he pulled the curtain swiftly over the door. He stepped inside looking for signs of a burglary.

'I'm here, Wyn.'

He looked over the counter, watching as she struggled to her feet.

'What are you doing here at this time of night?'

'Nothing.' Averting her eyes, she went to the stockroom to get her coat.

He glanced at the floor where she'd been sitting and saw the pastie and book. 'It didn't work out between you and Tony, then?'

She left the stockroom in tears. He embraced her clumsily, pulling her head down on to his chest. 'It's not the end of the world. You've been through worse than this and survived. Come on, you're frozen stiff. Put your coat on and I'll take you home.'

'No!' she protested forcefully, between harsh, rasping sobs.

'You can't sleep here, you'll catch your death of cold.' Taking her coat from her, he wrapped it around her shoulders. Forgetting the stock he'd intended to ferry down to the other shop he led her to the door.

'I won't go home . . .'

'I'll take you somewhere else.'

'I'm not going to your house.'

'No.' He smiled at the thought of what his father might say if he brought Diana in her present state into the house. 'We're going for a drive to give you a chance to pull yourself together, then I'm going to buy you supper.'

'I can't go anywhere looking like this.' She rubbed her eyes with a grubby handkerchief she'd found in her coat pocket.

'You can eat fish and chips in the van.' He switched off the light and opened the door. 'And I'm not taking no for an answer.'

The silence was intense enough to send buzzing noises through William's head. Mr Ronconi sat at the head of the table; Mrs Ronconi closest to the range so she could serve everyone with ease. William had been placed at her right hand, Tina on her father's left, and in between five pairs of round, black eyes stared solemnly over the edge of the table scrutinising William, while everyone crunched on the crackling of the leg of pork Mrs Ronconi had bought for the occasion.

Aware of the sacrifice of the family's ration coupons in his honour, William took as sparing a portion of the meat as Mrs Ronconi would allow.

Used to the banter around his uncle's table, he found the silence imposed at mealtimes by Tina's father, disconcerting.

'More mashed potatoes, William?'

'No, thank you,' he replied politely, choking on nerves and a dry throat.

'Mama's mashed potatoes are *very* special.' Tina handed the dish down the table with a sickly sweet smile. He obediently heaped spoonfuls he didn't want on to his plate.

'Gravy?'

He could quite cheerfully have taken the jug from Tina and poured it over her head.

'No, thank you.'

'You can't eat potatoes dry.' Theresa took the jug from Tina and splashed gravy on his plate until it overflowed on to his trousers. 'I *am* sorry, I'll mop it up.'

'I'll do it.' Tina ran out of the back kitchen into the wash-house and fetched a tea towel.

'Tina!' Mr Ronconi's warning voice boomed before her hand touched William's trousers.

'I'll do it.' William took the towel from Tina, laid it over the puddle of gravy on his lap and hobbled out to the stone sink. He ran the tap and dabbed at the stain, wondering what he was doing in the Ronconis', apart from getting thoroughly embarrassed. He should have kissed Tina goodbye and cleared off to the Guards, then when the war was over he could have come back and married her. Just like that. No poncing about with permission and family inspections. Just a quick ceremony in a registry office and a long honeymoon.

'You all right, William?'

'Yes, thank you, Mr Ronconi, but I think this stain needs a little more cold water.'

Leaning on the sink he breathed in deeply, as the old man left the wash-house. For some peculiar reason he felt as though he'd had a close call. As though Tina's father had been able to read his thoughts – about the honeymoon.

'You see, no people.' Wyn jammed on the handbrake and reached in the back of the van for the two newspaper-wrapped parcels. Both were warm and appetisingly fragrant with the vinegary, mouth-watering smell of freshly fried fish and chips.

'It seems darker up here than it does in the town,' Diana murmured. Wyn had driven up to the Common. Somewhere below them, unseen and unlit, Pontypridd was going about its blacked-out life, so very different from its late evening life of a year ago played out beneath ribbons of street and house lights.

'This is what it must have been like for whoever dragged the standing stones and rocking stone up here.' Wyn handed her one of the parcels. 'Perhaps they waited until this time of night to sacrifice to their gods. Can't you just imagine it? A circle of people holding flaming torches while the priest stretched the victim out on the rocking stone, lifted the knife . . .'

'Andrew said the circle's not old enough to be druidic.'

'There goes another of my illusions about the town's history.'

'Even if it were true, people should have more sense than to creep around a deserted common in the middle of the night.'

'You don't like the dark?'

'No.' She shuddered despite the reassuring bulk of Wyn's presence. 'I feel that there's a huge black hole watching and waiting to swallow us up down there. One turn of the wheel, and we'll go crashing into it.'

'Holes don't watch and wait.' He unwrapped his fish and chips and started eating. 'But then, I like the dark. I always have. Mind you, I can't remember being in anything quite this black since I used to hide in the coal hole when I was a kid.'

'You hid in the coal hole? Whatever from?'

'Myself, I think. I started crawling in there when my mother was dying. I tried to tell myself that everything would be all right as long as I stayed in there. That she'd get out of bed and come looking for me, and when she did, she'd be well, happy and smiling, which was how I wanted her to be. Stupid, really.'

'That's not stupid. When Will and I were small and my mother used to cry because my father wasn't there, we made up a story about him. That he hadn't been killed at all, but he'd lost his memory and when he remembered who he was he'd come back. One night my mother overheard us talking. The following morning she explained that his body had been accounted for and buried. That there was no hope, that all we had of our father, all we'd ever have, was his photograph. You were lucky.' She peeled back the newspaper on her parcel of fish and chips. 'At least you can remember your mother.'

'Only to miss her all the more when she had gone.'

'Mam says you can't build your life around what might have been, just get on with what you've got.'

'She's right.'

'Right, maybe, but it's damned hard sometimes.'

Knowing she was regretting the loss of Tony, he put his hand over hers. 'I think I know how you feel.'

'How can you?' she burst out angrily. 'I loved Tony. I'll always love him, and now there's nothing left. I can't even dream about meeting someone else. Even if I could find a man who'd forgive me for what Ben Springer did, no man would want a woman who couldn't stand him near her. And I can't . . . I really can't bear the thought of a man coming near me ever again . . .'

Abandoning his fish and chips on the bench seat, he held her in his arms. Her chips had tumbled on to the seat between them; he could feel warm, sticky grease oozing through his trousers. 'I know what it is to love someone and lose them, Diana. And I couldn't even go to his funeral.'

It was the first time Wyn had ever mentioned his private life to her. Struggling to regain control of her emotions, she drew the back of her hand across her eyes, wiping away her tears.

'You remember the boy who gassed himself over in Pwllgwaun a month ago?'

'It said in the *Observer* that he was depressed at being out of work.'

'His father's on the council, so they didn't print the truth. The police caught him.'

'Caught him?'

'With another man.'

She sat back, not knowing what to say. Although she was aware of the names Wyn was called, she had never really considered what being 'a queer' meant. In a few words he had painted a picture of his personal life which shocked her to the core. Not the fact that he had loved, or could love, another man, but the persecution that would follow if anyone in authority found out.

'You really . . . loved him?' It seemed odd to use the word in conjunction with two men.

'I loved him,' he reiterated bitterly. 'Not that it did either of us any good.'

'But you said he was with another man. If he loved you, why was he with someone else?'

'It's not as easy for us as it is for you. You meet a boy, you start courting, you go for walks in the park, sit side by side in the pictures, go to a café and no one will bat an eyelid. We have to sneak around in the hope that no one will notice us. The police stopped my van a couple of times when he was in it. They told his father, and he warned him to stay away from me. He threatened that if he didn't, he'd make sure the police picked both of us up. That we'd be dragged through the courts. The last thing either of us could afford to risk was a prison sentence. Apart from what the scandal would do to our families, they don't treat our kind very well behind bars.'

'I didn't realise, Wyn. I'm sorry . . .'

'So am I. You've managed to spread your fish and chips all over me, and I can't even see to scrape it up.'

'You've got a torch?'

'Front pocket. Make sure you hold the tissue paper over the lens.'

It took five minutes to return all of Diana's fish and chips to the newspaper. She used the time to regain control of her emotions. Wyn had made her realise just how selfish she was being. She wasn't the only one with problems. Her mother couldn't be finding the adjust-ment to freedom easy after years of harsh, regimented life in prison. William was leaving Pontypridd to go heavens only knew where, and having to abandon Tina. Wyn was living on a knife edge of respect-ability, an edge he could tumble from at any moment. Her mother, Tina, Will, Wyn – they all had reason to be as miserable as her. Maybe she could help them if she stopped wallowing in her own misery.

'I shouldn't have told you as much as I did about my friend.' As soon as their meals were back on their laps Wyn switched off his torch.

'I won't tell anyone.'

'It's not that. You've enough worries of your own without listening to mine. I don't even know why I told you. I've never talked like this before to anyone who wasn't . . . like me, if you know what I mean.'

'I know what you mean.' She gazed at his silhouette outlined against the half-moon. 'I'd be happy to listen to your problems, any time. I can't help, but after all you've done for me it would be nice to be able to do some small thing in return, if only listen.'

'You're the best friend I've ever had, Diana,' he declared suddenly. 'I don't know what I'd do without you.'

'You'd be all right. It's me who would be broke and in the workhouse.' She reached over and squeezed his hand. It was good to talk to and touch a man who would never want anything from her in return. Not in the sense that Tony and any other normal man would.

'More jam roly-poly, William?'

William shook his head as he scooped the last of the custard-coated roly-poly from his bowl. His stomach felt as though it was on the point of bursting, like a balloon pumped too full of air.

'We've all finished, Mama,' Alfredo, the oldest and boldest of the younger Ronconis, ventured. 'Please may we leave the table?'

'And please may we listen to the radio?' Theresa asked.

'Not until the table's cleared and the dishes washed,' Mr Ronconi decreed.

'Would you like a cup of tea, William?' Mrs Ronconi asked.

William shook his head again, not trusting himself to open his mouth in case he burped.

'You can bring a pot into the parlour for us, Mama.' Mr Ronconi rose from the table and felt in his pockets for his pipe. 'It's time William and I had a smoke.'

'Thank you very much for the meal,' William said politely as he eased himself out of his chair.

'Come along, young man.'

William looked helplessly after Tina, who had bolted through the wash-house door with a pile of dishes. Feeling like a sacrificial lamb, he followed Mr Ronconi from the passage into the front parlour.

The room looked and smelt differently from any he had been in before. He sensed that he had stepped not only into another culture, but into Italy itself. The pictures on the wall were a mixture of turn-of-the-century sepia tinted photographs and highly coloured landscapes captured in vivid primary colours and shades of light that spoke of warmer summers than Pontypridd with its damp, cool climate would ever know. As he studied them, his cousin Maud's letters came to mind and he realised that the pictures had been hung to remind the Ronconis of the sunny land they had left behind.

The furniture was highly polished mahogany of a quality found in any comparatively well-heeled Pontypridd home, but the ornaments and china were not. Standing on the round table that dominated the centre of the room was a plastercast Madonna, dressed in a gown that matched the brilliant blue sky in the paintings on the walls. She was holding a plump toddler wearing a sleepy, contented expression that reminded William of Brian. There were framed texts on the wall in Italian that he couldn't read, and a large glass case that held many photographs of small black-haired girls and boys with enormous rounded dark eyes. The boys were dressed in sober suits with white shirts and ties, the girls in multi-layered, white lace communion dresses. He thought he recognised a diminutive Tina amongst them, but he couldn't be sure.

'Sit down.' Mr Ronconi offered him a seat opposite his, next to the fire that flamed high, but which the temperature in the room suggested had been lit only a short time before.

'Thank you, sir. Cigarette?' William sat forward to offer Mr Ronconi his packet. The older man set his pipe on the mantelpiece and took one. Rolling it between his fingers he sniffed at the tobacco as though he disapproved of the brand.

'Tina said you wanted to speak to me?' Mr Ronconi moved on abruptly from polite preliminaries.

Glad to be finally confronted by what he had come to do, William nodded before lighting Mr Ronconi's cigarette then his own. 'Yes, sir.' He leaned back in the chair and desperately tried to look at ease. 'I'd like to get engaged to Tina.'

'So she tells me.'

William shifted uneasily on his seat, uncertain whether Mr Ronconi expected him to continue or not. The seconds ticked on into a full minute that he counted off on the mantel clock.

'I overheard Tina telling her mother that you've bought her a ring.'

'Tina saw one she liked in Cardiff. An old one.' 'Old' sounded better than second-hand, and not as pretentious as antique. 'I was afraid it would be sold if I didn't get it for her there and then.'

'You could have put a deposit on it.'

'It might have been sold by mistake, and if someone else had bought it we might never have found another that Tina liked as much . . .' William's voice trailed away. He was conscious of gabbling about trivia.

'Sure of yourself, aren't you?'

'Not at all, sir.'

'Tell me then, what are you going to do with the ring if I don't give Tina permission to get engaged to you?'

'Give her the ring as a present. It doesn't have to be worn on the third finger of her left hand.'

'And if I refuse to allow her to see you again?'

'I'll live in hope that you change your mind before the war is over.'

'So, you intend to wait until the war is over before marrying my daughter?'

'Yes, sir.'

'That will give you plenty of time to take instruction. You do intend to convert to the one true faith?' he asked sharply.

'Catholicism, sir? I haven't given it much thought.'

'I've had one son married in a heathen Church. I'm not about to allow a second child of mine to make the same mistake.'

'As you say, sir, I've plenty of time to take instruction,' William echoed, feeling that conversion was a small price to pay for Tina. Mr Ronconi puffed on his cigarette without making any further comment.

'I know everything's unsettled at the moment, sir, but that's why Tina and I want to get engaged, so we both have something to look forward to at the end of the war.' He looked expectantly at Mr Ronconi and when no reply was forthcoming, he said the first thing that came into his head. 'If Charlie's shops are still open at the end of the war, he'll give me my old job back . . .'

'And if they're not?' Mr Ronconi broke in swiftly.

'I'll go back down the pit.' William concealed one hand beneath the other and crossed his fingers. A pithead was one place he was certain he never wanted to see again from the bottom of a shaft. 'I earn good money now,' he insisted, anxious to prove himself a dependable prospect. 'And I've saved some. More than enough to buy furniture and set up a home.'

'Tina has some money of her own too.' The old man glowered at him as though he suspected William of having designs on it.

'She told me, sir, but I think it's a husband's place to support his wife.'

'Do you, now?'

'It's not as though we're too young to know what we're doing. We're both over twenty-one – '

'Only just,' Mr Ronconi snapped.

'I promise you, sir, I'll do everything in my power to make Tina happy.'

'You could start by getting killed.'

'Pardon?' William blinked, uncertain whether Mr Ronconi was joking, or not.

'You've joined up. Soldiers get killed.'

'Not me,' William protested indignantly.

'That's just what Tony and Angelo are saying. It makes me wonder if you boys know what you've got yourselves into.'

'We'll take care of one another.' Anxious to get back to the topic of Tina, William risked pushing his case again. 'Sir, about Tina and me . . .'

'As she insists she can't live without you, I suppose I'd better let you get engaged.'

'Thank you very much, sir.'

'We'll have a party in the Taff Street café on Sunday. It can be a goodbye party for the boys as well.'

'That's very generous, sir, thank you,' William enthused, scarcely daring to believe he'd met with so little opposition.

'Don't thank me too much; a lot can happen in a war, boy.'

'I hope you're not banking on me not coming back?' William smiled anxiously.

'I might be, and then again, with all the hotheads out of the way, the steady fellows who think and test the water before they jump in with both feet will be left with a clear field. Your going away will give Tina time to reflect, and who knows –' Mr Ronconi tossed the end of the cigarette into the fire and reached up for his pipe – 'she may do better for herself yet. Particularly as you won't be around to interfere.'

'Time to take you home.' Wyn screwed the paper that had been wrapped around the fish and chips into a ball and flicked it into the back of the van.

'I suppose so.'

'Don't you want to go?'

'I'm fed up with pitying glances and silences whenever I walk into a room.'

'Once Tony has gone it'll soon be forgotten.'

'By everyone except me.'

'I'm sorry.'

'I'm the one who should apologise. I'm turning into a right minnie moaner. You deserve a medal, and not just for buying me supper.'

He started the engine and inched back to where he thought the road might be, eventually picking it up from the markings the council had painted down the middle of all the roads when the blackout regulations had been enforced. Peering through the windscreen at the faint glow that escaped the cardboard hood over the single headlamp, he followed the line down the hill, over the new bridge that flanked the arched old bridge that had become Pontypridd's landmark, and up Taff Street. As he drew alongside the New Inn a policeman stepped in front of the van. Wyn slammed on the brakes and Diana was thrown forward, banging her head against the windscreen.

'Bloody fool,' Wyn shouted angrily. 'You all right?' he asked Diana anxiously, ignoring the constable who was hammering on the door.

'I think so,' Diana replied in a dazed voice.

Wyn wrenched down his window. 'You could have killed her,' he shouted furiously.

'Her?' The policeman shone a torch inside the car. 'Miss?'

'Diana, Diana Powell,' she answered faintly.

'I hope you had a good reason to stop us?' Wyn demanded indignantly, knowing full well why the rookie had picked on his van. The arrogant young constable had taken exception to him one night when they'd both been training in the gym and hadn't missed an opportunity to harass and belittle him since.

'I thought you were showing too much light.'

'I had the covers checked in the garage on Broadway. If there's anything wrong I'll go back to them.'

'No, now that you've stopped I can see they're fine.'

'Problems?'

Diana recognised the deep baritone of the oldest constable in Pontypridd, her mother's brother, Huw.

'This idiot stepped in front of us,' she complained through Wyn's open window.

'Diana?'

'A sore and aching Diana.' She rubbed her head as her uncle shone his torch inside the car.

'I suggest you get your young man to drive you home so you can put some cold water and vinegar on that bruise before it starts to swell.'

'I'll get her home now.' Wyn started the engine and began to wind up the window, but not quickly enough to cut out the conversation between the two officers.

'But he's a bloody pansy!'

'Language, lad, and I'd be very careful what I'd say if I were you. Particularly about one of the town's retailers and employers. You could get caught with a massive fine for repeating slander of that nature.'

'Looks like you've done wonders for my reputation.' Wyn turned the wheel and followed the road up the Graig hill.

'Any time you need a girlfriend you know where to come,' Diana replied flippantly.

'You mean that?'

'I'd be only too happy to be of some use to a man,' she replied, unable to keep the irony from her voice.

'Then how about coming to tea on Sunday?'

'Tea? In the New Inn?'

'At home with my father and sister.'

'I'd like to if I can.'

'You don't have to.'

'I didn't mean it that way. It's just that Will might be getting engaged.'

'To Tony Ronconi's sister?'

'Now that's an idea. I'll make a deal with you. If there's no party I'll have tea in your house, and if there is, you come to it with me. That way no one can shower me with sympathy over Tony.'

'Is that what you want?'

'That's most definitely what I want,' she answered firmly.

Chapter Six

'EARLY for chapel, aren't you?' Wyn's father carped from the depths of the bed set in front of the fire.

'I'm not going to chapel.' Wyn walked in from the passageway. When his father had become bedridden, he had insisted on taking up residence in the 'middle room' of the comfortable semi-detached he shared with his son and daughter. Wyn would have preferred him to have moved into the rarely used front parlour because it could be shut off from the rest of the house; Myrtle the largest bedroom because it was close to the upstairs bathroom, but he insisted on the middle room because in addition to serving as living room it also acted as the sole passageway between the kitchen and the hall, a distinct asset when his only interests in life were monitoring the comings and goings of the household and eliciting sympathy from visitors.

'Then why are you all prettied up like that?' the old man enquired scathingly. Wyn was wearing a white boiled shirt and starched collar, his favourite dark red tie and his best suit which had been brushed and pressed to pristine condition.

'Going out.'

The invalid lifted his head from the pillows Myrtle had plumped up for him and looked out of the window at a vista of grey skies and gathering stormclouds. 'Can't go for a walk in the park on an afternoon like this.'

'I'm going to Ronconi's.'

'To sit with the tram crews?'

'There's a private party in the restaurant they've opened in Taff Street,' Wyn said evenly, ignoring the gibe about the crews.

'And *you've* been invited?'

'A girl asked me to go with her.'

'Girl? *You* with a girl?'

'Diana, the one who works in our High Street shop.'

'Our? There is no "our", boy. It's all mine and don't you forget it.'

Wyn walked into the back kitchen where his newly polished shoes lay where he'd left them, outside the wash-house door. 'If you've no 'objection, I may bring her back for supper,' he murmured casually as he carried them through.

'Objection! I've been waiting for you to bring a girl into this house for ten years.' For the first time since his father had taken to his bed, Wyn actually saw a smile on his face. 'It's serious then?'

'Diana's a friend. A good one.'

'But she could be more?'

'Don't push, Dad.'

'If I don't, you never will.' His father settled back on the bed.

'Is there anything I can get you before I go?' Wyn asked when he'd finished lacing on his shoes.

'Myrtle can see to me when she gets back from the Troop Comforts Fund meeting.'

'That might not be for hours. You know how committees go on, so if you want anything, ask now.'

'Just the radio on low, perhaps.' Wyn obliged. 'Not that low,' he snapped, 'and not that loud either.'

Eventually Wyn hit a sound level that elicited no criticism. 'Do you want a cup of tea, Dad?' he asked

'So soon after my dinner? You want me to die of indigestion?'

'You might get thirsty. How about I bring you a bottle of lemonade?'

'That would be fine if I had the strength to lift it.'

'I'll pour you a glass.'

'And let it get flat before I drink it? You know I can't abide flat lemonade. No, you go off and have a good time. Don't worry about me, Myrtle will see to me when she gets back.'

Wyn counted silently to ten in a desperate effort to ignore his father's air of whining martyrdom. 'Here —' he propped a cane his father used to rap on the dividing wall between their house and next door, against the bed. 'I'll warn Mrs Edwards I'm going out and you'll be alone for an hour or two.'

'There's no need to bother the neighbours,' his father interrupted sharply.

'Would you rather I waited until Myrtle came back?'

'As your social life is obviously more important to you than my health and comfort, just go, will you.'

'Well if you're sure you have everything you need, I will,' Wyn answered smoothly, knowing full well that the last thing his father wanted was to be taken at his word. 'See you later.'

'With the girl?'

'If she's not too tired.'

70

It wasn't hard to walk away from the cantankerous, manipulative old man. It was only later, after Wyn had crossed Gelliwastad Road and was halfway down Penuel Lane, that he remembered the strong, upright, proud man his father had been. He almost turned back before recollecting that man had gone for ever. The whining invalid who ruled his and Myrtle's every waking minute with a rod of iron had supplanted him, transforming their lives into a never-ending routine of tedious, joyless duty. The last thing he could afford to do was yield to the tyrant's demands any more than he already had. For Myrtle's sake as well as his own.

Diana had been too busy on Saturday and Sunday morning to visit Ronconi's café even if she'd had the inclination to do so. Saturday was taken up with work, and Sunday morning went in helping Phyllis and her mother bake for William's engagement party. As Evan had invited her Uncle Huw and Charlie and Alma up for Sunday dinner to celebrate Megan's homecoming, the house was full of noise and high-pitched brittle laughter that accentuated the tension caused by the war and the imminent departure of William. Everyone was being far too cheerful, especially her mother, but for a few hectic hours she managed to relegate all thoughts of Tony to the back of her mind; however, when she found herself packed alongside her mother, Bethan and the baby in Andrew's car on the way down the Graig hill to the Ronconis' Taff Street restaurant, she remembered, and wished she'd had the sense to plead illness – any excuse rather than face Tony after the embarrassment of that night.

Wyn was waiting for her outside Penuel Chapel. He smiled when he spotted her climbing out of the car with a pile of biscuit tins balanced in her arms.

'You're early.' She forced a reciprocal smile as he came to greet her.

'Mrs Powell, Mrs John, Doctor.' He lifted his hat to Megan, Bethan and Andrew.

'You must be Wyn Rees, I've heard a lot about you.' Andrew, the only one with a free hand, extended it to Wyn who shook it vigorously.

'Allow me, Mrs Powell.' Wyn relieved Megan of the pile of tins she was carrying.

'Seems I have a lot to thank you for, Mr Rees.' Megan looked Wyn up and down, anxious to form her own opinion of Diana's boss, after listening to William's less than flattering description.

'I'm lucky to have found Diana, Mrs Powell. She's a good worker.'

'Are you lot going to stand outside all day gossiping?' William was waiting in the open doorway, Tina wearing an enormous smile and a new, red and green crêpe dress, hanging on to his arm.

'Do I get to kiss my new cousin-in-law?' Without waiting for a reply Andrew kissed Tina on the cheek.

'Hey, John, lay off, there's no such thing as a cousin-in-law,' William protested.

'Looks like there is now,' Bethan laughed, shifting the baby to a more comfortable position in her arms.

'You look far too gorgeous to be with him.' Determined to give no one cause to pity her, Diana nudged Tina with her elbow as she carried the tins into the restaurant towards a long table that was already groaning with sandwiches that must have taken up the whole of the Ronconis' ham and butter ration for a month. Besides the ham, cheese and chicken sandwiches, there were pies, pasties, sausage rolls, biscuits and a multitude of cakes of every sort, size and description, including a selection of fancies spread with icing that had attracted crowds of sugar-starved children. Diana opened her tins and moved the plates around in a futile attempt to make room for her family's offerings.

'You're going to need another table,' Wyn advised as he hovered at her elbow with the tins he'd taken from her mother.

Diana looked around the crowded room for someone to help them. Charlie and Alma were standing talking to Bethan and Andrew, the baby's tiny hands curled around Charlie's powerful fingers; William and Tina were still at the door surrounded by friends, Tina half buried beneath a mounting pile of parcels that had been presented to them. There was no sign of Tony, but she spotted Angelo filling the tea urn behind the counter and called to him.

'You've met Wyn Rees.' She effected the introduction as Angelo and Alfredo brought another table to join the bank against the wall that held the buffet.

Angelo nodded as he set down the table. Alfredo spread a cloth and Wyn and Diana moved plates on to it. The boys left them and returned to the counter with a cursory nod, but Diana looked up in time to catch Angelo's eye. She wished she hadn't. There was condemnation and anger in his fleeting glance, and something else, something she suspected wouldn't have been there if she'd brought anyone other than Wyn to the party. She looked back to William and Tina. Her brother's arm was wrapped around Tina's waist and there was a subdued look about him she hadn't seen before.

She wondered if Tina had 'volunteered' to sleep in the café one night so she and Will could experiment as she and Tony had done. If

72

they had, it must have ended more successfully than her episode with Tony.

'Isn't that your uncle?' Wyn asked as Evan walked in with Phyllis and their small son Brian, Huw Davies trailing behind them.

'Both uncles.' Her heart missed a beat as Tony walked up the stairs from the basement kitchen with lipstick smeared over his cheek and collar and Judy Crofter, a short, incredibly silly blonde from Leyshon Street in tow. 'Doesn't Uncle Huw look odd without his uniform?' she babbled, scarcely knowing what she was saying.

'That's Constable Davies?'

'His helmet hides his bald patch and what's left of his ginger hair. Come on, I know you've met him, but he'll sulk if I don't formally introduce you.'

Wyn gripped her fingers reassuringly as she slipped her hand into his. 'You all right?' he whispered as he saw Tony staring at them.

'Perfectly,' she gushed.

'I don't think I should have come.' Tony's gaze made him feel like a gatecrasher. 'It looks like this is a family occasion.'

She gave him as close an approximation of Tina's adoring look at William as she could manage. 'Don't be a silly goose, and thank you,' she said in a voice designed to carry to Tony. 'I'd love to have supper at your house.'

William wound up the gramophone Trevor Lewis had brought down in the back of his car while Tina turned the pages of the record book carefully so as not to chip the delicate edges of the fragile records.

'I'm amazed you're still with us, Laura,' Andrew declared tactlessly as he carried his daughter over to where Laura was sitting.

'It's not through choice.' She patted her swollen abdomen. 'Tina?' she called to her sister, 'put on a rousing jazz piece. A whirl with Andrew round the floor just might be the kick-start I need to get young Laura going.'

'Oh no you don't.' Andrew took the vacant chair next to hers, and clutched his daughter close. 'If anyone's going to be responsible for that, it has to be Trevor.'

'But he can't dance.'

'No one's perfect.'

'And you are?' Bethan raised her eyebrows as she joined them.

'Far from it, but I'm not foolhardy enough to foxtrot with Laura.'

'Are there no brave men left?' Laura wailed theatrically.

'Only in the army,' William crowed.

'I'll speak to you after you've met your first Sergeant-Major,' Andrew responded.

'No one will be able to resist this piece,' Tina set the needle down on the rousing refrain of 'I can't dance, don't ask me'. Glan Richards made a beeline for Tina's sister, Gina. Alma dragged a reluctant Charlie on to the square that the Ronconi boys had marked out for use as a dance floor in the back room, Wyn Rees and Diana joined them, and soon they were lost to sight behind a dozen other couples.

'I think your parents must have invited half the Graig,' Andrew commented to Laura as he looked around the crowded restaurant.

'Just family and friends, plus everyone who has boys leaving in the next week or two.'

'All these boys have joined up!' Bethan exclaimed.

'Let's hope they all come back,' Trevor said as he carried a tray of orange juices towards them.

'Why is Diana with Wyn Rees?' Tina asked as she bounded up to change the record. 'I know she and Tony have had a spat, but someone should tell her she's picked the wrong sex to make Tony jealous.'

'I'm not sure she is trying to make Tony jealous. She always has been rather fond of Wyn,' Laura answered in a flat tone that she intended as a warning to Tina to drop the subject.

'But he's a — '

'Exceptionally nice chap,' Andrew broke in speedily, as Wyn and Diana walked towards them. 'And a fair and decent boss, from what Diana says.'

'Boss? He's a . . . ow!' she exclaimed as Laura kicked her ankle. 'What did you do that for?'

'Testing to see if movement can make junior here budge. I'm fed up of carrying her around, it's time someone else had a turn.'

'You're that sure it's a her?' Andrew said.

'She wouldn't dare be anything else. I need reinforcements to keep Trevor in check. Tell you what, Tina, put on 'Begin the Beguine' and I'll get lazybones here,' she rose majestically to her feet and took the tray from Trevor's hands, 'to take a turn around the floor.'

'I'll start the car engine and keep it running,' Andrew joked.

'Laura in labour?' Diana asked as she joined Bethan.

'Not yet, but she's hoping.'

'Would anyone like some buffet?' Wyn was anxious to be of service. He felt uneasy surrounded by people he sensed would never willingly have chosen his company.

74

'I'd love a sandwich,' Bethan said as she took Rachel from Andrew, 'if you really don't mind getting them?'

'Not at all.'

'Make it a plateful, please,' Andrew called after him.

Diana stood against the wall and watched the dance floor. Half the girls on the Graig seemed to be there and Tony was in the middle of an adoring group of them. Reason told her she should be pleased that he had recovered so well from his disastrous experience with her. She loved him, she wanted him to be happy, but all the well-intentioned good wishes in the world couldn't put her in a reasonable frame of mind. It was unbelievably painful to stand back and watch him flirt and laugh, especially with Judy Crofter, whom he had always dismissed as an empty-headed ninny. But Diana didn't doubt that she was a virginal empty-headed ninny and that was the one thing she had learned really mattered to men, and the one thing she no longer had to give.

A sharp tap on her shoulder startled her. She turned to find herself staring at Angelo.

'Dance?'

She looked around for Wyn. He was deep in conversation with her mother and uncle Huw at the buffet table. 'Do you know enough not to tread on my toes?' she demanded, suspecting an ulterior motive behind the invitation.

'Tina's been giving me lessons.'

'Lessons don't necessarily mean that you've learned anything.'

'You and Tony quarrelled?' he asked bluntly as he led her on to the dance floor.

'That's between Tony and me.'

'He's really miserable and we're leaving first thing tomorrow.'

'He doesn't look miserable.' She couldn't stop watching Tony. He'd left the dance floor as soon as she and Angelo had stepped on to it and was now standing at the counter, Judy still fawning all over him, although he was now talking to Eddie's wife Jenny who'd turned up unexpectedly with a large and, she suspected, expensive parcel for William and Tina.

'That's an act, Diana. You know he likes you.'

'He told you that?'

'Not exactly,' he hedged.

'He'd be furious if he knew that you were talking to me.'

'Probably,' Angelo admitted. 'But he's my brother, and you two have been happy all summer. I hate to see you fall out now, when we're going away and anything could happen. We might not come back . . .' his voice faltered as he realised he'd finally put his greatest fear into words.

'You're scared, Angelo, aren't you?'

'Not me,' he bluffed defiantly.

'Then you're a bigger fool than I thought you were, and that's saying something. How could you let William and Tony talk you into joining up at your age? Especially now, with Laura having a baby, Ronnie gone, and Tony leaving. Who's going to run the cafés?'

'Tina and Gina will manage.'

'Poor old Tina and Gina. It's not too late. All you have to do is tell them your real age. They'd never have let you join the Guards if they knew you were only seventeen.'

'I want to go.' The music had ended and he and Diana were the only two on the floor. 'But I'd rather you and Tony made it up before we went.'

'Angelo, you're a sweet boy, but there are some things that don't bear meddling in, and one of them is other people's business.'

Diana took refuge in the toilet. Opening her bag she took out her comb and a small bottle of eau-de-Cologne. Unscrewing the top she dabbed the scent on her temples as she stared at her face in the mirror. Was it possible to tell? Were men already calling her the names they reserved for the women in station yard?

'Hiding?' Tina slammed the door against the wall as she walked in and pulled a lipstick out of her handbag.

'Getting my breath. You didn't do a good job of teaching Angelo to dance.'

'He wouldn't listen.'

'I've hardly seen you since Thursday. It's going to take some getting used to, you and Will engaged.'

'Thanks for the bedlinen you and your mother gave us, Di. It's gorgeous, I love the embroidery. I only wish Will and I could sleep under it tonight.'

'Tina!'

'Don't pretend to be shocked. I bet you wonder what it's like to sleep with a man as much as I do. I really wish Will and I were getting married instead of engaged.'

'You will when the war is over.' Diana's cheeks burned as she tried to tone down the colour with lavish applications of powder.

'I'd rather make it embarkation leave.'

'You might be separated for a long time. Anything could happen.'

'Does lecturing run in the family? You and Will are beginning to sound like my father.'

'Probably only thinking of Jenny and Eddie. They rushed in and look where it got them.'

'Give me credit, I've a lot more sense than her, and unlike Jenny who couldn't make up her mind between Eddie and Haydn I've never gone out with anyone other than Will.'

'I know. It's just that . . .' Diana soaked her handkerchief under the cold tap and dabbed at her eyes in an effort to stem the tears that threatened to run down her newly powdered cheeks.

'I'm sorry, that was tactless. I should have remembered you and Tony,' Tina apologised. 'I don't know what happened between you two, but he's pretty cut up about it. He said you wouldn't marry him.'

Diana grasped the revelation, and clung to it. Tony might consider her soiled goods, but he still thought enough of her to spare her feelings. Gentleman to the last, even if he was a gentleman who didn't want her.

'It wasn't meant to be,' she said shortly.

'It's a shame. I rather liked the idea of you being my sister-in-law twice over.' Tina hugged her, smearing powder from Diana's face on to her dress.

'Come on, this is your big day.'

'Not the biggest, that will come when we get married.' She stood back and eyed Diana. 'It seems wrong to be this happy when you're miserable.'

'Whatever makes you think I'm miserable?'

'Your face, and Tony's.'

Diana glanced in the mirror and tried to widen her smile to make it look just a little more natural. 'How can we be miserable when we've got you and Will to be happy about?'

'You eat any more and you're going to be sick.'

'Between you nagging and this one kicking I wouldn't be at all surprised.' Laura eyed Trevor warily as she stuffed half a custard-filled éclair into her mouth.

Andrew laughed as Bethan handed Rachel back to him.

'If you two want to dance I'll have my god-daughter,' Diana offered.

'That's right,' Laura moaned, 'rub it in.'

'Rub what in?' Diana asked mystified, as Andrew wrapped his arm around Bethan and led her off to dance.

'The fact that Rachel's born and this one isn't.'

Diana burst out laughing. 'Judging by the size of you it really can't be much longer.'

'Cake, Mrs Lewis, Diana?' Wyn asked arriving with a plate.

'I think even Laura's had enough,' Trevor said as Laura blanched visibly at the array of confectionery.

'I think Laura wants to go home.'

'To throw up?' Trevor suggested.

'To give birth. Get Bethan.'

'Laura . . .'

'I don't want any doctors around. Bethan and I are trained mid-wives, we know exactly how useless men are when it comes to the important part of having babies.'

The party dissolved into chaos. A white-faced Trevor and unnaturally calm Bethan helped Laura to Trevor's car. Mrs Ronconi, who'd run round in clucking, aimless circles for five minutes, insisted on climbing into the car with Bethan and Laura, despite her husband's and Trevor's protests that she would be more use in the restaurant. Megan, Evan and Phyllis relieved Andrew of Rachel and, offering to look after her for as long as necessary, carried her off to Charlie and Alma's across the road. Andrew, who had decided to follow Trevor in his own car in case he was needed to run errands or help out, had started the engine before Mr Ronconi decided to run after him and beg a lift to Trevor and Laura's, using the excuse that he'd be able to keep his wife, who was already semi-hysterical, in check. But it was obvious that he wanted to be at hand for what he hoped would be the birth of his first grandson.

'I feel sorry for Laura,' Tina said as she waved off her father and Andrew. 'She can't win. If she has a girl Trevor and my father will be disappointed, and if she has a boy Mama and my sisters will be upset.'

'If she has any sense she'll have a boy. Girls are useless.'

'You –' She hit William's arm too hard for the blow to be mistaken as playfulness.

'Glad to see you beginning as you mean to go on.' Diana stood with her arms raised so Wyn could help her on with her coat.

'Don't tell me you're going as well?'

'I promised Wyn's sister I'd have supper with them,' Diana apologised, knowing that she should have volunteered to help with the clearing up but feeling totally unequal to facing Tony for a moment longer.

'I'm sorry, Tina, William.' Wyn pulled an envelope from his inside pocket. 'I know it's customary to give the happy couple a present, but I didn't have time to buy one, and even if I had, I wouldn't have known what to get. So I hope you'll take this and get something you want.'

'Thank you, Wyn.' Tina took the envelope. 'I'll put it in the bank, and there it will stay until we're married. The less money William has to waste on beer before then, the better.'

'I'm going to need all the beer I can get where I'm going.'

'The memory of what you've already drunk will serve well enough.'

'Bossing me around, and not even married.'

'More fool you for letting her,' Tony shouted from inside. 'Who's going to help me put this place back together for the morning?'

'Who's going to run it now that Laura won't be able to?' Gina asked.

'Me,' Tina said briskly. 'And before you ask, you'll have to manage the Tumble by yourself, it's as much as Papa can do to keep the one on the Graig hill going.' She flashed an insincere smile at Angelo and Tony who were moving tables back on to the area they had cleared for a dance floor. 'I hope the army treats you like slaves.'

'I love you too, dear sister,' Tony retorted caustically.

'It will serve you right for joining up and leaving all the work to me and Gina. Oh, don't tell me you're going as well?' She turned from kissing Diana goodbye to see a crowd from Leyshon Street with their coats on.

Soon there was hardly anyone left. Glan helped William to move the last of the tables back while Gina, Tina and Maria finished the washing up.

'We could go to Charlie's to say goodbye,' William suggested when even Tina was finally satisfied with the state of the place.

'You go ahead.' Tony gave Glan a hard look as he moved close to Gina. 'I'll see Gina and the children home. And if you call in Laura's, tell Mama I'll see that they're all in bed on time.'

'Tony,' Alfredo whined.

'Ten minutes sooner for anyone who whinges.'

'Thanks, Tony.' William fetched Tina's coat.

'I hate saying goodbyes,' Tina said fiercely as he draped it over her shoulders. 'I always end up crying and making a fool of myself.'

'You'd better get used to them.' William opened the door and stepped out into the street. 'Something tells me there's going to be a lot more goodbyes before this war is over. But, to look on the bright side, there should be an equal number of hellos.'

'Not necessarily to people we want to see.'

'You thinking of the Germans?' he asked as he closed the door behind them.

'Among others.'

'They wouldn't dare invade Wales.'

'Who's going to stop them?'

'We are.'

'In France? Hasn't it occurred to you brave volunteers that all we'll have left to protect us when you're gone are the Home Guard and people like Dai Station who are only good at bullying children and little old ladies who've forgotten to pull their blackout curtains.'

'And hasn't it occurred to you that in order to reach here, Hitler's army will have to go through our forces in France, which is why we volunteered?'

'What's to stop them going round you?'

'The Dutch and Belgian armies.'

'Seems to me they didn't do much stopping last time.'

'That was last time, this is now.'

'Well I've news for you, you'll never make General. It's obvious to anyone with ears, eyes and a brain in their head that Hitler is going to invade us.'

'He told you?'

'Very funny. Better men than you must think he's on his way. Why else would they erect barbed-wire barriers on all the beaches? Just think of the money they could have saved by not bothering, and then there's the cost of issuing all the gas masks, and warnings to dig shelters . . .'

'The shelters and gas masks are only precautions in case Hitler decides to bomb us. And if you want my opinion I don't think he'll do that either.'

'Why not? According to Eddie he's already dropping leaflets.'

'There's a world of difference between leaflets and bombs.'

'I wonder if the army will be able to teach you what it is?' she asked innocently as he knocked on the door set to the side of Charlie's shop.

Charlie ran down the stairs to let them in, his square-jawed, normally pale skin flushed, William assumed, by a liberal helping of vodka.

'Came to say goodbye,' William explained as Charlie ushered them in. 'I won't get a chance tomorrow.'

'The best way is with a toast,' Charlie declared as he led the way up the stairs to his living room. 'Wine or vodka?'

'Wine please, Charlie.' Tina followed William into the apartment over Charlie's shop. It was the first time she'd been in Charlie and Alma's home and she was amazed, not by the furniture, which was old, dark and conventional but by the fabric Alma had used to cover the table, easy chairs and sofa. A swirling pattern in blue, red and green it dominated the room, lending it an exotic, Eastern atmosphere.

'Striking, isn't it?' Alma asked when she saw Tina staring. 'One of

Charlie's Russian friends gave us a bale as a wedding present. I've grown to like it, but it might be as well that my mother is blind.' There was a ghost of a smile hovering around her mouth and Tina wasn't sure whether she was serious or not.

Charlie went to the sideboard and pulled out bottles of wine and vodka. He opened the wine while Alma fetched glasses for Tina and William. Topping up Phyllis, Alma and Megan's glasses of wine, he poured out some for Tina. Handing them over he solemnly poured another helping of lemonade into the tiny glass Alma had given Brian. Brian turned his eyes to Evan, seeking approval. Evan nodded and Brian picked up the glass, but he didn't drink it. Like the women he held back, sensing that something important was about to happen. Charlie pulled the cork on the vodka bottle and poured out three half-tumblerfuls. William, who'd drunk vodka once or twice before at Charlie's instigation, blanched when he saw the measures, but he still took the tumbler.

Surprisingly ceremonious for once, Charlie lifted his glass to the room and to Rachel who was sleeping in a basket in the corner. 'To life, to us and victory for the Allies.'

They all raised their glasses.

'And to William and Eddie, the best men I could have hoped to have had working for me, and to us working together again at the end of the war.'

'I'll drink to that.' Evan made a wry face as the vodka disappeared down his throat.

Charlie put down his empty glass and picked up the bottle ready to refill his and Evan's glass. William hung on to his tumbler as he walked over to Alma. 'Am I allowed to kiss the boss's wife goodbye?'

She hugged him. 'You take care of yourself.'

'I'm only going training. I'll see you again before I get sent overseas.'

'You can still take care.'

He turned to Charlie. His boss was only nine years older than him, but perhaps because he had been Evan's friend first, he had always seemed older, more mature like his uncle. William held out his hand but Charlie ignored it. Lifting him off his feet he crushed him in a bear hug.

'See you back at the house,' Evan said as William turned away so no one would see the emotion mirrored on his face. William reached for Tina's hand, calling a last goodbye as he led her out of the room and down the stairs.

Chapter Seven

'MYRTLE, I told you that we'd be eating at the party,' Wyn admonished his sister when he saw the table in the parlour laid with enough sandwiches and slabs of cake to feed a dozen people.

'I wasn't sure how much you'd eat there.' She turned to Diana, her soft, grey eyes clouded with resignation and exhaustion. 'Pleased to meet you.'

'I've heard a lot about you.' Diana pulled off her glove and shook Myrtle's hand.

'You should have laid this in the kitchen, Myrtle.'

'Dad wouldn't hear of it, and you know what he can be like.'

Wyn nodded grimly as he helped Diana off with her coat. 'I suppose I'd better introduce you, but I warn you now, he can be difficult, and downright rude.'

'It's the pain,' Myrtle apologised, with a readiness that revealed that she was accustomed to making excuses for her father. 'He suffers constantly and it wears him down. It's no wonder he gets cross occasionally.'

'When doesn't he get cross?'

'Wyn!' Myrtle reproached her brother with an expression that reminded Diana of a whipped puppy.

Diana followed Wyn into the middle room. The first thing that struck her was the smell. A dense, sickroom odour of medicines and liniment mixed with cabbage and stewed tea; stale scents that lingered, imprisoned in the atmosphere. It was difficult to resist the temptation to rush to the window, haul down the casement and allow in draughts of cool, fresh air.

'Dad,' Wyn led Diana to the bed pushed close to the fire: 'This is Diana, who works in the High Street shop.'

'I'm very pleased to meet you, Mr Rees.' Diana offered her hand to the withered figure sunk deep in immaculate, linen-sheathed pillows. She took the fleshless claw he presented, and shook it. His skin was sallow, yellowed by sickness and stretched as dry and lifeless as old parchment over his skull. But there was nothing frail or sick about his eyes. Dark, alive, they rolled in their sockets like cockroaches trapped in sour milk, absorbing every detail: her clothes, her hair, the expression on her face as she glanced at his son.

'I can't tell you how pleased I am to meet you after all this time. Tell me,' he demanded in a high-pitched voice, 'when's the big day?'

'Pardon?' Diana blanched, wondering how this old man, locked up as he was in this sickroom, had heard about her and Tony Ronconi.

'Dad!' Wyn protested furiously.

'I told you I wanted a daughter-in-law. Well this one looks healthy enough. What are you waiting for, boy? Don't tell me you haven't asked her yet?'

'That's my business.'

'It's family business,' his father contradicted sharply. 'And if I've warned you once I've warned you a dozen times, I'll disown you if you don't marry, and soon. I'll cut you out of my will, I'll – '

Diana retreated to the parlour as the old man's ravings grew louder and more insistent.

'Please, sit down, make yourself at home,' Myrtle gabbled red-faced, before running past her to help her brother try to quieten the old man. Diana hesitated for a moment, then closed the door. The last thing she wanted to do was eavesdrop on the ugly scene. The noise the old man was making filled the house. Feeling a certain sympathy for whoever lived next door, she crouched in front of the fire, picked up the poker and, without thinking, broke the crust of small coal that was keeping the fire in. Flames darted high, dancing up the chimney, reminding her of the fires she had stared into as a child on cold winter evenings. William and her sitting side by side, sharing their father's easy chair as they had gazed at reddish-gold plumes and sparking fountains spurting between banks of glowing coals, seeing knights mounted on magnificent horses, towering castles, beautiful damsels in distress and evil, people-munching dragons. The last image had been one of William's inventions – she had always looked for the fairy-like and ethereal; he, the grotesque and evil.

So many dreams. Where had they all gone? Had William found his damsel in Tina? She hoped so, especially now when she knew she would never find her knight.

'I'm sorry you had to witness that.' Wyn walked in, his face flushed from humiliation and the unnaturally high heat in the middle room. 'It was a mistake to bring you here. Dad's not himself . . .'

'Really, it didn't bother me,' Diana broke in, wanting to save him embarrassment. 'And I promise I won't say a word, to anyone.'

'Thank you.' He pulled back one of the chairs from the table and sat close to where she was huddled on the hearthrug. 'I've taken the coward's way out and left Myrtle to it. She's always been better than me at calming him down. She'll join us when she can. In the meantime I think we should start.'

'I couldn't eat a thing.'

'Myrtle will be offended if you don't. Please,' he pulled out a chair alongside his. 'Tea?' he picked up a potholder from the fireplace and lifted the kettle on to the fire.

'Yes, please.'

'Milk and two sugars?'

'You remembered.' She looked back to the fire, strangely reluctant to release the memories the flames evoked; almost as though the simple act of repeating a childhood pastime could roll back the years and restore the innocence and youth that Ben Springer had destroyed.

'Looking for dragons?'

'You know?'

'When I was small I used to spend hours staring into the fire, imagining dragons living in the glowing caverns between the coals.'

'And castles and beautiful ladies . . .'

'And heroes in shining armour. So children aren't that different after all?'

'It doesn't look like it.'

Myrtle must have boiled the kettle once already. It started hissing and Wyn reached for the teapot and caddy. Warming the pot with a splash of water that he poured into a slop bucket he spooned in tea-leaves and poured on the water. 'To tell the truth, I'm glad in a way that you saw what you did. It's going to make what I'm about to say easier. There's something I've been meaning to ask you for a few days. It's not a spur of the moment decision, I've been thinking about it for some time.' He paused for a moment and she turned away, afraid that he was about to ask her to marry him. Much as she valued and respected Wyn as a friend and boss, and wanted marriage, and a normal life with a husband and children, she knew that she could never be happy with him. Quite aside from the gossip, after what he'd said about loving the boy from Pwllgwaun, she realised life with him would be anything but normal.

He took her hands into his. 'I won't be offended if you say no, or want time to think about it, but I'd like you to take over the running of the business. I'm all too aware that what I'm asking is no small thing.'

'But why?' The notion of him abandoning the shops shocked her even more than a marriage proposal would have done. 'What are you going to do?'

84

'Join up.'

'Wyn, how can you, your father needs you . . .'

'My father needs nursing, and that's woman's work. There's nothing I can do to help Myrtle on that score. You saw how he is with me. He hates me. I've always been a disappointment to him. I wish I could be the son he wanted, but I can't and that's an end to it. And no matter what I do, how much I try, all I ever succeed in doing is upsetting him. Every time I go near him he starts shouting, and it takes hours for Myrtle to calm him down. Please, Diana, just keep the shop running in the theatre with whatever stock you can get. The round will have to go, but since sugar's been rationed I've practically nothing to sell anyway.'

'What about the shop on the Graig hill?'

'I'll put it in the hands of a letting agency. I don't think there'll be any problem in renting it out. There's no talk of vegetables being rationed and one or two of the market boys are looking to open up a greengrocer's on the Graig. I know it means that you'll be on your own, that you'll have to make all the decisions about the shop and stocking it, and do the banking after you've taken your wages out of the takings, but I'll increase your wages to match the responsibilities. What do you say?'

'I think you're mad to consider joining up.'

'William and the Ronconi boys have.'

'They're mad too.'

'Diana, this war isn't going to last a few months, it's going to last for years. I know nothing much is happening at the moment, but it soon will, and when it does, the army is going to need every man it can get.'

'And because you've lost the person you loved, and you think no one else needs you, you've decided to be in the forefront when the killing starts?' She looked up to see Myrtle standing in the doorway, a shocked expression on her tearstained face, a handkerchief clutched to her mouth.

'I'll be going whether you decide to run the business for me or not, Diana, and if you don't, Myrtle may crack under the strain of trying to look after both my father and the shop.'

'But you don't have to go. You can wait until the call-up . . .'

'As I said, I've been thinking about it for some time. I'm going to the recruiting office first thing in the morning, and I'd really appreciate an answer before I go. What is it to be?'

'I'll run your business,' Diana said softly, but she was looking at Myrtle not at Wyn. If she had nothing to look forward to, Myrtle had even less. Besides, wasn't Wyn offering her exactly what she needed?

A business to throw all her energies into? If she could a run a shop successfully for him, one day she might be able to do it for herself.

'I'll walk down with you to the station in the morning and wave you off.'

'No,' William protested. 'I'd rather say goodbye to you tonight.'

'I'd settle for that, if I could think of somewhere private we could spend a couple of hours together.' Tina shivered as they made their way across the deserted Tumble.

'Cold?' He put his arm around her and turned up the collar on her coat.

'A bit,' she admitted. 'Come on, Will, there has to be somewhere we can go. Can't you smuggle me into your house?'

'My mother would have a fit.'

'It looked like she, along with your uncle and Phyllis were settling into Charlie's for the evening.'

'Don't you believe it. They won't be far behind us. Phyllis won't let Brian stay up late, and they've Bethan's baby to look after as well, remember?'

'And Angelo is sleeping in the café,' she grumbled, looking back under the railway bridge at the shadow that was all that could be seen of the Tumble café. 'But,' she hooked her arm into his, 'if we call in to see how Laura is doing, we might find out how long Mama and Papa are likely to be.'

'Tony and all the others will be in your house.'

'Sometimes I think you don't want to be alone with me.'

'If by that you mean I'm likely to lose my head, I'll agree with you.'

'The same way you lost it with Vera Collins?'

'You promised you'd never mention her name again.'

'I hate to think of you and her . . .'

'It meant nothing.' Drawing her close, he kissed her lightly, gently, as though she were so delicate that even the simple act of placing his lips on hers might hurt her. 'Not like you and me,' he whispered as he hugged her shoulders and carried on walking.

'You're a funny boy, William Powell.'

'For getting engaged to you?'

'That's just one reason. Look, there's two flashes of white running boards parked outside Laura's house. That means Andrew's still there. Let's walk up and find out if I'm an auntie.'

'You like babies?'

'I hope I'll like mine better than I've liked my brothers and sisters, but I must admit even most of them were all right until they started to talk and were able to answer back.' She tapped quietly on Laura's door before tentatively opening it. 'Anyone around?'

'In the kitchen,' came an answering masculine cry.

'You too.' She pushed William ahead of her.

'Not likely.'

'Laura won't be having the baby in the kitchen, stupid. Go on.'

William reluctantly walked down the passage and into the tiny kitchen. Mrs Ronconi was scrubbing the top of the already immaculate range with a blackleading brush. Mr Ronconi, Andrew and Trevor were sitting around the table, an untouched bottle of brandy and four glasses laid out in front of them.

'If you've come to toast the baby's health you're in for a long wait,' Trevor greeted them dolefully. 'Bethan says it could be hours yet.'

'Trust Laura to rush off and break up my engagement party for nothing,' Tina complained.

'The poor girl is having a dreadful time,' Mrs Ronconi countered resentfully, 'and all you can do is think of yourself.'

'Tina was joking, Mama,' Mr Ronconi cut in, all too aware of his wife's ability to create a three-act drama out of a small crisis, let alone a birth. 'Here,' he handed Tina a bunch of keys. 'These are Laura's keys to all three cafés. You'd better keep them if you're going to take over the Taff Street place tomorrow. In by six to supervise the pastrycook, and open by eight, mind you,' he ordered. 'And a good night's sleep first, which means you take her straight home, young man.'

'I will, Mr Ronconi.'

'Don't worry about a thing, Papa. And I'll help Tony to put the little ones to bed.'

'Check they wash behind their ears, clean their teeth and – '

'Don't worry, Mama,' Tina kissed her mother's cheek. 'Tony and I will see to everything between us. Give Laura my love, and tell her I'll call in on my way to work tomorrow.'

'If you do, you may find all of us in bed with exhaustion,' Trevor griped.

'One thing's certain: Laura couldn't look any worse than you.'

'I wouldn't be too sure of that if I were you,' her mother disputed. 'Men, they always get off lightly, they – '

'Don't worry, I think both father and mother will survive the experience,' Andrew reassured her.

Hearing a sound upstairs, William backed down the passageway. Tina followed. She couldn't wait to leave. She had a key to the café in High Street and it was only five minutes down the road. William couldn't possibly object to stopping off there to make sure the premises were locked properly, could he?

The flat above the grocer's shop on the corner of the Graig hill and Factory Lane was shrouded in silence, just as it was every Sunday evening. Jenny's mother had returned from chapel and gone to bed early, not that she ever went late, and her father was drinking illicitly in the Morning Star next door, as he did every Sunday night. Even before the war the landlord had kept the back door open for regulars.

Jenny lay on her bed and listened hard. She could hear footsteps on the hill. William and Tina, perhaps? She closed her eyes tightly, trying to fight a tide of jealousy that she knew from bitter experience would do nothing to ease her own pain, or terrible sense of loss at Eddie's absence.

It was ridiculous! When they had been together she hadn't wanted him except as bait to make his brother Haydn jealous. And afterwards, when Haydn had made it plain that he no longer wanted her – at any price – and she had allowed Eddie to make love to her, it had been nothing more than lust. A burning, all-consuming passion that had driven all thoughts other than when, where and how they could arrange the next time, from her mind. She had learned the hard way that passion and sexual fulfilment, no matter how exciting or pleasurable, was no basis for marriage.

But at moments like this, when she was totally alone and had time to remember the small things, she suspected that for Eddie their relationship had been based on more than simply lust.

Closing her eyes she pictured the bruises on Eddie's face and the gleam in his eye when he had asked her to marry him after the last boxing match he had fought in Pontypridd. The pride with which he had showed off the expensive engagement ring he had bought her to his family and friends. That one magic night when they had gone swimming without clothes in Shoni's pond and made love – for what had turned out to be the last time. Because after Eddie had seen her kissing Haydn in the wedding reception in a way no bride should kiss a best man, there had been no more lovemaking.

She longed to be with him. Ached for the feel of his naked body against hers, the cool touch of his lips on her bare skin, the sheer strength of his physical presence; a glimpse of his dark brooding eyes that could magically lighten at a smile from her. His quiet, undemonstrative dependability, that would have been such a good quality in a husband, if only she had given him a chance to be one.

She picked up the writing pad and fountain pen from her bedside cabinet. She had persuaded William to stop off at the shop on his way down the hill in the morning. If Eddie was still in the Guards camp 'somewhere in France', and she had no reason to think otherwise, William had promised to find a soldier bound for the place. Someone reliable and trustworthy who would seek Eddie out, and put her letter in his hand.

She knew that Eddie had been given embarkation leave, because every soldier was given at least forty-eight hours free between training and active service, and it grieved her to think that Eddie had preferred to spend that precious time somewhere other than Pontypridd. But there had to be other leaves. There *had* to. And in the meantime there were letters that she could send – but could never be quite sure he received.

She clung to the hope that Eddie would feel duty bound to answer one that was put directly into his hand, although he hadn't replied to the daily missives she had sent since his father had given her his address. She looked down at the writing pad and read what she had written for the tenth time, wondering if these particular words would elicit a response when so many others had failed.

She had tried to make her letter light, appealing, wanting to make him miss her, and more important still, return to Pontypridd for his next leave. She stared at the paper, trying to imagine him unfolding it for the very first time.

My darling husband,
    I thought it would be easier once you finally left Pontypridd and there was no chance of my seeing you, but, if anything, I love and miss you more with every passing hour. I try to keep busy helping my father in the shop, but every time the bell clangs on the door I look up, knowing it won't be you, yet hoping against all reason that it will. Please Eddie come back to Pontypridd the minute you have leave. I have saved some money, enough for us to stay at a hotel for two weeks, if you can get that long. Perhaps we could go to Cardiff, or Swansea, or Porthcawl or Barry Island? I know it won't be like having a holiday in the summer, but it would be so wonderful if we could spend time together, just the two of us.

She stared at the words until they danced before her eyes. Should she mention their disastrous honeymoon, the quarrelling that had led him to punch his brother, Haydn, through a plate-glass window in a jealous rage? How much she wanted to make up for everything he had suffered on her account! Or should she plead with him to give her one more chance?

Everyone said that soldiers' letters were censored. Did that mean the officers read the incoming as well as the outgoing mail? Picking up the pen again, she unscrewed the top and held it poised over the writing pad until a large blob of ink fell from the nib, disfiguring the creamy white paper. Eventually she began to write, quickly, instinctively, without thinking too hard about what she was saying, concentrating instead on an image of Eddie. But it was no use. Every time she succeeded in picturing his tall, hard, lean body, his dark curly hair and handsome, bruised boxer's face, the image faded before she could imprint it on her mind. It was worse than trying to catch water in her fingers. Elusive, quick-tempered, impatient Eddie. No different in her imaginings than he was in life.

Of course if you want to stay in Pontypridd, I'll understand. I'll get rooms for us somewhere. I just want to be with you, wherever that is. Please my darling, write soon, let me know how you are and if you need anything that I can send. I have saved every penny of the army wife's one pound thirteen shillings a week allowance, as my father is still paying me for working in the shop. It is surprising how it's mounting up. I don't want the war to last a day longer than it has to, but already between your money and what I've saved from my earnings, we have quite a bit set aside to put towards a home of our own.

*I wish you were here, Eddie so I could give you a great big kiss goodnight, and a whole lot more. I **long** to hold you in my arms . . .*

She stopped writing . . . was it wrong for her to feel this way? No one had ever told her that a woman could want a man this much. Naked and in bed, the same way men were supposed to want women.

Please my darling come to me the minute you can,
*   Your ever loving wife, Jenny*

She'd written from the heart, she could do no better. Resisting the temptation to read what she'd said, she etched a line of crosses beneath her name, pressed blotting paper over the page and folded it into an envelope. Now it was up to William – and Eddie. If only she could be sure he'd open the envelope and read every loving word.

'Tina I don't think we should do this. What if someone sees us?'

'You know anyone who can see in the dark?' she whispered as she fingered the keys and the lock, scraping metal on metal in an effort to home in on the right one.

'I promised your father I'd take you straight home.'

'We're checking his property to make sure it's safe.'

'A constable or an air-raid warden could come . . .'

'So what? I've every right to be in my own family's café. Open Sesame!' The door swung open and she stepped inside. 'Come on, quick!'

He followed her, standing in darkness while she checked the blackout. Only when she was satisfied that all the drapes were drawn across the windows did she finally switch on the light.

'There, want a cup of tea or something?'

'No.' He moved behind the door and leaned against it, as though to emphasise the fact that he had no intention of remaining long.

'Would you rather I switched off the light?'

'I'd rather we went. Someone could come.'

'Who? Laura's in labour, Tony's home with the children, Angelo's in the café; Papa and Mama are with Laura.' She moved behind him, rammed the bolt home on the door and switched off the light. Lifting her hands around his neck she kissed him. Unbuttoning his coat and jacket, she slipped her fingers beneath his waistcoat. 'This is the way I wanted to say goodbye.'

As the warmth of her hands radiated through the layers of his shirt and vest, his defences weakened. Unbuttoning her coat he pulled her to him, holding her close, luxuriating in the soft, warm, deliciously feminine feel of her body against his.

'I love you, Tina, but we shouldn't be doing this.' Summoning every ounce of willpower he possessed, he pushed her away.

She stood back and he heard the swish of cloth falling as she laid her coat over a neighbouring table.

'Tina?' he called softly, alarmed by her absence and the darkness that closed around him like a blackout curtain, dense, suffocating and totally blinding.

'I'm here.'

'What are you doing?'

'Trying to make a comfortable place for us.' She switched on the kitchen light; it filtered through into the café, filling the room with a soft, subdued glow. 'Don't worry, it won't be seen from the street. Here.' She dropped a bale of blackout material into a corner. Unrolling it, she transformed it into an improvised *chaise-longue*, with the roll acting as a pillow.

'I don't think . . .' His voice died in his throat as she sank to her knees and opened her arms to him.

He hesitated for barely a moment before discarding his coat and jacket. He knelt beside her and kissed her, his hands exploring her face as his mouth closed over hers. She clung to him tightly, fiercely.

'There'll never be anyone else for me, you do know that?' She stared at him intently. 'So no doing anything stupid when you're away.'

'No French girls, I swear it,' he smiled.

'Or English, or Dutch . . .'

'No other girls, ever.' He lay on his back and pulled her down on top of him, so he could kiss her again. Her breasts strained against the thin material of her dress. Reaching up he caressed them through the layers of cloth. She pulled away from him.

'I'm sorry,' he murmured contritely.

Her fingers set to work unhooking the row of mother-of-pearl buttons that ornamented the front panel of her dress.

'No . . .' he reached up and gripped her hands, imprisoning them in his own.

'We're engaged. I think I'm entitled to send you off to war with more than the memory of a few kisses.' Tugging her hands free she slipped the dress over her arms and tossed it aside. As she knelt over him, shivering in an opalescent silk shift, his self-control dissolved. He fingered the thin straps of the petticoat. She pulled them down before unlacing and discarding her bust-shaper. Slowly, tentatively he reached up and caressed her naked breasts, his fingers lingering over the perfect pink aureoles of her nipples.

'You're beautiful.'

'All I want is to make you happy.'

'You do, Tina and you will. But you're going to catch cold.' Reaching for his jacket, he draped it over her shoulders as she sank down on to his chest. 'I love you.'

'And I love you, which is why I want to be here with you like this.' She gazed up at him, her eyes dark, bewitching pools.

'And why I should never have come. I wanted our first time to be special. After a huge white wedding with my sister and all of yours as bridesmaids. We'd be in a sumptuous hotel room with a four-poster bed, there'd be flowers and champagne . . .'

'Can't you smell the flowers? They're carnations and freesias.'

'White ones?'

'What other colour is there? And the champagne bubbles have gone up my nose, I'm going to sneeze at any moment.'

'This is hardly a four-poster bed.'

'It's a little smaller than I would have wished, but just as comfortable.' She closed her arms even more tightly around his chest. 'So kiss me, and let's make the most of this room while it's ours.'

While he kissed her, she unbuttoned his shirt. She helped him to remove his waistcoat and draw down his braces. He pulled his vest over his head, and drew in his breath sharply as her naked breasts brushed against his bare chest. Trailing the tips of his fingers over her back and arms, he lingered over every inch of skin, every curve, imprinting the shape and feel of her into his memory. When he came to the flat of her stomach which was still covered by her petticoat, he rolled over, taking her with him, so he lay above her. He kissed her again, his senses reeling, lost in a kaleidoscope of colour, sounds, images, scents and jumbled memories.

The sweetness of their first stolen kiss at the back of the Catholic Hall, the damp, cloying darkness of the blacked-out night when he had first told her he loved her and wanted to marry her. The parlour in the Ronconi house where he had asked Tina's father for her hand, and her father's and his own voice echoing back from the Lewises' kitchen not an hour before.

'And a good night's sleep first, which means you take her straight home, young man.'

'I will, Mr Ronconi.'

He sat up abruptly. Leaning forward, he sank his head into his hands.

'Will!' Tina was beside him, her hand on his shoulder. 'What's the matter?'

'So help me, I can't do this. I'm sorry, Tina, I can't. It will be different when we're married I promise you, but this isn't the time or the place for us.'

'I'm beginning to wonder if there'll ever be a time and place for us,' she cried angrily. 'Will, I'm prepared to give you all I have to give. Everything! Why won't you take it like any other man would?'

'Because I'm not any other man.' He was on his feet pulling his vest over his head. Scooping up his shirt, tie and waistcoat he flung them on top of his jacket on the table, and continued to dress.

Turning her back, Tina picked up her bust-shaper. He was dressed before her. Lifting the blackout material he re-rolled it and carried it into the kitchen. She pointed to a shelf and he stacked it on to it. Taking the keys from her hand, he walked her to the door, opened it and locked it carefully behind them.

They climbed the hill in silence. Only when they stood outside her front door did he kiss her again, and this time she sensed it was a final goodbye:

'I love you.'

'I love you too, which is why I had to end that back there. I'm sorry, but if anything had happened between us I know I couldn't have left you afterwards. Not even if it meant going to prison. And that wouldn't have done either of us any good.'

'There's nothing to be sorry about.' She clung to him, her face pressed against the rough wool of his overcoat. 'You'll write?'

'Every chance I get.' Disentangling her arms he turned away. His footsteps rang out into the darkness and she was left on her doorstep, cold and more alone than she'd ever felt in her life before.

Chapter Eight

'I THINK that's the cry you've been waiting for.' Andrew stirred, and nudged Trevor's foot as he forced himself out of the half-waking, half-dozing stupor in which he'd passed the night.

Trevor needed no spur to move. He was out of his chair before Andrew spoke, and halfway to the door when Mrs Ronconi shot out of the parlour where she'd finally been persuaded to retire in the early hours of the morning.

For once Trevor abandoned all courtesy. Pushing Mrs Ronconi aside, he bounded up the stairs two at a time. Bethan was waiting on the landing.

'Are they . . .'

'Your wife has something to show you.' She pushed open the bedroom door. Picking up a bundle of soiled linen she walked slowly down the stairs.

'You look exhausted,' Andrew commiserated as he took the bundle from her.

'I don't know why, it was a textbook delivery. Although Laura isn't very pleased.'

'It's a boy?' Mr Ronconi enthused from the passage. 'I knew it would be.'

'I'll stay and look after them,' Mrs Ronconi announced from the stairs.

'Looks like you're redundant.' Andrew went to the table and poured Bethan a cup of tea from the barely warm pot.

'And you've got Trevor's rounds to do as well as your own.'

'The patients can wait until we've picked up Rachel and I've taken you both home.'

'Andrew,' Trevor shouted down the stairs. 'Come and see him! 'He's positively beautiful and perfect.' Dashing down the stairs, he burst into the kitchen, picked Bethan up and swirled her around. 'Thank you.' He kissed her soundly on the lips.

'If I'd known how you were going to pay my wife for her mid-wifery services I might not have allowed her to volunteer.'

'Come on, Andrew.' Trevor dragged him up the stairs.

'Just for a minute, then I'd better go and keep the practice running.'

'I'll give you a hand.'

'Absolutely not. Take a week off, you're not indispensable yet.'

Bethan dumped the bedding in the wash-house before following Andrew and Trevor upstairs. Laura was sitting up in bed, exactly as she'd left her, a tired but triumphant smile on her face as she cradled her newborn son.

'And here's your godmother back to see you,' she crooned as Bethan appeared behind Trevor, Andrew and her parents.

'I'll call in this evening to check on you.'

'My husband's a doctor, I have my mother who's had more children than hot dinners to fuss over me, and you want to leave your own baby to check on me?'

'He's my handiwork, I don't want him spoiled.'

'Got a name for him?' Andrew asked.

'Angela Bethan,' Laura chipped in quickly.

'He'll hate you for it when he's older.'

'I like John. It's plain and simple and you can't do anything to it,' Trevor said.

'With all due respect to Andrew, it's a reasonable surname but a boring Christian name,' Laura protested.

'Time we left,' Andrew turned to his wife.

'See you later.' Bethan kissed the baby on the head and Laura on the cheek. 'We'll see ourselves out,' she said to Mrs Ronconi.

'Anything special I should do?'

'As Laura said, you've had more babies than any of us.'

'But not recently.'

'Nothing changes. Keep the baby warm, dry and fed and see the mother rests.'

Andrew went ahead of Bethan. He paused at the foot of the stairs to lift down their coats from the hooks behind the door. While he was patting his pockets in search of his keys, the postman pushed a bundle of letters through the letterbox. He picked them up, slipping one from the top of the pile to the bottom, but he wasn't quite quick enough. Bethan had seen enough to work out that it was addressed to Trevor. She had also seen the address of the sender on the back. Ministry of War.

Harry Griffiths's wife was short-tempered and difficult at the best of times, and on the rare occasions when Harry risked depression by contemplating his married life, he inevitably came to the conclusion that for him and the woman he'd married there had been no 'best of times'. Even their courting had been conducted under the eagle eye of his future mother-in-law, who'd arranged a magnificent wedding as measured by the Pontypridd yardstick, only to put the finishing touches to the day by dispatching her daughter on honeymoon with the advice that the 'private side of married life was disgusting, but a woman had to put up with it', thus setting the scene for a disaster of titanic proportions.

Harry's wedding night had been the first and last that he'd shared a bed with his wife, and the one and only time his wife had permitted him to lay his hands on her. He had left the honeymoon hotel in Porthcawl for the debt-ridden shop he had inherited from his father, tired, and aching from sleeping on the floor. But their initial cata-strophic encounter had resulted in the single saving grace of his marriage: his daughter Jenny. He'd done his best to stop his wife from priming Jenny in the art of frigidity, but when Jenny's husband, Eddie, had returned to his father's house the day after their wedding he had seen his own frustrations mirrored in Eddie's anger, and he'd been deeply saddened by the thought of history repeating itself. But the final blow had fallen a few days later when Eddie had left Pontypridd to join the Guards, amidst a welter of scandalous rumours about Jenny and Eddie's brother, Haydn.

He'd tried to discuss Eddie's abrupt departure with Jenny without success. It pained him to stand impotently by and watch his beloved daughter move between the shop and the flat upstairs, rarely going out, and then only as far as the post office to forward the latest in a flow of letters that, to his knowledge, hadn't elicited a single reply. But Eddie's protracted silence didn't stop him from standing at the window of his shop every morning at about the time the postman climbed the hill, to watch and wait for an envelope that might – just might – bring a smile to Jenny's face.

Bert Browne pushed open the shop door, setting the bell clanging. Still puffing, he dumped his sack on the floor and handed over a small pile of buff envelopes. 'Three today, Harry.'

'Bills by the look of them.' Harry pushed them aside in disgust.

'You know what Percy said in the *Observer* last week. Patriots pay their bills promptly to aid the war effort.'

'I can't see how paying George Collins for his cheese before I need to will help anything besides George's bank balance. Ten Wood-bines?' he asked as Bert dug in his pocket.

'I need something to keep me going.' Bert glanced slyly at Harry. 'Heard Megan Powell is out?' he asked, feigning a casual air as Harry turned to the tobacco shelf. It had been common knowledge on the Graig that Harry's feet had been 'under Megan's table' for years before she'd been sent down. And no one had thought any the less of him for it, except the strict chapel goers. Everyone knew Harry's wife wouldn't give him his dues, courtesy of old Mrs Evans whose bedroom window faced the single-bedded box room Harry slept in – alone.

'Megan has years more to do.' Harry's hand shook as he scooped the coins Bert had laid on the counter into the wooden drawer that served as a till.

'Police sergeant told me they're letting out all the non-violent convicts to make room for the Nazis. As long as they lock up Mosley and all those like him, that's what I say. Mind you I feel sorry for Megan. Saw her in town yesterday with her brother-in-law. She's not what she was, but then what can you expect after years of hard labour? Shame,' he shook his head as he balanced a Woodbine on his lower lip. 'She was a pretty little thing. I remember turning green at the gills when I heard William Powell had snapped her up. Lucky sod, he might not have had her for long, but then a year spent with a woman like Megan would give a man more to crow about than twenty with some I could name, including my own missus.'

'What's all this about Megan Powell?' Harry's wife – slim, blonde, better looking and better dressed than any woman had a right to be at her age and at that time in the morning – stood glowering in the doorway that separated the shop from the stairs that led up to the living quarters.

'They let her out because of the war.' Bert opened the shop door, setting the bell ringing again. 'Well, must be off. See you, Harry, Mrs Griffiths.' He touched his cap.

Harry turned his back on his wife and fiddled with the boxes of sweets laid out in the window while the silence between them grew more and more ominous. His wife was the first to break.

'If you think I'll stand idly by and let you take up where you left off with *that* woman, Harry Griffiths, you're making a big mistake.'

'Keep your voice down,' he growled. 'Our Jenny's upstairs.'

'She's married, she knows what men are like. Driven by what's between their legs the same as alley cats. After every woman who lifts her skirt – '

'I'll not have you talking that way about Megan Powell,' he broke in harshly.

'Why? Because you're one of the pack who lifted her skirt?' she taunted. 'You didn't think you were the only one, did you? I've seen her stop on the hill and talk to a dozen men, one after the other . . .'

'Talk, and only talk. Because unlike you she's a pleasant friendly soul who thinks the best of everyone.'

'You expect me and every other decent woman on the Graig to think the best of her? To turn a blind eye when she's moved in with that brother-in-law of hers who's living in sin with the mother of his bastard? Like everyone else I'm wondering if she takes turns with Phyllis Harry, or if they sleep three in a bed.' She stepped back as Harry moved swiftly from behind the counter.

'You say one more word about Megan Powell and I'll hit you into the middle of next week, woman,' he warned grimly, as he stood in front of her with a look on his face that sent her reeling back into the door.

'I'm your wife,' she shouted defiantly. 'I have a right – '

'A wife has every right. You, being no wife, have none. I suggest you remember that.'

'I'll leave you.'

'I'll give you a hundred quid to see you on your way.'

'After I suffered all the agonies of hell to give you a daughter. Not to mention the best years of my life . . .'

'If it had been up to you, Jenny wouldn't have been born. You've given me nothing, woman. Nothing except heartache and frustration!'

Lip quivering, she stared at him for a moment before bursting into tears and running up the stairs.

'Wrong time of the month, Harry?'

The colour drained from Harry's face as he turned to see Huw Davies standing in the shop.

'Sorry, didn't hear the bell,' Harry muttered, as he moved back behind the counter.

'Ten Players, please.' Huw pulled a shilling from his uniform pocket.

'How long have you been there?'

'Long enough.' Huw pocketed his cigarettes and his change. 'Don't take this the wrong way, Harry. I've nothing against you personally, but Megan's my sister. She's been through a rough time, and it's not going to get any easier with her boy leaving today to join the Guards. The last thing she needs right now is trouble.'

'She won't get it from me.'

'Just see that she doesn't, Harry. Because if she does, you'll have me as well as your wife on your back.'

★

99

William opened his wardrobe door and checked its contents for what he sternly told himself had to be the last time if he was going to make the train. It was ridiculously full, as though he and Eddie were still living at home. Eddie's best suit hung next to his. The light grey flannels, boiled shirts and coats they'd worn to work in Charlie's shop had been pushed to the end of the rail. Shirts, ties, socks, underwear – Eddie had taken two changes of clothes with him and he'd written to tell William not to bring any clothes at all. That the army liked to set their mark on recruits by dressing them in khaki from the skin out, and as there was precious little free time, there was no point in wasting a second of it by changing into civvies when no one else bothered.

He closed the door and checked his bag. Shaving gear, towel, brush, comb, cologne – he lifted the bottle out – was there any point in taking it when he wouldn't be seeing Tina?

'William?' Megan tapped the door. 'You won't have time for breakfast if you don't hurry.'

'I know.' He glanced into the bag before shutting it. What he hadn't packed he'd have to buy, beg or borrow. Opening the door he gave his mother a wry smile. 'I'll be back before you know it.'

'To go again. Only it will be to France next time.'

'Mam, how many times do I have to tell you I'll be all right?'

'I promised myself I wouldn't cry,' she asserted illogically as she dammed the flood of tears pouring down her cheeks with a handkerchief. 'I only came to give you this.' She thrust a small parcel into his hands. 'It's your father's cigarette case. They sent it to me along with the letters I'd written him. God knows what it's made of, it certainly isn't silver, but he must have got someone to decorate the front for him. He couldn't have done it himself. He was never useful with his hands.'

'Like me.' William opened the small box and looked down at the flat, battered metal case.

'Just as well you have the same name. There'll be no mistaking the owner if you lose it.'

William traced his fingers over the lines that had been hammered into the smooth surface. WILLIAM POWELL, and beneath it, Verdun 1916. He flicked the catch. 'There's cigarettes in it.'

'It's safe to smoke them, they're not left over from your father. I got your Uncle Evan to buy them for you yesterday.'

He pushed the case into the pocket of the sports coat he was wearing.

'You'll take good care of it?'

Both of them knew it wasn't the case she was referring to. 'I promise,' he agreed solemnly.

'I won't come down to the station, if you don't mind.'

'I don't mind. In fact, I'd prefer it.'

'Well, breakfast isn't going to wait for ever. You coming, or what?'

'Or what?' He picked up his bag, wishing that the next hour was over so the goodbyes were only a memory.

Bethan tucked Rachel into her day cot and carried it into the dining room. The maid had laid the table for breakfast, although she couldn't possibly have known whether they'd be back or not. She found what she was looking for amongst the mail laid on a salver next to Andrew's plate. She picked it up and put it down again. She could hear the sound of water running overhead: Andrew was having a bath before doing his rounds. She went into the kitchen and washed her hands and face, checking the progress of breakfast and leaving only when she heard Andrew's footstep on the landing.

Mouth dry with anticipation – and fear – she laid her hand on the banister rail in the hall and waited for him to walk down the curving staircase. The stress of the wakeful night was beginning to exact its toll. Her head was swimming, she felt giddy, faint, the hall around her taking on an unreal, almost surreal quality.

'Rachel asleep?' Andrew asked.

'Yes.'

'Then I suggest you make the most of it and catch up on some sleep yourself.'

'I will later.'

'Later she may be awake.'

'As you're always reminding me, I have help in the house. I'll get Annie to take over if I'm tired.' They went into the dining room. The maid came in from the kitchen and laid a dish of scrambled eggs and a loaded toast rack on the table. Bethan thanked her before turning to Andrew, who was already opening his letters. She lifted the teapot and poured herself a cup of tea. The maid had placed the coffee pot in front of Andrew, who preferred to drink coffee at breakfast.

'Scrambled eggs?' Seeing her looking at him, he pushed the chafing-dish towards her.

'I'd rather you told me what the Ministry of War want with you and Trevor.'

'What they want from everyone.'

'You've been called up?'

'Told to register. It doesn't mean a thing.'

'No? They're just collecting names for the fun of it?'

'They're short of doctors. It's my guess they're checking on numbers, giving everyone of military age who's registered with the BMA medicals, to clear us in case we're needed at short notice some time in the future.'

'When do they want you to register?'

'Thursday.'

She rose abruptly and walked over to the window that overlooked the garden. It was the tail end of winter, but for once it wasn't raining and the branches on the trees and shrubs bore the first tiny buds, evidence of the coming spring.

'It doesn't mean that I'll have to go, darling.' He was behind her, his hands locked around her waist, his chin buried in her hair. 'You and Rachel are my whole world, I love you. The last thing I want to do is leave you.'

'Until now, this whole stupid war has seemed unreal, like one of the games we played as children. Eddie, Haydn and now William and the Ronconi boys have been knocked out, so they have to disappear from the scene. The only casualties have been the ones we've read about in the Pontypridd *Observer*, like the poor woman who fell off a stepladder when she was hanging blackout curtains.'

'Enough seamen have gone down with their ships to prove it's real enough.'

'And afterwards they're just a list of names in the newspapers to everyone except those who know them. Our side sits in their camps in France and the Germans bomb them with leaflets, and we retaliate by bombing Germany with pieces of paper. The headlines tell us that ships have gone down, planes have crashed, we get given gas masks, ration books and endless lists of things to do, but nothing seems real to me except the boys going away, and now you.' Her eyes were dark, frightened pools in her pale face. 'I'm terrified none of you are ever going to come back. That you're all going to disappear for ever.'

'We'll be back. We'll all be back. That's if I go at all.'

Rachel mewed softly in her sleep.

'Here, let me.' He lifted her out of her day cot. 'Nothing will change. Whatever happens, I'll go on loving you just the way I do now.'

'How can you say that when we don't even know how long this war is going to last? The men who marched away in 1914 came back in 1919 to a changed world. Five years will be a lifetime to Rachel, and will seem like a hundred to me if we're forced to spend it apart. No one will be the same, or feel the same way . . .'

'We will.'

'I wish I could be as sure as you.'

'Trust me.'

'Promise me one thing,' she demanded urgently.

'What?' he asked warily.

'That you won't go unless they make you.'

'Beth . . .'

'Promise me? I won't be fobbed off. Please, Andrew.'

'How can I when you're asking for the impossible? I'm a doctor, I've taken a solemn oath to save lives.'

'Even at the cost of destroying your own and mine? You're no different to the boys,' she continued, pain and exhaustion lending an uncharacteristic sharpness to her tongue. 'You think this war will be all glory, medals and marching.'

'No,' he countered evenly. 'I think there will be shooting, shelling, bombing, killing and maimed bodies that will need healing. And that's what I'm trained to do.'

'And your patients in Pontypridd?'

'My father and old Dr Evans will be here to see to them. Beth, don't ask me to opt for an easy war when so many others can't. God only knows none of us want it, and I have more reason than most to stay, but now that it's here we all have to do our bit.'

'In case people like Dai Station sneer?' she mocked.

He looked down at his daughter sleeping peacefully in his arms. 'No. So I can look her in the eye and tell her I took my chances along with everyone else.'

William was almost at Temple Chapel when he remembered he'd promised Jenny he'd call into the shop to pick up a letter for Eddie. He checked the time on his watch and raced back up the hill, panting for breath as he opened the door.

'I thought you'd forgotten.' Jenny took the envelope from the shelf where she'd stowed it next to the cigarettes and tobacco.

'I almost did. No time to stop.'

'William –' she walked around the counter and opened the door for him – 'you will remember to tell whoever takes the letter that I miss Eddie?'

He looked at her. Pretty, blonde and scheming, in his opinion she'd only begun to behave the way a wife should after Eddie had left. He held up the letter. 'You've told him in here?'

She nodded. 'But you could try reinforcing it. After the way I behaved, I need all the help I can get.'

'I'll do what I can.'

'Tell him to try and get leave soon. I couldn't bear it if he didn't come home next time. I **have** to see him, William. I need to set things straight between us to make up for all the awful things I did.'

'I'll try to find the right messenger, but you know what Eddie can be like.'

She bit her lip as he wrenched open the door with one hand and stuffed her letter into his inside pocket with the other. Knowing what Eddie was like and how much she'd hurt him didn't stop her from hoping for the impossible.

Diana was in the back of the shop when William came running in. Holding back her tears, she hugged him.

'You'll take care of Mam?'

'You don't have to ask that.'

'No.' He checked his watch again: he had five minutes at most. Why did he always leave the most important things until there was no time to deal with them? 'You and Wyn – is it serious?'

'I work for him, we're good friends. You know I like him,' she added, 'and you don't have to tell me what you think of him, I already know.'

'You won't do anything stupid?'

'With Wyn? What exactly do you mean, Will?'

'I'm not sure.'

'I doubt that I'll do anything quite as stupid as join the Guards – I'm sorry, I didn't mean that. Come back safe.'

'I intend to. I have to go.'

'And remember your promise to write,' she called after him as he ran down the hill. 'Whatever else you do, don't forget to write.'

'Does that go for me too?' Wyn was behind her.

'Why do men always feel the need to dress up in their best clothes to join up?' she asked tearfully as she eyed his suit.

'Perhaps in the hope of impressing enough to be made officers.'

'I heard you have to be English to be one of those.' She returned to the counter, trying to pretend she didn't care that he was leaving too. 'When are you going?'

'About a week, according to the recruiting officer.'

'Told your father?'

'Last night when I came back from taking you home. He was still awake. I told him you'll be running everything and that you can be trusted.'

'And he approved?'

'Of you, yes. I think he'd like you for a daughter-in-law,' he said lightly, turning his father's obsession into a joke. 'Well, I can't stand here chatting all day, I have a shop to let with an agent, a round to do, and warnings to give out that I won't be around with the van again after this week.' He hesitated. 'I don't suppose . . . no, never mind. Sorry I spoke.'

'Don't suppose what?'

'It doesn't matter.'

'I'll brain you if you don't finish what you've started.'

'There's a special showing in the New Theatre tonight for the Troop Comforts Fund. It's *Marie Antoinette* with Tyrone Power and Norma Shearer. The management insists on everyone being seated before it starts. I thought we could shut the shop early and go and see it.'

'And I could give you a hand to cope with the interval rush, and afterwards to close the shop?'

'I did say forget it.'

'It's just what I need to help me forget Will going away.'

'You mean it?' He stared at her in astonishment.

She nodded. 'I'll be down straight after I close this place.'

'You're not just doing this because my father wants us to get married?'

'I'm doing it because I want to see *Marie Antoinette*, and apart from Will and my uncles, you're the only man in Pontypridd who doesn't make me feel sick. And I happen to like your company, I always have. Are those enough reasons for you?'

He tipped his hat. 'See you later.'

'Had a warning phone call from Cardiff station. They're all bloody conchies.' Dai Station cleared his throat and aimed a stream of spittle at the feet of a small group of men who'd stepped off the incoming Cardiff train. The leading man paused, watching and waiting to see where the missive landed before walking on. Tall, with light brown hair and better dressed than his companions, he had an air of culture and quality that Dai had taken instant exception to. 'Come here hoping to hide away from guns, bullets and Hitler in our valleys, have you?' Dai spat again, with better aim this time. 'Bloody cowards, the lot of you. You're not welcome here, so you may as well crawl back into whatever hole you slithered out of!' he exclaimed, in a voice loud enough to carry to everyone standing on the platform.

'I wonder if he's got calluses hidden under those kid gloves?' A porter drew alongside Dai and kicked one of the pigskin cases the man was holding.

'Not likely. Idle bloody sods like these have never got their hands dirty in their lives. Have they, conchie?' Dai hurled the last word like a missile. Elbowing his way aggressively forward he stopped only when he stood nose to nose with the man. The rest of the group shrank back, but not him. He stood his ground, looking down his long, thin nose at Dai's squat figure.

'He's going to get them dirty now, Dai, so why don't you lay off and leave the man in peace.' Huw Davies pushed his constable's helmet to the back of his head and stared coolly at Dai and the group of belligerent porters who had gathered behind him. Despite the presence of a policeman, the grumbling escalated. Wearing a slightly abstracted look, deliberately designed to lull would-be troublemakers into a false sense of security, Huw folded his arms and listened intently, picking up on every insulting phrase.

'Scum of the earth . . .'

'Won't last half a day down the pit . . .'

'No decent lodging house in Ponty will take them in . . .'

'Too bloody cowardly to stand and fight like our boys . . .'

It was as much as Huw could do to keep his mouth shut. The only contribution that particular porter had made to the war effort had been illegal food hoarding – as much as he could get away with.

'Taking jobs from them that need them . . .'

The last comment was one too many, even for Huw. 'The jobs are only for the duration, Dai. Same time the miners who've joined up will serve. Now go about your business, there's good boys, before I have to arrest you for disturbing the peace.'

'You're taking their part against us?' Dai demanded truculently.

'I'm paid to keep trouble off the streets and the railway station, Dai. Now, I suggest you carry on and do your job so I can do mine, and that means leaving these gentlemen be.'

Setting a course straight through the knot formed by Dai and the porters, he walked towards the conscientious objectors. His sergeant had told him what to look for, but he couldn't have missed them if he'd tried. They stood out like sore thumbs. The one Dai had spat at was better turned out than any of the crache on the Common, and that alone was enough to make him a curiosity in Pontypridd. Camel-hair coat, soft felt trilby, kid gloves, matching leather suitcases – Huw knew instinctively that the inside pocket of the three piece pinstripe suit the man was wearing would hold a gold-monogrammed, solid silver cigarette case and lighter. But the conscripts behind him seemed to be cut from a rougher, more serviceable cloth. Most were wearing caps, even the minority who were dressed in ill-fitting suits; and there was a sprinkling of collarless shirts and cheap jackets that were too thin for the time of year. They looked like, and may have been for all he knew, farm labourers. One way and another if they learned to keep their heads down they'd survive. It was the man in the kid gloves he felt sorriest for because crache ways and soft hands were the first things to be crushed underground, and the crushing inevitably proved an agonisingly slow and painful process.

'I take it you're here to work in the pits?'

'Alexander Forbes.' The elegant man pulled off his right glove and held out his hand. 'Pleased to meet you, constable.'

'Wish I could say the same,' Huw replied as he shook the man's hand.

'We've been sent here by the Ministry of Labour.' Alexander looked Huw in the eye without flinching. His voice was cultured, educated, just as Huw had suspected it would be. His eyes were grey, and as he lifted his trilby in deference to Huw's status, Huw noticed that his hair was well cut and lightly pomaded, confirming his view that the man was crache all right. 'There's twelve of us.'

'I'm here to take you to the police station so you can get sorted with billets and work.'

'Will we be starting today?' one of the other men asked.

'You're that keen?' Huw asked drily.

The man shrugged. 'Just like to know where I stand.'

'You'll most probably find out tomorrow. I may as well warn you now, boys, you're not going to be all that popular. There's still a lot of unemployment around here and some men will think that you're taking jobs away from them, and bread from the mouths of their families.'

'Then why did the Ministry send us here?' Alexander Forbes asked.

'Since when have those in charge ever needed a reason to do anything? Right, boys, if you pick up your bags and follow me we'll start getting you organised.'

Huw herded the men along the platform towards the stone steps that led down into station yard, stopping to send a warning look towards Dai and the group of porters who stood, poised to spit again as the group passed. 'A word?' Huw took Dai to one side as the men descended the steps.

'Bloody conchies, they've no right to be in this town . . .'

'I don't see you in any uniform, Dai.'

'Home Guard and ARP, and I would have joined up if – '

'If there's one thing I've found out, it's that there's always an "if" with men like you.'

'I'm doing my bit!' Dai exclaimed defensively.

'Your bit may not amount to very much in the scheme of things, Dai. Now I've seen a nephew who's like a son to me, off today, and I tried to join up myself, but they put me on the reserves because of my age, so I reckon I've as much a right to speak out as any other man here. As I see it, everyone's entitled to their own way of thinking, and if these men have volunteered to go down the pit instead of shoot Nazis, that's their choice and no one's business except their own. I was in the trenches in the last show and I've worked down the pits, and as I remember there's not much between them. And if any of you feel that strongly about the lack of manpower in France, you know the way to the recruiting office.'

'I . . .'

'I don't want to listen to any of your excuses, Dai. Just give you a word of advice. Stay out of the way of anyone you don't like, and keep your nose clean. Or I'll have to lock you up. And we wouldn't want that now, would we?'

Chapter Nine

Aᴸᴇxᴀɴᴅᴇʀ Forbes could discern hostility in the air as he walked through the industry-blackened streets of Pontypridd, the first Welsh town he'd seen, let alone been in. But then he was growing accustomed to hostility. He'd existed in an atmosphere fraught with animosity since his principles had led him to register as a conscientious objector.

Before he'd made his decision, he'd discussed the implications *ad nauseam* with his colleagues and friends in the university town he'd lived in; read Rupert Brooke and every essay he could lay his hands on that examined the concepts of war and patriotism; and all the time he'd tried, really tried to allow himself to be swayed by notions of right, glory and heroic meaningful death.

But when the time came to examine his conscience coolly and dispassionately, he realised that he'd remained unswayed by the fundamental argument – that every man could be turned into the killing machine that was a soldier. That no matter what his basic moral standpoint, any man would return the fire of an enemy shooting at him or his mates.

It was the thought of 'mates' that had given him the courage to own up to his convictions. He had no way of knowing for certain, but he suspected he was incapable of killing another man, even if that man was about to shoot him or his best friend; and from what he'd been told by the survivors of the last show, comradeship was the best and only mitigating factor in war: that men learned to entrust everything, including their lives, to their mates, especially in battle. And feeling the way he did about shedding blood, he refused to allow himself to be engineered into a position where his inability to take life could jeopardise the lives of others.

But his aversion to killing didn't lessen his animosity towards the Nazi creed, which was why he'd been one of the first conscientious objectors to volunteer his services for non-combative war work, or whatever use his country saw fit short of what he privately saw as 'legalised murder'. So he hadn't been surprised to find himself bound for Wales and the coal mines, but he did find it difficult to understand why the men of the valleys with their history of free thinking and Communism should show so much hostility towards one small group of 'conchies'.

'Left at the next corner,' Huw Davies shouted from the back of the line. 'That's it, up through the Arcade.'

Alexander hung back, studying the hills that hemmed in the town. 'I don't see any pits.'

'We don't keep them in the centre of town, sir.'

Alexander glanced at the constable's face. There wasn't a trace of humour. 'Then we're going to be billeted out of town?'

'No idea, sir. We only had the telegram to say you were on your way an hour before you arrived. But don't worry, the sergeant will soon have you all sorted into nice pits and billets.'

'That's good to know,' Alexander replied drily as he shifted his heaviest case from one hand to another.

'If you don't mind me saying so, sir, you don't look as though you've held a pick much less been down a pit in your life.'

'None of us has, sergeant, and I wish you'd call me Alexander, or Forbes.'

'What are you good at then, Mr Forbes?'

'My last job was in a museum, but I've also been a teacher.'

'Grammar school?'

'University.'

'The lads in the miners' institute will be happy to hear that. They've got a programme of classes going.'

'I'd be glad to help out.'

'If I were you, I'd wait to see how you take to working a twelve-hour shift, six days a week underground before you volunteer for anything.' Huw looked across Gelliwasted Road. 'There it is, boys. The grey building. If you'd like to go through the front door –' He stood back and saw the ragged column of men across the road. 'Were you a teacher long, Mr Forbes?' he asked as he and Alexander brought up the rear of the column.

'Five years.'

'That explains it, then.'

'Explains what?'

'Why you're a conscientious objector. Seems to me anyone who's studied the past can't fail to come to the conclusion that war never solves anything.'

'You're a scholar, Constable?'

'I wouldn't call myself that, sir.'

'A Communist then.'

'I was never one for extremes. Socialist will do.'

'From what I've seen so far I think it would be difficult for any man to live around here for long and remain a capitalist.'

'If you intend to live around here for more than a week or two, Mr Forbes, you might be glad of a little advice.'

'I'll be glad of anything you can give me, constable.'

'Speak only when you're spoken to, and don't talk about socialism or Communism until you learn to live Owain Glyndwr's ways like the natives. And last, but most important, watch your back. Given time, the boys may get used to you, but for the moment jingoism has taken over, and I'd hate to see you or any of these lads get hurt.'

'I'll remember that, constable, and thank you.'

'You've nothing to thank me for, sir.'

'The first civil word, constable,' Alexander said as he walked into the darkened interior of the station. 'It means a lot.'

Harry Griffiths tried to ignore the slamming of doors and the scraping of furniture being dragged over the floor upstairs as he went about serving his customers and unpacking the boxes that the delivery boys had humped into his stockroom. His wife was angry and letting the whole world know it. But he didn't want to think about his wife, he wanted to remember Megan Powell. Her warm smile, her welcoming arms, the quiet, companionable evenings he had spent at her fireside. The way she had listened to his problems, calmly, attentively without ever passing judgement.

He wished he had known she was about to be released. He would have rented a house for her in Leyshon Street. Not her old house, that had been let a long time ago, but another one. He would have arranged to have all her old furniture moved from her brother Huw's house where it had lain in storage ever since William and Diana had been forced to give up their home. He would have . . .

He suddenly recalled the reality of his relationship with Megan. Having to creep down the back lane of Leyshon Street after dark. Opening the door in the garden wall and sneaking into Megan's kitchen when no one's curtains were twitching. Never being able to say more than 'Hello' to her in public. Never being able to give her a present ostentatious enough for her to wear or display, lest she have to account for its origin.

Megan was a woman who deserved much more than lies and subterfuge. This time it would be different between them. He'd divorce his wife and marry Megan — not straight away, of course.

Divorce took time – years, even. But then as Bert had said, a wife like Megan was worth having. The only wonder was why he hadn't left his wife and moved in with Megan years ago. But it wasn't too late. He had time. Time to make up to her for all she had suffered. Time for them to be happy.

'I can't take any more of them and that's final.' The manager's representative from Lady Windsor colliery glowered with an expression hardened miners had learned to back away from. Crossing his arms over his barrel chest, he faced the sergeant square on.

'Then where am I supposed to put them?'

'There are other pits.'

'I've tried them. They've all been very helpful,' the sergeant lied, 'but it's not just the pits, it's the billets. And there's a handy lodging house within walking distance of the gates of the Lady Windsor that's prepared to take all twelve.'

'I don't doubt it. It's renowned for its bedbugs and rats, which is why the landlady's always prepared to put up men at short notice.' The representative pretended not to notice the alarm registering in the eyes of the men sitting on the bench in the waiting area. 'I can understand why people aren't queuing up to take them in,' he continued as though they were dumb animals incapable of either thought or comprehension.

'You can?'

'You're a working man, sergeant. Imagine how you'd feel if you came off shift and found one of these sitting with his feet under your table.'

'These?' Huw Davies queried innocently, looking to Alexander Forbes who was sitting at the end of the line, listening attentively to the conversation.

'They can call themselves whatever they want, but I can see the yellow in their skin.'

'It'll soon turn black, same as all the other miners around here,' Huw said shortly.

'Well, thank you for your help, sir,' the sergeant curtailed the conversation. 'If you take yours, we can see to what's left.'

The man nodded to the two clerks he had brought with him. Within minutes they had ushered half the men out of the waiting area.

'How many does that leave us with, sergeant?' Huw asked.

'Two, if the Lewis Merthyr take four.'

'The Maritime?'

'Still waiting to hear, but as I said, it's not persuading the pits, they'll do whatever the Labour Board directs them to do, it's finding the billets. You've got contacts on the Graig, haven't you?' he asked, knowing full well that Huw had family there; the constable had asked for enough blind eyes to be turned towards their doings in the past.

Huw was slow of speech and slow of action, but only a fool took him to be slow witted, and the sergeant wasn't usually a fool. 'The answer's no.'

'Come on. Evan Powell's two sons have joined up, and I hear your nephew went today. They're swimming with room up there.'

'My sister's moved in, and my niece is still living there.'

'The boys must have slept somewhere. Bed and board for two men for a couple of days, that's all I'm asking. We all have to do our bit now there's a war on.'

'I don't see the crache doing much except draw their one and threepence an hour when they're on fire-watching duty.'

'We're having enough trouble with the unemployed in this town grumbling about those payments without you starting, Davies.'

'I'll ask around when I cover my beat.' Huw lumbered towards the door. 'I can't do more.'

Alexander watched the constable leave, and prepared himself for another hour or two of hungry, mind-numbing boredom. The railway warrant and summons to Pontypridd had come so suddenly, he hadn't had time to consider what he'd find at journey's end. He'd seen newsreels of the Rhondda, filmed when the pits had closed during the depression. He'd helped serve meals in church halls to miners when they'd walked south on hunger marches, and he'd been amazed at how widely read and intelligent they'd been. Talking to them had consolidated his belief in Communism and a fair share for all, and he'd expected to find plenty of other like-minded people in the valleys. But as the day wore on and the mutterings in the waiting room grew louder every time someone looked their way, he began to despair of finding anyone in Wales capable of understanding his motives for declaring himself a conscientious objector.

By six in the evening he was exhausted from travelling, aching from sitting on the hard bench, and in urgent need of a wash and something more substantial than the tea and biscuits the sergeant had doled out at inadequate intervals. And still half a dozen of them waited. After some hard telephone bargaining the sergeant had exacted a promise from the Lewis Merthyr colliery to take three men, but that had been hours ago and there'd been no sign of any movement since.

'Trust this government,' a whisper came from the top end of the bench as Alexander rose to his feet to stretch his legs. 'They couldn't organise a piss-up in a brewery, let alone a war. I knew there was no way they'd be ready for us here.' The speaker was a pasty-faced cockney who looked as though he'd never breathed a lungful of fresh air in his life, and probably wouldn't be given the chance to now, Alexander reflected grimly. He put him down as a troublemaker, a man who enjoyed manufacturing grumble bullets he handed to others to fire. Ignoring his moans Alexander paced to the door.

'Hey, you there! Where do you think you're going?' the sergeant shouted from behind his desk.

'Work off cramp,' Alexander answered.

'No further than the door,' the sergeant warned, as though he expected Alexander to add whatever energy was left to him after his long day, to the German war effort.

Alexander leaned against a noticeboard screwed to the wall and surveyed his fellow sufferers. There was an intense fidgeting and whispering around the troublemaker. The only one who hadn't joined in the activity was a young lad sitting at the end of the bench. He looked nearer sixteen than eighteen, and his worn corduroy trousers and jacket spoke volumes about his class and financial status. With nothing better to do, Alexander watched him for a while, but the boy continued to sit, eyes down, cap in hand, completely withdrawn from the others and the scene around him.

Alexander tried to follow his example and retreat within himself. He had a rich store of literature to tap into. A choice selection of the works of the great poets, Chaucer, Milton, Donne and Shakespeare that he had committed to memory and heart, but although they had proved a diversion on the journey down, they eluded him now. The muse clearly didn't feel at home in a gloomy police station in Pontypridd on a Monday evening in late winter.

'You –' the sergeant beckoned to the three men clustered around the troublemaker, but not the troublemaker himself. 'If you go with this man he'll take you to your billets.'

'And us?' Alexander enquired hopefully.

'There's a chance you'll be taken on at the Maritime if billets can be found for you. There's a housing shortage in the valleys,' the sergeant added superfluously.

'In that case why didn't they sort it out before sending us here?' the troublemaker demanded.

'Probably because the Ministry has more important things to concern itself with than the fate of a group of untrained miners.'

'I never wanted to be a miner,' the man retorted belligerently.

The sergeant laid down his pen with the resigned air of someone who'd seen and done it all before, and of choice wouldn't be doing it again. 'What's your name, boy?'

'I'm not a boy,' the man responded sullenly.

'I asked you a question.'

'Alfred Hawkins.'

'Well, Mr Hawkins. You don't want to be a miner and you'll meet plenty around here who don't want you on the job. By the look of you,' the sergeant flicked a critical eye over the man's scrawny physique, 'I doubt you're up to the rigours of life underground, but time will tell. In the meantime I suggest you sit down, shut up, and get on with what you've been ordered to do.'

'No one's ordered me to do anything.'

'Precisely.'

Having finally silenced Hawkins, the sergeant picked up his pen again. Another half an hour ticked by. Alexander watched the clock; the hands had never moved so slowly. No one entered or left the station. No noise came from anywhere within the building. Seven o'clock came and went. Perhaps the town ate an early dinner or late tea and the inhabitants were too engrossed in their food to cause trouble.

The huge policeman, Huw Davies, who had been on the platform to greet them, returned. He removed his helmet to reveal a balding head of greying, ginger hair and a moon-sized face.

'Maritime will take three,' the sergeant gestured to the remaining men, 'but there's no billets arranged.'

'Then tell the Ministry we can't accommodate them.'

'I wish it was as simple as that,' the sergeant replied with a patience Alexander found remarkable, considering how many hours he had already devoted to sorting out the problems of twelve unwanted conscripts. 'They've been assigned to this area; forerunners, the Ministry spokesman said when I telephoned.'

'You should have told them to read their own unemployment statistics. Why didn't they use their heads, and put them in civil defence or firefighting in their home towns?'

'That's what I told them,' Alfred Hawkins chipped in.

'Don't suppose you thought to ask round for a billet?' the sergeant pressed, ignoring Hawkins.

'I asked.'

'No joy?'

'I wasn't even sure what pit they were going to.'

'Maritime. The Graig would be handiest, which was why I mentioned your connections earlier. See what you can do, constable, there's a good man.'

'Is that an order?'

'If you want a quiet life.'

Huw Davies knew what that particular set of the sergeant's jaw meant. He replaced his helmet on his head.

'Best you take them with you. I'm fed up with them cluttering this place, and people find it harder to say no when they're confronted with lodgers that mean an extra couple of bob in their pockets.'

Resigned to his task, Huw looked at the two men sitting on the bench. 'You'd best come with me.'

'Do you want me as well?' Alexander moved away from the wall. Huw looked to the sergeant, who nodded his head.

'Didn't they tell you that things are difficult in the valleys?' Huw questioned as they left the gloom of the station for the damp, freezing night air and blackout.

'They didn't tell us nothing,' Alfred protested resentfully. 'And before you say any more, we don't want to be here any more than you want us to be.'

'Well, seeing as you are here, all we can do is make the best of it.' Huw led them across the road down Church Street and into Market Square. 'I take it you're all conscientious objectors?' All three nodded. 'Communists?'

'Fully paid up member of the Fascist Party, me,' Alfred Hawkins announced proudly. 'And there's no way I'm lifting a finger against Hitler or the Germans. In my opinion, we need one like him in this country.'

'Best keep your opinions to yourself while you're here,' Huw cautioned.

'Because the valleys are full of the red menace?'

'Either of you two Communist?' Huw asked, doing his best to ignore Hawkins, lest he be tempted to thump him.

'No,' the boy answered in a small voice. Huw didn't press Alexander Forbes because he'd already formed his own opinion about him. He contented himself by wondering how the pit management would react to the government sending more Communists to add to the troublesome strength of the ones they already had. Every strike brought out infiltrators working for the mine owners and all of them seeking Communist subversives.

'If you're not a Communist, why are you a conscientious objector?' Huw asked the boy.

'My family are Quakers,' he mumbled, keeping his head down as he lugged his worn carpet-bag.

'Where are you from?' Huw asked in a kindlier tone.

'Cornwall.'

'What work have you done?'

'Basket weaving.'

'Well there's not much call for that down the pit, but I'll do what I can to get you a decent billet, for tonight at least.' He turned to Alexander. 'You're not saying much.'

'You warned me to keep my mouth shut.'

'So I did,' Huw smiled. 'Glad to see you're prepared to take advice.'

Harry Griffiths opened the cupboard under the stairs and took out the clothes brush. Lifting his best trilby from the hat stand he began to clean it.

'And where do you think you're going?' his wife demanded from the landing above him.

'Civil Defence League.'

'Let others volunteer for that nonsense. You can't afford the time with a business to run.'

'If everyone took that attitude we may as well surrender to Hitler now.'

'If you think I'm serving in the shop . . .'

'Jenny's offered to go in the shop until closing time.' He rammed his hat on his head and reached for his coat.

'And where is this precious meeting of yours?'

'Graig Hotel.' He could hear her sharp intake of breath from where he was standing.

'If I find out . . .'

'If you find out what?' He shrugged his coat over his shoulders and stared up at her. 'You'd refuse to allow me into your room? Your bed? The only thing of mine you have, Mrs Griffiths, is my name. And I'm giving you fair warning, you won't have the use of that much longer.'

'I'm a decent – '

'Respectable married woman?' He raised his eyebrows as he put his hand on the door handle. 'Try divorced. You may even get used to it,' he said brusquely as he walked out.

Phyllis had finished washing the tea things, and was tidying the kitchen in readiness for the evening. Megan had insisted on helping, and was stacking the clean dishes in the pantry, although both Phyllis and Evan would have been happier if she had sat down and conserved what little strength she had left. A sharp knock at the front door, followed by the sound of the key turning in the lock, disturbed them.

'It's only me,' Huw's voice echoed down the passage.

'You're too late for tea.' Megan walked to the pantry door. 'Although I could do you egg and chips.'

'Not now, love.' He picked his sister up from the pantry step, lifting her so he could kiss her cheek.

'I hate it when you do that,' she complained.

'Hurts my back to stoop to your level.'

'Two visits in one week.' Evan looked up from his paper as Phyllis took an extra cup and saucer from the dresser. 'We are honoured.'

'There'll be a blue moon tonight,' Megan said, closing the pantry door and joining them in the kitchen. 'Come to see if I'm crying over William?'

'Much as I love you, Megan, I must confess it's Evan I've come to see.'

Evan laid his pipe on the mantelpiece and folded his newspaper. Huw couldn't help reflecting that no matter how much effort Phyllis put into taking care of him, Evan was looking tired, and a lot more washed out since he'd given up his rag and bone round to go back underground.

'Well at least none of the boys have done anything. Have they?' Evan demanded, suddenly realising that if there had been an accident in training camp, or London, where his eldest son Haydn was living with his wife Jane, Huw would be the obvious choice to bring the bad news.

'Not that I'm aware of, although knowing those three it's my guess they'll be up to something if they've got any energy left after a day's square-bashing, even if it's only a few jars in a pub.'

'Well if it's not the boys, what is it?'

'Sergeant had a surprise parcel this morning. Conscription board sent us a dozen conscientious objectors.' Huw lowered himself into the seat opposite Evan's and took the tea Phyllis handed him.

'What for?' Evan asked.

'That's what the sergeant wanted to know. He rang up the Ministry of Labour and asked if they knew we had more miners in the valleys than jobs. They didn't. Apparently some silly sod up there decided we could use a few more, untrained at that, and now they're here we've no choice but to keep them. Sergeant split them between the pits, there's three for the Maritime.'

'And you want me to keep an eye on them?'

'Bit more than that. They've nowhere to stay. No billets arranged.'

'And you thought they could stay here?'

'I wouldn't have come unless I was desperate.' Huw pulled a creased handkerchief from his top pocket and wiped his forehead. The Graig hill was steep, it had been a long haul up it at the end of a full twelve-hour shift, and it was warm in the kitchen. 'I had three of them. One was a Fascist so I persuaded Richards next door to take him in, I thought he'd feel at home there.'

Evan appreciated the irony. His neighbour was well known for supporting Mosley. The only man on the Graig to do so.

'There was a bit of a fracas when they arrived at the station this morning. Dai organised a reception committee and you know what he can be like.'

'I know,' Evan said drily, thinking of the tough time the Communists in his own pit who'd tried to register as conscientious objectors had been given by people like Dai, and they had the advantage of being local.

'The ones who shout the loudest and kick the hardest are always the ones who've never fought, and wouldn't know how to if they came face to face with Hans or Fritz.' Huw was thinking back to his own time in the trenches. A time he wished he didn't still remember and rarely mentioned.

'So, you feel sorry for these two conscripted miners and thought we'd take care of them for you?'

'Well, I did wonder, what with the boys' room being empty and everything, if you could put them up until we have time to get things sorted. They'll be paying normal lodging rates of seven and six a week.'

'Only a bachelor could ask a man a question like that. The decision isn't mine to make. I'm merely the head of this household, it's the women you should be looking to.'

'As long as it is only for a few days,' Phyllis began hesitantly. 'The boys' room is empty now, but they'll be needing it when they come home on leave.'

'When they come home it will only be for a few days, and I can always move in with Diana,' Megan volunteered.

'And Brian can come in with Evan and me,' Phyllis added.

'Looks like it's sorted,' Evan said to Huw.

'We have to do all we can to help the war effort, don't we?' Phyllis looked to Megan for confirmation.

'Seems to me, this particular copper,' Megan picked up the teapot and refilled Huw and Evan's cups, 'knows where to come for a soft touch and a pot of tea just brewed.' A suspicion crossed her mind as she went to the pantry to fetch more milk. 'Huw, where are these men?'

'Outside the door.'

'Huw Davies, it's cold enough out there to turn an Eskimo blue.'

'I couldn't be sure Evan would say yes.'

'You best go and get them before they freeze to death.' Megan lifted down another two cups while Huw went to the door.

Evan rose to his feet and extended his hand as Huw ushered them in. He wasn't sure what conscientious objectors should look like, but he doubted Huw could have found two more disparate men if he'd tried.

One was tall and thin with clothes that spoke of money, and a fair amount of it; the other, a young boy dressed in a shabby jacket several sizes too large for him, a cloth cap, collarless shirt and muffler, clean, but more darn than cloth.

'Evan Powell.' Evan shook the hand of the older man. 'This is my wife, Phyllis,' he said avoiding laborious, embarrassing explanations, 'and my sister-in-law Megan Powell.'

'Pleased to meet you, ladies.' Alexander removed his hat and shook hands with Phyllis and Megan before Evan.

Huw unbuttoned his jacket as the boy shook hands with everyone. He'd heard Megan shuffling around in the pantry and he knew his sister. She wouldn't allow the new lodgers to go to bed hungry, and if there was a supper going it would save him the trouble of slicing bread and cheese in his own house.

'Well as you're staying, you'd better take your coats off, you can hang them in the hall. Put the light on for them, Huw. I hope you've pulled the blackout curtain, because the last thing we need is Dai Station snooping around.'

'I think we've already met him,' Alexander said wryly.

'You did,' Huw confirmed.

'You look as though you could do with a cup of tea.' Evan smiled at the younger boy, who hadn't said a word since he'd come into the house.

'We don't want to put you to any trouble, Mr Powell.'

'Have either of you eaten since breakfast?' Megan asked as she emerged from the pantry.

'We had tea and biscuits in the police station.'

'I know what police station tea is like.' Megan lifted the kettle and took it out to the wash-house to fill it. Phyllis followed her.

'We've all the ingredients for a Welsh rarebit,' Phyllis said practically. 'If you don't mind making it, I'll sort out the boys' bedroom.'

'Be glad to. If you're short of space to put the boys' things you're welcome to store them in my room.'

'I think there's room in the second wardrobe in Diana's room. Do you think she'll mind?'

'Looks like she's never home long enough to notice what's in her room.'

'This really is very kind of you,' Alexander said. He opened the door to take his and the boy's coat into the passage.

'I'm trying to stay on the right side of the law.' Megan earned herself a frown from her brother, who had found it difficult to come to terms with her incarceration.

'Can I do anything to help?'

'Looks to me like you need a warm. Go and sit by the fire.'

As Alexander returned to the kitchen and pulled a chair close to the cooking range he was struck by two things: the warmth and cleanliness of the room, and the hours of work that had gone into making the rag rugs and patchwork cushions and curtains, which brightened the scuffed and battered furniture. He had never sat in a kitchen before, never seen well-scrubbed flagstones, nor a cooking range at close quarters. Above all he'd had no social contact with the working classes, and he hoped it wouldn't show.

Megan cracked eggs, grated cheese and sliced leeks into a basin. 'Ten minutes and you'll have a meal in front of you. I hope you both like Welsh rarebit.'

'After what we've eaten today it sounds like a banquet,' Alexander answered politely.

The boy, who had been screwing his cap into a ball, looked up warily.

'Did you volunteer for the pits?' Evan asked as Megan continued to bustle between the range and the pantry.

'I volunteered to do anything other than actual fighting,' Alexander said briefly.

'What were you doing before the war broke out?'

'Working in a museum. The artefacts were sent to a secure location for the duration so I found myself redundant, and the Ministry stepped in. I think it's only fair to tell you, Mr Powell, I'm a Communist as well as a conscientious objector.' Alexander looked Evan in the eye, half expecting him to throw him out of the house then and there.

'So am I. But being a Communist doesn't necessarily make a man a conscientious objector.'

'It's a personal thing. I can't bear the thought of killing another man – any man.'

'You'll soon discover that you haven't picked the easy option. It's hard work underground.'

'So I've heard.'

'What about you?' Evan asked the boy.

'My family are Quakers.'

'Well you're both welcome to stay here until something more

permanent can be arranged, though I warn you now, I'm not too sure how the boys are going to take your presence down the pit. They've only just reopened and there's plenty still out of work.'

'I told them that,' Huw said from his corner where he was almost nodding off.

'I hope they'll understand when we tell them we had no choice.' Alexander rubbed his hands in an attempt to restore the circulation.

'So do I.' Evan smiled as Phyllis opened the door with their three-year-old son in her arms.

'Brian was awake so I thought we should introduce him to our guests.'

'I'm Alexander.' He extended a hand to the boy, who shrank back against his mother.

'And I'm Luke.' The Quaker boy held out his hands and Brian went to him without a murmur.

'You have brothers and sisters?' Megan asked as she opened the oven door to push in the finished rarebit.

'Five brothers and six sisters. I'm the eldest.'

Megan looked at his worn, but clean and mended clothes. The size of his family explained a lot, including the way Brian, who was normally shy of strangers, had taken to him. He sat contentedly on Luke's knee allowing himself to be bounced up and down. It was evident that Luke felt more at home with children than adults.

Brian smiled, pushed his thumb into his mouth and snuggled down on Luke's shoulder.

'Back to bed for you, little man.' Phyllis lifted him out of Luke's arms.

'Megan's daughter lives with us too.' Evan picked up his pipe from the mantelpiece and opened his tobacco tin. 'She's working late tonight, but hopefully we'll be able to warn her that you're in the house before you collide in the wash-house. Now, if you've finished your tea I'll show you round.'

Evan started with the lean-to wash-house. That summer he had moved the tap in from the back yard to the wash-house to make things easier for Phyllis. He pointed in the general direction of the ty bach, warning them to make sure the curtains were pulled before they left the house, so as not to show any light and risk incurring a fine. 'Dai Station is our ARP warden, so there'll be no warning.'

'Especially for conchies,' Alexander agreed.

Luke looked around, relieved and pleasantly surprised. His father had told him to expect harsh treatment and workhouse conditions, and as the day had worn on, events had seemed to confirm his father's prophecy. This house was far larger, better furnished and much more luxurious than the two-up, two-down cottage his parents rented, and because Evan hadn't gone out of his way to be over-friendly he was already beginning to thaw – enough to return Megan's smile when they walked back through the kitchen on their way upstairs.

Harry didn't hear a word that was said in the Civil Defence League meeting. He was too busy keeping a lookout for Evan Powell and thinking over the harsh words he'd exchanged with his wife that evening. He needed to talk over his problems with someone, and he couldn't think of anyone better than Evan, and not only because he was Megan's brother-in-law. Evan had been married to a shrew of a woman who had made not only his but his children's lives hell until she had finally walked out on him. And when she had, Evan hadn't wasted any time in moving the woman he loved and their bastard into his house to ensure that his wife wouldn't be returning. A few people who'd been shocked to the core at the time, had now unbent enough to nod to Phyllis in the shop, and he felt that Evan, more than any other man in Pontypridd, would understand the situation between Megan and himself.

The meeting was over and the serious drinking had begun in earnest when Evan put in an appearance with Huw Davies. As Harry had no desire to face Megan's brother so soon after the warning Huw had given him that morning, he lingered next to the bar, listening to the gossip centred around the barmaid until Huw left. Then he made a beeline for Evan.

'Pint?'

'I was just going home.'

'Just one. I need to talk to you about something.'

Evan glanced around the crowded bar. 'It's worse than auction bell time in the market in here.'

'We could go in the snug?'

Harry picked up their beers on the way to the cheerless back room. It was cold and dismal, the wallpaper so stained by nicotine it was impossible to determine what its original colour had been.

'Here's to victory,' Evan toasted as Harry plonked a full pint glass before him.

'Cheers.' Now Harry actually had Evan's undivided attention, all his carefully planned and mentally rehearsed speeches were forgotten. 'How's Eddie?' he blurted out.

'Fine, or at least I think so. We had a letter from him yesterday. He seems to be enjoying his free time in France, if not the rest.'

'Glad to hear it.'

'He still hasn't written to Jenny?'

'I don't think so, but then she doesn't say much.'

'Well, we can't live their lives for them,' Evan observed, closing the conversation.

'I heard Megan is living with you,' Harry said, quickly seizing the initiative.

'She is.'

'I was wondering . . . wondering . . .' Harry looked at Evan and stammered into silence. It was evident Evan was reluctant to discuss his sister-in-law with him. 'How is she?' he finished lamely.

'Weak, worn out, worked half to death. How you'd expect a woman to be after years of hard labour.'

'I was hoping to see her.'

'She won't be out for a bit. Not until the weather's warmer if Phyllis and I have our way.'

'I'm very fond of Megan.'

'I gathered that,' Evan stated, wondering what was coming next.

'I'd like to see her again.'

'With or without your wife?' Evan pulled out his pipe.

'Everyone knows my wife and I lead separate lives.'

'Your marriage is no concern of mine, or Megan's.'

'I've asked my wife for a divorce. I want to marry Megan. I thought you of all people would understand my position.'

'All I understand is that Megan's had a rough time. In my opinion she needs a bit of peace and quiet away from the gossip-mongers.'

'I'd like to see her.'

'Your daughter is married to my son, Harry. You and your wife are welcome in my house any time you care to call. You wanting to see Megan on your own is something else.'

'And if my wife leaves me?'

'Is she likely to?'

'I don't know,' he confessed dismally.

'Seems to me there's enough trouble in this world without going looking for it.'

'Then you won't help me?'

'Megan's a grown woman. I'll tell her about our little chat, but after that it's up to her.' Evan drained his glass and rose from the table. 'Next time I see you, it'll be my round.'

Chapter Ten

'You've taken in conscientious objectors as lodgers?' Diana dropped the porridge pot on to the table and stared dumbfounded at her uncle.

'They had no billets. From what your Uncle Huw said, it was either us or a police cell.'

'But the boys . . .'

'When they come home on leave your mother can move in with you, and Brian back with us. Eddie can have the downstairs and William the box room.'

'And Haydn and Jane?'

'It's unlikely Haydn, Jane, William and Eddie will all come home at the same time, but if they do, either Haydn and Jane can stay with Bethan, or Eddie with his wife.'

'I suppose so,' she said doubtfully, wondering, like everyone else in the family, the extent of the estrangement between Eddie and Jenny. 'It's just that . . .'

'It's just that you think the boys have no sooner moved out than these fellows have moved in to take their place? I know exactly how you feel because the same thought's crossed my own mind. But they're not here for good, just the duration, and as the boys are away for the same, however long that is, it seems crazy to allow their room to stand idle when it can be put to good use.'

'I just wish everything was back to normal!' she exclaimed in exasperation.

'Don't we all.' Evan nodded towards the door as it opened. 'Good morning. Alexander, Luke, this is my niece, Diana Powell.'

Diana wiped her hands on her apron before shaking their hands. Alexander's handshake was firm and confident, in sharp contrast to Luke's nervous, hesitant touch.

Evan scrutinised the clothes his lodgers were wearing. Luke was dressed in the same rags as yesterday. Neither the trousers nor the shirt were strong enough to protect him from the conditions he'd encounter underground, but by the look of the boy, he'd need his first month's money before he'd be able to foot the bill for something more serviceable. Alexander, however, was dressed for a Sunday afternoon stroll round the park. 'Those clothes are going to get ruined down the pit,' he warned.

'I'm afraid these are the oldest I have,' Alexander said, apologising for his grey flannels, white shirt and tie.

'Well at least take the collar and tie off. There's no point in wearing either to wield a pick and shovel.'

'Breakfast is ready.' Diana set a rack of toast alongside the porridge. 'Help yourselves. If I don't make a move, I'll be late.'

'Wyn's working you hard,' Evan commented, reaching for the teapot.

'Not for much longer. He joined up yesterday.'

'The Guards?'

'They're the only ones actively recruiting at the moment.'

'That means he'll be going soon.'

'And guess who'll be running the business while he's away?'

'You?'

'His father's worse than ever, and Myrtle's too busy looking after him to help out.'

'No wonder you've been working late. How are you going to manage both shops?'

'I'm not. Wyn saw the agent yesterday about letting one. We're clearing out High Street today. Porridge?' She pushed the pot towards Luke who was sitting opposite her looking lost and far too uncertain to do anything so forward as help himself to food. It didn't take much imagination to put herself in his place; thrust among strangers miles from home, family and friends. 'If you're not too tired after your first day's work I could show you Ronconi's café tonight,' she suggested, trying to be friendly.

'Café, for a meal?' Alexander asked, confused by the offer that Diana hadn't intended for him.

'I don't know what you do in the evenings where you come from, but we don't eat out very often in Ponty. But we do go down to the cafés to drink tea or coffee.'

'Is there anywhere else to go?'

'Two theatres and three picture houses in the town centre, another one in Treforest, a couple of dance halls, a roller-skating rink, and lectures in the YMCA and unemployed institute, but if I were you I'd start with Ronconi's café. It's *the* place to be in Pontypridd on a Tuesday night.' Diana regretted her half-hearted attempt at a joke when she saw a light in Alexander's eye that she'd had no intention of kindling.

'What time will you be going down?'

'After tea, whenever that will be. But there's no need to give me an answer now. I'm meeting friends there anyway. I suggest you wait until you know how you feel after work.' Leaving the table, Diana took a saucer of salt and the mug that contained her toothbrush from the cupboard next to the stove and went into the wash-house.

'What do you think, Luke?' Alexander asked. 'Would you like to see Pontypridd?' Bypassing the porridge, Alexander reached for the toast and jam.

'Perhaps,' the boy replied, wondering how much a cup of tea in Ronconi's would cost.

'If you're going to make the pit by six, boys, you'd better hurry.' Megan carried a collection of battered tins out of the pantry into the kitchen. Dropping them on the table she kissed Diana goodbye.

Evan saw the quizzical look on Alexander's face. 'Snap boxes,' he explained.

'But we haven't paid you yet, Mr Powell,' Luke protested as Megan began stuffing the sandwiches she'd cut into the boxes.

'It's Evan, and you can pay for your lodge on Friday when you get your wages.' He only hoped that the boys wouldn't have to work a week in hand. That might stretch the family budget too far.

'But we will need your ration cards.' Megan poured tea into three metal bottles and screwed the tops on firmly. It would be stone cold by snap time, but she'd never met a miner who didn't prefer cold tea to any other drink underground, and it hadn't occurred to her to ask if either of the lodgers had a preference.

'I'll go upstairs and get it.' Luke spooned the last of his porridge into his mouth as he pushed his chair away from the table.

'Mine's in the drawer in the bedside cabinet on my side of the bed. Would you get it for me please, Luke?' Alexander took a second piece of toast and spread butter on it with a lavishness that earned him a reproving glance from Megan; he saw it, but failed to understand its significance. He was having too difficult a time adjusting to the vagaries of working-class life to notice disapproval in the reactions of others.

For a start he'd never shared a bed with anyone, male or female, in his life, yet Luke appeared to be used to the arrangement, and to be fair to the boy he'd kept to his own side. And this hectic idea of breakfasting was totally alien to him. Only a few days ago he'd been sitting in the dining room of his parents' house, waited on by a black-garbed, white-aproned maid, who'd enquired in suitably deferential tones if he had a preference for tea or coffee, orange or tomato juice, cereals or porridge.

'Right, let's go.' Evan tightened his leather belt over his coal-encrusted clothes and pulled his cap down over his head. Picking up his snap tin and bottle he led the way to the door. Luke followed, leaving Alexander to bring up the rear.

'If you keep your head down, and put your back into anything you're asked to do, you'll be all right,' Megan advised.

'I hope so, Mrs Powell,' Alexander answered doubtfully as he looked at his camel-hair coat, and left it where it was, hanging on the wall behind the front door.

Harry Griffiths was alone in the shop's storeroom when his wife walked in.

'I thought you'd be working behind the counter this morning?'

'Divisional Food Officer has asked all retailers to notify him of ration book and stock levels. I'm making an inventory.' He slashed open a box with his penknife. Pulling back the cardboard covers he revealed twin rows of tins. He lifted one up as though he doubted the veracity of the label that proclaimed it to contain tomatoes. Replacing the tin, he folded the top over and lifted another box on to it. His wife had never shown any interest in the business before. On the few occasions he had been desperate enough to appeal to her for help, she had told him in no uncertain terms that her job was to see to the house, and with a husband like him and a daughter to look after she had more work than she could cope with as it was. He hadn't liked her reply, but as they'd settled into the sterile patterns of their respective lives he had learned to accept it, and he hoped that now, of all times, his wife would have the sense to let sleeping dogs lie. The last thing he needed after Evan's reception of his plans for him and Megan, was a reconciliation scene engineered by his wife.

'You saw Megan Powell last night?'

He sat back on his heels, while continuing to attack the top of the box.

'Well, did you?' she demanded in a shrill voice.

'I went to the Civil Defence League meeting,' he replied evenly.

'You came in very late.'

'It dragged on. There was a lot to discuss.'

'I don't want to be stopped on the road to be told that you and that woman have picked up where you left off before she was put behind bars.'

'I was at a Civil Defence League meeting,' he repeated forcefully.

'I know you, Harry Griffiths. You and your filthy mind. You want to leave me to live in sin with Megan Powell. Go on, admit it.'

'What's there to admit? I've already told you I love Megan and I want to spend what's left of my life with her.'

Now that he'd had time to think through the implications – social and financial – of continuing his affair with Megan, she had half expected, half hoped for a denial. More of the same lies and evasion that they had used to paper over the cracks in their marriage since that first catastrophic night.

'I want a divorce. I can't put it any simpler than that.'

'Over my dead body!'

'A different man might tell you that could be arranged.'

'Are you threatening me?'

'No, just telling you that I want to live with the woman I love.'

'And do disgusting, revolting, bestial things with her. Things no decent woman would allow.' She screwed her mouth and eyes into tight little slits of repugnance.

'I'll give you a hundred pounds cash and a pound a week allowance. You could live with your sister.'

'Not for all the tea in China. I'm your wife. I'm entitled to half of everything you own.'

'Then I'll move out. You can have this flat, but the shop remains mine and Jenny's.'

'The law and God are on my side, and I'll hold you to the vows you made in church.'

'How would you like it if I held you to yours?' he threatened as he rose to his feet. 'Starting right now.' He took a step towards her. She backed away. He reached the connecting door before her. Slamming it shut, he turned the key in the lock.

'Don't you dare touch me!'

'Perhaps it's time to do what I should have a long time ago.' Moving swiftly he grabbed the neck of the thin woollen dress she was wearing and yanked downwards. The cloth tore, breaking away at the shoulder and side seams, exposing an expanse of bright pink elasticated corset with satin brassière cups. She screamed, clutching her hands over what little cleavage could be seen.

'You beast! You filthy, vulgar, disgusting – '

'Is everything all right, Mam? Dad?' Jenny hammered on the door.

'Your mother tripped over a box and tore her dress,' Harry answered coolly. 'But she's not hurt. Be a good girl and nip upstairs and get a cardigan for her. She can't walk through the shop looking the way she does.'

He stared at his shivering, terrified wife as Jenny's footsteps echoed on the wooden stairs. 'If you're sure it's what you want, I'll stay with you, darling,' he spat out the last word caustically. 'But it's only fair to warn you that the sight of you in your underclothes has excited my filthy, disgusting depraved appetites. I'll be in your bed tonight and every night from now on. And I'll be faithful, because I intend to see that you satisfy me in every way, and I mean *every* way. We'll be doing things you never knew men and women were capable of. But that's the bargain. I keep my vows, as long as you keep yours. One lapse and the person responsible leaves and foots the bill for the divorce. Agreed?'

Jenny's knock on the door interrupted them. He turned the key and opened it, almost knocking his wife over. 'Hand it through the gap, your mother's too embarrassed to be seen the way she is. She wants to cover herself before she goes back upstairs.'

'Could you use another butty, Evan?' the under-manager asked as he looked along the line of waiting miners who were deliberately cold-shouldering Evan's lodgers. News travelled fast in Pontypridd and the men on the day shift were making it plain that none of them wanted to take on either of Evan's conchies.

Evan breathed in a lungful of dust-laden, pithead air. He knew what the men were doing, but there was a way of turning it to the advantage of one of his mates. 'It's probably time Ieuan went out on his own.'

'He's only eighteen.'

'With the back of a twenty-five-year-old. Ieuan could take the boy, Luke and I'll take the older one.'

The conscripted miners looked from Evan to the under-manager. They'd scarcely understood a word that had been said other than their names. It wasn't simply the use of alien words like 'butty'; it was the incomprehensible Welsh accents.

'You two prepared to give it a try?' the under-manager asked.

'If Evan thinks it's all right, that's fine by me.' Alexander didn't have a clue what he was agreeing to, but he nodded anyway.

'You?'

Evan looked at Luke and realised that the boy hadn't grasped the first principles of what was expected of him. 'Most pits, including this one, are worked on the butty system,' he explained. 'That means as a newcomer you'll be put to work with an experienced miner as his mate, or "butty". All miners get paid on production, one shilling and eightpence a ton for the coal he and his butty cut. He pays his butty a share of what they make which varies from week to week, but there's a minimum set at fifteen shillings, so you'll never make less than that.'

'Fifteen shillings!' Alexander was clearly appalled by the paltriness of the sum, but Luke was already picturing the postal orders he'd be able to send home.

'If you work hard, you may get promoted to fully fledged miners,' the under-manager continued. 'But don't go looking for advancement soon. If sales and markets don't pick up, we won't be able to keep the men we've already got on the books, let alone take on more. As it is, I don't know what the miners without jobs are going to say when they find out you two are working here.' The whistle blew. 'Take them to the stores and get them kitted out with helmets and lamps, Evan, and make it quick. I don't want the cage held up.'

Evan walked alongside a stone building to a stable door. He pushed the top half open and shouted for attention, watching as the store-keeper booked out helmets, lamps, picks and shovels against Luke and Alexander's names.

'Your pay will be docked to cover the equipment,' Evan warned. 'Mark everything with your name and don't take your eyes off any of it, especially the lamps: your lives may depend on them.'

Alexander smiled as he pushed the helmet on his head, but there was no answering smile on Evan's face. It was then he remembered the newsreels he'd seen of women waiting at the top of pithead cages just like this one. He suddenly realised that this was no longer a noble political gesture, but his life for the duration; and if he was careless, it also could be his death.

The waitresses were screaming at the woman who made the teas and coffees because she wasn't making them fast enough; the girls who served cakes over the front counter of the café were quarrelling with the boy who was ferrying trays of newly baked confectionery up from the basement kitchen, because none of the cakes he brought were the ones they wanted, and Tina was shouting at everyone, principally the cook who had baked four times the usual quota of sugarless 'sugar' buns, because the sugar ration had run out.

The door clanged open. At that moment she would have given everything she had to see William framed in the doorway. It was bizarre. He'd been gone for barely twenty-four hours, he wouldn't be home for at least six weeks and already she was having difficulty remembering his face, his smile, the expression in his eyes when he had slipped the ring on her finger to the accompaniment of clapping from the girls and jeers and catcalls from the boys, especially Angelo.

'Miss Ronconi?'

She looked blankly at the small, thin man in front of her.

'You are feeling all right, Miss Ronconi?' He raised his hat, and she couldn't help comparing his wizened frame and yellowed skin with William's robust physical presence and strength.

'Yes, sorry, just discussing the day's baking with the cook.'

'Sorry to be calling so early, Miss Ronconi, but I have to start my rounds somewhere. My name is Henley, Ministry of Food, here to discuss your food allowance for the cafés.'

'I think you should discuss that with my father in our High Street café.'

'It says here that I should discuss it with a Miss Laura Ronconi,' he said, referring to a sheaf of papers in his hand.

'She had a baby yesterday.' Suppressing an urge to leave the shocked expression on the man's face, she relented. 'She's married to the local doctor, but because this is a family business she uses her maiden name when she's here.'

'Yes, quite.'

'As I said, you'll find Papa in our High Street café.' While she gave him directions she searched her mind for somewhere quiet she could go. She needed time to herself, time to think. Retrieving her handbag from behind the counter, she poured herself a cup of coffee and climbed the stairs to the banqueting room which was opened only when they had a function booked.

Sinking on to a chair she placed her handbag on the table next to her. Opening it, she pulled out the writing pad and fountain pen she'd dropped into it that morning in the hope of finding time to write to William. She wrote her address neatly in the top right-hand corner of the page just as she'd been taught in Maesycoed school, then she put down her pen, folded her arms, sat back – and remembered.

William winking at her every time she dared turn her head from the teacher, because he'd fought Alwyn Collins from Danygraig Street for the desk in the 'boys' row opposite hers. Playtimes when William had led her into forbidden corners so they could experiment with kissing. The excitement of her début dance in the Catholic Hall in Treforest when William had claimed every dance despite her eldest brother Ronnie's presence. Their first real kiss behind that same hall after she had run outside with William when Ronnie had assumed she'd been fetching her coat.

Closing her eyes she tried to imagine William holding her. It was no use. She couldn't *feel* his presence – his arms around her, his lips on hers as they had been that last night. No matter how hard she concentrated, she failed to conjure the sensation and intensity she craved for. And, worst of all, William's face persisted in eluding her.

The face of the man she loved, had promised to marry, and now had difficulty in recalling.

Sliding her hand inside the neck of her dress she pulled out the gold locket Laura and Trevor had given her when she had been their bridesmaid, and pressed the catch. The chain was long enough for her to study the photograph of William that she had placed inside. He was laughing, his dark curly hair tousled, blowing in the breeze outside St John's church. It was his most recent photograph, taken at Eddie's wedding to Jenny. Smooth featured, too good-looking for peace of mind as Laura had said. Had he already found another girl at the camp? Everyone said that there were girls in army camps. Cooks, laundry maids . . .

'Miss Ronconi!'

'Yes?'

'The dried goods rep is here.'

'Tell him I'll be down in a minute,' she retorted more sharply than she'd intended. This was it! Her life. With her brothers gone and Laura a mother there'd only be work, work and more work for her from now on. Five minutes snatched here and there for daydreaming if she was lucky, and no time at all if she wasn't. Nothing to look forward to except reading and writing letters and planning for leaves, and after William's embarkation leave, even that would be uncertain. She had to persuade him to marry her. If she didn't she'd run the risk of becoming a dried-up spinster like Myrtle Rees. And any fate, even the unmarrieds ward in the Graig Hospital, had to be better than that!

'What is he doing?'

'Searching everyone in case they're carrying cigarettes and matches.'

'We can't smoke underground?'

'Not if you want to stay in one piece.'

'Does he have to pat everyone down like that?'

'Regulations.' An amused grin crossed Evan's face as he watched Alexander check his pockets.

'I've brought my cigarette case and lighter. What do I do with them?' he asked helplessly.

'Hand them over. One forgetful moment down there could ignite a pocket of methane gas and then we'd all be fried to a crisp.'

'Save Hitler the bother,' a tired voice muttered from the front of the queue.

'Not sure if that isn't seditious, Richards,' another answered.

'Just make sure you get a receipt for those,' Evan advised as he watched Alexander hand over his silver cigarette case and lighter.

'Don't trust us now, Evan?' The man on duty grinned, his teeth two gleaming lines of white set in a grimy face barely visible against the background of dark grey morning.

'When did I ever, Dafydd?'

'That's a harsh thing to say when you've known a man as long as you've known me.'

'That's why I'm saying it.'

'Get a move on there.'

Alexander pocketed the hastily scribbled receipt and stepped into the cage. It was packed solid with warm bodies. He listened while the winding mechanism emitted increasingly alarming creaks and groans as more and more men joined them until there was no room for him to move or even draw a breath that someone else hadn't exhaled.

'Take it down!'

A loud slam was followed by a grating and high-pitched screech. Slowly, infinitely slowly, the cage descended from the sombre half-light that had passed for morning into a dense, turgid darkness where the air was thick, close, and warmer than on the surface. The fetid odours of male sweat, foul breath, coal dust, damp, earth and other things he'd rather not think about, closed suffocatingly around Alexander. He couldn't see Luke, but he sensed the boy trembling behind him. He gripped his lamp hard as a tide of sheer panic rose from the pit of his stomach and threatened to swamp his self-control. If there had been something to hold on to – if he hadn't been hemmed in on all sides by bodies – he might have been tempted to grab whatever came to hand and fight his way back up to the morning that had seemed dark until he had descended into this Stygian gloom.

Just as it occurred to him that hell might be this never-ending descent the cage rasped and shuddered to a halt.

'From here we walk.'

He recognised Evan's voice, but his figure was no more than a shade amongst shadows, thrown into relief by the flickeringly inadequate light of the lamps.

'Ieuan? Where are you, boy?'

'Here, Mr Powell.'

'Take Luke with you. And by the way you've been promoted to miner.'

'The under-manager told me. Thank you, Mr Powell.'

'It's Evan now. Don't let me down.'

'I won't.'

As Alexander's eyes became accustomed to the patchwork glow of lamps he saw men striding purposefully forwards. Someone laughed and he jumped as the sound echoed eerily from the walls.

'All right?' Evan asked as they set off down a fairly wide, and mercifully, because they were both tall men, high tunnel.

Alexander's lamp picked out twin snakes of metal tracks festooned with piles of horse manure on the left-hand side of the pathway, but he couldn't see any trucks. 'Entombed is the word that springs to mind,' he muttered, struggling to subdue a claustrophobia that could turn him into a gibbering idiot at any moment.

'It's a peculiar sensation and it never goes away, not entirely.'

'I didn't think it would be like this.'

'What were you expecting?'

'I don't know. Just not this.'

'This isn't the coal face, this is only the walkway to the face. There's miles of these tunnels. Some even connect up to other pits.' Evan turned a corner. 'Watch your head!' The ceiling shelved sharply and Alexander ducked just in time. Even Luke who was a good few inches below six feet had to walk bent double. 'Watch these,' Evan pointed to one of the wooden pit props that supported the ceiling at random intervals, 'and listen to them. The second you see one split or hear one crack, shout at the top of your voice and run, because once they go, they bring down tons of rock and coal with them.'

'Does it happen often?' Alexander asked, trying, and failing, to make the question sound casual.

'Once in a while.' Evan halted in front of an area heavily shored by an odd assortment of timbers. 'This is our face. They've promised us electric cutters, but they haven't appeared yet, and not many of the boys are in a hurry to get them. If you'll pardon my French, the buggers are rumoured to throw out more dust than Hopkin Morgan's bakehouse when they're emptying the flour bags, and dust is one thing we can do without more of.' He slapped his hand on the flaking black wall in front of him.

'We'll start using the picks here. If we hit a good seam, we'll work it for all it's worth. Ieuan, you go to the right with Luke, and both of you,' he looked hard at Alexander and Luke, 'watch your lamps. They're the only thing down here that gives prior warning of gas.'

Alexander removed and folded his coat. As he looked around for somewhere to put it, he wondered if the atmosphere was oppressively warm, or if he was still suffering from the effects of claustrophobia.

The hammering of picks and scraping of shovels filled the air as men began to hew great lumps from the earth. Head down, a pony walked slowly towards them, dragging a row of trucks.

'About bloody time too,' a miner grumbled. Exchanging his pick for a shovel he began to fill a truck.

'You waiting for Christmas?'

Alexander looked back to the coal face. There was a pile of loose coal in front of Evan, and sweat had already etched white streams in the crust of dust on his face.

'Sorry.'

'Not so quick,' Evan warned as Alexander hurled his all into his first thrust. 'There's a twelve-hour shift ahead of us.'

'What time do we go up top for a meal break?' Alexander had lowered his voice but he sensed a hundred or more ears waiting for Evan's reply.

'We get a break, but we eat here.'

'Here?'

'There's no canteens underground, which is why Megan packed snap for us.'

'We eat here?' Alexander repeated incredulously.

'Right here, at the coal face.'

'Where's the washroom . . .'

'Hear that, boys, the fancy Englishman wants a ty bach.'

'I'm not surprised, given some of your habits, Richards.' Evan continued to swing his pick without breaking his rhythm. 'If you need to relieve yourself, there's an abandoned face down there to the left. We try to make it the furthest from where anyone is working.'

'These conditions are not fit for animals . . .'

'It's work, boy, and when you've gone hungry you come to realise that any work is better than none. Just be grateful you've got a job.'

Chapter Eleven

ALEXANDER pulled a rickety three-legged stool that Eddie had made in school against the wall of the wash-house and collapsed on to it. Even that small movement took more effort and energy than he felt he could spare. He stared down at the broken, bloody, swollen remains of his hands. The pain was intense, all consuming. His fingers were skinned, covered with sores so ingrained with black dirt he doubted they'd ever be clean again. The fingernails he'd so carefully manicured twice a week were split, chipped, dented and host to minute nuggets of coal. His palms were raw, the few areas still covered by skin distended by fat, slug-like blisters.

'Your hands hurt?' Luke rose from the shallow depths of the narrow tin bath set close to the yard door. Reaching for a towel he tucked the ends around his pale, skinny body and walked over to where Alexander was sitting, his feet leaving large damp prints on the flagstones.

Alexander nodded dumbly, too tired to speak. Evan had taken first bath. It had taken ten minutes for the women to fill it with hot water from the copper boiler set in the range in the kitchen, a quarter of an hour of hard scrubbing for Evan to get himself clean and, Alexander reflected ruefully, Evan was well practised in the art of bathing after a shift spent underground, and another ten minutes to empty the water down the drain in the back yard and clean the bath ready for the next man. By which time the fresh water Megan had carried through to the kitchen had warmed to a sufficiently high temperature for it to be hauled back to the wash-house so the whole procedure could be repeated.

Despite a deep-seated, bone-aching weariness, Alexander had insisted Luke take second bath. His body cried out for a long soak in scalding, hot water, but one glance at the tin tub Megan had unhooked from a nail on the garden wall had dashed any hopes of a proper bath. Luke was smaller than him and he had only managed to submerge his feet and a scant few inches of his backside by resting his chin on his knees. He'd also noticed that Evan and Luke had been hard pushed to work the soap into a lather powerful enough to remove the coal grime that coated every inch of their bodies, clogging ears, noses, mouths, and lining their eyes with black smudges reminiscent of a vamp's make-up.

Alexander gazed disconsolately at the scum that crusted the water Luke had left in the tub. Just the thought of pushing his maimed and swollen fingers through the narrow handles, so the bath could be carried outside to be emptied, made him wince. And he doubted he'd be able to hold the bar of carbolic soap. Quite apart from the pain, his fingers no longer seemed capable of carrying out his bidding.

'My hands aren't just hurting,' he complained. 'They've been tortured to the point where amputation seems the only option.'

'You should go out to the ty bach and piss on them. It's the only thing that will harden up hands that have never been put to manual work.'

'What?' Alexander couldn't have been more shocked if Evan had suggested he do it in front of the women.

'Mr Powell's right,' Luke agreed shyly.

'It'll sting like blazes, but you won't find a better disinfectant to pour over those cuts, or toughen up what's left of your skin,' Evan continued from the window where he'd set up his shaving mirror and was busily engaged in scraping his chin with a cut-throat razor.

'I'd rather not, if it's all the same to you two.'

Evan looked over his shoulder at Alexander and shook his head in sympathy. His own first day down the pit had been over a quarter of a century ago, but he could still remember the agony. 'It's well meant advice. What you do with it is up to you. Can you manage to empty the bath on your own, or do you want help?'

'I can manage,' Alexander asserted unconvincingly. Feeling the way he did, he doubted he'd be able to put one foot in front of the other, but he was loath to admit that to Evan.

'Here, grab the other handle.' Evan wiped his chin with the towel he'd slung around his neck, and hooked his fingers through one handle. As Alexander tried to push his hand through the other, his eyes creased in pain.

'Out to the ty bach with you, boy,' Evan said kindly. 'Luke and I will empty this and refill it for you.'

It took Alexander an agonising half an hour to wash, by which time he was chilled to the bone. It was cold in the wash-house, and the water that had been heated for a scant twenty minutes in the copper boiler next to the oven had been barely warm to the touch when brought in, and freezing after thirty minutes of painfully slow washing.

Shaving was out of the question: he could never have gripped the brush let alone the razor. Fastening his buttons was a torment that expended blood as well as tears, so he concentrated on the vital ones, his fly and the shirt buttons closest to his waist. When he looked around for somewhere to dump his washing, Evan saw him and pointed to a row of hooks on the back wall.

'There's no point in changing clothes from one week's end to the next in the pit.'

'But they're filthy,' he protested.

'And whatever you'll wear tomorrow will get just as filthy. Besides, as the saying goes, a good layer of dust holds the threads together. Hang them up there, underclothes as well.'

'Don't you ever wash them?' Alexander was horrified at the thought of having to don dirty clothes in the morning.

'On washday. Mondays the women throw them in the tub after they've done everything else.'

Alexander scooped up his clothes between his wrists and carried them to the peg.

'Ready for tea?' Evan asked.

'I'm not sure I can stay awake long enough.'

'I suggest you make an effort. Without food, our tonnage will drop tomorrow.'

'All set for a night on the town?' Diana asked as the men emerged from the cold wash-house into the warm steamy atmosphere of the back kitchen.

'I'm not even sure I'm up to climbing the stairs for a night in bed,' Alexander complained, irritated because the grumbles he'd intended to sound lighthearted came out anything but.

'That looks good, Mrs Powell,' Luke enthused as Phyllis lifted an enormous pan out of the oven. Thin slices of liver and onions continued to bubble in a rich, brown gravy as she set it on a wooden block on the table.

'Nothing like a hard day's work to give a man an appetite.' Megan finished mashing the potatoes she'd carried out of Phyllis's way, into the pantry.

Evan took his customary place at the head of the table, smiling at Brian who was laying the miniature fork and spoon Diana had bought him end to end on his tray, playing trains. The new lodgers sat at the table and Megan began dishing out the meal.

Ever since William had told Evan he'd joined up, he'd been dreading his nephew leaving. Last summer had been hectic with both his sons and William living at home. He was glad Megan was back, but despite all her efforts to be her old bright self, she couldn't conceal the fact that prison had shattered her spirit, and William's departure what was left of her heart. Diana had been totally preoccupied since she had broken off her courtship with Tony Ronconi, and the spring had promised to be a subdued one. But now things were different. Not that the lodgers could take the place of his sons and his nephew, far from it.

Luke was quiet, and unsure of himself, Alexander had all the charm of the self-centred, flat-footed crache but they were people, and hopefully their companionship would go a little way towards filling the void left by the boys' departure. And he still had a lot to be grateful for. He'd hung on to his own house, more by luck than judgement, during the depression; he was in work, and he was living with the woman he loved. It was a time to count his blessings. If only he could be sure that all the boys would survive the fighting, he would be almost happy.

Harry's wife had fled to town, and later her sister's after the ugly scene in the stockroom; but whereas it had been easy for her to avoid Harry's presence, she hadn't been able to put his threats out of her mind for an instant. Just the thought of him, naked and hairy in her bed as he had been on their wedding night, was enough to make her physically ill. She spent the day quaking and nauseous, but as the clock ticked on and it drew closer to teatime she forced herself to leave the sanctuary of her sister's kitchen and climb the Graig hill.

She wished she could have told her sister about Harry's insane outburst, but the idea of discussing the intimate details of married life with anyone sickened her. So it was with a rapidly beating heart and a cold clammy skin that she finally opened the side door that led directly into the family's living quarters. She glanced into the shop. Jenny was behind the counter.

'Have you seen your father?' she asked.

'He's upstairs changing. He's going out.'

'But what about tea?' Mrs Harry Griffiths, who prided herself on the perfection with which she executed her domestic duties, had for once bought the ingredients for a ready-made tea in town. Her carrier bag was packed with three 'off the coupon' meat pies, which meant that meat represented less than half of the filling, and it was anyone's guess as to what the rest was. She'd also bought half a dozen baps, and a custard pie which had eaten heavily into their sugar ration. The guilt engendered by her rare extravagance was assuaged by the thought that Harry was solely responsible for her improvident expenditure. She wouldn't have even gone to town that morning if he hadn't driven her from the house.

'Dad and I have already eaten. He cooked bacon and egg.'

'No doubt using up all our ration for the next month?'

'He didn't seem too worried,' Jenny replied absently. She had pushed the beginnings of yet another letter to Eddie behind the cheese, out of sight of her mother's probing eyes, but not out of mind. She was midway through a beautiful, touching sentence, half her own, and half culled from a romantic weepie she had seen in the White Palace. It would be *the* sentiment that would make her absent husband realise just how much she loved him. He'd come back, forgive her and they'd live happily ever after – if she could get the sentence down on paper before she forgot it.

The door slammed and she heard her mother's step on the stairs; she pulled out her writing pad and tried to visualise Eddie in her mind's eye.

'I've been wondering where you got to.' Harry looked up from the table in the over-furnished and ornamented living room as his wife walked in.

'Shopping.' She carried the bag through to the kitchen.

'You must have had a lot to buy, judging by the time you've taken.'

'Is it any wonder I wanted to stay out after the way you behaved this morning?'

'Did you buy some new underwear or nighties to excite me?' he mocked.

'You . . . you . . . beast!' Fear surfaced through her anger. She crumpled on to the Rexine sofa and began to sob.

Long since inured to her emotional outbursts, he looked at her coldly. 'All you have to do is grant me a divorce.'

'I'll never be able to go to chapel, or hold my head up in this town again if I'm divorced.'

'Then stay married to me. But I warn you now, I won't let you get away with separate bedrooms any longer.'

'But it's not right. What you're doing isn't right. You'll make me ill . . .'

'We'll find out just how ill tonight, won't we?' He left the table and went to the door.

'Where are you going?' she demanded, suddenly fearful that he was going to a solicitor.

'To play cards in the Queen's Hotel with George Collins. We arranged it when he delivered the dairy goods.'

'Then you'll be home late.'

'Not that late. I suggest you wait up for me. It will save me the trouble of waking you.'

'I'm not sure I'm up to this.'

'I've never heard anyone for moaning like you, Alexander Forbes,' Diana said as she walked down the Graig hill between him and Luke. Night had settled, dismal and drizzle laden over the streets. 'Why don't you take a leaf out of Luke's book. If you can't find something cheerful to say, don't say anything at all.'

They walked under the railway bridge, their footsteps echoing upwards to the massive steel girders that supported the tracks. Leaving the confines of the short tunnel for the open area of the Tumble, Diana crossed the road, opened the door to Ronconi's café, pulled back the blackout curtain and fought her way inside.

'Watch it,' Gina called from behind the counter. 'Dai Station has already been in here once tonight to give us a warning.'

'So what's new?' Diana held the cloth back so Luke and Alexander could enter.

'He said we allowed a chink of light to escape last night.' Tina emerged from the back where she'd been eating her tea of beans on toast.

'Gina, Tina, I'd like you to meet our new lodgers, Alexander Forbes, who's feeling very sorry for himself after his first day down the pit, and Luke Grenville.'

'I would shake hands,' Alexander said smoothly, 'but they're in no condition to be placed near a lady's.'

'I'll vouch for that.' Diana winked at him, smiling at Tina when she succeeded in bringing a sheepish look to his face.

'You're one of the conchies?' Tina asked Alexander in a loud voice.

'Tact's never been Tina's strong point,' Diana commented as half a dozen men in the back room turned their heads to stare at the newcomers.

'And it's not likely to be now I've a restaurant to run. You wouldn't believe the day I've had.'

'It can't possibly have been any worse than mine,' Gina remonstrated.

'Don't you believe it. How many covers has this place got? Fifty?'

'Sixty-two,' Gina interposed swiftly.

'The Taff Street place has two hundred.'

'A hundred and twenty of which are shut off upstairs for functions,' Gina bit back. 'And you close the doors down there at six o'clock.'

'But we sell cakes, and I have to manage the main confectionery kitchen . . .'

'But you have a chef you can rely on to work unsupervised . . .'

'Happy families,' Diana said to the two men. 'What do you want?'

'I'm sorry, I should have asked you.' Gina flashed a smile at Luke that turned the whole of him, especially his knees, to jelly. He had never seen a girl as exotic, dark and beautiful as Gina outside of a book illustration.

'Tea, coffee, hot chocolate?' she prompted.

'Yes, please.'

'All three?' she smiled in amusement.

'Tea please,' he stammered awkwardly.

'Sugar and milk. We have to put the sugar as well as the milk in now that it's rationed,' she explained.

'Two sugars and milk please.'

'You'll get one sugar and like it,' Tina told him as she asserted her authority over her younger sister.

'I'll have a tea too please, Tina.' Diana opened her purse.

'Please, let me get them.' Alexander pushed his sore and swollen hand into his pocket and attempted to close his fingers over the change nestling in the bottom.

'Tea for you?' Gina asked, taking one look at Alexander's expensive clothes and unshaven face, and deciding she didn't like what she saw.

'I'll have a coffee please.' He gave her the benefit of his most devastating smile, but to no avail.

'We'll sit in the front, Gina.' Diana and Alexander walked over to a table set in the corner behind the door away from the draughts, but Luke lingered at the counter studying everything so he could write to his younger brothers and sisters about the novelties in his new life. He had never been in a café before for the simple reason that even if his strict Quaker father had approved of his children visiting such places, there weren't any within walking distance of the tiny hamlet they lived in.

By Pontypridd standards the second largest café the Ronconi family owned and ran in the town, was average, by Cardiff standards it was poky and rudimentary, but to Luke's naive eye it was an awesome wonderland.

The long side wall was mirrored and shelved, the space in the centre dominated by an enormous mock marble fountain. Even now after rationing had begun to bite, the shelves were crammed with confectionery, more dummy than real, but all wrapped in glittering swaths of silver and coloured paper. The aromas of coffee, hot chocolate, tea and raspberry ice-cream sauce vied for supremity in the warm, smoky atmosphere, with the splendidly appetising fragrance of coffee winning by a margin.

'Would you like anything with your tea?' Gina asked Luke, as Tina took the coffee and two teas from the counter to join Diana and Alexander at their table.

'No, thank you,' he faltered.

'The cakes aren't up to our usual standard.' She gestured to the glass stand where a few tired-looking pastries were set amongst an array of cinnamon-dusted custard tarts, 'but we have some biscuits, and there's a couple of teacakes in the kitchen that I can toast for you if you're hungry.'

'I've just eaten an enormous meal.' He'd consumed double the amount his mother could afford to feed him at home, and it hadn't just been the liver casserole, mashed potatoes and vegetables. There had been an enormous rice pudding afterwards, rich and creamy, sprinkled with nutmeg, and made with scrapings from the butter dish and the top of the milk; luxurious touches Phyllis had warned everyone to make the most of, because they weren't going to last.

'You're lodging with the Powells?'

Lost in admiration of the dark velvet of her eyes, it was as much as he could do to nod assent.

'Then you'll be all right for food. Evan and Phyllis believe in setting a good table, unlike some around here I could mention.'

'You know the Powells?'

'Diana's a good friend, her brother Will is engaged to my sister, Tina. That's her, sitting next to your friend, Alexander.'

'Alexander's not really my friend. I never saw him before yesterday.'

'But you're both conchies.'

'Yes,' he conceded as he stirred the tea she put in front of him.

'Two of my brothers joined up with Diana's brother. Strange, isn't it?' She stopped to take money off a tram crew who were leaving. 'They leave, then you come into Ponty.'

'Perhaps that's why people hate us, they think we're trying to take their place.'

'Who says anyone hates you?'

'There were men at the station . . .'

'The railway station?'

'Yes.'

'You don't want to take any notice of anything they say.'

'But they're right. We are here because we refused to fight.'

144

'I don't see any of them in khaki.'

'But they've probably registered for the army.'

'And they'll fill their pants if they get called up.'

'Pardon?'

'Sorry, crudeness comes when you've been brought up with brothers like mine. If you don't mind me asking, why did you register as a conscientious objector?'

'Because it was what my father wanted.'

'And you always do what your father wants?'

'Don't you?' he asked as though it had never occurred to him to hold, or voice, an opinion of his own.

'When I have no strong feelings one way or the other.'

'And if you do have strong feelings?'

'I don't tell Papa what I've been up to. Why didn't your father want you to join the army?'

'We're Quakers.'

'Don't they wear funny hats?'

'Not any more.'

'You must have worked before you came here,' she probed.

'Weaving baskets in between helping out on the land. The farmer my father works for didn't mind me assisting at busy times, like harvest, but he wouldn't put me on the books because he had no real call for me. When we were told to register, I had to tell them I was unemployed.'

'Times have been hard for everyone,' she commiserated. 'You think you're going to like the pit?'

'As Mr Powell says, it's work.'

'And Pontypridd?' she asked archly.

'From what I've seen so far it seems like a very nice town,' he answered without taking his eyes off her.

Gina's laugh, light, silvery, echoed across the café.

'Little sister's flirting,' Tina commented acidly.

'With Luke?' Diana looked up in surprise. 'He's just a boy.'

'Which suits her, seeing as how she's just a girl, and a lucky one at that. As he's just got here he won't be going anywhere.'

Diana glanced at the clock on the wall. 'Time I was off.'

'You're not staying?' Alexander asked, disappointment evident in his voice.

'I promised my boss I'd help him close up the sweet shop in the New Theatre.'

'You'll be back?'

'Later perhaps. See you later, Tina.'

'Do I detect romance in the air?' Alexander asked as Diana disappeared behind the curtain.

'Romance?'

'Diana and her boss?'

Tina burst out laughing. 'You've picked the wrong pair there.'

'He's married?'

'Of the other persuasion. "One of those", as my mother would whisper. A queer,' she explained as the expression on his face remained bemused.

'Then Diana's not going out with anyone?'

'She was courting my brother, Tony, but they quarrelled before he went away. Why do you ask?'

'I was just wondering. She's a pretty girl.'

'And you're thinking of making a move in that direction?'

'I think I have enough to get used to at the moment without adding any more complications to my life.'

'It's obvious you're not used to hard work,' she said bluntly as she looked down at his hands.

'I was working in a museum. It's closed for the duration.'

'What did you do, in the museum I mean?'

'Arrange displays, study artefacts and documents as they came in and categorise them for the archives.'

'It sounds like thrilling work.'

'I enjoyed it.' He ignored the sarcasm.

'Well, much as I'd like to, I can't sit here all night. I have a sister to supervise, and a café to run.'

'Can I help?'

She looked down at his raw and bleeding hands. 'You could wash the dishcloths out in washing soda.'

The answering expression on his face was so peculiar, she burst out laughing again. 'I was joking.' She walked to the counter. 'Honestly.'

'Myrtle's asking if you can come to tea again on Sunday?'

'Won't that rather reinforce the wrong impression we've given your father?' Diana asked Wyn as she helped him bag the copper he'd taken.

'I think that's why she's asked. He's been a lot quieter and easier to manage since last Sunday.'

'You should tell him it's going nowhere between us, Wyn.'

'Why?'

'Because it's the truth.'

'I'm not so sure it is going nowhere between us, Diana,' he countered quietly.

'Come on . . .'

'No, listen. I've been thinking. We get on incredibly well. You've already said you like me. Why shouldn't we set up something more permanent than a business arrangement?'

'A business arrangement suits me fine,' she answered swiftly.

'What I'm trying to say, and very badly, is that I trust you totally, Diana. And not only with the day-to-day running of the business. You're very special. I'm fond of you and I can't think of anyone I'd rather live with . . .' Doors banged upstairs and down in the theatre, and noise flooded the corridors as the audience spilled out into the foyer. ' . . . so why shouldn't we get married,' he blurted out abruptly.

'You know why,' she whispered, turning away from him.

'Marriage to someone like me would be very different to marriage to Tony.'

'Wyn . . .'

'Please, just think about it.'

'You sure you're not asking me to marry you because your father's threatening to cut you out of his will if you don't silence the gossips by finding a wife?' she challenged.

'That is the one thing I am sure of. If anything happened to my father, Myrtle would hand over half of his estate whether I wanted it or not. I know my sister, she'd never be able to live with herself if she did otherwise. But to be honest, as far as I'm concerned she's welcome to the shops. My mother had her own money and she left it in equal shares between Myrtle and me. It's not a fortune, but it's enough to set me up in a business of my own if ever I've a mind to try.'

'Then why haven't you done so?'

'Because I couldn't bring myself to leave Myrtle to cope on her own. My father's difficult, but he is still my father, and Myrtle deserves a better life than the one he's been giving her of late.'

'Marrying me wouldn't solve Myrtle's problems, or yours.'

'I didn't ask you to marry me to solve my problems, but because I thought we might be able to make one another happier than we are now. It doesn't take much to see that you're as miserable as sin, and with good reason, and I can't bear the thought of carrying on the way I am now for the rest of my life. Always having to look over my shoulder, always having to be careful who I talk to in case it's a policeman out to book me. I'm lonely, Diana. I'd like a home of my own, to live with someone I can talk to, someone I care for . . .'

'While having someone to go out with like that boy you told me about?'

'Not if we were married. There are other things in life besides sex,' he argued with an honesty that startled Diana. 'I'd try to be content with what we had. We're good friends . . .'

'There's a world of difference between being good friends and living with someone.'

'It was just a thought,' he murmured apologetically, rebuffed by her refusal to even consider the idea.

'And a sweet one. Thank you,' she said firmly, wanting to put an end to the conversation.

'You'll think about it?' He found it difficult to give up, even now.

'It wouldn't work, Wyn.' She tried to deflate the fairy-tale world he'd dreamed up as gently as she could.

'I was afraid you'd say that.'

She pushed the last pile of coppers into a small paper bag and dropped it into the large canvas bag he was holding. 'But I'd still like to be friends, good friends. And I'll stand you a tea at Ronconi's so you can meet our new lodgers.'

'The conscientious objectors?' he asked, accepting her change of subject – for the present.

'You've heard?'

'No one can sneeze in Pontypridd without your uncle knowing, and he was in here earlier buying his ration of pear drops.'

'Good old Uncle Huw.' She opened the door in the side of the kiosk as he pocketed the bag. The crowds had gone, the foyer was in darkness.

'I'll never get used to this absolute blackout,' she said as he joined her on the step.

'You will. It's going to be here for some time.'

'You think the war's going to last more than a few months, too?'

'I wish I could say otherwise.' He turned up his collar and tucked the ends of his white scarf inside his coat.

'Haven't you read your blackout advice? You should leave those dangling, and pull your shirt tail out of your trousers.'

'There's no point when I'm wearing an overcoat.' He led the way up to the crossroads on the Tumble. The sound of a man and woman arguing floated across from station yard.

'Streetwalkers are hard at it tonight.'

'I didn't know young ladies knew such words.'

'Who said I'm a young lady?' Stepping off the pavement she walked confidently into the middle of the road.

'Diana!'

She froze at his cry. Turning her head she looked back, but all was pitch darkness. Something large and heavy bowled into her. She fell on to the road, hitting the crown of her head painfully on the kerb. A heavy weight pressed her on to the tarmac. The soft purr of an engine was close, too close. She could smell the petrol, see the outline of the single headlamp almost, but not quite, obliterated by the cardboard hood. She screamed as the white lines painted on the running boards loomed above her; there was a nauseating crunch that she knew – simply knew – was wheels crushing bone. The screech of brakes drowned out her cry. Then a terrible silence settled over the Tumble, broken seconds later by the reverberation of feet running towards her.

'You all right?' She recognised the voice of the manager of the New Theatre. A circle of torchlight shone down into her face. In a ridiculous moment of clarity she noticed that the lens wasn't covered with tissue paper.

'I think so,' she stammered uncertainly.

'Just lie still while I get help.'

'But I'm all right.' She moved her right leg gingerly, then her left. Apart from whatever was on top of them, they seemed fine.

'You might be, Miss Powell, but the poor devil with you isn't.'

More running feet thundered over the pavement.

'I saw it. I saw it all. He was speeding recklessly, at least thirty miles an hour, and everyone knows the limit's twenty in the blackout.' A man pushed his way to the front of the rapidly thickening crowd.

'Go into the theatre,' the manager ordered briskly, 'and telephone for a doctor before this fellow bleeds to death.'

A car door slammed and another torch shone down on them, this time covered with tissue paper.

'It's Wyn Rees,' Dai spat out the name contemptuously. 'I bet that's the first time he's been on top of a woman.'

'We'll have less of that,' the manager said firmly.

'But he ran out in front of me without warning. Everyone must have seen it. I didn't stand a chance . . .' Anthea Llewellyn-Jones, the bank manager's daughter, appealed to the shadowy figures behind the torchlights.

'I saw you speeding, girl. Just who in hell do you ARPs think you are? Requisitioning cars for your bloody war games and killing innocent pedestrians.' The man was shouting at Anthea, but it was Dai who answered.

'Trying to save the country and your bloody neck.'

'Trying to add to your own self-importance, more like. When have either of you two ever driven a car before?'

'All of you. Quiet!' the manager ordered sternly. 'There's a badly injured man here.'

149

The shock of what had happened finally sank in. Diana tried to sit up. It was only then she realised what the weight on her legs was. 'Wyn . . .' she murmured weakly. 'Wyn . . .'

'Please, Miss Powell, try to stay still for both your sakes.' The manager was rolling Wyn gently away from her. 'The doctor will be here soon and then we'll get you both into hospital.'

Chapter Twelve

Harry Griffiths left the Queen's early. George Collins was on a winning streak, and after he'd counted up his losses halfway through the evening and found they amounted to more than a pound, he threw in his cards and settled for half an hour of serious drinking.

All he could think about was seeing Megan again. There were so many things he wanted out of life: Megan; his wife out of his house; Eddie to start writing to Jenny; and above all happiness for everyone he cared for, principally Megan. And he couldn't see his way clear to achieving any of them.

When he'd been young and penniless, he'd assumed money to be the panacea for all ills. Now, with the pits reopening and most of his customers settling their 'tabs' on a weekly rather than 'catch can' basis, the shop was doing better than it had done since his grandfather had set it up. And with luck, the reserves he was building would enable him to hold out through any damaging influences the war and rationing might have. But he had learned a long time ago that happiness depended on a lot more than a successful business or a bank account in credit. His shop was as secure as any in Pontypridd, he had a little money, and he was wretched; and what was worse, he had no one to blame for his misery other than himself.

He should have sent his wife packing years ago. The morning after his wedding, if he'd had any sense. Why hadn't he?

The more he considered the question, the more an answer eluded him. It hadn't been the advent of Jenny that had kept them together. His wife had been so appallingly ignorant she hadn't even realised Jenny was on the way until she had been almost six months gone. Then what? No other woman to love until he had noticed Megan Powell? And Megan's insistence, even after he'd taken to visiting her house three or four evenings a week, that she didn't want a permanent relationship at the cost of breaking up his marriage?

He pushed his hands deeper into his pocket and carried on walking up Taff Street, seeking solutions to problems that were insoluble. He had to see Megan. It was no longer a wish, but a burning need, well worth risking Evan's wrath and being thrown off his doorstep. He wondered if all that nonsense about sleeping with his wife had frightened her enough to grant him a divorce. The only thing he had enjoyed about the ridiculous scene between them that morning had been her mortification when she had realised he was staring at her corset. The thought of sharing a bed with her after all these years repulsed him, probably as much as the thought of rolling over to make room for him, did her.

It was still comparatively early, no more than a quarter-past ten if the clock in the Queen's had been right. He would walk past the shop, carry on up the hill, confront Megan and tell her once and for all that no matter what, he intended to spend the rest of his life with her.

He heard the sound of women sobbing up ahead against a background of raised voices, saw flashes of torchlight, an unheard-of infringement of lighting regulations.

'Who's that?' The torch shone full in his face, blinding him.

'Harry Griffiths,' he answered, recognising Huw Davies's voice. 'What's going on?'

'Wyn Rees and Diana Powell have just been run over.'

'By a van that was doing over thirty, when regulations limit traffic to twenty miles an hour in the blackout. Dai Station was in it . . .'

'Shut up,' Huw interposed swiftly. 'We could do with a hand, Harry.'

Harry stepped forward and saw Tina and Gina sitting either side of Diana on the kerb and Andrew John stooping over a figure laid out on the ground. Behind him Anthea Llewellyn-Jones was crying on Dai Station's shoulder.

'He can't afford to wait for an ambulance. Constable Davies?' Andrew rose to his feet and looked for Huw.

Both Huw and the manager of the New Theatre stepped forward.

'I'm carrying some splints and strapping, but not enough for injuries as extensive as these, and I dare not risk moving him until both legs are immobilised. Do you have any spare wood that I can use in the theatre?'

'The shutter over the booking office is four feet long.' The manager was already halfway to the foyer door.

'Get it, and something to cut it up with, please. Constable, help the girls move Diana into the front seat of my car, she's going to have to go to the hospital too.'

'What about me?' Anthea wailed. 'I feel awful. I think I'm going to faint . . .'

'Put her down before she falls down,' Andrew ordered Dai brusquely.

'I'm all right,' Diana protested in a voice that was anything but, as the girls helped her to her feet.

'Just do as you're told, there's a good girl,' Andrew commanded.

'I feel awful, Andrew,' Andrea cried, imposing on an old courtship and a friendship between their respective parents.

'Go home and take two aspirin.'

'Here's the board, and the fire axe.' The manager rushed back carrying both.

'Right, Harry over here. Need anyone else, Andrew?' Huw asked.

'We should manage it between the three of us.'

Harry stepped closer, and blanched. Andrew had placed his torch on the road to throw the maximum light on to Wyn's legs. Below Wyn's knees both legs were bloodied and crushed. His trousers were torn, soaked in blood, and between the dark spreading stains Harry could see the white of splintered bones.

'On the count of three,' Andrew directed as soon as he had finished strapping Wyn's legs to the rough boards Huw had chopped.

They lifted Wyn slowly and carefully into the back of Andrew's car. To his amazement Harry saw that Wyn's eyes were open. He didn't make a sound when they moved him, but his teeth showed white in the torchlight, and when he was finally propped on the back seat of Andrew's car, blood ran from his lips where he had bitten through them.

'I'll go straight to the Cottage Hospital,' Andrew looked to the threatre manager: 'if you could telephone ahead and warn them I'm on my way, I'd be grateful. And tell them to get the operating theatre ready. I'll need a scrub nurse and the X-ray machine, and you'd better ask them to call out my father. Diana's going to need a check-up.'

'Don't worry about telling the families, I'll see to it,' Huw said. He closed the door gently on Wyn.

'Be sure to tell Mam I'm fine,' Diana called from inside the car.

'And that she won't be home until tomorrow,' Andrew warned.

'I'm going home, I could call in on the Powells, Huw,' Harry volunteered.

'There's no need.'

'It's no trouble, and you'll be busy with Wyn's family. I've heard his father is in a bad way, and his sister already has a load on her shoulders without this.'

'All right,' Huw conceded, too preoccupied with the task in hand to think through the implications of Harry going to Evan's house. 'Perhaps you'll take the boys up with you.'

'I think we should walk Tina and Gina home, Constable Davies,' Luke interrupted.

'Good idea,' Huw agreed, uncertain whether Tina and Gina were shocked or just appeared unnaturally pale in the torchlight.

Andrew started his engine, and Huw pushed the crowds back. Harry didn't wait to see them off. He had his chance and he intended to make the most of it. He had a valid excuse to see Megan, and he was going with her brother's blessing.

'Wyn's legs looked a real mess. Do you think they'll be able to save them?'

'Wyn's Diana's boss, the one you were telling me about earlier?' Alexander asked, neatly sidestepping Tina's question as he followed her into the café.

'Yes. The manager of the New Theatre said he pushed Diana out of the way of the van. God knows what the ARP wardens think they're doing commandeering trucks and careering round town like that. They could have killed Diana and Wyn.'

'Don't you read the papers, love?' a tram conductor asked as he waited patiently to pay his bill. 'Accidents have rocketed since they brought in the lighting regulations.'

'That particular accident happens to be my best friend . . .' Tina began, before succumbing to tears and fumbling blindly for the kitchen door. Gina intercepted her and soon both girls were sobbing. Luke took the money from the tram conductor and put it in the till.

'Girls!' Alfredo exclaimed in disgust as he stuck his head around the door. 'For all the good you're doing you may as well go home.'

'Not until the café's closed.' Tina made an effort to pull herself together.

'I can do it.'

'You're only twelve.'

'And a boy, which makes me more sensible than either of you.'

'We'll all help,' Luke offered. At that moment he would have walked on red hot coals if it meant he could stay with Gina for a little while longer.

'Here's the brush.' Alfredo handed Alexander, who happened to be closest to him, a long-handled brush and pan. 'You can start by sweeping under the tables.'

As Alexander closed his hand over the handle, two blisters burst, soaking the wood with blood. He had a sudden longing for his cramped, dusty office in the museum; the quiet, if dull routine of academic life, and polite, deferential people who didn't have the warped sense of humour of the working classes.

'It's good of you to call, Evan, seeing as how I'm under house arrest.'

'I wouldn't call confining you to your house at night, house arrest.'

'No? Then what would you call it?' Charlie turned off the light and opened the door wide to admit Evan.

'The government being over-cautious about spies,' Evan suggested mildly as he followed Charlie up the stairs and into his living room.

'Did you come into town just to see me?'

'I've just been to a lecture in the Institute on the Jewish situation in Nazi Germany.'

'Is it any worse than the Russian situation in Wales?'

'Everyone there agreed that the restrictions on people like you should be lifted.'

'Drink?' Charlie opened the sideboard and brought out the vodka bottle.

'A small one, please.' Evan looked around. 'Where's Alma?'

'Gone to bed to escape my boorishness.'

'I was going to ask how the interview went with the recruiting office, but I think I already know.'

'They don't want me in their army, but maybe they will find me special duties. Like sweeping their floors, or cleaning their latrines.'

'They didn't say that.' Evan took the half-tumblerful of vodka Charlie offered him.

'Not exactly. They won't make me a soldier but they'll use me as a spy once they are sure of my loyalties.'

'They didn't say that either.'

'Not in so many words, but it was obvious. How many countries have you lived in? How many ports have you docked in? How many languages do you speak?'

'Just out of interest, how many do you speak?'

'Now you're an undercover agent too?'

'Even an uneducated miner like me can see that a man who speaks Russian and English has got to be an asset to the war effort.'

'Particularly when you remember that the Russians marched hand in glove with the Germans into Poland.'

'I can't see the Fascists bedding down with Communists for the duration.'

'That's what I told them.'

'But they want to use you as an interpreter?'

'You know I was a seaman?'

'I knew you jumped ship in Cardiff. I presumed you were a seaman not a passenger.'

'I worked on Russian ships and later German ones, mainly the Baltic and the North Sea routes. Like every other sailor I learned the rudiments of as many languages as I could. It was either that, or risk not getting a berth.'

'But you don't want to work as an interpreter?'

'It's not what I volunteered for. I want to be an ordinary soldier, like Will and Eddie.'

'The government are utilising people to the best of their abilities, which is why Haydn's been drafted to ENSA and set to work on the radio. It would be a criminal waste to relegate someone with his stage experience and singing voice to the ranks.'

'A waste – that's what they said. "It would be a waste, to put someone with your linguistic ability and knowledge of foreign ports in the ranks, Mr Raschenko." '

'Then it looks as though they have something more than interpreting in mind,' Evan said shrewdly.

'As long as it remains between me and you, Evan, I think so.'

Evan pulled out a packet of cigarettes and offered Charlie one.

'I don't mind taking my chances as a footsoldier, but this is something different.'

'You're worried about Alma?'

'You've been a good friend, Evan. You've taken me as I am, never asked any questions. There's a lot of things you don't know about me. I have another wife.'

'There's nothing wrong with that. I'm living with one woman and married to another.'

'But I didn't want to leave my first wife. She disappeared. In fact my whole village vanished while I was away one day. I came back to find the houses flattened and the people gone. Officials said they had been resettled in the East. That's your Communism for you. When I asked too many questions I was arrested and sent to a labour camp. I escaped and became a seaman. For years I continued to look for someone . . . anyone from my village but I never found a single person. And now Alma is afraid that if I go to fight in this war I'll find my wife again and forget about her.' Charlie picked up the vodka bottle and refilled both their glasses, to the brim this time, emptying the bottle. 'That's why I wanted to join the ranks. What they want is something else.'

'You think they'll send you behind enemy lines?'

'If you were in charge, what would you do with a Russian who speaks German, Polish, Finnish, Norwegian and English?'

'Send him behind enemy lines. But you have a right to refuse, Charlie. This isn't Russia . . .'

'And have the finger of suspicion pointed at me more than it already is? No, my friend,' he shook his head. 'I'll do what they want me to.'

'And Alma?'

'You'll look after her?'

'The best I can. You have my word on that.'

'I promised her I'd come back. But that was when I thought I'd be an ordinary soldier.'

'Charlie . . .'

'Please,' he lifted his vodka glass. 'Just look after her. That's all I ask.'

It was then Evan realised it was already arranged. Charlie had made his choice. 'When are you going?'

'Tomorrow.' He drained his glass in one swallow. 'I have one more bottle of vodka, what say you we open it, and to hell with the war?'

Evan rose to his feet. 'I think you should take it to your wife, tell her what you've just told me, and drink it with her.'

'That wouldn't be wise. She thinks I'm going to translate documents in a country house outside London. You won't tell her otherwise will you, Evan? There's no point in her worrying before she has to.'

'I won't tell her, or anyone.' Evan rose to his feet and braced himself to receive one of Charlie's bear hugs. 'Just take care of yourself,' he whispered, his voice hoarse with vodka and suppressed emotion.

'One more for the road?'

'A small one,' Evan answered with a forced smile.

Freda had locked her bedroom door, but the closer she scrutinised the lock, the less she trusted it. It was a box type, screwed below the knob on the inside, and she was afraid that one good push from Harry would dislodge it. She looked around her bedroom for something to wedge against the door. She took a chair and propped it beneath the knob just as she'd seen someone do in a film, but the chair was spindly legged and she couldn't see how it would stop a determined man like Harry. Clearing her dressing table of glass bottles and face creams she laid them out on the linoleum. Removing the drawers to lighten the load she dragged it towards the door.

'You all right, Mam?'

'Perfectly well, thank you,' she called to Jenny through the door.

'I heard a noise.'

'There's an enormous spider's web behind the dressing table, I'm pulling it out to clear it.'

'But you hate spiders.'

'I know, that's why I'm pulling it out. Now go to bed, there's a good girl.'

'I am not a girl, I'm a married woman,' Jenny bit back, annoyed by her mother's tendency to baby her which had become even more pronounced since Eddie had walked out on her. Retreating into her room she slammed the door and picked up her pen to continue yet another letter to her husband. Minutes after she had posted the one she'd written in the shop she had begun to have doubts about its power to affect Eddie, and had taken a clean sheet of paper to start another.

Freda surveyed the mess she had made of her pristine bedroom. Her perfume, face cream and cut-glass dressing-table set lay strewn over the lino. The dressing table was firmly wedged beneath the door handle, the chair propped in front of it. She had caught the heel of her shoe in the candlewick bedspread and torn it. The blackout curtains that had been hidden behind the dressing table were grey, filmed with dust and stained by damp from the time she had left the window open during a thunderstorm.

Emotionally and physically drained, she sank down on the bed to catch her breath and compose herself. It was no use: the sight of the dust that had settled on the blackout curtains irritated her. Leaving the bed she caught her heel in the long fringes of the bedspread again and fell headlong among the mess on the floor. Shards of glass and pots of cream skidded over the linoleum, glancing off the skirting boards and the door frame behind the dressing table. She stretched out towards her crystal trinket bowl. She kept the amethyst earrings she had inherited from her grandmother in its satin-lined depths. The lid had disintegrated in a welter of splinters. And it was all Harry's doing!

Tears of rage and frustration coursed down her cheeks as she struggled to her feet, slipped again on a pool of spilt cream and slid towards the earrings, miraculously still intact in their bowl. Her hand closed around the crystal just as the bowl began to waver before her eyes. The room grew dark. Shadows stole inwards from the walls, great, dark, slow-moving mists that gradually blotted the room from view. She lifted her hand to her neck, saw the red on her fingers. Deep red. Blood? It was the last thing she registered before the darkness overcame her. She cried out before slipping downwards through the floor into a wonderfully warm, comfortable world, lined with gossamer grey, miraculously silken and downy to the touch.

Jenny heard the crash. Still angry, she carried on writing. If her mother couldn't be bothered to talk to her in a civil manner why should she bother to help clear up whatever disaster had befallen her in the bedroom?

'You're sure I can't go to him?'

'There's no point in you going up the hospital at all, Miss Rees,' Huw assured Myrtle. 'Dr John said he was going to operate on your brother. You wouldn't be able to see Wyn until he came round, and that won't be until late tomorrow afternoon at the earliest. Now the best thing you can do is get a good night's sleep.'

'But he will be all right?'

'Can you think of a better doctor than Dr John? Or a better equipped hospital than the Cottage?'

'And Miss Powell?'

'Knock on the head and a bit shaken up, that's all. She'll be fine in a day or two. Come on over here, and sit down. You've had quite a shock.'

A banging on the wall disturbed Huw just as he was settling Myrtle into a chair.

'It's my father. I must go to him.'

'He's in the parlour?'

She nodded, tight-lipped, trying not to cry.

'Let me tell him.'

'You, but . . .'

'It's my job. What I'm paid to do. Now why don't you make us all a nice cup of tea. I think your father's going to need it.'

'Yes. Yes of course.'

Myrtle pulled her old cardigan closer to her as she reached for the kettle in the hearth. She could brew tea automatically, without thinking. And it was a marvellous luxury not to have to make any decisions after hearing the news Constable Davies had brought.

'Constable?' Mr Rees struggled to sit up in bed as Huw tapped the door and walked in. 'What's happened?' he demanded, a police presence making him think the worst. 'If that son of mine – '

'He's hurt, Mr Rees.'

'Someone give him the hammering he deserves?' The old man's beady eyes focused on Huw.

'He was knocked down by a van.'

'Serve the silly bugger right. Too slow to get out of the way, I suppose . . .'

'He saved Diana Powell's life. If it hadn't been for your son's quick thinking and action she would have been mowed down.'

'Is he all right?' It was the first time the invalid had enquired about his son's health, and the significance wasn't lost on Huw.

'Young Dr John is operating on him now. The van went over his legs.'

'And Miss Powell?'

'She'll be fine in a day or two.'

'Glad to hear it. That girl's going to be my daughter-in-law.'

'I didn't know.' Huw struggled to keep his features impassive.

'Boy's too dozy to know it yet. But she will, you mark my words. Now tell me, who's the silly bugger who mowed them down?'

The key protruded from the lock on Evan Powell's front door, as it did from the front door of every other house on the Graig. Harry could see its outline, dark against the pale paintwork, but after the conversation he'd had with Evan in the Graig Hotel, Harry didn't feel he ought to turn it and walk in as he would have with most of the other houses in the street. Instead, he knocked on the door softly, hoping that the sound would carry down the passage to the back kitchen.

He had to knock twice more before a door opened, and when it did, he heard a burst of music. They were obviously listening to the wireless.

'Who is it?' Phyllis's voice echoed down the passage.

'Harry Griffiths.' Curtain rings grated over a pole, a light switch clicked, and he found himself facing Phyllis, her eyes round, straining into the darkness.

'Can I help you, Mr Griffiths?'

'Huw Davies sent me.'

'Huw? I don't understand, has Diana or Will . . .'

'It's Diana, she's not badly hurt. But I was there just after the accident happened. I think I ought to see Megan.'

A door opened behind Phyllis, flooding the passage with light.

'You'd better come in.'

Harry stepped inside and closed the curtain.

'Is it one of the children?'

Harry had difficulty in containing his shock. Everyone who had seen Megan had told him she had altered, but he hadn't been prepared for the sight of the worn, lined old woman in front of him. She could have been her own mother. The hair he remembered as jet black was heavily streaked with grey, the lips creased with age, pain and worry lines, and her once magnificent eyes were weak and watery.

'Huw sent Harry up to tell us about an accident,' Phyllis faltered.

'Accident!' Megan's hand flew to her mouth. As Phyllis helped her into the kitchen Harry saw how frail she was. Evan was right: he had no right to put any more pressure on her, no matter how well meant.

'Sit down.' Phyllis indicated a seat next to the table. 'Would you like some tea?'

Harry shook his head, conscious of his beer and whisky-laden breath. He told them in as few words as he could, about the accident, and how it had happened. '. . . the last thing Diana said was to be sure to tell you she was fine,' he emphasised to Megan, looking at her and wondering how he could ever have been naive enough to imagine picking up the threads of their relationship as though nothing had happened.

'And you say Andrew is going to bring her home?'

'Probably in the morning. By the look of Wyn Rees he's going to be in the operating theatre most of the night.' Harry glanced at Phyllis. It was easier than trying to meet Megan's clouded eyes. 'Dr John has sent for his father to take care of Diana. I'm sure they'll find a bed for her while he operates on Wyn.'

'And Wyn pushed Diana out of the path of the van?'

'There's no doubt she would have been killed if it hadn't been for him. Stupid ARP – '

'What are you doing here?' Evan demanded as he walked in.

'Harry came to tell us that Diana's had an accident,' Phyllis explained hastily. 'She and Wyn Rees were knocked down by a van tonight on the Tumble.'

'But she's going to be fine. Probably be home first thing in the morning,' Harry said quickly.

'What have the ARPs got to do with it?'

'They requisitioned just about every spare car and van in the town for tonight's exercise, then they went charging round in them pretending it was an emergency. Anthea Llewellyn-Jones was driving the one that knocked down Wyn and Diana, but Dai Station was with her.'

'The most she's ever driven in her life is a bicycle,' Evan pronounced contemptuously. 'Every time I've seen her, the chauffeur or her father has been ferrying her around.'

'Does it matter? What's done is done.' Megan was trembling uncontrollably. Evan nodded to Phyllis, a movement so slight, Harry might have missed it if Phyllis hadn't risen from her seat, opened a door in the sideboard and produced a bottle of brandy.

'I'll put it in the tea.' She reached for the kettle and lifted the cover on the hotplate of the stove. 'I think we all need it.'

'She really was all right,' Harry insisted. 'I helped her into Dr John's car. Her stockings were torn, her skirt dirty, a small cut on her chin, her hands were skinned but that was it. Dr John told me to tell you that he was taking her up to the cottage only as a precaution.'

'What about Wyn?' Evan asked for the first time as Phyllis laid cups out on the table.

Harry fell silent, not wanting to say too much in front of Megan lest he upset her even more.

'It's bad?' Evan pressed.

'The wheels went over his legs.'

'Oh my God!' Megan exclaimed as Phyllis splashed brandy into their cups.

'But from what I could see Dr John was there within minutes. I'm sure he'll do all he can.'

'Andrew's a good doctor,' Evan reassured her.

'His poor father. He was going into the army . . .' Phyllis began.

'Then at least his father will have him for a while longer,' Megan said with a touch of bitterness. 'If his injuries are as bad as Harry says, he won't be going anywhere.'

'It's good of you to walk us home.'

'Not at all,' Alexander demurred. 'It's the least we can do after the nasty shock you and your sister have had.'

Tina tried telling herself that's what it was. A shock. No other emotion could explain the way she'd felt when Alexander had put his arm around her shoulders. It was a combination of shock and missing William, that was all. Who had told her that the first few days of absence were the worst? She couldn't remember. Had she dreamed it?

'I think you and your sister are incredibly courageous.'

'Courageous?' She looked towards his silhouette.

'Taking over the family business.'

'There's nothing courageous about that. The family has to eat, and with the boys away we had no option but to take over.'

'Most women would have shut down the cafés.'

'As if Papa would let us. Here we are.' She turned the corner into Danycoedcae Road. 'You know where to go?'

'The road below this one?'

'There is a short cut, but I wouldn't recommend it unless you know the area. It's the one William used. He grew up here and he was still falling down it last week,' she added, feeling the need to bring William's name into the conversation, although she had already talked about her fiancé at length to both Alexander and Luke.

'He's a lucky man. Well, goodnight, Miss Ronconi. Thank you for an interesting and eventful evening, and the pleasure of your company.' He touched her hand with his. 'I hope we can repeat the experience.'

'I'd be happier if it wasn't so eventful next time.'

'So would I.'

'Gina,' she called to her sister, who was standing so close to Luke they'd merged into a single large shadow next to the wall.

'You'll be down the café tomorrow night?' Gina whispered to Luke.

'Yes,' he murmured, his heart thundering at the thought of this enchanting, fascinating girl actually wanting to see him again.

'Until then.' Gina pressed her fingers briefly into the palm of his hand.

'Gina!' Tina repeated crossly from the doorstep.

'Coming.' Gina tore herself away and ran up the steps.

'Pretty girls,' Alexander observed as Luke joined him for the walk back down Llantrisant Road to Graig Avenue.

'Beautiful,' Luke agreed in a rare display of eloquence.

'Going to the café tomorrow night?' Alexander asked, his voice wavering in amusement.

'Yes. You?'

'See how I feel. At this moment I'd rather not imagine what another day down that pit is going to do to me. But, if I survive, I'll be happy to join you.'

'Thank you for coming up specially to tell me, Harry.' Megan opened the front door to usher Harry out. Evan and Phyllis had tactfully remained in the back kitchen, Evan deciding that as circumstances had thrown Harry and Megan together, he had no right to interfere with their reunion.

'It was the least I could do. That's a brave girl you've got there, Megan,' he complimented her.

'I know.'

'Would you mind if I called in tomorrow to ask how she is?'

'I'll get Evan to drop by the shop and tell you.'

'Megan, nothing's happened to change the way I feel about you.'

'A lot has happened to me. I'm not the person I was.'

'I can see that, but I still love you,' he blurted out suddenly, realising he might never get another opportunity to tell her.

'You're also still living with your wife, Harry.'

'Not for much longer.'

'I'm tired, Harry. Bone tired. I haven't the strength to face your wife cutting me dead every time she sees me on the hill, or the gossips watching everything I do and say, making me feel grubby and dirty, like a streetwalker.'

'Supposing I left my wife, got a divorce? What then, Megan?'

'Didn't you take a long, hard look at me? If I was ever worth the sacrifice, I'm not any more. Goodnight, Harry, and God bless.' She closed the door on him, leaving him to his thoughts and the walk down the hill.

Harry turned his steps towards Vicarage corner. All the time Megan had been in prison he had looked forward to her release as a watershed that would mark a new beginning for both of them. But now he'd actually seen her he realised that he should have made the changes years ago.

He'd condemned himself to living the stale, sterile life he detested, by taking the easiest option. Remaining with his wife, because leaving her would have meant embarking on an emotional trauma he'd been too cowardly to instigate or confront.

And now he had reached a point when he was prepared to renounce the whole of his past life, Megan had turned him down. All his grand schemes shattered, and for what? So he could stay trapped in a sham marriage with a woman who didn't love him.

More bitter than he would have believed possible, he opened the side door and walked upstairs. The flat was silent and in darkness, just as it usually was when he came home late. He went into the kitchen, opened a cupboard and found a tumbler. The taste of the brandy Phyllis had poured into his tea lingered. He wanted more.

He went into the living room and opened the sideboard, finding what he was looking for behind the sherry: a half-bottle of brandy, all that was left of the Christmas cheer he had bought for visitors, who apart from his sister-in-law and her henpecked husband hadn't materialised.

Pouring half the brandy into the tumbler, he settled back to continue with some serious drinking, so serious it didn't seem worth the effort of leaving the living room for the single bed in the cramped, uncomfortable box room. And, as his eyes finally closed, he lay back and relaxed, forgetting all the threats he had made to his wife about sleeping in her bed that night.

Chapter Thirteen

ANDREW leaned wearily against the door of the operating theatre and tore the cap from his head.

'Operation go well?' His father was sitting in the small room the doctors used as a changing room.

'Not wonderfully.'

'From what the admitting sister said, it was bad. Both legs crushed beyond repair.'

'I've tried to save one.'

'The other?'

'I had to amputate below the knee. It should heal well enough. It's the other one I'm worried about. God only knows if the bones will knit back together. If they don't, he'll be facing another major operation, probably an amputation, within the week. He told me he joined the Guards yesterday. Poor devil, one thing's certain, they won't want him now.'

'Look on the bright side: this accident may have saved his life.'

'Are you saying he's better off crippled in Pontypridd than dead on the fields of France?'

'A lot of men would have given a great deal to be offered that option in the last show.'

'I suppose they would, but I can't see Wyn being overly grateful for his present state.' Andrew pulled off the operating gown he was wearing and tossed it into a linen bin. 'What are you still doing here? I thought Diana's injuries were superficial?'

'Apart from mild concussion they are. Cuts, grazes, contusions, and a bad case of worrying about Wyn Rees. I gave her a sedative and they found her a bed. She's been sleeping for the past two hours.'

'You could have gone home and gone to bed yourself.'

'I wanted to have a word with you. You always seem to be in a hurry when you're in the surgery, and you and Bethan never call in to see your mother . . .'

'Don't start that again, Dad.'

'Your mother would like to see more of Rachel.'

'I know.' Andrew resigned himself to receiving yet another lecture. His father was a doctor, his parents 'crache' who looked down on Bethan and her family because her father was a miner. But class differences hadn't prevented him and Bethan from falling in love, and staying in love, even through the trauma of the death of one baby, and a temporary estrangement that at one time had threatened to become permanent.

'I think you should teach Bethan to drive.'

'What?' Andrew had been expecting many things, but that suggestion hadn't been one of them. 'You know something about my interview on Thursday, don't you?' he asked warily. His father had influential contacts. It wouldn't take much for him to find out exactly why his son and the other junior partner from the practice had been called to register.

'They're expecting trouble to break out in France at any moment, and they're doubling the number of field hospitals to cope with the expected casualties.'

'You mean we're going to start dropping more than paper on the Germans?'

'There may be a way to get you out of this . . .'

'Oh no you don't.' Andrew turned on his father. 'If I find out that you've pulled strings to keep me out of the army, I'll go to the recruiting office and enlist in the first regiment that will take me as a private.'

'It's not just me and your mother, it's Bethan and the baby.'

'I've discussed it with Bethan. She doesn't want me to go any more than I want to, but the one thing we're both agreed on is that if I'm called up, I go.'

'You always did have a stubborn streak.'

'And I know who I got it from.' He glared angrily at his father. The older man returned his stare for a moment, then his face crumpled into a grimace that might have been a smile, or some other emotion Andrew didn't care to think about.

'If you insist on going, your mother and I would consider it a privilege to do whatever we can for Bethan and Rachel.'

'I know you mean well, Dad, and I'll tell Bethan what you said.'

'We only want to help . . .'

'How much time do I have?' Andrew cut in abruptly.

'Not much. They want you to report for duty next Monday.'

A sick, hollow feeling rose from the pit of Andrew's stomach as he reached for his jacket.

'Dr Evans and I can run the practice until then. Take some time off.'

'Don't be stupid.'

'What's stupid about it? We're going to have to do without you and Trevor after this week, so we may as well get used to it now.'

'Surely you're going to get replacements?'

'If we can. But a town like this isn't going to be high on the list of priorities when there's a whole army in France waiting for a war that's due to start any day. I mean it. Make a holiday of what's left of the week. I'll take it as a personal affront if you don't. I was running the medical side of things in this town before you were born.'

'And it looks as though you might be running them when I'm gone. Sorry – I didn't mean that the way it came out.'

'You'll take my advice, about teaching Bethan to drive? She'll need to, stuck all the way up Penycoedcae hill.'

'She passed her test last week.'

'You could have told us.'

'I intended to.'

'You'll come to tea? Thursday would be nice. I know your mother would prefer to hear the news from you.'

'We'll be there.' He walked his father to the door. The silence between them was palpable. For the first time in his life, Andrew had an urge to hug the old man, but something, probably the stiff upper lip instilled in him during childhood, held him back. He shook hands with his father at the door, and watched him walk down the steps holding the regulation torch downwards, shining the spotlight on his feet as he headed for home.

The brief moment of intimacy had passed. Andrew knew better than to try to recapture it. He regretted its passing but he wasn't to find out just how much, until later. Much, much later.

'You awake, Tina?' Gina whispered in the depths of the double bed they shared.

'I was trying to sleep.'

'Do you think Diana will be all right?'

'Dr John said so, and he should know. I'm not sure about Wyn Rees though.'

'He looked . . .'

'Gina, there's no point in talking about it. We'll find out what state they're in tomorrow.'

'What do you think of Luke?'

'So that's who you really wanted to talk about. In a word, scruffy.'

'Tina!'

'Ssh, you'll wake the others.' Tina pulled down the bedclothes and peered over the edge. The blackout curtains were so thick she couldn't even see the bed her three younger sisters were sleeping in, let alone the girls.

'He is not scruffy!' came an indignant whisper from beside her.

'He's a conchie.'

'You walked home with Alexander, he's a conchie, and you're engaged.'

'I didn't walk home with him in that sense.'

'I'm not sure William would agree with you. I saw the way Alexander was ogling you, and he's crache. You know what William thinks of crache.'

'I could hardly leave you alone with Casanova, now could I? It's obvious what he's after.'

'He's not after anything. He's all alone here. Everything's strange . . .'

'And you're a sucker for a sob story.'

'I am not. I can tell when a man – '

'A man? How old is he?'

'Eighteen.'

Tina giggled mockingly.

'There's nothing to laugh about, we're of age,' Gina asserted indignantly.

'To get married? You meet him for the first time tonight and already you're planning your wedding?'

'Just because it didn't happen that quickly between you and William, you're jealous.'

'You know nothing about the way it happened between me and William.'

'I do know that if I loved a man who'd joined up I wouldn't bother with an engagement. I'd get married straight away.'

'Oh, shut up!' Tina turned over, pulled her pillow over her head and pretended to sleep.

Before William had left she had wanted to marry him, but now, only one day later, her mind was filled with images of Alexander Forbes. She didn't want to think about the man, but aspects insisted on intruding into her thoughts: the cut of his clothes, the quality of the cloth in his camel-hair coat, his exquisite manners, his accent – the way she'd felt when he'd put his arms around her after she'd seen Diana lying on the road.

How could she even think of Alexander when she'd promised to marry William? Was it possible to love two men at the same time? Why couldn't she remember William's face clearly? Why couldn't she *feel* him close to her? Why couldn't she think of him every minute of every day and ignore Alexander? And what was she going to do for the next six weeks when William wouldn't be around and Alexander would?

Concerned at the possibility of Wyn going into clinical shock from loss of blood, Andrew spent the night at the hospital. After telephoning Bethan to warn her he wouldn't be home until morning, he dozed fitfully for a few hours in the sister's office. It brought back memories of his early courtship, when Bethan had still been nursing and he'd used every excuse he could to visit her when she'd been on night duty.

He looked in on Diana a couple of times. The sedative his father had prescribed had certainly done the trick. She continued to sleep soundly. Eventually the night sister came into the office bearing a cup of tea. He sat up stiffly and took it from her.

'Dawn broken?'

'I have it on good authority that it's on its way.'

'How are our patients doing?'

'The same as when you looked in on them half an hour ago.'

'I was trying to be discreet and not disturb the ward.'

'You have a home to go to and, knowing you, rounds to do.' The sister wouldn't have dared be so familiar with Dr John senior, but Trevor and Andrew were proving to be quite a different breed from the older generation in the practice.

'My father is taking over for me.'

'And Dr Evans will be in shortly to take over here. Your patients will be in safe hands.'

'I'll wait for Diana Powell to wake so I can take her home. She's my wife's cousin,' he added in answer to her quizzical look. Taking his tea he left the office and walked out into the corridor to stretch his legs. The lights were still dimmed to night-time strength. He tweaked back a blackout blind. The Common was swathed in darkness. If dawn was on its way, there was no sign of it.

'How's Wyn?'

He turned to see Diana, up and dressed behind him, the bandage on her head only marginally whiter than her face. 'How are you?'

'Fine,' she replied irritably. 'How's Wyn?' she repeated urgently.

'He's going to live.'

'His legs?'

'I've had to amputate one below the knee. I'm sorry, Diana, I had no choice. He would have bled to death if I hadn't operated.'

169

'When we came in, one of the nurses warned me that he might lose his legs.'

He pushed the cup and saucer he was holding on to the window-ledge and put his hands on her shoulders. 'I've tried to save his other leg. It's early days yet, but it may recover.'

'Even if it does, Wyn will still be crippled.'

'If the bones knit back together he'll be able to use it again. The other leg will be fitted with an artificial limb and after physiotherapy hardly anyone will notice.'

'He'll be crippled,' she reiterated bitterly, 'and it will be my fault.'

'None of this is your fault, Diana. If anyone's to blame it's the driver of that van.'

'Wyn wouldn't have even been on the road if he hadn't pushed me out of the way. He was going into the army.'

'Once his leg heals he still may be able to. There are plenty of jobs a man with his disability can do.'

'Who are you trying to kid?'

'The first thing Wyn said when he came around after the operation was, "How's Diana." He obviously thinks a lot of you. Perhaps it's time to repay the compliment. He's going to need all the help and friendship he can get in the coming weeks.'

'Can I see him?'

He looked at her, wondering if she'd heard the gossip about Wyn Rees's sexual preferences.

'Please, Andrew.'

She looked so wretched, he capitulated. 'Only on condition that you don't try to talk to him. Then I'm taking you straight home, and no arguments.'

'I've got to sort out the shops.'

'Pontypridd can do without its sweets for one day.' Putting his arm around her shoulders he led her down the corridor. He opened the door quietly and looked at the nurse sitting beside Wyn's bed and nodded. Taking Diana by the hand he guided her through the door. She bit her lip and clenched her fists as she stared at Wyn lying, ashen and bloodless against a background of snowy hospital bedlinen. She stared at the tent that had been placed over his lower legs to keep the weight of the blankets from his injuries.

'I'll let you know when he's well enough to receive visitors,' Andrew whispered as he pulled her back into the corridor.

'Promise?'

'I promise,' he answered mechanically, wondering if he'd be around to let her know. First he had to make a telephone call to Trevor to tell him what lay in store for them, then he had to go home. And facing Bethan was going to be the hardest of all.

Harry dreamed there was a fire. The bells of the fire-engine were ringing, loud, aggravating, as the engine raced up the Graig hill, louder, louder . . .

'Dad!'

He woke with a start to find Jenny shaking his shoulder. She was wearing a cotton nightgown that was too thin for the time of year. Then it came again, that loud sharp ring.

'Do you want me to open up the shop?'

Totally disorientated, he looked around and realised he'd slept in the living room. He glanced at the clock on the mantelpiece. Five-thirty. The shop should have been opened for the early-shift miners half an hour ago. He tried to move and realised he was still dressed. 'No, you go back to bed, love, I'll see to it.'

'You sure, Dad?'

He was already on his way down the stairs, the walls swaying precariously around him courtesy of the brandy that still flowed in his veins. His head hurt, his mouth felt as though he'd been eating sawdust laced with mould, and his body was ten times larger and clumsier than it had been the night before. 'Coming!' he shouted angrily, as he opened the door that led into the shop. Pulling up the blind, he thrust back the bolts on the shop door.

'Heavy night?' Mr Richards enquired sarcastically.

'Late night,' Harry bit back. 'Usual?'

'Five Woodbines, on the slate.' The shop filled quickly. Men jostled in front of the counter complaining in loud voices at the shop being opened late. Harry served them as quickly as he could, but he was glad when Jenny appeared twenty minutes later, washed, dressed, her hair neatly arranged and looking one hundred per cent better than he felt. As the door closed behind the last of the early-shift customers, she stood back and studied her father.

'If I were you I'd go upstairs, shave, wash and change. Mam will have forty fits if she sees you looking like that. And you'd better hide that suit in my room. I'll sponge and press it before putting it back in your wardrobe. Pity I can't do anything about the bloodshot eyes.'

'I look that bad?'

'Worse. When you come down I'll go up and make breakfast.'

'You're a good daughter, Jenny.'

'Flattering me won't make you look human. Now go upstairs, before Mam gets up.'

Harry tackled the living room first. Feeling very sorry for himself he eyed the pitiful remains in the brandy bottle. He had hit it hard last night. From half-full to barely registering a level. If his wife knew how much he'd drunk in one sitting there'd be hell to pay. He debated whether to top it up with water but decided there wasn't enough left to colour another inch. It wasn't until he pushed the bottle to the back of the cupboard and picked up the glass he'd used that he remembered his ultimatum to his wife. It said something for his state of mind last night that he hadn't even thought of trying the door to her bedroom.

He went into the kitchen and soaked the tumbler in cold water before lighting the gas and putting the kettle on to boil for tea and shaving water. The bleak routine of the domestic chores depressed him even more. It was as though the vengeful God of the chapels had sentenced him to interminable purgatory for his sins – life with a woman he loathed – without hope of remission or pardon.

After all his grandiose plans of yesterday, nothing had changed. He couldn't bear the idea of carrying on as he was, but seeing Megan had finally convinced him that too much had happened for them to plan a life together. What could he do? Join up like his son-in-law to escape his problems? Would they want a man of his age?

He went into the cheerless box room and fetched his shaving tackle. Pouring warm water into a bowl he lathered his chin. It was so unfair. He only had one life, and he was doomed to spend it in grief and heartache without even the glimmer of a better horizon around the corner.

'Where's Annie?'

'I gave her the afternoon off.'

'Rachel?'

'Down for her afternoon nap. We have at least an hour before she stirs.' Bethan slid the coffee she had brought Andrew on to his bedside table and lay on the bed next to him. He reached out to her, his bare skin warm from sleep, his arms strong as they imprisoned her in a grip she knew from experience she had no chance of escaping until he chose to release her.

'Then how about you undress and join me here?'

'To make the most of every moment we've got left?'

He looked in her eyes and saw that she knew. 'I'm sorry, I should have told you when I came home this morning. But Rachel was crying, and – '

'And you were tired and you wanted to put it off. It doesn't matter.'

'Yes it does. Who told you?'

'Laura, she telephoned to invite us down on Friday night. She thought we'd want to keep the weekend for you to say goodbye to your family.'

'Beth . . .'

'It doesn't matter, darling, really. It's strange, this is the one thing I've been dreading since war broke out. Now it's actually happened all I feel is relief that the waiting and uncertainty is over.'

'I'm sorry.'

'Let's not talk about being sorry.' She reached up and unclipped the hook at the neck of her dress. 'Let's pretend we've all the time in the world.'

He pulled the pin from her long hair, burying his face in its scented depths as it cascaded over her shoulders. 'I'd like to try. Do you think it's possible to make one hour last a lifetime?'

'Mam hasn't stirred all day. She always has dinner on the table by now.' Jenny looked to her father, who was weighing sugar into small bags for the weekly rations. The goods weren't usually made up until Thursday night, ready for Friday delivery, but he was trying to keep himself busy. Anything rather than think.

'I knocked on her door with tea this morning. She wouldn't answer.'

'Perhaps she's ill.'

'Perhaps,' he answered in a tone that said he didn't care.

'I think I should check, don't you?'

'If you want,' he answered, half hoping that his prayers had been answered and his wife had packed her bags and left.

Jenny ran up the stairs. He heard her knocking at his wife's bedroom door, just as Mrs Richards, the nosiest busybody on the Graig, walked in. Mrs Richards had the shortest weekly goods list of any of his customers, not that the Richards consumed less food than other families but because she made a point of running out of something essential practically every morning. It gave her an excuse to walk down to the shop and glean as much gossip as she could along the way. She had a better reputation than the Pontypridd *Observer* for accumulating and disseminating news.

'Heard about Wyn the queer?' she asked as she plonked her basket on the counter.

'I saw Wyn Rees being taken to hospital after he'd been knocked down by a van in Taff Street last night, if that's what you mean.'

'You were there? Then you know Diana Powell was with him?'

'She does work for him,' Harry said firmly, hoping to discourage her. 'Have you a list?'

'A tin of blacklead. I saw Andrew John bring Diana home in his car this morning. By the look of her, she'd been out all night.'

'Chances are if Dr John brought her home, she'd been in the Cottage Hospital all night.'

'She looked all right to me.'

'She didn't when I saw her lying in the road.'

'I just saw Dai Station's wife by the post office. He was there when it happened. According to him Wyn Rees was a right mess. His legs were all mangled. He may never walk again . . .'

'Dai should know.' Harry slammed a tin of blacklead on the counter and reached for the red book where he recorded the credit purchases. 'He was in the van that knocked Wyn down.'

'Oooh, Dai's wife didn't tell me *that*.'

'Will there be anything else?' Jenny's knocking upstairs was growing louder, more insistent, then he heard her try to open the door. It rattled, but there was no sound of hinges creaking.

Mrs Richards consulted her list. 'A quarter of a pound of suet, and half a pound of washing soda. Problems upstairs?'

'Sticking door.' As he spoke the air was filled with the sound of wood splintering.

'Shouldn't you go and see to it?'

'Jenny can cope. I'll help her when I've finished serving you.'

'It's a long list.' Mrs Richards smiled insincerely.

'Shall we continue, then?'

'Now let me see, blacklead, suet, washing soda – '

'Dad!'

'In a minute, Jenny.'

'I think you should come right now.'

'I can wait,' Mrs Richards assured him. He didn't hear her; he was already halfway up the stairs.

'Snap time.'

Yesterday Alexander had been horrified at the thought of eating sandwiches with grimy unwashed hands. Today he was glad of the opportunity to sink on his haunches and rest his back against the coal face. Silence, blissful and edifying, lapped around him as picks and shovels were dropped to the ground.

'How are your hands, Alexander?' Evan asked.

'Stiff and dead.'

'That's good,' Luke congratulated him chirpily.

'How are you doing?' Evan smiled at the boy.

'Working underground has its advantages.'

'I can't think of any,' Alexander countered.

'You're not bothered by the weather. It gets pretty cold and wet in the fields at this time of year.'

'As opposed to dusty, dark and damp.'

'There's no wind.'

'Just the sound of scurrying rats whenever the work stops.'

'You get them everywhere. I always think of their scampering as a friendly sound. At least you know you're not alone.'

'I believe that if you were put in jail you'd find something good to say about the place,' Alexander grumbled.

'You'd probably get three square meals a day.'

'See what I mean?' Alexander leaned back and opened his snap tin.

'Seems to me we could all do with a little of his contentment.'

Evan bit down on a beef-heart sandwich, grimacing as his teeth crunched on coal that had fallen on the bread from his helmet.

'That's not contentment, that's love.'

'Love? You've left a girl behind?' Evan asked.

'No, he's found one here.'

'But you two boys only went out in Pontypridd for the first time last night.'

'That's all it took.'

Evan looked at Luke in a new light. 'Do I know her?'

'It's nothing really, just one of the girls who works in the café, she was being friendly . . .'

'The Ronconi girls?'

'They were on the scene of the accident minutes after it happened. As it really upset them Luke and I helped to lock up the café and walked them up the hill afterwards. And that's when Luke did his very best to make the younger one feel better.'

'Gina,' Evan breathed in relief. The last thing he wanted was gossip some busybody felt they had to write to William about.

'I think the lad's really smitten.' Alexander rose to his feet and brushed the crumbs off his filthy trousers, before reaching for his bottle of cold tea. 'I almost heard the violins playing in the background.'

Harry could hear Jenny talking to him, could see her lips moving, but his brain failed to grasp the significance of a single word she said.

Through the chink between the door and the jamb he could see his wife's feet clad in the silk stockings and high heels she insisted on wearing, even around the house.

Whatever else, he had never been able to accuse her of 'letting herself go'. Twenty-two years of marriage and he had never seen his wife without make-up, or with her hair in curlers or her stockings rolled down around her ankles like some of the other women on the Graig. But neither had he seen her with her skirt hitched up as high as it was now.

'Dad!'

He continued to stare vacantly at Jenny.

'She must have fallen behind the door. Shall I get help?'

He nodded dumbly. He could push the door open, it wouldn't be difficult, but he didn't want Jenny there to witness it. He wasn't sure what his wife had done, but he had a feeling that whatever it was, she'd intended it to be a punishment for his eyes only.

'Mr Griffiths. Coo-ee, Mr Griffiths, is everything all right up there?'

'It's Mrs Richards, keep her in the shop,' he ordered Jenny, thinking clearly for the first time since he'd climbed the stairs. 'Then go next door . . .'

'The pub?' Jenny asked, horrified at the thought of her father actually telling her to go into a public house when no decent woman would dream of stepping over the doorstep of one.

'Ask to borrow their telephone. Get the doctor. Quick as you can now, girl.'

When she was halfway down the stairs he gave the door an almighty push. The key clattered noisily to the floor. He pushed again. There was a crash of falling furniture and a scraping of wooden feet over lino, but he succeeded in creating a gap wide enough for him to squeeze his way into the room.

His wife was lying on the floor in a pool of congealing blood. He bent down and picked up her wrist. It was limp but warm, and he could feel a pulse: weak, but definitely there. He stepped over her body and crouched between her and the bed. There was blood around her head but he couldn't see where it was coming from. Gently, very gently he lifted her head. Then he saw it – a jagged piece of crystal stuck in the side of her neck. Forgetting everything he'd been taught in the St John's basic first-aid class, he closed his fingers over it and tugged. A warm tide of blood gushed out over his hands. He panicked, pressing on the wound, desperately trying to stem the flow. He must have cried out without being aware of it, because Jenny came running back up the stairs, Mrs Richards hot on her heels.

Jenny halted in the doorway, staring at her mother lying, red lipped and blue faced in her father's lap.

'I killed her, Jenny,' Harry whispered. 'I didn't mean to, but so help me God, I killed her.'

Mrs Richards didn't wait another moment. Charging back down the stairs she ran through the shop and into the street. She saw Huw Griffiths just starting on his afternoon changeover shift from nights to mornings. It was the best and biggest piece of gossip she had ever been privilege to, and she made the most of her moment. Waving her hands in the air, she shouted 'Murder!' at the top of her voice and didn't stop until Huw crossed the road to meet her.

As the telephone rang in the hall, Bethan burrowed her head down on to Andrew's shoulder.

'I should answer it.'

'Your father promised us a few days.'

'It could be important.'

'What could be more important than this?'

'Laura's baby getting colic, Diana suffering from delayed shock, a mining accident . . .'

'You win.' She reluctantly disentangled her arm from around his waist, allowing him to reach for his silk dressing gown. He left the bed and went downstairs. As he picked up the telephone receiver and silenced the bell she heard another sound, barely audible to anyone not attuned to it, but one she instantly recognised. A series of quiet whimpers that preceded Rachel's wake-up cry by a few minutes. Leaving the warmth of the bed she went to the bath-room.

She was sitting on the bed rolling on her stockings when Andrew dashed upstairs.

'Harry Griffiths's wife is seriously injured. Some kind of accident in the shop. They tried and failed to reach my father or Dr Evans, so I'm it.'

'Could you take Rachel and me down the hill with you as far as Graig Avenue?'

'If you don't delay me.' He pulled on his socks and reached for his shirt.

'We're ready.' Bethan picked up Rachel, and the bag of clean nappies and other necessities she left packed at all times in preparation for her next trip to her father's house.

'Better warn your father when he comes home. Jenny might need help. Perhaps Megan could stay with her.'

'I'm her sister-in-law.'

'You have Rachel to look after, and this might be an overnight job, or even longer. I spoke to Huw Davies. Apparently Harry is rambling about killing her.'

'Killing her!'

'Wouldn't you kill a wife like Harry's if you had one?' He kissed her on the cheek. 'Come on, let's go.'

A young constable was standing guard outside the door to Griffiths's shop when Andrew pulled up. He was doing his best to keep the crowd pressing around the window at bay, although there was little point in the exercise. Even if he'd allowed them to draw closer there was nothing for them to see because the blackout blinds had been pulled down over every window. The constable looked at the car and the bag Andrew lifted out.

'You the doctor, sir?'

Andrew was tempted to make a witty observation on the young officer's powers of detection but thought better of it. 'I am. I take it the patient's inside?'

'Yes, sir.' He opened the door to the shop, closing it again as soon as Andrew stepped through it.

A light shone beyond the doorway that separated shop from living quarters. Andrew could hear voices upstairs. He followed the sound and found himself in a room crammed with heavy, old-fashioned furniture. Jenny was sitting on a sofa with the landlady of the Morning Star, a bottle of brandy and a glass on the table beside them.

The landlady glanced up at Andrew. 'In the bedroom,' she mouthed, nodding to the back of the house. Andrew walked down the landing, finding it peculiar to be in rooms lit by electricity in the middle of the afternoon. The door to the bedroom facing him was hanging off its hinges. He walked around it.

Harry Griffiths was sitting slumped forward on a double bed. Huw Davies stood next to him, the sergeant, notebook in hand, was sitting in a Lloyd Loom chair on the other side of the room, and lying on the floor at their feet was the body of Harry's wife.

Andrew didn't need to feel for a pulse to pronounce her dead, but he crouched down and went through the motions all the same.

'She been dead long, Dr John?' the sergeant asked.

'Difficult to say. Her temperature's higher than the room, but not by much.'

'We know she was alive an hour ago,' Harry said flatly. 'So why bother to ask how long she's been dead?'

'The doctor's here to ascertain cause of death,' the sergeant intoned as though he were quoting from a manual.

'I told you, I killed her.'

'Killed her?' Andrew looked up from the deep cut he was examining on the side of the corpse's neck.

'I pulled this out of the wound.' Harry opened his fingers to display a chunk of bloodied glass.

'You'd better give that to me.' The sergeant held out his hand and Harry obediently dropped the glass on to his palm.

'Did you push this into her neck?' the sergeant asked.

'No.'

'Then how can you say you killed her?'

'Tell them,' Harry prompted Huw in a bleak monotone. 'Tell them she was still alive when you came into the room. You saw the blood pumping out of her after I pulled the glass from her neck. I killed her. Tell them.'

Andrew took the sharp chunk of crystal from the sergeant, matching its size and shape to the wound. 'Her jugular's been severed. It would have taken a miracle-worker to sew it back together, even if he'd been present when the accident happened. And you're not a doctor, Harry. You weren't to know that removing that piece of glass would hasten her death. And that's all you did, hasten it. Take it from me, there was no way of saving her once that glass cut the blood vessel.' Wiping his hands on a towel he'd pulled from his bag, he rose to his feet.

'No?' Harry looked at the three men through cold, dead eyes. 'Ask him,' he pointed to Huw. 'He knows I had good reason to want my wife out of my life. And when she wouldn't go, I pleaded with her, I offered her money, but she still wouldn't go.'

'Wanting your wife out of the way and killing her aren't the same thing, Harry.' Andrew surveyed the upturned dressing table, the drawers heaped in a higgledy-piggledy pile, the smashed chair and the mess of broken cosmetic and perfume bottles, spilt cold cream and shattered glass strewn over the linoleum. 'Looks to me like she was rearranging the furniture, slipped, fell and landed on this lot. There's no killing in that.'

'Things have never been good between us, and lately they've got worse. Yesterday I threatened her. Said she could either be my wife in every sense of the word or go. She didn't go. I killed her.'

'Harry you've been cautioned,' Huw pleaded.

'I don't care. I confess. I wanted her dead, she's dead. I killed her,' he repeated dully. He looked at the sergeant who was noting every word he was saying in his book. 'Is there anything else you want me to add?'

Chapter Fourteen

IT was strange to be back in Pontypridd after a whole winter away. Strange to be surrounded by hills again after the flat lands of France; strange to look out of the window of the train and see signs of spring in the buds on the trees and early primroses in the hedgerows; and stranger still to walk familiar streets in uniform and not be going to or from work in Charlie's shop; to be shouldering a kitbag – to be back – to want to, and yet in some ways not want to be home. Which was why Eddie Powell walked straight past Griffiths's shop on his way up the Graig hill from the station, and went directly to his father's house.

It was teatime. He knew it would be, but there were two men he had never seen before sitting at his and William's place at the table. His father and Diana jumped up to greet him as he walked in. Brian put his head to one side and looked at him quizzically, a peculiar expression on his small face that told Eddie his half-brother didn't remember him, and that, more than the presence of outsiders in the old, familiar kitchen, disturbed him. He loved Brian, had spent a lot of time with him, and within the space of a few short months the child preferred the company of strangers.

'You should have told us you were coming, son,' Evan said as he grasped him by the shoulders.

'They handed me a pass three days ago, with a message that the train was leaving in half an hour. I've been travelling ever since.'

'You look exhausted.' Phyllis's mind immediately turned to the practical. 'I'll make you something to eat.'

Eddie looked at the remains of the meal on the table. Stew and jam roly-poly. He could have polished that off in no time, he thought resentfully, as he glanced at the interlopers.

'Eddie, I'm sorry, I should have introduced you. These are our lodgers . . .'

'Alexander Forbes.' Alexander rose from his chair. 'I would have recognised you from your father's description anywhere. Pleased to meet you.'

Eddie pulled the cap from his head and shook hands with the man, but he didn't return his sentiments.

'And Luke Grenville.'

'It's time we were off, Luke. Thank you very much for the tea, Mrs Powell.'

'Mrs Powell?' Eddie asked his father as the men left the room.

'It's easier to introduce Phyllis as my wife. Saves explanations.'

'What are they doing here?'

'Conscripts working in the pit,' Diana answered. 'Tell us, have you seen Will?'

'And Tony and Angelo. I spent last night in base camp, and before you ask, they're all fighting fit and drinking hard.' He looked around the room. 'Where's Auntie Megan? You said in your letters she was home.'

'She's with Jenny. Someone had to stay with her. When I wrote to the army authorities I didn't know if they'd grant you compassionate leave or not. In the meantime we couldn't allow Jenny to stay in the shop by herself, and she wouldn't come up here, so the simplest solution was for Megan to move in with her until everything was over.'

'All my CO told me was Jenny's mother was dead. I was still getting letters from Jenny and she made no mention of her mother being ill. Was it sudden?'

Diana disappeared into the pantry with Phyllis, and Evan could hear the sound of eggs being cracked and beaten. The women were obviously intent on depleting the larder in honour of Eddie's arrival.

'No, she died in an accident. At least that's what Andrew said it was, and he was there shortly afterwards. The problem is, Harry insists he killed her.'

'Killed her?' Eddie stared at his father, dumbfounded.

'From what little I've been able to gather, not that the police are giving much away, Harry says he quarrelled with her the day before she died. Apparently he asked her for a divorce and she wouldn't give him one. Unfortunately Mrs Richards was there when Jenny and Harry broke down the door of her bedroom and found her lying on the floor in the middle of a pile of broken glass. One piece was in her neck, Harry took it out, she started bleeding, and died soon afterwards.'

'Mrs Richards would have to be there.' Eddie pulled a packet of Senior Service out of his tunic pocket and offered his father one.

'That woman has a sixth sense for trouble.'

'Can't say I blame Harry for wanting his wife out of the way. She was an old cow from what I saw, and I only saw her when I had to.'

'As Andrew said, wanting someone dead isn't the same as murdering them. He was the attending doctor, and he insists it was an accident. He did what he could to help Harry before he left, but with Harry persisting in repeating that he murdered her, it wasn't enough. Harry's been taken to an asylum . . .'

'Left? Andrew's been called up?'

'Him and Trevor. And Charlie. They went over three weeks ago.'

'The boys said Charlie had tried to join up. I didn't see him in camp.'

'He's been detailed to special interpreting services.'

'Omelette, sausage and chips, with apple pie for afters?' Diana asked as she carried a bowl out of the pantry.

'Sounds like heaven after army rations, but I'd prefer ham to sausages.'

'Eddie, we haven't any. It's rationed and when we can get hold of it we're only allowed four ounces a week.'

'That's why I want big thick slices.' He opened his kitbag, and produced an enormous cooked ham.

'Eddie!' Phyllis gasped, wide eyed. 'Wherever did you get it?'

'France, of course. Best French ham that.'

'But haven't they got rationing?'

'Of course, but then,' he winked at Diana as he tossed her a pair of silk stockings and a bottle of perfume. 'You know me. There's always people prepared to do a bit of bartering.'

'So I see,' Evan said drily. 'And what exactly did you have to offer them in exchange for all this?'

'Bit of this and that.'

'Not the kind of "this and that" that could land you in the glass-house, I hope?'

'Me, do anything illegal?' He handed his father a packet of tobacco and a bottle of brandy. 'Here's more perfume, one for you Phyllis, and Megan, one for our Beth, and this,' he smiled as he handed Brian a tin car with a key in the side. 'Wind that up, nipper, and see what it can do.'

Brian unbent enough to come forward and take it from him.

'This is just like Christmas.' Diana unscrewed the top of the perfume and sniffed it before giving her cousin an enormous hug and kiss.

'I just hope you've something in that bag of tricks for your wife,' his father prompted as Phyllis laid an enormous plate of bread before him.

'Something for everyone,' Eddie answered ambiguously.

'You haven't been to see her?'

'Not yet.'

'We'll go as soon as you've eaten.'

From the tone in his father's voice, Eddie knew it was useless to try and put off seeing Jenny until morning. Picking up a piece of bread he eyed the scraping of real butter on it before biting down hard.

'It really is very good of you to help me, but you don't have to, Constable Davies.'

'That's all right, Miss Rees.' Huw lifted down one of the heavy shutters that fronted the sweet kiosk and reached for the other. 'Diana told me she was taking the night off to visit Wyn. I guessed you'd be taking over, and I'm doing no more for you than I do for her.'

'It's still very kind of you. These are heavy.'

'Tell me, how is your father?' he asked as he stacked the shutters behind the door.

'About the same. Mrs Edwards from next door is sitting with him tonight.'

'You finish here about half-past nine don't you?'

'Nearer ten by the time I count and bag the money.'

'I'll be here to lift the shutters back and walk you home.'

'No, really, I couldn't put you to all that trouble.'

'No trouble. We can't have young ladies walking around in the blackout, carrying money and tempting the crooks in town, now can we? Call it preventive policing.' He tipped his helmet to her before going on his way.

'You've missed your mother-in-law's funeral.' Evan closed the front door and followed Eddie down the steps.

'That's the army for you. She dies a month ago and I get compassionate leave now.'

'The police wouldn't release the body until after the inquest two days ago. We buried her this morning.'

'I can't say I'm that sorry to have missed the service. What was the inquest verdict?'

'Open.'

'How does that affect Harry.'

'We'll find out more when we talk to Spickett's the solicitors. They're dealing with it. How long have you got?'

'I have to be back in base camp Tuesday night.'

'Three days. That's not a lot of time.'

'You're lucky to get forty-eight hours these days. By the time I get back I will have been away for almost ten days.'

'I was thinking of the time you need to spend with Jenny.' Eddie remained obstinately silent, just as Evan knew he would, but for once Evan broke his golden rule of not interfering in his children's lives. 'You wanted to marry her, Eddie. No one made you. We all advised you to wait, but you couldn't get to the altar quick enough.'

'Don't remind me.'

'You must have loved her then?'

'I was a fool.'

'For hitting Haydn through a plate-glass window when you thought he was having an affair with Jenny, and for leaving her afterwards without any explanation or apology, perhaps.'

'I should have known Haydn wouldn't have had anything to do with Jenny after I married her.'

'Neither would Jenny with Haydn,' Evan said quietly. 'You've got a good girl there, boy.'

'I don't want to talk about it, Dad.'

'You have to. Don't you see you have to resolve the situation between you one way or another. If you don't love her, divorce her, then you can both make a fresh start.'

'Divorce!' It was evident from the shock in Eddie's voice that he hadn't considered the idea.

'On the other hand if you do love her and want to save your marriage, you've got a lot of sorting out to do in three days.' Evan waited for Eddie to pick up the conversation. When he didn't, he risked Eddie's temper by continuing. 'If you want my opinion, I think Jenny wanted to marry you for the white dress and the big wedding . . .'

'I know that,' Eddie broke in savagely.

'I was going to add, and after you left, she realised how much she really cares for you. She's hardly left the shop since. Harry told me before this happened that she spends all her free time writing to you. She's only been out once that I know of, and that was to William and Tina's engagement party. Every time I see her, she asks after you. You haven't written to her?'

Eddie shook his head as he felt in his pocket for his cigarettes.

'Take my advice, son. Talk to her and lay whatever's between you to rest.'

Eddie looked up. Judging by the sound of piano music and the gleam of moonlight on blackened glass they were outside the Morning Star Hotel. 'You'd rather I stayed with her, wouldn't you?'

'No.' Evan watched while Eddie lit two cigarettes. He took the one Eddie handed him. 'All I want, all I've ever wanted is for you children to be happy. Bethan is.'

'After a sticky start.'

'No one waved a magic wand. It only got sorted between her and Andrew because they made an effort and worked at it together.'

'No matter how much work you put into some things, they still go wrong.'

'You think I don't know that? I could have tried to appease your mother until kingdom come, and we would have been just as miserable. But with Maud and Ronnie blissfully happy in Italy from what I understand from her letters, and Haydn and Jane making a go of it in London, and Bethan waiting for the war to end so Andrew can come back . . .'

'He's only just gone.'

'That's what I'm trying to tell you. Bethan and Andrew love one another, which means he has something to come back to. If you haven't, better to end it now and find yourself a Mademoiselle, and free Jenny so she can look around as well.'

Eddie was glad his face was shrouded in darkness. His father was blessed with an uncanny ability to home in on the truth. There was a Mademoiselle in France, and not only one. There were always girls around army camps. Girls who could be bought for a few drinks and a cheap present. He'd even managed to fool himself into thinking he was happy with the situation – until now.

'Tell your Auntie Megan I'll be waiting in the snug of the Star for her.'

'You're not coming in?'

'The place will be full of women clucking over the sermon, the flowers and the service. If you take my advice you'll get Megan to throw them out before you see Jenny. You'll be up tomorrow?'

'Around teatime if not earlier.'

'Good luck. Whatever decision you make I know it will be the right one.'

'Don't you ever have a night off?' Luke pleaded as Gina emptied a bag of coppers into the till, counting it out into the farthing, halfpenny and penny drawers.

'I suppose if I pleaded with Tina she might take over for me one night, but then she'd expect me to do the same for her, and it's hard work running this place by yourself.' She looked towards the back room where Tina was sitting with Alexander, both apparently engrossed in a book.

'It's just that I'm going to get paid tomorrow, and I'd like to take you somewhere special.'

'By the time Tina closes the restaurant and reaches here, there's nowhere special to go.'

'One of the boys said there's a benefit dance for the town's Troop Comforts Fund in the Catholic Hall in Treforest a week Saturday.'

'You can forget Saturday night. It's always bedlam here.'

'Supposing I ask Alexander to give your sister a hand?'

'Alexander?' Gina laughed. 'I couldn't see him soiling his hands to make a cup of tea let alone serve a tram crew.'

'You'd be surprised at what Alexander can do,' Luke asserted. After a month of taking everything that the men underground could throw at him and not retaliating, Alexander had earned a grudging respect. So much so that a few of the miners had already dropped the appendage of 'conchie' when they spoke to them.

'You can still walk me home tonight, if you like.'

'You know I'd like to, very much.'

'And there's always tomorrow morning. I don't suppose Quakers go to Catholic churches?'

'No.'

'Pity, we could walk to mass together.'

'I could wait at the door.'

'For two hours in Treforest? There's nothing to do over there.'

'It would be worth it for the walk back.'

'I leave before seven in the morning so I can be back to open this place up for the Sunday dinner trade.'

'I could pick you up.'

'No,' Gina looked across to where Tina was sitting, 'don't do that. I'll meet you. Mountain end of Graig Avenue at ten to seven?'

'Here, as you persist in hanging around my baby sister all night you may as well make yourself useful.' Tina dumped a tray of dirty dishes into Luke's arms.

'Would you like me to carry them through to the kitchen?'

'Yes please, Luke,' Gina smiled broadly at Tina. 'It's my break time, I'll make us both a cup of tea.'

'Sometimes I wonder if Gina will ever grow up,' Tina grumbled as she took Gina's place behind the till.

'I rather think she just has.' Alexander put his hand in his pocket and pulled out half a crown with difficulty. He was beginning to wonder if his fingers would ever get back to normal after the battering they were being subjected to in the pit.

'And what's that supposed to mean?'

'It's obvious Luke is besotted with her.'

'She's a child.'

'And how old were you when you started seeing your fiancé?'

'Older than her.' She took a shilling from a customer and dropped it into the till, ramming the drawer shut. She turned to Alexander. 'And what's your interest in all this?'

'Friendship, and the glow I get from seeing young love.'

'Really?' she enquired sceptically.

'And if I was entirely honest –' he lifted her hand in his damaged paw and kissed the tips of her fingers – 'the pleasure I get out of taking a certain young lady home.'

Tina glanced up at him, the caustic quip she was about to make dying in her throat when she saw the expression in his eyes. It wasn't just his attractive face, or even the look he was sending her way, there was something between them. An empathy she didn't want to examine too closely for William's sake, because she was afraid it might be rooted in more than simply loneliness.

'Hello Auntie Megan.'

Megan whirled around to see Eddie standing in the Griffiths's kitchen behind her.

'Eddie?'

He swept her off her feet. 'You've lost weight.'

'It's all the running up and down stairs I've done for the past couple of weeks letting people in and out of here.'

'Seems like a bit of a mess from what I've heard.' Dropping his kitbag to the floor he shoved it into a corner with the toe of his boot.

'A right mess,' Megan agreed, 'and Jenny's had nothing but an endless string of visitors since it happened. And the worst of them was Jenny's mother's sister. She was hysterical when she came in, and in a dead faint when she left.'

'Dad said you've been doing everything here. Thank you.'

'You've been home?'

'I wasn't sure where everyone would be,' he lied.

'Jenny wouldn't leave here, even before her mother was brought back.'

'Dad told me the funeral was today. I'm sorry I wasn't here.'

'It went well. Jenny insisted on everything being done traditionally.

I tried to keep the worst of the sightseers and gossips at bay, but it wasn't easy. You know what Mrs Griffiths was like.'

'Better than most,' Eddie said, tight-lipped. 'All I can say is that if Harry did kill her, I wouldn't blame him one little bit. If ever a woman needed murdering it was her.'

'You shouldn't speak ill of the dead.'

'If I can help Harry justify her death, I will.'

'There's a fair chance there won't be any charges. At least that's what Mr Spickett told Jenny tonight.'

'Dad said Harry confessed?'

'He has. But Huw says the only real evidence against him is his own testimony, and the doctor in the asylum says Harry's had a complete breakdown. He's not expected to leave the place for at least a year, if then.'

'Anyone who confesses to murder without waiting to be charged has to be off his trolley.'

'What am I thinking of? You must be starving . . .'

'Phyllis cooked me a month's rations.'

'But you'll want to see Jenny, not stand here gossiping with me.'

'Is anyone with her?' he asked swiftly.

'A roomful. As I said, poor Jenny's had nothing but people in and out since it happened. I've tried to keep to close friends and relatives, but it's been difficult. Dying the way she did, I think more have come from curiosity than any desire to express their sympathy.'

'If you mean that Mrs Griffiths wasn't liked . . .'

'Eddie, talk like that isn't going to help Jenny.'

'I see the shop's still open.'

'Your father found a reliable girl in Leyshon Street who was willing to take over at short notice. It's doing better than it ever has.'

'Moral is, to improve trade, stage a gruesome death on the premises. Sorry,' he apologised. 'Sick sense of humour.'

'It seems to have got sicker since you've been in the army.'

'You wait until you see the change in Will. Which reminds me –' he pulled an envelope out of his inside pocket – 'letter for you. I came via our home base camp.'

'He's all right?'

'Fit as a fiddle, in all ways. You know Will.'

'That's why I can't help worrying about him. But look,' she untied the apron from her waist. 'You really should be with Jenny.'

'Dad's waiting in the snug of the Morning Star for you.'

'I'll get rid of everyone.'

'Do me a favour, don't tell Jenny I'm here.'

'But you are going to see her?'

'Of course, but not with people around.'

'And I'll tell the girl to lock up downstairs. The shop can close early for once. I'm sorry you had to come home this way, Eddie, but it's good to have you back.'

'You are coming back tonight?' Suddenly he was alarmed at the thought of being left alone with his wife.

'There's no point now you're here. Besides, I'd like to see Diana before she goes up to the Cottage Hospital to visit Wyn, and it will be nice to sleep in my own bed instead of Harry's box room for a change.'

'Dad told me what happened to Diana and Wyn.'

'It's shaken her badly. But come on, boy, you're holding me up. This is time you should be spending with your wife, not me.' Picking up her apron, Megan left the room.

Eddie switched off the light and opened the curtains. He stood in front of the window staring out at the view of Factory Lane and the shadows of the coke works towers outlined against the rising moon. Behind him he could hear Megan ushering people out. She returned just once to remind him that there was a pot of stew in the oven that needed warming up.

'You haven't told Jenny I'm here?'

'No, she thinks I'm just going home for an hour. See you tomorrow.' She kissed him and left. The stairs creaked, the door closed and she was gone. He waited, half expecting Jenny to come and put the stew on the stove, but there wasn't a sound in the flat. The bell rang downstairs. He heard a key turning; 'the girl', whoever she was, had locked up. He had no reason to delay any longer.

He walked along the passage to the living room. Megan had left the door open. The curtains were drawn and the room smelt stuffy, as though fresh air hadn't blown through it for days. But then it wouldn't have, he reflected. The curtains were always kept drawn in a house of death.

Jenny was sitting on the sofa, sunk deep in thought. His heart beat faster as it always did whenever he saw her silver blonde hair, slender figure and smooth white skin. She was motionless, so still he wondered if she was sleeping. Then she looked up and saw him.

'Eddie?' She whispered his name softly, as though she were afraid he was a dream that would dissolve at the slightest sound.

'They gave me compassionate leave.'

'Your father said he'd try, but I didn't dare hope they'd let you come. Oh Eddie.' She was off the sofa and in his arms in an instant.

Burying her face in his shoulder she began to cry, quietly at first, then as her tears flowed freer her throat constricted with harsh, rasping sobs.

He held her and stroked her hair, his mind awash with conflicting emotions. This was the girl who had married him, loving his brother. A girl he had left after three days of bitter fighting and arguing. A girl he loved, but who he'd never dared speak to of love.

'It's all right, Jenny,' he said wearily, leading her to the sofa. 'It's going to be all right.'

'But Dad . . . Mam . . .'

'I know.'

'Eddie . . .'

'Just cry it out. We'll talk later.'

Her grip tightened around his chest. He could feel her heart beating against his, and something of the old familiar emotions stirred within him. This was what he'd been most afraid of. Falling prey again to feelings that were unrequited and he could no more control than he could his need to breathe.

'I've cleared it with the matron. You can stay with Wyn until eight. That's an hour beyond normal visiting, so you'll have to be quiet and not upset any of the other patients.'

'I won't,' Diana assured Andrew's father.

'I'll take you home afterwards . . .'

'There's no need.'

'I have an ulterior motive. Andrew handed Mr Rees's care over to me when he left and, well, to be perfectly honest the patient isn't making the progress he should. I'd appreciate any help you can give me.'

'Me? But I don't know anything about nursing injuries like Wyn's.'

'I'm not asking you to nurse him, but tell me what you know about his likes and dislikes and the things that make life worthwhile for him. The only time he shows any signs of animation is when you're here. The nurses can't get a word out of him, he spends all day staring out of the window. He doesn't read or talk to anyone, he won't eat. He might be my patient, but if he's going to recover from this it's you, not me, who's going to have to pinpoint the reason as to why he should make the effort.'

'But last time I was here, you said his injuries were healing.'

'Oh, physically he's making reasonable progress. However, no matter how well he adapts to an artificial limb he'll always walk with a pronounced limp, and unfortunately he knows it. But that accident did more than cripple him. It damaged his mind. He's angry, with the kind of destructive anger that can worm into a man and destroy him if he's not careful. I've seen it before with miners after pit accidents. Losing a limb makes some men, especially the younger ones, feel less than human. They're labelled cripples and it's as though the label detracts from their manhood. It takes a lot of courage to resume a normal life, or as near to one as they can manage, afterwards.'

'But Wyn will be able to walk again?' Diana asked anxiously.

'First with crutches, then eventually with a stick, yes, there's no reason why he shouldn't. But it will take months, possibly as long as a year or two, and in the meantime he'll have to undergo a slow, painful course of physiotherapy – a humiliating, dependent process for a proud man. Don't forget he wanted to go into the army.'

'He signed up for the Guards.'

'Quite, and like most volunteers he probably had mixed feelings about going, and now it almost certainly won't happen. He might even believe that he's cheated death at the cost of becoming a cripple. To say he feels worthless is no exaggeration, and that coupled with the fact that he can't even leave his bed to go to the bathroom at the moment without a nurse's help, has turned him into an extremely withdrawn, resentful invalid.'

Dr John wasn't telling Diana anything new. She had seen it for herself during the visiting hours that first Andrew, and then his father, had arranged for her over the month since the accident. But she hadn't wanted to believe Wyn's depressed state of mind was serious, or permanent. She still held herself responsible for the accident, and her guilt coupled with Wyn's embittered frame of mind had made the past weeks extremely difficult. The last thing she remembered every night before she went to sleep was the look of pain and anguish that settled over Wyn's face every time she caught him unawares. The first thing that came to mind every morning was the screech of brakes followed by the sight of Wyn's horrific injuries in the puddle of torchlight.

'You'll remember what I said, and try to think of ways we can help him?' Dr John led her out of the office to the door of Wyn's private room.

'I'll try,' she echoed, 'I just wish there was *something* I could do that would make it all come right for him.'

'That, young lady,' he said drily, 'is the something we doctors have been trying to find for the past two thousand years.'

Chapter Fifteen

Eddie's shoulder was numb, his arm tingling with pins and needles.

'Come on.' He moved slightly, easing the weight of Jenny's head higher up on to his chest. 'It's time you had tea.'

'I don't want to move, not yet.'

For the first time since he had walked into the room her voice was free from tears.

'We can't stay here all night.' Gripping her by the shoulders he moved away and rose from the sofa.

'No, but we could go to bed.'

'Jenny . . .'

'No, please Eddie. Just answer me one question. Did you read any of the letters I sent you?'

'Yes.'

'All of them?'

'All of them,' he repeated as he walked to the door that led to the kitchen.

'Then why didn't you answer them?'

'You've no idea what it's like in the army. They keep you busy from dawn to dusk. There's no time for anything except spit, polish and parade grounds.'

'Don't give me that, Eddie. William's in the army and he writes to Tina every day.'

'She gives you his letters to read?'

'Of course not, but she talks about what's in them when she calls in here, generally finishing every sentence with, "but you'd know that anyway, Jenny, Eddie would have told you about it".'

'If I didn't write, it was because I didn't know what to say.'

'I poured my heart out to you.'

Turning his back on her he went into the kitchen. Pulling the blackout, switching the light on, getting the stew out of the oven, putting it on the hob and lighting the gas gave him something to do. He was glad of an excuse to look anywhere but at her.

'Aren't you going to say something?'

'Like what? Ask if you're still sorry you married the wrong brother?'

'Eddie, I thought we had settled all that. Haydn's married to Jane, we're married . . .'

'But you still would have preferred to have been Haydn's wife?'

'At one time, perhaps,' she said slowly, admitting to no more than he already knew. 'Not any more.' She moved towards him, but he still refused to face her. Resting her head against his back she stroked his arms through the rough khaki sleeves of his tunic. 'I've grown up a lot since you've left, Eddie. I love you. The only thing I really regret is not finding out just how much until after you'd gone.' She waited for him to react in some way. If only he'd say something – anything. 'This material is horribly itchy, as bad as Welsh flannel, how do you stand it?' It was an absurd question, but she couldn't bear the silence between them a moment longer.

'I wear a shirt underneath.'

She stood on tiptoe. Her breasts brushed against his arm as she kissed the side of his cheek – all she could reach. She had never failed to arouse him with her kisses, but for the first time since she had undressed for him in Shoni's woods last summer, she wasn't sure how he'd react to her lovemaking. When he didn't push her away, she reached around and began unfastening the buttons on his uniform. He grabbed her hands, clutching them in a vice-like grip.

'Eddie . . .'

'If we're going to do this, I want to do it properly, in a bed, and for the right reasons.'

'Like I love you and I'm your wife?'

'You sure about that first bit?'

'I'm sure, although it's hard being married to a man who's never once said he loves me.'

Closing her eyes she buried her face in the back of his tunic, certain that she'd lost any chance she'd ever had of him returning to her. Then suddenly, without warning, he spun round and swung her into his arms.

'My bedroom, you remember where it is?'

'I remember leaving my suitcase there the day after we married, and picking it up later.'

'This time you'll stay?'

'Only for a while, Jenny,' he breathed as he kissed her neck. 'It can only be for a while.'

'You've done all the banking?'

'I put every night's takings in the night safe, as soon as I've locked the kiosk.'

'My sister said you'd been up to see her. You've even persuaded my father to move into the parlour.'

'My uncle's carried his bed in there. Being able to close the door on his sickroom is easier for Myrtle. It gives her a little time to herself.'

'I don't know how you did it. Myrtle and I have been trying to get him to move out of that middle room for years.'

'I told him the draught from the doors constantly opening and closing was affecting his arthritis.'

'I wish I'd thought of that.'

'The shop's doing well, and now that rationing's settled down we seem to have hit roughly the same level of trade every week. Myrtle said the takings aren't far off what they were before the war.'

'The fruiterers paying the rent on the shop in High Street?'

Diana swallowed hard and forced herself to look at him.

'Is there a problem?'

'They never moved in there, but I saw the agent this morning. He's doing his best to let it.'

'I bet he is.'

'It's a difficult time, Wyn. With most of the men being away, trade is down . . .'

'You don't have to remind me.'

'I'm sorry.'

'I most probably would have been with them by now.' His mouth settled into a grim line.

'Are you in much pain?' she asked gently – too gently.

'As the doctor says, it's something I'll have to learn to put up with,' he snapped.

'I'm sorry – '

'For pity's sake stop saying sorry! What do you have to be sorry about?'

'If I had seen that car, you wouldn't have jumped in its path to push me out of the way, and then none of this would have happened.'

'If it's anyone's fault it's Anthea Llewellyn-Jones's and Dai Station's,' he said, softening his tone a little. 'And please stop crying. You know how I hate to see you cry.'

She opened her handbag and rummaged in its depths for a handkerchief.

'Here,' he pulled open the door of his locker and extracted one of the freshly laundered handkerchiefs Myrtle had brought in the last time she'd visited. 'I've never known you to have a handkerchief at any crisis point in your life.'

'As soon as you leave here, I'll look for another job.'

'Why?' he demanded furiously.

'Because there's only one shop now. You can manage that on your own, you won't need me.'

'Take a good look, Diana. I can't even walk to the bathroom unaided. Haven't you noticed I'm a cripple now?'

'I saw Dr John, he says you'll soon be up and about.'

'On crutches. For pity's sake how do you think I'm going to run a shop when I can't even stand like a man?'

'You won't be on crutches for ever.'

'Oh yes, I forgot, the great aim is a stick, isn't it? If you think I'm going to serve behind a counter – '

'Why shouldn't you serve behind a counter?' she interrupted, finally beginning to lose patience with him.

'I was going to say "only to have every customer point at me and regard me as a freak" if you'd let me finish.'

'You served behind a counter often enough before.'

'I wasn't a cripple before.'

'So you're going to allow this accident to ruin your life?'

'There's no "allow" about it. It has.'

A nurse came to the door and he realised he'd been shouting.

'Can I get you anything, Mr Rees?'

He shook his head. 'I'm fine, thank you,' he answered in a subdued voice.

'If you could keep it down. Some of the other patients are trying to sleep.' She gave Diana a hard look.

'I think it's time I went.' Diana rose and picked up her handbag.

'If you like I could get you a wheelchair so you could accompany your lady friend to the door, Mr Rees?'

He stared at the nurse as though she was insane.

'You did well in the chair earlier.'

'I'd rather not put on a display right now, if you don't mind.'

Diana looked despairingly at him, then walked slowly to the door. 'I'll see you again on Wednesday, Wyn.'

'If you bring the books in, I'll go through them.'

She gripped the door frame as a sudden giddy spell weakened her legs. Wyn either didn't see her reel, or chose to ignore it. As soon as she recovered she walked away, not knowing what else she could do or say. For the first time since she'd struck up a friendship with Wyn, he'd retreated into a shell she simply couldn't break through. Dr John

196

was wrong. If Wyn was going to make a recovery, it wouldn't be down to anything she did. Not while he chose to close her out of his life like this.

'That has to be the best ever.' Jenny ran her fingers through the thick mat of curling hair on Eddie's chest.

'Oh, I don't know – ' he leaned over the edge of the bed and rummaged through the pockets of his uniform until he found his cigarettes and matches – 'there have been one or two other occasions I can think of.'

'Eddie Powell!' She picked up a pillow and hit him on the head with it. Then she looked around. 'What's that smell?'

'Oh God, Auntie Megan's stew.' He shot out of bed and into the kitchen. Without stopping to switch on the light, he picked up the pan, dropping it almost immediately into the sink.

'You clown, you've burnt your hands, haven't you?' Without waiting for an answer Jenny turned on the tap, grabbed his hands and pushed them under the running water. 'There goes a week's meat ration,' she said as hissing water splashed back at them from the burning pan.

'I have some money. Knowing Ponty, there has to be a black market. I'll talk to the people in the slaughterhouse on Monday morning.'

'I wish we could go away, if only for a few days.' She clung to his naked back, running her hands down to his thighs.

'I have to report back on Tuesday night.'

'Eddie that gives us no time!'

'Forty-eight hours is normal, a pass like this, unheard of except in special circumstances.'

'But we're only just . . .'

'Getting to know one another?' He turned around and cupped her breasts with his wet hands. She stood there, trembling as his fingers roused her nipples while his eyes appraised every inch of her body. 'Don't you think I feel the same way?' He slid his hands downwards between her thighs.

'I hate this war.' She pressed herself against him, kissing the back of his neck so he couldn't read the unspoken question in her eyes. 'What did you want to go and join up for?'

'There's a lot will agree with you on that. But if we go back to bed for ten minutes I'll guarantee you'll forget about the war.'

'Promise?' She stepped towards the door and switched off the light.

'Why don't you come and see?'

★

Dr John led Diana to a chair in the foyer of the hospital and made her sit down while he fetched his car.

'Are you feeling ill?' he asked, as he helped her down the steps, 'or was it just the hard time our patient gave you?'

'You were listening?'

'The whole ward was. You know I'm not sure you gave yourself a chance to get over that concussion. A bang on the head can be quite a serious thing and my wife said you were back in the shop within three days of the accident.'

'Someone had to run Wyn's business.'

'Better the place stay closed than you risk your health.' He squinted at her through the darkness as he started the engine. 'You haven't been getting any headaches? Seeing flashes of lights that aren't there?'

'No.'

'Nausea?'

'I have been feeling sick lately,' she admitted.

'Just sick? No headaches?' he repeated.

'No headaches.'

'If you don't feel better soon, come and see me or Dr Evans in the surgery.'

'I will, but it's probably just running the shop for Wyn. I open it first thing in the morning and it has to be kept open until the interval in the second house of the cinema. By the time I get home it seems too late for tea.'

'I'm not surprised, eating late at night is no good to you. Stays on the stomach and gives you nightmares. Can't you get Myrtle Rees to take over to give you a meal break?'

'I don't like to bother her. She has Wyn's father to look after.'

'An hour out of the house would do her good, and it certainly wouldn't harm Mr Rees. Do you want me to ask her for you?'

'No, there's no need, thank you, Dr John. I'll ask her myself.'

'Be sure you do, because I'll be seeing her some time this week, and if you haven't talked to her, I will. The last thing that boy in there needs is to start worrying about how he's going to replace you if you fall ill.'

The only light in the bedroom was the glow of Eddie's cigarette as it arced from his mouth to the ashtray on the floor. Jenny was asleep, her head on his shoulder, her arm tightly wrapped around his waist. Her naked body was warm, comforting and sensuous against his bare skin, but he couldn't help thinking that nothing had changed. The sex between them had been bloody marvellous, it always had been. When it came to lovemaking Jenny always had been game for anything. He'd met French whores who were more inhibited. But then, there'd never been any shortage of girls willing to take their clothes off for him. He wanted more, much much more from his wife.

Physically he knew Jenny: every curve of her body, the feel of her skin, the scent of her hair, the lilt in her voice, the way she smiled – in fact everything about her except her thoughts. Some of her letters had been too gushing, too glib as though she'd copied them from a book. He'd even dreamt up a title: 'Letters to cheer a serving soldier'. The problem was he wanted to believe what she had written, that she *was* missing him, that she **did** love him, that there was a wonderful life waiting for them at the end of the war.

He felt for the packet of cigarettes on the bedside table and tipped them forward. Extracting one, he lit it one handed on the dog-end that still burned in his mouth. Exchanging them, he stubbed the spent cigarette in the ashtray and continued to smoke blindly, mechanically without enjoyment.

Two more days, and nights. Tuesday would be taken up with travelling back. Tomorrow he wanted to see his sister Bethan, and he'd promised William that he'd look up Tina and give her a letter from him, one that hadn't been read by a censor. And he had to talk to his father and pretend that everything was fine, even when it wasn't. His father had enough problems without worrying about him.

He'd been such a fool. Far better to have kept on courting Jenny. But his father had been right: blinded by lust and her sweet, willing body he couldn't wait to marry her – God knows why when she was already sleeping with him. What was that saying Mrs Richards was so fond of? 'Marry in haste, repent at leisure.' Well, repenting was certainly what he was doing now. And three days was nowhere near long enough to put the whole world to rights.

'Can't you sleep, Eddie?'

'I feel as though I'm still travelling.'

'What's France like?'

'Flat.'

'No mountains at all?'

'Not where we are. You can stand in a field and see for miles, rivers, trees, houses . . .'

'I'd like to see it.'

'Perhaps you will when the war is over.'

'Are the French girls as exciting as everyone says they are?' Her fingers moved lightly downwards from his chest, teasing, tickling, tantalising.

'We don't see many.'

'Everyone says they flock around the British boys.'

'Perhaps I just don't look,' he lied.

'I know you. The day won't dawn when you stop looking.'

'Or you. There's enough men left in Ponty. And there'll soon be more now they've started using conscripts in the mines.'

'There's only one man for me.'

'Is there?'

She wished she could shout back at him, 'How can you say that?' but the past lay too heavily between them. Would it always be there? Would she end up with the same kind of silent, sterile marriage as her parents? 'Eddie, if there's any way to prove to you how much I love you, just tell me and I'll do it. Anything you want.'

Squashing out his cigarette he turned and grabbed her head between his hands. Lowering his face to hers he kissed her. It was easier to make love to Jenny than try and talk to her, particularly when they had so little time left.

It was just getting light when Luke, dressed in the Sunday suit he had bought for ten shillings on the second-hand stall in the market, sneaked out of the house and walked to the end of Graig Avenue. He could see a small pale figure standing at the beginning of the mountain path at the end of the terrace. Gina, dressed in her Sunday-best outfit of grey coat and hat.

'You made it?'

'You thought I wouldn't get up?'

'You have to get up early every other day of the week. Most people like a lie-in on Sundays. Where does everyone think you are?'

'I told them I was going for a walk.'

'Then Alexander will think you're seeing me?'

'What if he does?'

'I don't mind Alexander knowing, as long as it doesn't get back to my father.' She set off down the rough track that led over to Treforest. 'Papa wouldn't approve of my being so friendly with a boy at my age. I tried telling him and Mama that I'm grown up now, but they wouldn't listen. It's so unfair. Particularly when I consider that Mama was *married* at my age, and Maud Powell was only sixteen when she married my older brother Ronnie.'

'I think sixteen is old enough to know what you want from life.'

'You agree with me?'

He slipped his hand shyly into hers.

'I can feel the calluses on your hands through my gloves.'

'I'm sorry.'

'What's to be sorry about. It's real work, man's work. You should be proud of them.' She grabbed his arm. Since the first night they'd met and he'd taken her home after Wyn's accident, he'd walked her home every night; but the presence of her sister coupled with his shyness had kept him from doing more than holding her hand. He longed to kiss her, even at this unearthly hour of the morning, but uncertain how she'd react, he held back.

'You could come to mass with me,' Gina suggested.

'I don't think so,' he murmured hesitantly.

'Your father wouldn't like it?'

'From what little I know, I think your religion is at the opposite end of the spectrum to mine.'

'Quakers believe in God, don't they?'

'Of course.'

'And the saints?'

'Not to worship.'

'We don't really worship them. But as they're in heaven and closer to God than us, we light candles under their images when we want them to intercede for us.'

'Intercede?' He looked at her blankly.

'We ask for their help when we want something.'

'And what do you want?'

'The war to end, so my brothers will come home and take over the cafés again so Tina and I can have the occasional night off.' She looked up at him and smiled, 'and the usual things every girl wants. A home, husband, children.'

'This husband of yours? You have anyone in mind?'

'Yes.'

'I see.'

She stood in front of him. The sky had lightened to a cold grey, casting her in a silvery glow. He had never seen her looking so beautiful, or so remote. Standing on her toes she put her arms around his neck and kissed him, hurriedly and inexpertly. By the time he'd plucked up courage to put his arms around her, she had walked on. 'That's the first time I've ever kissed anyone.'

'Me too,' he confessed.

'Have you had breakfast?'

'No.'

'Me neither. You're not supposed to eat before mass. I could mitch off for once and cook us both breakfast in the café in High Street. Papa doesn't open it on Sunday mornings.'

'Won't that get you into terrible trouble?'

'Only if Papa finds out. You're not going to tell him, are you?'

He shook his head.

'Come on then. We can cut down here to Graig Street. Just duck if you see Laura looking out through her window. Not that she'd tell on me, but she wouldn't half give me a lecture.'

Tina finished serving breakfast to a crew from the railway station in the Tumble café and returned to the counter. Trade hadn't diminished since the advent of the war, but the amount the customers were prepared to spend had. Times were still hard, and more people called in for tea and biscuits and tea and bread and butter than cooked meals or breakfast. So much so, she was beginning to wonder if it was worth paying a cook's wages every day. It had been different when Angelo had been doing the cooking. Family never took a full wage out of the business.

Business? She was actually thinking about business for the first time in her life. And she'd shouted at the staff in the Taff Street place she'd taken over from Laura. If she wasn't careful she'd end up grumpy and miserable like Tony and Ronnie, and then no one would go near her.

Looking around to check no one needed her, or was likely to for a few minutes, she opened her handbag and slid out a bundle of letters tied in blue ribbon. Every one that Will had sent her since he had left. Twenty-eight days, and twenty-eight envelopes. She opened the one at the top of the pile, the one that had come second post yesterday. Hopefully there would be another waiting for her when she got home after midday mass.

She glanced up at the clock. Another two hours before she could reasonably expect Gina to take over from her. Opening the envelope she spread the letter on the counter and began to read.

Dear Tina,

Not my dear Tina, or Darling Tina! She always wrote 'my dear William' or 'Darling' hoping he'd take the hint, but he hadn't so far.

I am well, I hope you are well.

He might have been writing to a maiden aunt.

As I wrote yesterday they are keeping us very busy. Nothing but square bashing and drills, so we will probably all be half the size we were, and worn out by the time they finish with us.

Not much has happened to write about. Tony perseveres with the cook. As I wrote to you, we play cards with him nearly every night, and he has lost so much money to us he's paying us in kind. Last night it was three bacon sandwiches. The bacon was destined for the officers' mess, so it was really good. We are hoping to have a pass to go into the nearest town this weekend. Angelo is trying to find himself a girl, although Tony and I have warned him no girl is going to look twice at him. You should see him in his short back and sides military haircut. And he hasn't learnt to wear his uniform properly, but at least he has learnt to polish his buttons without getting polish all over his tunic. Two weeks to go and we should get embarkation leave. I must go now, there's another card game starting and Tony and Angelo (and me) are hoping for more sandwiches.

Best wishes
William

'Miss! Miss!'

She looked up from the page.

'Any chance of two teas and two slices of bread pudding?'

'Milk and sugar in the teas?' she asked.

'Yes, please.'

She set about serving the man and his wife, all the while thinking of William and the letters he wrote. How could a man kiss a woman the way he had her before he'd left, and then write a letter so totally bereft of emotion?

She carried the teas and the thick glutinous slices of pudding to the table and returned to the counter. Folding the letter she stuffed it back into the envelope. Not even a cross at the foot of the page to denote a kiss. Not a single mention of love from beginning to end. Where did that leave her? Or him? Had he taken up with a camp follower? Was it only Angelo and Tony who were out looking for girls? Or had he joined them? Only four weeks ago they'd got engaged and it already felt like four years since she'd seen him.

'Breakfast?'

Eddie, who'd only fallen asleep as dawn broke, opened one eye to see Jenny, still in her nightdress, standing next to the bed with a tray in her hands.

'I've raided the shop. There's eggs, toast, sausages – tinned, I'm afraid – and jam. And tea of course.'

'Thank you.' He struggled to sit up. The bedclothes fell back, and a cold draught blew across his shoulders.

'If you clear the clock away I'll put the tray down on the bedside table, and get back into bed.'

He did as she asked, conscious that when she climbed in beside him she left her nightdress on.

'Here put the tray between us, and I'll feed you.'

'No one's done that since I was a baby,' he laughed.

'Open your mouth.' She spooned egg into it. 'Good?'

'Not bad.'

'Do you realise this is the first time I've cooked for you?'

'I hope I survive the experience.'

'I'm a good cook,' she informed him gravely.

'Let's hope we have the time one day for you to prove it to me.'

'It is going to be all right between us from now on, isn't it, Eddie?'

'Do you want it to be all right because I'm all you've got left?' he asked, looking into her eyes.

'You mean because my mother's dead and my father's . . .'

'Ill,' he said for her. He saw the pain in her eyes, but some devil in him prompted him to press her. 'What happens when I go back?'

'I'll run the shop, write to you, hoping I'll get an answer. Wait for you to get leave, and . . .'

'Go out once in a while to meet people?'

'Hope that I have a baby to keep me in at nights.'

'A baby!'

'You don't want children?'

'Now doesn't seem a good time to have them. Not with a war on.'

'There's never been a good time to have a baby.'

'I'd like to wait until I'm in a steady job and we have our own place.'

'This is our place. My father always said he'd leave it to me. And if they do let him out next year, he's not going to be able to run the shop and look after himself, so he's going to have to live with us. You don't mind, do you?'

'At the moment I have nothing to mind about.'

'You'd better eat that before it gets cold.' She sat up and tugged her nightdress over her head, pulling the sheet up so it covered her breasts. 'Ever since you joined up I've dreamed of your first leave, but I never imagined it quite like this.'

'How was it different?' he asked, buttering a piece of toast and loading it with egg before pushing it into his mouth.

'You were different. More trusting, more loving I suppose. I should have known I didn't deserve it. Not after the way I treated you.'

'Jenny . . .'

'No, please let me finish. I've seen what bottling things up can do to a marriage. I'd rather have everything out in the open now, even if it means losing you, than go on the way I was, not knowing one way or another. I was a fool, Eddie. I fell in love with Haydn when I was thirteen, and carried on being in love, not with him, but the idea of him. Then there was you, and one thing you *have* to believe – no one, and I mean *no one*, not even Haydn ever made me feel the way you do. You're the only man I've ever made love to, the only man I want in my bed. Eddie, how much plainer can I make it?' Her blue eyes blazed in anger. She looked as though she were about to hit him.

'I don't think I've ever seen you like this before.'

'How?'

'Angry. It suits you.'

'Damn you, Eddie, do you have to joke about everything?'

He scooped more egg on to his toast.

'Eddie, either you tell me what you're thinking or get out of my bed this minute.'

He looked up at her, realising that she was deadly serious. 'Then you do love me?'

'I've been trying to tell you that one way or another since you left. The question is, do you love me?'

He picked up the tray and returned it to the bedside table.

'Aren't you going to say anything?'

'I'll go along with that.'

'What?'

'What you just said.'

'I asked if you loved me?'

'Something like that.'

'Eddie . . . say it. Just this once, please say it?'

Grabbing her, he kissed her.

'You taste of tea, cigarettes and egg,' she gasped when he allowed her to come up for air.

'And you taste of toothpaste and smell of Pear's soap.'

'You still haven't said it.'

'I love you, Mrs Powell. Just don't expect me to say it all that often.'

'Just once a day for the rest of our lives.'

'I won't be here.'

'You can write.'

'Not that. Not with the officers reading every bloody word when they censor my letters.' He tossed the bedclothes aside and leaned on his arm looking down at her.

'We can work out a code.'

'Like?'

'Just two words, for ever?'

'For ever.' He gazed into her eyes as he caressed her. For the first time in his married life he was about to make love not sex with his wife. And at that moment that was just how long he wanted his marriage to last – for ever.

Chapter Sixteen

'LEAVE the blinds,' Gina ordered as Luke stepped behind her into the café. 'Let's go and see what's in the kitchen.'

'Won't your father miss the food?' Luke asked nervously, afraid of being found out. He could imagine his own father's reaction if he'd discovered that one of his sisters had sneaked off to be alone with a boy, and he felt that the Papa Ronconi of formidable reputation and legendary temper would have every right to be just as furious.

'Papa doesn't know what's here from one day to the next. Oh fantastic, there's eggs. Thank goodness for all the people who keep chickens on the Graig, and there's bread. It's a bit hard but I can toast it. How does fried eggs on toast sound to you?'

'Wonderful if you're sure the eggs won't be missed.'

'Tea, coffee or hot chocolate?'

'I've never tried coffee or hot chocolate.'

'It's time you did. Come and talk to me while I cook.'

He followed her into the kitchen. She slipped a white overall over her clothes and began by breaking eggs into a bowl. A frying pan was already smoking lightly on the gas as a lump of lard dissolved over the heat.

'Can I do anything?'

'Slice the bread if you like. You do know how?'

'My mother taught us all to cook, boys as well as girls. She said it might come in useful if no one wanted to marry us.'

'Wise woman.' Gina tipped the eggs into the pan. 'This is more fun than mass.'

'I haven't been to a meeting since I came here. I don't even know if there is a Quaker meeting house in Pontypridd.'

'We'll have time to make up for our sins of omission when we're old and grey.' She took the bread and pushed it under the grill.

He summoned all his courage. 'Together?' he ventured uncertainly.

'Of course.'

'I love you, Gina,' he blurted out clumsily.

'I know,' she assured him blithely. 'I knew it the first moment I saw you.'

'And you?'

'Can't have you getting big-headed, now can I?'

'That was a good dinner, Diana.' Evan took his pipe and sank back into his chair. Brian, still clutching the tin car Eddie had given him, climbed on to his lap and reached for a picture book on the window-sill. He opened it out and looked expectantly to his father.

'No peace for the wicked,' Phyllis smiled as Evan turned to the first page.

'I agree with Dad, that wasn't bad, Di,' Eddie complimented her as he pushed his chair away from the table.

'Not bad? I'd like to see you do better,' she retorted.

'It's almost like the old days with you two arguing.' Bethan handed Rachel to Megan so she could help Phyllis and Diana with the dishes.

'Thank you for the meal, Mrs Powell. If you'll excuse me I think I'll go for a walk down town.'

'To the café?' Diana teased.

A deep blush spread over Luke's cheek. He wondered if Diana had seen him and Gina leave the High Street café. Not that they'd done anything wrong. He hadn't attempted to kiss Gina and she hadn't kissed him again after that once on the mountain, but he still felt guilty, sensing that he'd done something Mr Ronconi would have every right to be furious about.

'If you hang on, Jenny and I will walk down with you.'

'I thought you two would be a bit past courting in the café.' Diana stacked the plates and carried them through to the wash-house.

'I have a letter for Tina.'

'I'll give it to her,' Alexander offered.

'No, it's all right, the park's open until dark.' Eddie winked at Jenny. 'We thought we might do a spot of remembering.'

Evan pretended he hadn't heard, but he didn't fool Bethan. She could see the smile hovering at the corners of his mouth. She only hoped that her father's faith in Eddie was justified. Haydn might be the one on stage, but both her brothers had proved themselves consummate actors in the past.

'Why don't you come to the café, Diana?' Alexander said persuasively. Diana had walked down the hill with them, but not to visit the café. She had promised to call in on Wyn's sister, and intended to do just that.

'Come on, Di, I've hardly seen you since I've been back, and I'm leaving the day after tomorrow.' Eddie added his voice to Alexander's.

'Just one coffee,' she capitulated, 'then I really must visit Myrtle.'

'How is Wyn?'

'Not very good. He's finding it difficult to come to terms with his injuries, but I think he's even more devastated at not being able to join the army.'

'Tell him he's not missing much. The army's not all it's cracked up to be.' Eddie pushed open the door.

'Eddie!' Tina ran from behind the counter and kissed him on the cheek. 'I heard you were home, but I didn't think you'd have time to call in here,' she said with a sly glance at Jenny.

'William would have shot me if I hadn't.'

'You've seen Will? But I thought you were in France?'

'I was, but I came home via the base camp. Here.' He produced a letter from his tunic pocket and handed it to her.

'That's the last we'll see of her for an hour,' Gina complained as Tina disappeared into the kitchen.

'I'll give you a hand.' Luke went behind the counter as though he worked there every night.

'It's easy to see what you two have been doing since you've come to Pontypridd,' Eddie commented as he watched Gina squeeze Luke's hand. He eyed Alexander, waiting to see if he'd follow Tina into the back, but he stood in front of the counter and put his hand in his pocket.

'Coffee all round?'

'Just one, then Jenny and I have to go.'

A man lurched out of the back room. Staggering to the counter he elbowed Alexander aside. Diana turned pale and Eddie gave the drunk a hard look, recognising Dai Station.

'I want to pay,' Dai slurred, swaying on his feet.

'Be with you in a moment,' Gina answered as she continued pouring out coffees.

'I said I want to pay,' he shouted contentiously.

'I'll be with you right away, sir.' Gina left the coffees to Luke and went to the till.

Eddie had been watching Luke, but to his amazement it was Alexander who stepped in front of Dai.

'May I suggest you pay your bill, and leave quietly, sir?' Alexander asked politely.

'Bloody conchie, I don't have to ask what you're doing here with these bloody foreigners. Mussolini arse-lickers . . .'

'Less of your language, you're in mixed company,' Eddie warned, pushing Jenny behind him as he walked to the counter.

'That will be two and threepence please, sir,' Gina murmured nervously as she opened the till.

'Bloody people like you should pay us Welsh to come in your cafés.' Dai lurched towards the till, fingers spread as though he intended to scoop the coins out of the cash drawers. Alexander held him back just as Eddie drew alongside them.

'Shut the till and go into the kitchen, Gina,' Alexander ordered softly.

'What's going on?' Tina was standing in the kitchen doorway trying to sound braver than she felt.

'And who do you think you are? Bloody . . .'

'I've told you once. Gentlemen don't swear in front of ladies.'

Dai turned to Eddie, seeing his uniform for the first time. 'You're a soldier?'

'That's right.'

'You shouldn't be in here. These people are foreigners. You could give away secrets,' he mumbled.

'These people are as Welsh as you and me, Dai,' he replied with a coolness that amazed Diana and Jenny. Hot-headed, angry with the world Eddie had finally learned to keep his temper in check.

'They're not!' Dai protested.

'I promise you they are, and I'll tell you something else, I think you've had a skinful. Now why don't you go home and sleep it off before a copper runs you in.'

'You can't tell my mate what to do just because you're wearing a bloody uniform.'

Three porters from the station were standing in the archway that separated the front of the café from the back.

'Just giving him some advice.'

'Doesn't sound like it to me,' one of them said belligerently.

'No one wants any trouble,' Eddie replied.

'Then why don't these buggers go back where they belong? They're not wanted here.'

'You don't like the café, you stay away,' Tina intervened forcefully.

'You've no right to be here, taking money out of honest Welsh people's pockets.' Without warning Dai swept his arm across the counter, knocking over the four-tiered glass case that held the cakes. It shattered, sending glass splinters showering across the floor. Women screamed as they jumped up and ran from their tables, adding to the general confusion.

Eddie grabbed Dai. Pinning his arms behind his back he held him face down over the nearest table.

'No one, soldier or not, does that to my mate.' One of the porters swung a punch at Eddie that Alexander intercepted. Diana ran to the door, opened it and shouted 'Police!' She turned in time to take the full force of a blow that one of the men had intended to plant on Alexander, who'd ducked to avoid it.

Until then Eddie had kept his temper under control. By the time Huw Davies had run up from the Criterion doorway where he'd been talking to the minister of Penuel chapel, Eddie had knocked out the porter who'd hit Diana. Realising he was no longer restrained, Dai Station picked up a chair and smashed it against the wall. Wielding a broken leg like a club, he turned on Eddie. Diving forward, Luke picked up another chair and pinned Dai to the wall with the legs.

'Lion tamer act?' Huw asked Luke after he'd blown his whistle to summon assistance.

'For Christ's sake they're only bleeding, bloody Eyeties . . .' Dai mumbled, his voice slowing like a gramophone in need of rewinding.

Huw looked from Dai to the two men Eddie had cornered, and the one laid out cold on the floor. His experienced eye missed nothing: the broken glass and squashed cakes littering the café, the wrecked furniture, the bruise spreading darkly across Diana's cheek. Pulling out his notebook he began to write slowly and ponderously, detailing the charges as he inscribed them.

'Criminal damage . . . drunk and disorderly . . . swearing . . . blaspheming – and on the Sabbath, tut tut,' he shook his head as he looked at Dai before continuing: 'conduct likely to cause a breach of the peace . . . assaulting an innocent bystander . . .' he studied Diana who was sitting in a chair being tended to by Tina and Jenny. 'Are you going to have a shiner tomorrow, sunshine! Call out Dr John,' he directed one of the younger constables who appeared in the doorway.

'There's no need. I'll be fine,' Diana protested.

'Routine, love. That injury is evidence. Trouble seems to follow you, Eddie. You haven't been home twenty-four hours and look what you've got yourself into.'

'It was all Dai Station's doing,' Gina said warmly. 'He wouldn't pay his bill and he made a grab for the till when it was open. Then he smashed the cake case.'

'Attempted theft . . .' Huw continued scribbling. 'Boy, we're going to throw the book at you, Dai, and toss away the key.'

'Has this sort of thing happened before?' Eddie asked after Huw and two other constables had loaded the drunks into the Black Maria and Dr John had come and gone.

'Insults because we're Italians?' Tina asked as she saw the last customer out of the café and locked the door.

'There's been a bit of trouble,' Alexander admitted.

'So that's why you and Luke come down here so often?'

'Luke has his own reasons.' Alexander swept the last of the broken glass into a dustpan Luke was holding for him.

'You're handy with your fists. Glad you were on my side.'

'A public school education has some advantages.'

'Perhaps you and I should have a match some time.'

'Eddie was on the point of becoming a professional boxer before the war,' Jenny said proudly.

'You all right, Di?' Eddie asked, concerned at the swelling that was still rising on Diana's cheek despite the ice-cream poultice Dr John had suggested.

'You heard the doctor. It's just bruised. I'll be fine tomorrow.'

'I'll walk you home.'

'No, I really must see Myrtle. She's expecting me, and –' she glanced up at the clock – 'she's going to be wondering where I've got to.'

'Then I'll walk you over there.'

'No really. You and Jenny have so little time, and I'm perfectly capable of walking through town on my own.'

'Not after what's just happened.'

'I'll take Diana to the Rees's, wait for her and walk her home afterwards,' Alexander offered.

'That's silly,' Diana complained. 'I'd much rather go by myself.'

'And we'd rather you didn't,' Eddie insisted.

'But Dai and the others are locked up.'

'They might have been drinking with others who aren't,' Alexander pointed out logically. He turned to Eddie. 'Do I have your permission to walk your cousin home?'

'It's her you should be asking,' Eddie answered without a glimmer of a smile.

'I don't need an escort.'

'You're not going without one.'

Eddie had a stubborn look on his face that Diana had seen before. She knew what it meant. Turning to Alexander, she said, 'I'm going. If you're intent on coming with me you'd better make a move.'

'Why didn't you tell me that anti-Italian feeling was running so high in the town?'

'I've been out so seldom since you left, I had no idea.' Jenny opened the door to the shop.

'It's tough on the girls.'

'I don't think Tony and Angelo thought of everything before they joined up.'

'I wouldn't like to be Dai Station if they get to hear about tonight. Do me a favour, keep an eye on things down there and write to me if anything happens.'

'What good would that do?'

'I'd know about it.'

'But none of you would be able to come back from France to punch the next one on the nose.'

'No, but we know some of the bruisers who train in the gym with Joey. A nod and a wink and they'd do some sorting out for us if we asked them, and then again, Alexander packs a good punch for a conchie. Perhaps it's just as well Dad took him in.'

'Both he and Luke seem very nice.'

'Fancy one of them, do you?'

'You know better than to ask that. Alexander's crache,' she put just the right amount of contempt into the Welsh expression, 'and Gina would kill the first girl who dared make a play for Luke.'

'Young love.' He followed her into the shop, watching as she closed the door and pulled the blackout.

'What would you like for supper?'

He grabbed her waist and pulled her close. 'Nothing that's on the shelves.'

'You should eat.'

'Later. What I have in mind is best done on an empty stomach.'

'I can't bear to think of you leaving the day after tomorrow.'

'Then don't.'

'On the other hand I really envy you being able to go away.'

'What, so they can drill me from morning till night? Having every NCO and officer treat me as though I'm worth less than the dirt beneath their feet? You've nothing to envy me for.'

'Being in France would be better than running the shop. I feel as though I'm contributing nothing towards the war effort stuck here, on the Graig.'

'And you think I am?'

'Come on, Eddie . . .'

'There's no come on about it. We spend all our time spit, polishing and square-bashing. It's so tedious, sometimes I feel like crying out of sheer bloody weariness and boredom.'

'You have free time.'

'Some, but to be honest the way things are now –' he stepped towards her and held her in his arms – 'I'd much rather spend it with you.'

'You're not just saying that?' Her eyes were dark, questioning.

'No, I'm not just saying that, but I do want to have my evil way with you.' He kissed her. 'Now let's go upstairs and I'll explain to you exactly what I have in mind for tea.'

'This Myrtle is Wyn Rees's sister?'

'Yes.'

'You've been seeing a lot of her since Wyn has been in hospital.'

'Someone had to keep the businesses running.'

'He's lucky to have an employee like you.'

'I'm lucky to have an employer like him.'

Diana led the way up the steps of Wyn's father's comfortable, semi-detached villa. Alexander stood back in the shadows as she rang the doorbell. He watched and waited in a corner of the hall while Myrtle fussed over the dark swelling on Diana's face, and the story of what had happened in the café was briefly recounted for Myrtle's benefit. Eventually, Diana managed to draw him into the conversation, introducing him as they walked towards the parlour door.

'Dad's been waiting to see you all afternoon, Diana. I've no idea what he's going to say to that face.' Myrtle dropped her voice as she put her hand on the doorknob.

'I'll tell him I walked into a wall. Mr Rees is ill,' Diana confided to Alexander.

Myrtle opened the door. 'Diana's here, Dad. She had an accident, that's why she's late.'

Diana went in and kissed the old man's sunken cheek.

'I'll go and lay an extra place for tea,' Myrtle said with a shy glance at Alexander.

'Please don't trouble yourself, Miss Rees,' Alexander smiled. 'I see a chess set, is there any chance of a game, sir?'

'Who are you, young man?' Wyn's father demanded suspiciously.

'Alexander lodges with us, Mr Rees,' Diana explained.

'Oh, the lodger. Well, as long as he hasn't got any designs on you. I don't know that Wyn would approve of you walking around town this late in the evening with another man, especially when he's in hospital and in no position to stop you.'

'Are you aware that the old man thinks you're going to marry Wyn?'

214

Alexander asked Diana when they left the house, after Diana had drunk three cups of tea with Myrtle, and Alexander had played two games of chess with Mr Rees.

'Wyn has asked me.'

'Then you really are going to marry him?'

'I don't think so,' Diana answered carelessly, not wanting to discuss her personal life with Alexander.

'I'm not quite sure whether I should say this but . . .'

'You've heard Wyn is a queer?'

'You know?'

'Of course I know, but that doesn't mean we can't be friends.'

'I agree. I have a lot of friends who prefer to lead the more avant-garde lifestyle.'

'I'm not sure I understand that.'

'What I mean is I have a lot of friends like Wyn.'

'Is that supposed to impress me?'

'Is it me, or are you always this spiky?'

'What's spiky?'

'Spiky means I can count the number of times I've seen you smile on one hand since I've got here. Are you worried about the accident and your boss? Because if you are, people have recovered from far worse than what he's going through, and the accident really wasn't your fault.'

'I wish everyone would stop telling me that.'

'It's the truth. I know, because I was there just after it happened, remember?'

'I'd prefer to forget all about that night if it's all the same to you.'

'Diana, I haven't known you long, but it doesn't take a genius to work out that something is troubling you. If there is anything I can do to help, you only have to ask, you do know that, don't you?'

'I don't need anything, thank you. All I want is for people to leave me be and stop asking a lot of stupid questions.' She quickened her pace; he followed, catching up with her in Market Square. He walked alongside her, neither attempting to sympathise nor to press her further. It was only when they reached the railway bridge and he heard what sounded like a sob, that he dared to speak again.

'You're obviously unhappy about something. Your family has been so kind to me since I arrived here, I really would consider it an honour to help.'

The sympathy was more than Diana could bear. She faced the tiled wall that gleamed palely even in the blackout, and broke down. He put his hands on her arms, and when she didn't brush him away he turned her round, pulling her face down on to his shoulder.

'It's nothing,' she mumbled into his jacket. 'Just the shock of having my face thumped when I've done nothing to deserve it.'

'I think it's more than that. Just look at what you've been doing since the accident. Running the shop, visiting Wyn in hospital, trying to support his sister. You're only human, Diana. Can't you see you're wearing yourself out, without trying to cope with whatever it is that's worrying you. You need to talk it over with someone. Can't your mother . . .'

She shook her head. 'Mam's not well. I can't burden her with my worries.'

'Then Tina? She's your best friend.'

'She's Tony's sister. I can't talk to her.' It was only after she'd spoken that she realised what she had said. But Alexander was too tactful to probe.

'How about your cousin Bethan? She's a sensible lady.'

'She's got enough on her hands, looking after Rachel with Andrew away.'

'I think you're assuming that because your family all have problems of their own, they can't spare any time for yours.'

'I'll sort myself out.' Regaining her self-control she extricated herself from his hold and carried on walking up the hill.

'I didn't mean to interfere.'

'I know you're only trying to be kind, and I'm being horrible to you.'

'That doesn't matter, I'm only here for the duration.'

'I wish I was.'

'You want to leave Pontypridd?'

'I want to go away and come back new and clean.'

'In my experience no matter how far you run, you take your troubles with you. Look at me. I'm as reviled for being a conscientious objector in Wales as I was in England. In fact my problems have doubled. Here, I have a whole new way of life to contend with. I'm doing much harder work than I've ever done before, for longer hours and less wages and with fewer friends around to console me on my lot. So if anything, I've fallen right out of the frying pan into the fire.'

'But you're still a decent, honest and truthful person.'

'You flatter me.'

'If everyone knew what I was really like, no one would come near me.'

'That's nonsense.'

'You don't know me.'

'I think I do. Here,' he handed her a handkerchief as she wiped her eyes with the back of her gloves.

'I'm sorry, I'm being stupid. Wyn told me he's never known me to have a handkerchief when I've needed one.'

'That's hardly a sin. Look up there,' he pointed to the sky as they rounded Vicarage corner. 'The night sky was never this beautiful in the city. There was always too much glow from the lights, and the air here is fresher, cleaner . . .'

'Even with the coal dust?'

'Even with the coal dust,' he echoed with a certain amount of irony. 'Do you know the constellations?'

'Only the obvious ones like the Great Bear. William got a book out of the library when we were small, and we hung out of the bedroom window to try to spot them until Mam caught us and sent us back to bed.'

'I think I'll walk over the mountain a little way and look at what's in the sky tonight. Want to come?'

'Anything to delay Mam seeing my face.' She followed him to the end of the street. 'Do you have any brothers or sisters?'

'I'm an only child.'

'You must have parents.'

'They're getting on a bit, but yes I do have parents.'

'A girlfriend?'

'Not really. I suppose you could say I've had the Communist Party, and more of a political than a social life.'

'A political party doesn't sound much of a substitute for family life to me.'

'Are you saying you don't understand how someone of an advanced age like myself can remain unmarried?'

'How old are you?'

'Thirty.'

'That seems old to me.'

'That's because you're a child.'

'A child, at eighteen?'

'You are to me.' He looked at her and smiled. Silvered by the cold light of the moon and stars, she looked very young and very charming. 'I'd give my eye teeth to be your age again. On the brink of life, everything before you, that's why I can't understand why you're considering marrying a man like Wyn.'

'I didn't say I was considering it, only that he asked.'

'Fellows will soon be queuing up to ask. That's if they aren't already.'

'No they won't,' she burst out bitterly. 'I'm not fit to be anyone's wife.'

'What nonsense. Who on earth told you that?'

'I was raped.' She was so angry she no longer gave a thought as to what she was saying, or who she was saying it to. 'Do you understand, raped? I'm soiled goods. Used, dirty, good for nothing. No decent man will want me near him once he finds out.'

'Is that what this is all about?' he asked. 'Tina's brother raped you?'

Realising what she'd done, she fell silent for a moment, then it all came out. Ben Springer, the incident in the shoe shop, Tony's reaction when she told him about it, but not the circumstances of the telling – that was one thing she kept to herself.

'. . . so you see,' she said finally, 'I may as well give up now. I have nothing to look forward to. I'll never have a husband or a family of my own.' She turned away from him and looked back at the silhouette of the mountain, dark against the deep blue velvet of the spring night sky. 'I shouldn't have told you this.'

'I won't tell anyone about it, if that's what you're afraid of.'

'Thank you. And I'll understand if you don't want to be seen with me again.'

Taking her face into his hands, he bent his head and kissed her lightly on the forehead. 'And that's not the kind of kiss you have to slap my face for.'

'Then why?'

'Because you've had a foul time, because no girl should be sinned against as you were. You couldn't help what Ben Springer did to you.'

'I should have fought harder.'

'Like you should have had some kind of sixth sense that told you when that van was coming down the hill, although even Wyn didn't see it until it was virtually on top of you?'

'People make their own destinies.'

'I'll agree with you to a point. But there's no way a slip of a girl like you can fight a brute of a man intent on rape. Diana, forget it. You're still the same person you always were. It means absolutely nothing.'

'Would you marry a girl who'd been raped?'

'You asking? . . . Sorry, bad joke. But then I'd be lucky to find a girl who'd forgive me my sins.'

'Why, what have you done?'

'Made love with half the female members of the Communist Party cell when I joined.'

'It's different for men.'

'The Communist doctrine preaches equality in all things between the sexes. Sometimes I think the main attraction when I joined was the free love precept. I was young, in university and it all seemed very glamorous and exciting. Different girl, different bed every night, then after a while it became drink sodden and sordid. I learned then it's not sex but the person you make love to who's important.'

'But I lay a pound to a penny that when you finally do get married you'll want a virgin.'

'Now that's an overrated commodity.'

'You can't be serious?'

'I've just told you I've slept with dozens of women. What right have I, or any other man who has had more than one woman in his bed, to demand a guaranteed, chaste wife who's been locked away from men until her marriage night? That attitude belongs to Turks and harems, not the 1940s.'

'I never thought I'd hear a man say that.'

'Is that why you were considering marrying Wyn? Because he wouldn't expect you to sleep with him?'

'He knows about Ben Springer and it doesn't seem to matter to him. He cares for me, we're friends.'

'There's a lot more to a relationship between a man and a woman than friendship.'

'Like pain, humiliation and misery?'

'One day you'll find someone who'll prove to you that it doesn't have to be that way.'

'I wish I could believe you.'

'I wish you'd let me take you out to dinner in the New Inn so we could talk about it some more.'

'I think it's late and we should be getting back.'

'We haven't looked at the stars yet.'

'There'll be other nights.'

'They could be cloudy.'

'Not all of them.'

'There's a war on, we should grab what we can, while we can.'

'Now where have I heard that before?' She turned back towards the houses.

'A bad Hollywood film.' He wished he could see her face more clearly. Troubled, beset by problems that were enough to threaten any woman's stability, she had touched him in a way no woman had done in a long time. Even the ones who had shared his bed. Perhaps she was right. Perhaps friendship was the most important thing in a relationship between a man and a woman. And perhaps he should begin by cultivating a friendship with her.

Chapter Seventeen

THE best thing about being a member of a large family was having brothers and sisters to conspire with. Which was how Tina managed to keep the unpleasant incident in the Tumble Street café from her parents that night; the worst thing about living in a crowded house was the complete lack of privacy.

Making the excuse that she needed an early night, Tina left the kitchen soon after arriving home and searched for a quiet corner where she could read William's latest letter in peace. The parlour as well as being out of bounds except on what her brothers referred to as 'state occasions' was freezing cold, and her father had commandeered the middle room, which was only marginally warmer than the parlour, to do the business accounts. There was nothing for it except to climb the stairs, but instead of going to the bedroom she shared with her four sisters, she stole along the passage and shut herself into the tiny box room that had belonged to Ronnie and later Tony. Neither twelve-year-old Alfredo nor nine-year-old Roberto had thought to stake a claim on the room as yet, and as she looked at the single bed, chest of drawers, narrow wardrobe and two square feet of bare linoleum around the door, the only clear floor space, she was sorely tempted to make a bid for it herself. Sharing a room with four sisters was enough to try the patience of a saint, and she was growing more demon-like with every day she ran the restaurant.

Sitting on the bed she pulled down the blackout, switched on the rickety lamp Ronnie had made from a wine bottle and removed the promisingly fat wad of writing paper from the envelope Eddie had given her.

Although she had read the first page before the fight in the café had disturbed her, she began to read it again from the very beginning, lingering over and cherishing every precious word.

My darling Tina,
Eddie has just come into camp on his way home on special leave. He has gone to the canteen with Tony and Angelo, but I have decided to skip

supper and stay here to write to you, because for once, my love, I will be able to send you a letter that hasn't been censored.

Can you imagine what it's like to know that every time I write to you, an officer is going to read what should be my most private thoughts and our secrets? Besides which, I don't want to give the miserable, unimaginative, peanut-brained idiots any tips on how to romance girls. No self-respecting female, no matter how desperate, would go near one of our officers, she'd find more excitement in a nunnery. Funny, telling you exactly what I think of the clowns in charge of us wasn't nearly as much fun as I thought it would be.

I am sorry, my darling, if my letters have been distant and cold. There was so much that I wanted to put into them, but I only had to imagine one of the stupid crache who order us around smirking as he censored what I'd written, to end up writing about what we'd had for tea, or the latest scores in the nightly card game.

I know it's unfair on you, especially when I read yours. You write so well about what's going on at home I only have to close my eyes to imagine myself back in the Tumble café with you sitting next to me.

I never thought I'd envy Eddie, but tomorrow he'll be in Pontypridd and I won't. He'll be able to see you, hug you, kiss you (not on the mouth or I'll brain him) and talk to you for as long as he likes. I can hardly believe it's only four weeks since I left. It seems like half a lifetime, and that's when we're still more or less in the same country. (We're bound to take over England one day, if the English here are anything to go by they're all half wits.) I dread to think what it's going to be like when I'm in France.

I remember that last night we spent together often, especially after lights out when all the camp is in darkness and it feels as though the whole world is sleeping except me. Then I wonder why I pushed you away when I did. Believe me, I certainly wouldn't be capable of doing it now.

I was so worried about doing the right thing I messed up the little time we had. Can you forgive me? All I could think about was not wanting to leave you widowed with young children like my mother. I don't think she ever really recovered from my father's death, but now I can see that at least they had one another for a while. If I'd had the sense to talk to her about it, I think she would have told me that she wouldn't have wanted her life to have been any different, because when she does talk about my father it's always about the happy times. Is that what you were trying to tell me? That it's better to have a little time together as husband and wife, than no time at all?

222

The more I think about it, and the more I talk to the married boys in camp, especially the ones from London who've left their wives and children in what must be Hitler's prime target areas, the more confused I get. One of the boys managed to wangle a forty-eight-hour pass last week so he could get married. His girlfriend's in the family way, and he's quite open and unashamed about it, telling everyone that it's no one's business but theirs. When war was declared both of them decided to live every minute come what may, because no one can be sure just who's going to live or die in this war, especially if Hitler starts bombing our cities which everyone here seems to expect him to do.

Reading back over this, I don't know if I'm making any sense to you? I'm not even sure I'm making sense to myself, and I swear I haven't had a drink yet today, although we're all going down the local tonight in honour of Eddie's arrival.

What I'm trying to say, my darling, is how do you feel about a wedding on my next leave?

The problem is, despite all the promises they made in the recruiting office about leave after six weeks' training, no one really knows when we'll be able to get home next. It depends more on the availability of transports and the need for reinforcements in France, than any plans us poor squaddies might want to make.

Think about it carefully, darling, and let me know what you decide. If you've changed your mind and don't want us to marry until the war is over, I'll respect your decision and won't mention it again until after the peace treaties have been signed. I know it's the sensible thing to do, but when it comes to you, I'm afraid love and separation are driving any sense I ever had from my mind.

I'd give a month's pay to be coming home with Eddie. I can't wait to hold you, kiss you – and do a whole lot more. Promise me, that when I next walk through the door of the café, you'll close it so we can go somewhere quiet where we can be completely alone for as many hours as I have leave.

I can hear voices. That means that your brothers and Eddie are coming back to drag me off to the pub. I'd much rather stay here and carry on writing to you, but I know that if I did, I'd only repeat everything I've already written.

Tina, know that I love you with all my heart, miss you with every breath I take, and can't wait until you're in my arms again. And if you agree to marry me on my next leave, you'll make me the happiest man alive. Please send a letter back with Eddie.

Your own, very loving, Will

If letters could be worn out by reading them, Tina would have destroyed William's in the following hour. She read and reread every word until she had committed the pages to memory.

She heard Gina walk up the stairs and whisper her name, but she kept the door closed and Gina didn't think to look for her in the box room. Eventually the bedsprings creaked and she realised that her sister had gone to bed without her. Her parents followed soon afterwards. And still she sat on the narrow bed, hugging her letter to herself, her thoughts centred on William and the wonderful revelation that not only did he love her with all his heart, miss her with every breath, but on his next leave he would marry her, and then, no matter what, they'd truly belong to one another – for always.

Eddie was woken by birdsong. Somewhere behind the blackout, dawn had broken. He felt as though he had closed his eyes only ten minutes before. As he bent his head to Jenny's to kiss her, yet again, a key was inserted in the lock downstairs.

'It's morning,' Jenny whispered in dismay. 'We didn't make the night last for ever.'

'We have tonight,' he smiled lazily as he rolled back on to his own pillows.

'And after tonight?'

'Memories until the next time.'

'You think I'm likely to forget this after the next leave?' She snuggled her head down on to his chest.

'I'd say that depends on what we do on the next leave.'

'I wish you didn't have to go.'

'I've a war to win.'

'Try and make it soon.' She turned on her side and looked down at him, her face pale in the light of the bedside lamp they had allowed to burn all night.

He glanced at the clock. 'It's wonderful to lie in bed and not wait for the sound of a bugle call.'

'You want to sleep?' Mischief glowed in her eyes as her hands wandered beneath the sheet.

'What's that?' he asked, steeling his muscles against her touch.

'You're not going to fool me into giving you the advantage,' she laughed as she continued to tickle him.

'Someone's knocking.'

'Let them, the girl will open the shop soon.'

'It's not the shop door, it's the one downstairs.' Sliding out from under her, he left the bed. 'I'll go.'

'Not as you are. You'll cause a riot.'

'There'll only be miners around at this time in the morning.'

'And Judy in the shop,' she reminded him.

He pulled on his uniform trousers and buttoned the fly. 'Just a minute,' he shouted as he opened the door and padded down the stairs on bare feet. His father was waiting in the hallway.

'Telegram came for you, Eddie.'

Eddie took it and ripped it open.

'You have to report back immediately?'

'How do you know?'

'If Norway and Denmark was the end of the phoney war, Hitler's invasion of Holland and Belgium has to be the beginning of serious hostilities in Europe.'

'From what I've heard no one's expecting the Dutch and Belgians to hold out. After all, they didn't last time. It was us and the French then, and it will be us and the French now.'

'But don't you see, as soon as Hitler has occupied the lowlands he'll turn all his attention, and troops, to France.'

'Well, it was too much to expect the War Office to keep paying us to sit on our backsides in France doing nothing for ever.' He read the telegram again, focusing on the words *without delay*. He knew what they meant in military terms. 'I'd better dress.'

'Eddie?' his father laid a restraining hand on his arm. 'Everything is all right, isn't it?'

'It will be when I get back. Don't worry, we'll stop the Jerry bastards.'

'I wasn't talking about the war.'

'That is the only thing that's wrong, isn't it?'

His father smiled. 'I'm glad to hear it.'

Ignoring his father's filthy, coal-impregnated clothes, Eddie hugged him, raising clouds of dust as he patted his shoulders. 'Do me a favour, Dad. Look after Jenny for me.'

'Just as we have been. And you look after yourself. Do you hear?'

'As if the Nazi who came near me would have a chance.'

'War's a bit different to boxing, you know.'

'I know,' Eddie answered quietly. 'They've been training me for it harder than Joey Rees ever did in the gym.'

Eddie took a deep breath before he opened the bedroom door.

'What's wrong?' Jenny asked as he walked in.

'I've got to go, now.'

'But you have leave until tomorrow . . .'

He held up the telegram. 'It's cancelled, I've been recalled.' He reached for his underclothes.

'Come back to bed for just five minutes?'

He shook his head. 'I daren't. Knowing the army they had a Great Western timetable in front of them when they sent this, and they'll not give me long to get to the station. God only knows when the next train to Cardiff leaves, but I'd better be on it.'

'No time for breakfast?'

'No time for anything.' He leaned on the bed and kissed her.

She grabbed her dress. 'I'll cut some sandwiches, and come down to the station with you.'

'We could be hanging around for some time.'

'I don't care. I'd rather stay with you as long as I can, than sit around here moping and thinking about you. I could even get a ticket to Cardiff and travel with you as far as there.' She stared at him defiantly, daring him to say otherwise.

'I'd like that,' he smiled, 'but you'll have to keep reminding me that we're in public.'

'Tina, have you got a letter ready for William?'

Tina stared at Jenny in bewilderment. 'No, I thought I had plenty of time. Eddie isn't going until tomorrow.'

'He's been recalled.'

'To France?'

'No one knows, but it looks likely.' Jenny lowered her voice and looked around nervously for potential fifth columnists who might be listening in on their conversation.

'But that means Will and the boys could be going . . .'

'Eddie doesn't know anything, only that he has to report back to camp immediately.'

Tina remembered the news broadcast she had listened to that morning. Her father's warning that the German invasion of the lowlands might mean the boys going directly to France with no home leave. 'Eddie's going now?'

'The Cardiff train leaves in ten minutes. He went to the booking office to get me a ticket while I came here. I'll have to go or I'll miss it.'

'Wait!' Tina threw her keys at the senior girl behind the cake counter. 'Take over for me. Tell the cook to lock up, and check that he does everything I normally do, I'll pay you ten bob extra if it's done properly. You're in charge.' Grabbing her handbag and ringing open the till she scooped all the notes and a handful of silver into her purse. 'If you run out of change send up to my sister on the Tumble.'

226

'Tina, what are you doing?' Jenny asked in bewilderment.

'Going to camp with Eddie.'

'Don't be ridiculous, they won't let you see William . . .'

'There's no time to argue.' She pushed Jenny out through the door. 'Come on, let's go. And I promise not to sit in the same carriage as you and Eddie on the way to Cardiff. In fact, if you like I'll promise not to talk to him until we're at the camp.'

'You do realise that William may not even be able to leave the confines of the camp, and you certainly won't be allowed inside?'

Tina nodded apprehensively. What had seemed like a good idea in the restaurant had turned into a more and more ridiculous escapade with every passing mile. She already knew there was no chance of her getting back to Pontypridd that night, and she could just imagine the row she'd get off her father for that alone. She had nothing with her except the clothes she stood up in and a purse full of money. No soap, no towel, not even a toothbrush.

'You're crazy.' Eddie shook his head at her: 'but then I know a lot of fellows who'd give their eye teeth to have a girl like you running after them. I only hope William appreciates what he's got in you.'

'Do you think he'll be angry?'

'Bewildered, maybe, surprised certainly, but not angry. Here we are.'

She looked out of the carriage window. The rolling fields had given way to a sprinkling of stone cottages with low walled gardens crammed with multicoloured, bell-shaped spring flowers.

'Normally I'd wait for a bus, but seeing as how you're with me, I'll get a taxi to take us to camp.'

'I'll pay, I have lots of money. I raided the till in the restaurant,' she confessed.

'Knowing your father, you're going to have hell to pay for that alone when you get back.' He picked up his kitbag, opened the window and leaned out to open the door.

She stepped down after him on to the platform. 'How far is it?'

'A few miles. Look, thinking about it logically, there's no point in you going out there. It's in the middle of nowhere.'

'But if Will can't get any time off, then I could be sitting around on this station all night waiting to no purpose. I wouldn't even know if he could get away or not.'

'I told you there's no chance that they'll let you into the camp. You'd cause a riot, and there's nowhere for you to sit and wait. Not even a bus shelter.'

'Please, Eddie, I've come this far, don't turn me back, not now. I **have** to see him even if it's only through a wire fence.'

He stood and looked at her, an exasperated expression on his face. 'All right, but don't blame me if you end up sitting around for hours and not seeing him at all.'

Tina took one look at the barbed-wire fences and ditches that enclosed the camp and realised exactly why Eddie had been so reluctant to bring her out here. The camp was huge, sprawling. Through the wire she could see hordes of men, lorries and military vehicles, and surrounded as the place was by fields and countryside, there was no shelter, nowhere for her to wait except the side of a road.

'There's a pub. It's not much of a place. We drink there when we can get a pass.'

'I can't go into a pub,' she protested.

'The landlady's a bit of a rough diamond, but she has a couple of rooms upstairs that she lets out.'

Knowing that Jenny had never been near the camp, Tina wondered how Eddie knew about the rooms.

'They aren't up to much but they've got to be a better option than standing at the side of the road in full view of the animals.' He pointed to the men walking behind the wire.

'I don't know if I should . . .'

'It's only a mile away. If Will can get a couple of hours off he can go straight there. There's always transport available for a short hop, you won't miss more than five minutes of whatever time he can scrounge.'

He sensed her wavering.

'Here.' He pushed something into her hand. 'And don't tell anyone, especially Will and Jenny, where you got it. Drop me off at the main gates, mate,' he directed the taxi driver, 'and take Mrs Powell up to the Tally Ho.'

'You'll tell him . . .'

'That you're waiting? It will be the first thing I do after I've checked in. If I don't see you again before you go, take care of yourself, and look out for Jenny and my family for me.'

'Every chance I get.'

It was only after she'd watched him salute the guard and disappear through the gates that she opened her hand. There, nestling in her palm, was a wedding ring. She didn't dare speculate where he'd got it, or what he'd used it for.

Taking off her engagement ring she slipped it on to the third finger of her left hand, and secured it with the ring William had given her.

It was far too big. Eddie had obviously gone on the premise that any girl could wear a ring that was too big; a small one might cause complications. Her heart skipped a beat. Was this the sort of thing William would get up to when he was in France? Had she made a complete and utter fool of herself, throwing herself at a man who might already have moved on to someone else?

The pub was small and old. There wasn't a wall or floor that didn't dip or lean at an alarming angle. The ceiling beams were blackened and pitted and might well have been hoisted into position at the time of William the Conqueror's coronation and if so, certainly hadn't been maintained since.

The landlady, a hard-faced, brassy-haired woman, took Tina's money quickly enough, but as she walked her up the stairs and showed her into a dismal little room furnished with a cracked washstand, chipped toilet set, split chair and a double bed that probably had been stuffed with both the horse and the hair, her mouth set into a sceptical line that told Tina she no more believed she was married, than she was Princess Elizabeth. Making a sarcastic comment on Tina's lack of luggage she left with the injunction that the dining room would be open for the evening meal in two hours.

With nothing else to do Tina closed the door, kicked off her shoes and lay on the bed. She tried to sleep, hoping that when she opened her eyes it would be to find William kissing her, just like Prince Charming.

She woke with a start to find that the light had dulled to reddish gold. She sat up and looked out of the handkerchief-sized window sunk deep into the two-foot-thick wall to see the sun sinking slowly over the fields, then she heard a repetition of the noise that had roused her. There was a step on the rickety staircase. A floorboard creaked outside the door.

'Tina, are you in there?'

She leapt off the bed wishing she'd woken in time to run a comb through her hair and touch up her powder and lipstick. She wrenched open the door, pulling at the knob when it wouldn't move more than a few inches over the warped floorboards.

'It's you. It's really you?' Sliding into the room William kicked the door shut behind him, before gathering her into his arms. 'When Eddie told me what you'd done I couldn't believe it. Tina, what on earth possessed you?'

'I heard the news about Holland and Belgium. When Jenny told me that Eddie had been recalled I was afraid you'd be posted overseas and I wouldn't see you again before you left.' Leaning back, she looked into his eyes, seeing her own image mirrored in their depths. 'I had to see you, Will. I had to make sure you still loved me.'

'You think I make a habit of handing out engagement rings?' He sank on to the bed, pulling her down with him.

'Can you stay the night?'

'I'm lucky to be here now. The whole camp's been put on alert, all leave has been cancelled.'

'But you came . . .'

'Only because Eddie did a deal with one of the senior sergeants. It wasn't easy. We decided it wouldn't be politic to mention your presence here to either of your brothers.'

'What kind of a deal did Eddie make?'

'Don't ask.' He held up her left hand, twirling the outsized wedding ring around on her finger. 'Eddie?'

'I wasn't supposed to tell you.'

William laughed. 'I trust we'll be able to find one that will fit better than this before my next leave.'

'I wish we could be married now, this minute.'

'I take it that means you still do want to marry me?'

'How can you ask?' She clung to him as though she had no intention of ever letting go. 'How long have we got?'

He lifted his arm behind her back and glanced at his watch. 'As long as it takes the sergeant to drive into town and replace the whisky and brandy that disappeared mysteriously from the officers' mess. It will probably be nearer half an hour than an hour.'

'Then we've no time to waste.' Extricating herself from his arms she turned back the sheets.

'Have you thought what you're going to tell your father about this?' he asked anxiously.

'That I had to see you before you left. Please, Will, let's not waste any more time talking. I haven't come all this way to be fobbed off a second time.' Sliding up her skirt, she unclipped one set of suspenders then the other. Sitting on the edge of the bed she rolled down her stockings and flung them on to the chair. Rising to her feet she discarded her dress, then her underclothes. When she was completely naked she went to him, and as he held her she knew that this time there would be no turning back, for either of them.

The light had dimmed from old gold to cool silver. From somewhere below came a bar-room clamour of conversation and raucous laughter. The bed was as uncomfortable and lumpy as it looked, and a smell of stale beer, woodsmoke and dust that had lain too long on old surfaces hung in the air, but Tina didn't care. They were all wonderful sensations, smells and sounds that she would treasure for the rest of her days, because in this rickety room in this rather grubby, old pub she had made love with William for the very first time, and at that moment nothing mattered except the way they felt about one another.

Nestling her head against his arm, she entwined her legs into his and moved her hands lightly over the smooth skin on the flat of his stomach. 'I never thought anything could make me feel closer to you.'

'I always said we were made for one another. Now we've proved it.' He kissed her forehead as his hands explored her body.

'Promise me, Will. No more Veras?'

'If I had known it would be this way between us, it would never have happened.'

'Promise?' Her eyes were dark, earnest as they gazed into his. 'We could be apart for a long time. I can't bear the thought of you doing what we just did with anyone else . . .'

He laid his finger over her mouth. 'Do you think there could ever be another girl for me after this? From now on there'll only ever be you, I swear it.'

She snuggled down, revelling in the velvet feel of his skin against hers. 'I wish you could stay until morning.'

'So do I, but if I don't make a move now, they'll be sending search parties out to pick me up.' Kissing her again, he reluctantly extricated himself from her and the bed. Flinging back the covers too vigorously he succeeded in exposing her as well as himself. He stood and stared at her for a moment, mesmerised by the beauty of her naked body as he reached blindly for his clothes.

'You're going to put those pants on backwards if you're not careful.' She made no attempt to reach for the blankets, feeling no sense of shame or modesty as she basked in his admiration.

'And what would you know about a man's underpants, young lady?'

'A lot. I've washed enough pairs belonging to my brothers. You are going to France, aren't you?'

'No one tells us poor squaddies anything important, but we think so.' He pulled on his trousers, buttoning them but leaving his braces dangling as he reached for his vest and shirt.

'Soon?'

'It must be, now they've cancelled all leave. But it's you I'm concerned about, not me. Have you got enough money?'

'I have a return ticket, this room is already paid for and I have more than enough for a taxi, and a meal.'

'Moneybags.'

'I raided the till.'

'What are you going to tell your family?'

'The truth. That I went to the camp with Eddie, and we had half an hour to say goodbye, which was all the time you could spare. That you told me Tony and Angelo are fine, and then, as there was no train back I slept the night in a small hotel. That does sound better than a pub, doesn't it?'

'Infinitely better.' He leaned over the bed. Gently stroking her hair from her face, he kissed her for the last time. 'You are a mad, insane idiot, and I love you for it.' A sharp knock at the door interrupted them.

'Message for Private Powell.'

'Who's that?' Tina asked as he moved away.

'The sergeant who dropped me off here.'

'William Powell?'

'Coming.' William gave her a haunting look of love and tenderness that she sensed she would remember, and cherish for ever. 'I love you.'

'Think of me, and keep safe and well?' she begged, rising to her knees and holding him.

'Every minute of every day.' Disentangling himself from her arms, he turned abruptly, opened the door and walked away.

Chapter Eighteen

Sunday dinners remained a ritual in Evan's house, but when he glanced around his kitchen the following Sunday as he prepared to settle down after the meal to listen to the news, he couldn't help thinking that the tradition had become an empty one. Everything around him reminded him of the absent faces. Eddie, William and Andrew with the army, Haydn and Jane in London, Maud and Ronnie in Italy . . . he wondered what they were all doing. The post had been ominously sparse that week. He didn't even know if Eddie was back in France, or if William and the Ronconi boys had been sent out there with him. Alma hadn't heard from Charlie in over a week, and in the last letter Bethan had received from Andrew, he'd told her that he and Trevor had finished their military training and were awaiting transport, but either he didn't know, or hadn't been allowed to divulge, the destination of that transport.

Evan sat, patiently filling his pipe, trying not to look at the women's faces while the news reader lingered over the details of the Dutch Queen Wilhelmina's domestic arrangements for her British exile, and her grand gesture of placing the whole of the Dutch merchant fleet at the disposal of the Allies. Five minutes were spent recapping the fighting in Holland, and the command that had finally gone out to the Dutch troops the day after Eddie had left, ordering them to stop fighting; the humiliation and misery felt by the Dutch as the Germans had occupied the Hague, and as a final snippet, the replacement of one French General with another as Allied Commander-in-Chief.

'I trust he's a better man. The Germans are bound to turn their attention to France next.' Alexander voiced Evan's own thoughts, but that didn't stop Evan from wishing that his lodger hadn't expressed his opinion in front of the women.

'The worst thing is, not knowing what's happening.' Evan switched off the radio.

'Everyone says that the news is heavily censored these days. Do you think there could already be fighting in France?' Megan asked.

'They'd have to tell us if Hitler had crossed the frontier. It would be far too big a development to keep quiet,' Evan reassured her. 'It's not lack of war news I'm complaining about. It's not knowing where the boys are.'

'I wish I knew if William was already in France.'

'I doubt it, not after only four weeks' training,' he answered smoothly, going on the premiss that it was better for Megan to believe the best for as long as possible than allow her imagination to dwell on the worst.

'Mam, you're as bad as Tina. There's no point in worrying until we know where Will is for definite,' Diana said firmly.

'You going down the hill?' Alexander asked her.

'I promised Wyn I'd call in the hospital. Dr John said he might be able to go home in the next couple of days.'

'That's the first piece of good news I've heard all week.' Evan finally lit his pipe. 'If you're coming back between seven and eight, call into Alma's. Phyllis and I are going down later to see her. We'll walk back with you.'

'Is she managing the shop all right by herself?' Bethan asked.

'She doesn't say much but I think she's finding it a bit of a strain. Although the boy she's taken on to help her is supposed to be willing, and a hard worker.'

'It's hard on any woman who suddenly loses her husband's companionship, for whatever reason,' Megan said firmly. 'But it must be doubly hard on Alma. Not even married a year, and she and Charlie were so happy . . .'

'Are so happy,' Evan contradicted. 'He'll be back.'

'The question is when. And in the meantime she has a lot on her shoulders, what with the shop to run, and her mother the way she is. Mrs Jones told me that the old lady is none too well again.'

'That's all we seem to be hearing – people finding it hard to cope.' Evan held out his arms to Brian who was toddling towards him with the inevitable picture book in hand.

'The good thing is, unemployment has fallen again,' Luke chipped in.

'There goes our own home-grown, happy Harry again,' Alexander complained. 'The Germans are sitting in half of Europe, we're waiting for Nazi bombs to start falling, and he finds something to be chirpy about.'

'Seems to me we could all do with some of Luke's optimism,' Evan smiled.

'Come on then,' Alexander nodded to Luke as he left the table. 'Put your coat on so Diana and I can walk you down to the café and your own personal ray of sunshine. Perhaps then you'll be kind enough to continue to dispense it to the rest of us.'

'God knows we all need it,' Megan said fervently.

'So you see the shop's made a steady and clear profit varying between five and six pounds every week after the overheads have been cleared.'

'You've done well.' Wyn pushed the book to one side.

'I thought you'd be pleased.'

'I am, very.'

'You don't sound it.'

'It seems you're doing well enough without any endorsement from me.'

'Wyn, please . . . ' Diana's voice tailed away as she shifted awkwardly on the uncomfortably hard, upright hospital chair. Both Dr John and the sister had assured her that Wyn was walking well with the aid of his crutches. The leg Andrew had operated on was healing, plans were already in motion to fit an artificial lower limb and foot to the other leg, but despite the progress Wyn was making physically, there was still no sign of his depression lifting. He took a cigarette from a packet in his dressing-gown pocket and pushed it into his mouth.

'Are you allowed to smoke in here?'

'There's nothing else to do.' He flicked his cigarette lighter.

'Dr John told me you'll be out next week.'

'Tomorrow.'

'That's wonderful news.'

'What, that they've had enough of me in here?'

'When are you thinking of going back to work?' she asked, determinedly ignoring his cynicism.

'I'm not thinking of it, why?'

'Cohen's are advertising for an assistant to work in their optician's.'

'You've applied?' He had a peculiar expression on his face she couldn't quite fathom.

'I was thinking of it. After all, you really don't need me any more. You'll be able to manage the theatre shop – '

'Like this!' he broke in forcefully, looking pointedly at his leg.

'The cast will soon come off.'

'The pain is excruciating.'

'It will fade in time.'

'In the right foot?'

She looked down: it was his lower right leg that had been amputated.

'They call it a ghost pain. Sometimes it never goes away.'

'If you think like that, it never will.' It was the first time she'd snapped back at him.

'I'm a useless cripple who'll never be good for anything . . .'

'You'll have to walk with a stick. So what? Hundreds of men around Ponty who've been hurt in pit accidents use sticks. No one thinks any the less of them for it.'

'You've already got this job, haven't you?' he challenged.

'I've an interview on Monday,' she conceded. 'It's a good position, Wyn. I could wait years for another to come up like it.'

'And the High Street shop?'

'You've closed it.'

'I was thinking of reopening it.'

'Why would you do that? You said yourself you haven't enough stock to put in it.'

'Not sweets, something else.'

'Like what?'

'Like anything. I don't have to make a decision straight away – or ever, if you leave me in the lurch.'

'You know I would never do that.'

'I was under the distinct impression that is precisely what you are doing.'

'You can't afford to pay me to hang around and do nothing.'

'And I can't afford to allow just anyone to take over the business. Do you think there's a queue of people waiting to put the effort and care into running the shop that you have?'

'There's you,' she pointed out, consciously lowering her voice because his was escalating.

'I'm not ready . . .'

'You will be the week after next. If I get the job in Cohen's, I'll tell them I have to give you a week's notice.'

'And what if I can't manage to run the place? What if the bones in my leg don't mend any better than they are now? What if I end up losing both my legs?'

For the first time Diana fully understood what Andrew's father had been trying to tell her. She was angry with herself for not recognising the signs sooner. Wyn had been strong all his life. Strong enough to survive losing his mother, to take care of his sister when his father's health had broken, strong enough to withstand all the gossip about his private life – and strong enough to sort out her problems when she had no one else to turn to; but now he was facing something he didn't know how to fight. Something that held more terror for him than all his previous problems combined. He was frightened of becoming a useless cripple; one more liability for his overburdened sister who was already worn out from looking after his father.

'If you really need me, I could withdraw my application and stay until another job comes up.'

'Don't do me any favours. Not out of pity. Whatever else, Diana, spare me your charity.'

'Do you really need me, Wyn, or are you just being kind?' It was a last appeal and it fell on deaf ears. He turned away. She gathered her handbag and coat from the chair and rose to her feet knowing from past experience that it was useless to attempt to remonstrate with him when he was like this. 'I'll visit you at home tomorrow after work.'

'To give me another dose of pity? No thanks.'

'You've always been there when I've needed someone. I'd like to return the favour. Not out of pity, but out of friendship.'

He flung the most vicious thing he could think of at her. The one thing he knew would hurt. 'And guilt?'

She steadied herself against the doorpost, clinging to it as grey tides of giddiness washed over her. 'And guilt,' she echoed faintly. 'I'm sorry, I should have seen that van . . .' her voice faded, sounding distant even to herself. The last thing she heard before slumping downwards was Wyn's voice crying out for help.

'What's the matter with Tina tonight?' Luke asked Gina after her sister had shouted at the hapless cook for the tenth time in as many minutes.

'She finally had a letter from Will this morning. Apparently they're in transit.'

'To France?'

'We think so, but Will obviously wasn't allowed to say. All he did say was that he, Tony and Angelo are well, and there's no chance of leave in the foreseeable future.'

'Odd that he hasn't written home. Evan was only saying this afternoon that they haven't heard from the boys all week.'

'This letter took four days to reach Tina. The boys probably wrote to everyone, but their letters could be stuck in the post somewhere.'

'Then it looks as though all the available men have been sent to France.'

'You collecting information for Hitler?' Tina asked Alexander as she carried tea to him and Luke from the counter.

'No, just someone who follows the news.'

Tina superstitiously touched William's letter in her pocket. A bland censored letter, as different from the loving tome he had sent with Eddie as cold, cheerless slag from brightly burning coal, but she didn't mind. Not now she had her memories to draw on. Memories that had been worth every minute of her father's rantings.

She glanced around the café. Since the fracas with Dai Station, trade had fallen dramatically. Most of the business regulars like the tram crews still called in, but the station staff had taken their custom elsewhere, and there were no girls or women in the place. Word travelled fast. She had asked Huw Davies to play down the incident to her father and mother, but she hadn't been able to silence the gossips, or the Pontypridd *Observer*, and she was dreading the court case report appearing in its war-thinned pages. Enough families were paranoid about allowing young girls out in the blackout as it was, let alone to visit a café that had a reputation for trouble.

Gina and Luke had left Alexander's table and were whispering to one another at the counter. The rapt, loving expressions on their faces irritated Tina beyond measure, and there was something else, something Tina recognised as jealousy and bitterness. Not envy over Luke, his smooth, round, baby face reminded her too much of her younger brothers for that; but a resentment that came from Luke's presence and William's absence, which today's letter had warned was likely to be months, possibly even years, and after that stolen half-hour the thought was an unbearable one.

'Why don't you walk Gina home, Luke?'

Astounded, Gina stared at her sister. 'It's only eight o'clock.'

'And it's quiet. Go on, neither of you are serving any useful purpose by cluttering up this place.'

'Are you serious?' Gina asked warily, expecting Tina to come out with some caustic comment.

'Perfectly,' Tina answered coldly.

'If there's a sudden rush I'll help your sister,' Alexander offered.

'She means it. She really means it!' Gina sang out to Luke as she rushed into the back and grabbed her cardigan.

'Just don't do anything I wouldn't,' Tina cautioned, as Gina ran past her on the way out.

'That's easy. You'd do no end of things if William was here.'

'I'm trusting you to get her home in one piece and a lot earlier than she would have if she were working here,' Tina called out to Luke as he opened the door.

'That was nice of you.' Alexander followed Tina to the counter after Luke and Gina had left.

'Nice had nothing to do with it. I couldn't stand their stupid

238

mooning grins a minute longer. They always look as though they're auditioning for a cocoa advert.'

'I'm not sure I believe you. Could it be that you're thinking if you're kind to those two, the fates might be kind to you and send this William of yours home sooner?'

'You're a romantic.'

'Anything wrong with that?'

'Everything, if the person you want isn't around,' Tina said abruptly.

'Ouch. I know when I'm not wanted.'

'You'll do to talk to until something better comes along. More tea?'

'I wish I had an invitation to a formal ball or concert in my pocket and a scintillatingly beautiful, witty female hanging on my arm –' he pushed his cup towards her – 'but as I don't, I suppose I'll have to settle for your cold comfort and tea.'

Wyn waited for half an hour for a nurse to appear from the room they'd carried Diana into. Dr John came and went, and although Wyn called out to him, it was as much as the doctor could do to acknowledge him curtly before going on his way. The sister walked down the corridor and went into the room, staying for only a few minutes before emerging with a nurse and returning to the main ward.

Unable to bear the suspense any longer, Wyn swung himself up on to his crutches for the first time without help; balancing precariously he stumbled down the corridor towards the sister's office. The door was open and she was sitting at her desk, a cup of tea at her elbow and an enormous pile of forms in front of her.

'How is Miss Powell, sister?' he asked apprehensively.

She looked up and stared coolly at him as he propped himself against the doorway. 'You're doing well, Mr Rees. Won't be long before you're racing around, at this rate of recovery.'

'Miss Powell?' he repeated.

'She'll be fine.' She looked away from him and continued to write on the document in front of her.

'What's wrong with her?' he pressed, irritated by her offhand manner.

'Not a great deal that time won't cure, but then, Mr Rees, I should imagine you're in a better position to know that than anyone else.'

A door opened behind him and he turned to see Dr John walking back into the ward. Manoeuvring quickly, he blocked the doctor's path.

'Can I see Diana, please, Dr John?'

'Five minutes, then I'm taking her home,' the old man barked, gruffly. He hated situations like this, finding them embarrassing for everyone concerned.

Wyn swung his crutches around and limped back down the corridor. The worst was opening the cubicle door: turning the knob wasn't a problem, stepping back far enough for the door not to hit him was. Eventually he entered to see Diana propped up on a couch, a cup of tea in her hand and a blanket covering her legs.

'You all right?' he asked.

'Yes.'

'You don't look it. You're as white as a sheet.' He limped over and propped himself against the side of the couch.

'All that talk earlier about whether you want me to stay or not was pointless. Very soon I won't be able to work for anyone.' She gazed at him with wretched eyes. He was the one person who knew all her secrets, and she saw no point in keeping this one from him. 'I'm going to have a baby.'

'Tony's?'

She nodded dumbly, sending tears splashing down on to the blanket.

'I wasn't much to start with, I'm even less now, but if you're prepared to take on a crippled queer as a husband, the offer of marriage still stands.'

'Didn't you hear what I just said? I'm carrying Tony's baby.'

'I prefer to think of it as your baby, and if you marry me, it would be ours.'

'You'd take on another man's child?'

'I love kids. That's why I like working in the sweet shop. They're mercenary little sods, but unlike adults they're open and honest about what they want.'

'But if I married you, it would be for all the wrong reasons.'

'So, I'm asking you for all the wrong reasons. A cripple needs a wife to take care of him, and marrying you would make my father happy and guarantee me a half-share in his estate. What do you say, Diana? This could be a classic marriage of convenience, but I'll lay a pound to a penny neither of us will ever regret it.' Putting all his weight on one crutch he offered her his hand. 'Partners?'

'And when the baby's born?'

'It would be ours, yours and mine. I rather like the idea of being a father.'

'You promise to treat it as your own?'

'If you promise never to tell anyone it isn't mine. Especially Tony.'

'And if he guesses?'

'Tell him he guessed wrong.'

She looked him in the eye. 'Partners,' she echoed, taking his hand into hers.

'I can't believe Tina let me leave the café this early.'

'I think your sister is really nice.'

'Which only goes to prove you don't know her. Where do you want to go?'

'A walk. I love the spring, and it seems to have finally arrived.'

'It's too cold for walking, and it's getting dark.'

'You're too used to working in warm cafés. A bit of fresh air will do you good. Put roses in your cheeks.'

'There's enough roses there already.'

'I could take you to another café.'

'And give money to the opposition? No fear.'

'There's nothing else open on a Sunday except the churches.'

'I could make you supper in the High Street café,' Gina suggested as they crossed the Tumble.

'What about your father?'

'I keep telling you he won't find out. Besides, he's too furious with Tina for chasing after William to worry about anything I'm doing. Come on, I have the keys.'

'Does Tina know you have them?'

'Of course. Otherwise how could I open up the Tumble in the morning?'

'Then she'll guess where we've gone.'

'What if she does? I've no intention of doing anything wrong. Have you?'

He turned the colour of beetroot as she opened the door of the café and went inside. He followed her and she closed the door and pulled the blackout. Walking into the kitchen she switched on the light.

'Instead of supper you could kiss me again like you did on the mountain,' she prompted boldly.

Heart pounding like a piston in a steam engine, Luke leaned forward and touched his lips to hers.

'Now we're alone, I think we can do a little better than that.' Wrapping her arms around his neck she pulled him close to her and kissed him soundly, if a little clumsily, on the lips.

He drew back reeling from a heady combination of Evening in Paris that Gina had filched from Tina's handbag, and the warm sensation of her body pressed against his.

'Toast?' she asked.

'Yes, please.' Taking off his suit jacket he hung it on the back of one of the chairs. Under the pretext of adjusting his tie he surreptitiously loosened his collar. Embarrassment had sent his temperature soaring.

Gina lit the gas. 'I could make beans on toast?'

'Between what I get at the Powells, the tea in the café, and what you make me, I'm putting on weight.'

'You can afford to. Are they all as skinny as you at home?'

'It's working in the fields that does it,' he said solemnly.

'You don't like me teasing you, do you?' She waited until he sat on a stool before walking towards him. Linking her hands behind his neck she kissed him again. He pushed her gently away, holding her at arm's length.

'Kissing isn't a dangerous occupation,' she said pertly as his colour continued to heighten beneath her steady gaze. 'My sister does it all the time when William's around.'

'They're engaged.'

'They did it before they got engaged as well.'

'But we shouldn't be behaving like this, not when we're alone without anyone knowing where we are. I feel guilty every time we come here.'

'I don't see why. It's not a sin to want to be alone together once in a while.'

'Your father wouldn't like it.'

'What the eye doesn't see, the mind won't grieve.' Wrapping her arms around his neck she pressed her nose against his and looked into his eyes. 'Tell you what, you give me one proper kiss, and in return I'll make us a meal, then we'll go.'

This time as his lips touched hers, all his qualms about being alone with her and about the surroundings receded from his mind. He reached up, burying his fingers in her hair, fusing the length of her body to his.

'I said just one kiss.' Suddenly afraid of his mounting passion and the situation her innocent flirting had landed them in, she retreated behind the counter.

'I'm sorry,' he faltered. 'I don't know what came over me . . .'

'It will be a long time before I ask you to kiss me again.'

'I didn't mean to get carried away.'

'I know,' she relented. She chose a saucepan and put it down again. 'Perhaps I should take you straight home?'

'That might be a good idea.' She picked up her coat.

'This won't make a difference, will it? To us, I mean?'

'That depends on how you behave in future.'

'I promise – '

'No . . .' she interrupted as they walked out through the door. 'No promises.' She reached for his hand. 'You'll only break them when we get married.'

'I heard a car.'

'Dr John brought me home.' Diana pulled off her tam and dropped her handbag into a corner. She was glad to find her mother alone. She checked the time. Evan and Phyllis would soon be back from Alma's. Steeling herself for an outburst she said as casually as she could, 'Wyn Rees has asked me to marry him.'

Her mother dropped her knitting on to her lap. 'And what did you tell him?'

'I said I would.'

'Diana . . .'

'I know all about his reputation, if that's what you're going to tell me.'

'Do you think you could be happy with him?'

'Happier than I could be with anyone else. We're good friends.'

'There's a lot more to marriage than friendship.'

'I know and so does Wyn. There's already a baby on the way.'

'And Wyn's the father?'

'He's promised to take care of both of us,' Diana answered, neatly evading the question.

'Don't marry him just to give the baby a name, Diana. You know I would never let you go to the unmarrieds' ward in the workhouse. Neither would your Uncle Evan if it came to that . . .'

'It doesn't need to come to anything, Mam. As soon as it can be arranged, I'm marrying Wyn.'

'It's what you want?' The words were commonplace, but there was a wealth of pleading in Megan's eyes that Diana found hard to ignore.

'There's no one else I'll marry.'

'In that case there's nothing for me to do except wish you and Wyn well.' Megan would have liked to ask a lot more questions, but the years she'd spent in prison had estranged her from her daughter, damaging their once close, loving relationship. She longed to rebuild it, but she knew enough to tread carefully. If things were going to return to what they had been, it would take time, but for now Diana had retreated not only from her, but from everyone in the family. If Wyn had broken through Diana's reserve enough to want to marry her, and she him, who was she to stop them?

'He's coming out of hospital tomorrow. I'm going to his house after work so we can tell his father and sister.'

'About the wedding or the baby?'

'Both,' Diana replied shortly. 'I can't stand the thought of anyone gossiping behind my back. I'd rather it was out in the open so the scandalmongers have nothing to talk about.'

Megan left her chair, and hugged her.

'Tell Uncle Evan, Phyllis and Beth for me?' Diana avoided looking into her mother's eyes.

'Wouldn't you rather tell them yourself?'

'I won't have time. I want to go to bed now, and I'll be in Wyn's tomorrow night. If Wyn can get a special licence we hope to be married next weekend.'

'In the Registry Office?'

'It seems more appropriate than a church under the circumstances.' Diana went to the door.

'Just tell me one thing?'

'Yes, Mam.' Diana looked back.

'If I'd been here, if I hadn't gone to prison and been able to keep our home going, would it have been any different for you?'

Diana thought back to Ben Springer, remembered the cold welcome Evan's wife Elizabeth had given her when she'd returned from Cardiff Infirmary, the lack of money that had driven her to take the job with Ben. 'No, Mam,' she lied stoutly. 'No it wouldn't.'

'Time I was going.'

'You're a real nag.' Gina looked up at the stars shining down on Danycoedcae Road.

'Tina will have closed the café by now and I think you should be in bed before she gets home.'

'Yes, Papa.' She pecked Luke's cheek before crossing the road to the white cross that gleamed on her garden wall.

'I wish I could take you home with me to introduce you to my family,' he said, as he walked with her.

'Do you think they'll like me?'

'My mother, brothers and sisters will. I'm not too sure about my father. Not that he wouldn't like you as a person, but he's a very strict Quaker.'

'And like Papa with me, he'll expect you to marry into his own faith. Well that's going to make for one very disappointed Catholic and one very disappointed Quaker. What say you we get married in the Salvation Army Citadel?'

244

'Are you serious?'

'Of course not, silly.' She wrapped her fingers around his arm: 'but then, we haven't got to worry about religion until our wedding, and that isn't going to be for ages yet.'

'What do you think is the right age?'

'Eighteen for me, twenty for you.'

'We could get married on my twenty-first birthday.' He was thinking more of the opposition he was likely to encounter from his father than any romantic connotations.

'If my father agrees, but I'm sure he will, because by then we will have been going out together for two years. I'm glad you're not joining the army. The thought of you leaving Pontypridd makes me understand why Tina is so miserable these days.'

'I'm probably here until the end of the war.'

'You'll leave Ponty when the war ends?' she asked, aghast at the thought.

'I wouldn't if the pit was prepared to keep me on. I've no job to go back to in Cornwall.'

'I'd hate it if you left.'

'So would I. When I've saved some money we'll get engaged,' he promised recklessly, trying to work out how long it would take him to save enough for a ring, given that half of his wages went in lodgings, a quarter in postal orders which he sent back home, and so far the remainder had been swallowed up by replacing his clothes, and buying cups of tea in the café.

'I'll have to wait a while before I spring that on my father, but in the meantime we have a whole lot of courting to do, and I don't know about you, but I'm looking forward to it.' She squeezed his fingers lightly.

'And you've really forgiven me for what happened earlier?'

'I'm thinking about it.'

'I'm sorry . . .'

'Don't be. I'd better go inside. Goodnight.'

'I love you,' he whispered as she opened her front door.

'I know,' came an answering murmur out of the darkness.

Chapter Nineteen

THE moment Wyn and Diana informed his father they were fulfilling his wildest dreams by getting married, the old man began organising the event from his invalid bed. Not even the news of the baby Diana was carrying (discreetly mentioned by Wyn at an opportune moment when he and his father were alone) upset him. In fact, if anything, he drew strength from the potentially scandalous revelation. As he frequently insisted on repeating to Myrtle to her ever-increasing embarrassment, it meant that his line wouldn't end in a dried-up old spinster and her barren bachelor brother.

Although Wyn insisted on getting a special licence which would enable him to marry Diana within three days, their idea of a swift, quiet wedding with no fuss was quickly scotched by his father, who insisted on a reception after the registry office ceremony. The first people he invited were the chapel minister and his wife in the hope that they would lend some religious significance to his son's union. And while Wyn saw to the important things, like papers and certificates, and the old man fussed over trivial details harassing a flustered and hard-pressed Myrtle about the fare for the wedding breakfast he expected her to organise and provide, Diana drifted through the intervening days and nights like a sleepwalker; far more preoccupied with the German advance into France than the clothes that were to be worn and the food that was to be eaten on her wedding day.

Apart from demanding that the number of guests be kept to a minimum, she showed no interest in the arrangements. Haunted by newsreel images of the hordes of goose-stepping Nazis her brother and the other volunteers were facing in France, she simply refused to think about flowers, lace and veils, and the domestic details of the new life she was about to embark on.

With every bulletin released through official channels, and the lurid, generally baseless rumours that swept through Pontypridd like wildfire, Megan grew gradually paler and more withdrawn. Diana helped her mother to plot the German advance on a map in her uncle's atlas, but the exercise wasn't the reassuring device she hoped it would be.

Even the place names were the same ones that had sounded so many death knells in the last war. Amiens, the Somme . . . slowly, inexorably the line crept towards Paris.

The day before the wedding, Bethan insisted on dragging Diana, Megan and Myrtle off to Cardiff to buy wedding clothes, but despite all of Bethan's efforts, including a sumptuous lunch in Howell's, they remained a cheerless group. They looked at linen, china and household goods as well as shoes, dresses, handbags, hats and lingerie. Diana dutifully tried on the various costumes, dresses and hats Bethan picked out for her, acknowledged they were 'very nice' and attempted to walk away. If it hadn't been for Bethan's persistence, neither she nor her mother would have bought anything new, and the serviceable dark green coat and matching skirt she ended up with as a bridal outfit were much more Bethan's taste than her own.

On the rare occasions when Diana thought of her wedding in the days leading up to the event, she considered it in Wyn's term of a partnership. Neither the barbed congratulations from people she had a nodding acquaintance with, nor the bewildered expressions on the faces of those she knew well, disturbed her trance-like state. Once the letter came from William telling them that he was no longer in transit but 'somewhere in France' she could think only of him, what he was going through, whether he was alive or dead, and – God forbid – what his death would do to her mother.

Even the sincere, enthusiastic welcome Myrtle and Wyn's father extended to welcome her into the family and the look on Tina's face when she told her she was marrying Wyn Rees, failed to jolt her out of her numbed state; and in the meantime there was still the shop to open, stock to hunt down, packing to be done, and her mother to care for and constantly reassure that Will would be all right – even when she didn't really believe it herself.

The evening before her wedding Diana was lifting the kiosk shutters into place at the end of the night's trading when a shadow fell across the counter. She looked behind her to see Alexander standing in the foyer.

'I'll take those.' Hardened by weeks of swinging picks and shovels underground, he lifted one of the shutters and slotted it into place as though it were made of nothing more substantial than cardboard. After sliding down the bolts that held it in place, he crouched down next to its partner. 'You've been avoiding me lately?'

'Just busy,' Diana replied truthfully.

'Your uncle mentioned that you're getting married tomorrow.'

'I hope you and Luke don't mind not getting invitations, but it's going to be a very quiet wedding. Just the immediate family and the minister.'

'I was amazed to hear that you're marrying your boss after what we talked about the other night.'

'You promised you'd never bring that up again,' she cautioned in a whisper as the manager walked into the foyer.

'How can you think of doing this?' He followed her into the blacked-out kiosk where she picked up the money bags and the keys.

'Because I'm fond of Wyn, because he's kind . . .' she searched her mind frantically for a plausible reason that wouldn't involve any mention of the baby, 'and safe,' she finished lamely.

'Safe!' Alexander exclaimed in amazement. 'How can you even use that word when the Germans are practically on our doorstep?'

Ignoring the question she locked the door, walked through the foyer and stepped out into the street. Walking on the inside of the pavement she headed back into the town towards the bank and the night safe.

'I'll buy you a coffee in the café,' Alexander offered as he caught up with her.

'Not tonight, I'm going straight home, I'm tired.'

'You still haven't told me why you're marrying Wyn.'

'I told you. You just didn't listen.'

'I mean the real reason.'

'What else do you expect me to say? Because he asked me and no one else is likely to.'

'I don't believe that either. Perhaps I didn't make myself clear the other night. All of this – coming here, working in the pits, living in your uncle's house – has been a culture shock. I needed time to adjust, time I wish now I had devoted to you.'

'To me?' She stood and stared at his silhouette in the uncertain light of the moon.

'I thought I made it clear the other night that I was interested in you.'

'Interested?' she repeated caustically. 'We're used to plain speaking in the valleys. What exactly does "interested" mean in English crache terms? You're missing all that free love you were telling me about, and you thought you'd train a working-class girl to fill the gap in your life?'

'What I'm trying to say, and saying very badly is that I'd like to spend time with you, get to know you . . . what's the word Tina uses to describe Gina and Luke's relationship? . . . "court", that's it. I'd like to court you.'

'It's courting, not court, and I don't think we'd make a very good couple.'

'Why not?'

'Because you're used to best pork fillet and I'm used to tripe. Because you talk posh and I speak with a valleys accent. We're poles apart, Alexander. You might be bored and missing your free love now, but when the war is over you'll go back to your English museum and crache ways, and I'll stay here.'

'Would you want to come with me?'

'No more than you'd want me to.'

'Diana . . .'

'You're pinning an awful lot on one kiss, Alexander, and in case you haven't noticed, I've already made my decision,' she said firmly, trying not to think about what might have happened if she'd been in a position to begin courting him. 'I don't know what people do where you come from, but in Ponty it's customary to wish the bride and groom luck.'

'How can I, knowing what I do about the groom?'

'You know nothing about Wyn.'

He looked around. They were in the bank doorway, there wasn't a sound or a soul in the street. 'I know he'll never kiss you like this.' He swept her confidently into his arms, bowing his head to hers he kissed her; no chaste, brotherly peck this time, but deeply, thoroughly, with a savagery he hoped would make her realise what she was giving up by marrying a man like Wyn. Parting her lips with his, he pushed his tongue into her throat and unbuttoned her coat. There was none of the gentle tenderness there had been on the mountain, only the same brute passion and selfish disregard first Ben, and then Tony had shown her.

Diana's head began to swim, then it came again, that sickening sense of self-loathing that culminated in a bout of mind-spinning, stomach-churning nausea. When she finally managed to struggle free from Alexander's clutches she reeled against the door before lurching into the street. Bending over the gutter she retched violently, backing away from him as he walked towards her.

'I'm sorry. I shouldn't have . . .'

She pushed him aside as he walked towards her.

'If I ever needed confirmation that I was doing the right thing in marrying Wyn, you've just given it to me,' she muttered hoarsely when she could speak.

'I'll walk you home.'

She heard the shame and contrition in his voice but she still shook her head. 'I'd rather go alone. I really would.'

'To the happy couple.' Huw Davies had proposed the toast in the parlour of Wyn's house, cleared of all the sickroom paraphernalia for the first time since Wyn's father had taken occupancy; even the bed had been folded away and pushed under the stairs for the occasion. Wyn's father, looking more skeletal than ever in a shiny dark suit and boiled shirt and collar several sizes too large for his shrunken figure, radiated pride as he lay propped on a *chaise-longue*, his legs covered by a red and green tartan rug.

'To the happy couple.'

The toast was taken up by Evan, Phyllis, Bethan, Megan, Myrtle and the minister and his wife.

'And absent friends.' Wyn, who knew exactly how worried Diana, Megan and Evan were about William and Eddie, raised his glass a second time.

'May all the boys be home soon,' Evan echoed, thinking of, but making no mention of defeat.

Diana raised her glass along with the others. 'The boys.' She couldn't wait for Eddie and William to come home, but there was also Tony. What if he suspected that he was the father of her baby. Would he confront her? Make a scene? If he did would he believe her when she told him Wyn was the father of the child? If only she could stop thinking about him and concentrate on Wyn instead. It would be so much easier if Tony continued to ignore her as he had done the last few days he'd been home when there'd been nothing left between them except mutual misery and humiliation.

Forcing a smile, she looked at her mother, absently complimenting her for the third time that day on how well she looked in her new navy blue costume and serviceable black hat. Megan hugged and kissed her in return as conversations were resumed with everyone being too determinedly cheerful, and talking just that little bit too loudly. Despite the toasts and sumptuous buffet that had claimed so much of Wyn's father's money and so many hours of Myrtle's time, Diana could sense strain in the atmosphere.

Bethan was smiling indiscriminately at everyone and everything. Her Uncle Evan who had given her away, and her Uncle Huw who had served as best man, were drinking the beer and whisky chasers they had provided as their contribution to the wedding breakfast far too fast for the minister's liking, and Wyn who was balancing unsteadily on his plastercast, artificial leg and crutches, wasn't far behind them.

Myrtle, desperately anxious to please and dressed in a pale blue dress and hat that didn't suit her, was offering everyone plates of cakes, sandwiches and sausage rolls, oblivious to the fact that they'd all eaten their fill. Swept along on a tide of sudden sympathy, Diana left Wyn's side and went to Myrtle. Taking a plate from her hand she laid it on the table.

'Is the bride allowed to propose a toast to her new sister-in-law?' she asked the room in general. 'This wonderful buffet was all her work, and I think you'll all agree it was magnificent.'

'Hear hear!' Huw Davies's shout drowned out the minister's hesitant agreement.

Megan touched Wyn's arm. 'Just look after my girl,' she said. Intended to be a lighthearted comment, it sounded like a threat.

'I'll do everything in my power to make her happy,' Wyn assured her gravely, 'and I really appreciate you moving in with Myrtle and Dad so Myrtle can look after the shop. Diana and I would never have managed to get away otherwise.'

'It'll give me something to do instead of moping around listening to the news from France.'

'Diana's warned you about my father?' he murmured leading her to one side.

'That he can be difficult?' Megan smiled. 'Don't worry, I've coped with enough difficult men in my time. As long as Myrtle can manage the shop, we'll be fine.'

'Taxi's here.' Huw, who could never quite manage to forget he was a policeman, had commandeered a vantage point in the bay window that looked out over the street and the approach roads. 'You see to the bride, Wyn, I'll see to the cases.'

Diana kissed the women goodbye first, then the men, even risking a peck on her father-in-law's cheek. Wyn shook hands with her uncles, kissed her mother and Myrtle and picked up his coat and hat from the rack in the hall. He pushed his hat down on to his head, draped his coat over his shoulder, opened the door and stared down at the steep flight of steps that led to the street.

'Here, I'll help you, Wyn.' The minister stepped forward.

'No!' Diana's voice rang out clearly in the warm, spring air. 'Wyn can manage fine, thank you.'

The minister stepped aside, but Wyn sensed several pairs of eyes boring into his back as he put his crutches together and leant on the iron handrail screwed into the stonework. After three or four steps he fell into a rhythm, swinging his artificial leg alternatively with his crutches and plastercast. Gaining the street he stood next to the car, a small smile of triumph on his face as he held out his arm to Diana.

'Bride has to throw her bouquet,' Bethan reminded them as Diana reached him. Diana glanced down at the small posy of early spring flowers. She turned and looked at the people assembled on the steps, tossing the bunch towards Myrtle. It was neatly intercepted by her Uncle Huw, who presented it to Myrtle with a flourish.

'Good luck!' Bethan shouted as Diana stepped through the taxi door Wyn was holding open for her.

Someone else called out, 'Be happy!'

With the cries ringing in their ears, Wyn sat beside her in the taxi. His hand closed over hers.

'Well, Mrs Rees?'

'Well, Mr Rees?' Her eyes unaccountably filled with tears. Wyn produced a handkerchief. 'I know, don't say it.'

'Say what?' he asked, watching as she dried her eyes.

'That I never have a handkerchief at any crisis point in my life.'

'I was going to ask if you had any regrets for what you've just done?'

She shook her head.

'No worries?'

'None.'

He pressed her hand. 'Make that the last lie you ever tell me.'

When she dared to look at him, he was smiling. He squeezed her fingers again, and she tried to smile back, hoping against hope that she really had done the right thing.

'I think you need a hand with that, Miss Rees.' Huw Davies walked into the foyer of the New Theatre and took the heavy shutter from her hand.

'Thank you very much, constable. I don't think I could have managed it by myself.'

'You look worn out, Miss Rees, if you don't mind me saying so. After-effects of all that hard work you put into the wedding breakfast?'

'I enjoyed it.'

'You did Wyn and Diana proud.'

She blushed at the compliment. 'It did go off all right, didn't it?' she asked, seeking reassurance like an insecure child.

'I don't know that either of them could have asked for more, unlike me. I could have eaten a bucketful of those cheese straws. I resented every one Evan and the minister filched from under my nose. Somehow it doesn't seem right for a minister to have such a healthy appetite. His thoughts should be concentrated on more spiritual matters than food.'

'I made those straws from an old recipe of my grandmother's. I can give it to you if you like.'

'I'd rather you gave it to Megan. That way I might get to eat them again.'

252

'It can't be easy for you, living alone.' Realising the connotation of her words, her colour heightened.

'It made a nice change to go to a wedding where all the food was home-made,' Huw complimented her, as though he attended a wedding every week.

'It was nothing, really. I like cooking.' She walked into the kiosk and tipped the float into the drawer. Before she'd even finished separating the coppers from the silver the first customers had walked through the door.

'I'll be back about ten to walk you home.'

'There's no need to put yourself to any trouble, constable.'

'Trouble? Between the blackout and you having to drop the takings into the night safe, I call it preventative crime measures, not trouble. Promise you'll wait?'

'As you put it that way, yes.' She smiled uncertainly.

He tipped his helmet to her as he walked away. She tried to concentrate on her customers, but old Mrs Evans had to ask for her bag of cracked nut toffee three times before Myrtle finally handed over exactly what she wanted.

'Do you really like this place?' Wyn looked at Diana across the candlelit table in the upstairs dining room of the Mermaid Hotel in Mumbles.

'I love it. I've been in the New Inn in Ponty for tea and dances on special occasions, but this is the first time I've ever actually stayed in a hotel.'

'I haven't been here in years. We used to come for holidays when my mother was still alive.'

'That must have been wonderful. I've never slept away from home except for the time I worked as a ward maid in the Cardiff Royal Infirmary. Mam used to take us to the seaside on day trips, mainly Barry Island and Porthcawl, but that's not quite the same, is it?'

'This place was Dad's idea. I've never asked, but I suspect it's the only hotel he's ever stayed in. He brought my mother here on their honeymoon. She loved Swansea and Gower.'

The waiter stepped forward and poured more wine into both their glasses, emptying the bottle Wyn had ordered. Diana suspected that Wyn's injuries had been mistaken for war wounds, but as Wyn appeared not to notice the extra service they were getting, she decided not to draw his attention to it.

'More of anything?'

She shook her head. 'I couldn't eat another thing. I think I'm tired,' she murmured, suppressing the desire to hit the waiter, who smirked knowingly when he overheard her remark.

'It's been a long day. That journey down was horrendous, especially the wait when we had to change trains in Cardiff.'

'It felt as though we were going to be stuck there for ever,' she agreed. 'But I'd still like to find out if there's a radio around here that we can listen to.'

'I'll look for one. If there's any news I'll come up and tell you. I promise not to hold anything back, good or bad,' he added, sensing her reluctance to entrust the task to him.

He left her outside their room. She walked in and closed the door behind her. It was a well proportioned room that could have swallowed her bedroom in her uncle's house four times over. High ceilinged, elegantly decorated in a light floral wallpaper that complemented the gilt mirrors and mahogany furniture, it looked out over Swansea Bay, affording a view of sands and sea that had taken her breath away when she had seen it for the first time that afternoon.

The maid hadn't pulled the blackout, but there was sufficient moonlight to guide her path to the window. The beach was shrouded in shadows that mercifully hid the wartime barbed-wire fortifications, but no blackout could darken the brilliance of the stars and full moon that cast a shimmering path on the glistening, inky waters that filled the bay.

She couldn't help feeling that Will and Tina should be here, not her and Wyn. It was the perfect romantic setting she and Tina had sighed over in so many Hollywood films. Everything was right – the view, the wax roses on a side table that could almost pass for real in this light, the enormous double bed, its crisp white linen perfumed with starch and lavender; there was even a bottle of champagne that Bethan had ordered and sent up in Andrew's name as well as her own that she and Wyn had decided to leave until after dinner.

She clung to the curtains, lightheaded at the enormity of what she'd done in marrying Wyn. The whole day had been diffused with a sense of unreality, and now everything about this room and the hotel seemed far too good for her. She felt like an impostor, a maid perhaps, who had wandered into a guest's bedroom. Any moment now the door would open, voices would be raised in anger and she would scuttle back to the kitchens and linen rooms where she belonged. The familiarity of menial work seemed a safer, easier option than the unknown quantity of married life.

Tearing herself away from the vista of night sky and sea, she opened the smart leather suitcase Tina and Gina had bought her as a wedding present and removed her toilet bag and the silk négligé set Bethan had insisted she buy as part of her trousseau. Opening the door she walked along the corridor to the bathroom.

Ignoring the signs prohibiting baths of more than four inches, she filled the tub half full of scalding hot water, shook a few drops of Evening in Paris into its depths, added a burst of cold and got in. Resting her head on the lip, she stretched out until her toes touched the tap, revelling in the unaccustomed luxury of immersing her whole body in water. After ten minutes of indulgent wallowing she felt inordinately guilty and unpatriotic. Here she was, living in the lap of luxury while William and Eddie were probably fighting for their lives in God only knew what dreadful conditions in France.

Trying not to think about much of anything, she washed and dried herself, cleaning the bath after her before dressing self-consciously in her bridal nightwear. Opening the door a fraction of an inch she scanned the corridor, checking it was empty before slipping back into her room.

On closer acquaintance the bed proved softer than the one in her uncle's house, and the fragrant linen sheets colder than the flannelette she was used to. She lay there, shivering in the moonlight waiting for Wyn, recognising the thud of his crutches on the stairs long before the door opened.

'Is there any news?' she demanded as soon as he walked in.

'It's not good.' He shrugged off his suit jacket. 'Ghent's fallen.'

'I hate it when they say a city's "fallen". It makes it sound like it's tripped over.'

'I think when they say fallen to the Nazis, they mean flattened. The bastards like using bombs to soften up the opposition before they go in.'

'Did they say anything about our troops?'

'No.' He moved closer to the bed: 'but if I know your brother, he'll be all right, and they did say that none of our troops are anywhere near Ghent.'

'There was nothing else?'

'Nothing, I swear it.' He went to the window. 'Do you want me to draw the blackout?'

'No. I've never seen anything as beautiful as that moon and the view from the window. If I wake up in the night I want to be able to look at it.'

'Do you want the window open or closed?'

'What are you used to?'

'Open.'

'Then open it. We'll be able to hear the sea as well as see it.'

'Diana,' he looked towards the bed but it was difficult to make out the expression on her face in the gloom. 'Don't throttle this marriage at the outset with politeness.'

'What do you mean?' she asked nervously.

'Any marriage, even one like ours, has to be a matter of compromise, of rubbing off the edges of personal preference to accommodate another's inclinations. It's not going to be easy for either of us, but you're going to make it a whole lot harder if you're the one who always bows to my wishes.' He opened his case and took out what he needed for the bathroom. When he returned she lay curled on her side, her face buried in the pillow.

He knew before he went to her that she was crying – for Will – for her mother – possibly even for herself. As he sank down on to the bed alongside her she shuddered, bringing a vivid memory to his mind of that dreadful night two years ago when he had found her wandering along Taff Street dazed by shock and pain, her face and body battered and bruised by the violence Ben Springer had used to rape her. By some miracle neither his father nor sister had been home, so he had taken Diana back to his house, found her some of Myrtle's old clothes to replace the ones Ben had torn off her, patched her up as best he could, and walked her up the Graig to her uncle's house. That appalling, traumatic night had marked the beginning of their friendship. Try as he might, he couldn't forget what Ben had done, and dismayed by Diana's refusal to go to the police and have fingers pointed at her as a 'fallen woman', he had cornered Ben one dark night not long afterwards and made sure that he would never be able to do to another girl what he had done to Diana. But revenge had never tasted as sweet as he hoped, not even when he'd heard that Trevor Lewis had operated on Ben Springer, finishing what he'd started, but although Ben's injuries had destroyed his manhood, they hadn't helped Diana in any way. Not then, and certainly not now.

Lifting her by the shoulders, he held her against his chest.

'I'm sorry, I didn't mean to cry. You've been so kind. This beautiful room, the hotel, the trip . . .'

'You're worried about Will and your mother?'

'Yes,' she murmured in a small voice.

'We'll go back to Pontypridd whenever you want.'

She looked up at him, her eyes luminous in the cold light. 'You mean it?'

'I told my father this honeymoon idea was stupid, he was the one who insisted on booking it. It feels wrong to be here enjoying ourselves with a war on.'

'You really don't mind going back?'

'Of course not.' He slid carefully into the bed alongside her, still holding her against his chest.

'I'm sorry.'

'What for now?' he teased gently.

'For being the way I am.' She trembled even more violently as his body stretched out warmly alongside hers.

'I promised you'd be safe with me, and you will.' Despite her trembling he drew even closer to her. 'Do you mind sharing a room and a bed like this?'

'It will take some getting used to,' she confessed, struggling to subdue the tide of nausea that threatened to engulf her even though it was Wyn, not Tony or Ben, who was holding her.

'I think the hotel would have found it odd if we'd asked for separate rooms on our wedding night.'

'I know.'

'And Myrtle and my father will expect us to share a bedroom at home, but I promise to keep my side of the room clean and tidy. I'll put all my dirty clothes into the linen bin just as my mother taught me, and I'll try not to snore.'

She couldn't raise a smile at his poor joke. 'It's just that . . .'

'You can't help remembering Ben Springer?' He locked his arms around her, cradling her as though she were a child. 'You told me you shared a bed and a room with Maud before she married Ronnie.'

'Yes.'

'Well, think of me as Maud.'

That time she did laugh.

'What's so funny?'

'You. You're ten times the size of Maud.'

'I'm also tired. Come on, time for sleep.'

He wrapped his arms around her, imprisoning her against him as the hotel closed down for the night. Snatches of conversation floated up from the stragglers who were leaving the bar. She tried to decipher their cries as she continued to lie in Wyn's arms, muscles tensed in a vain attempt to still her trembling, but her fear didn't finally fade until long after Wyn fell asleep. Only then did she allow herself to relax and enjoy the novelty of her surroundings. The hiss of the waves breaking amongst the pebbles on the shore, the throb of Wyn's heartbeat beneath her head, and a new, and wonderful sensation of quiet and absolute peace that she hadn't known since the night Ben Springer had robbed her of her innocence.

257

Chapter Twenty

'HEARD the news this morning, Tina?' one of the waitresses called-out as she walked into the restaurant.

'Fat chance, when I have to be here early to get this place ready to open.' Tina poked a wary finger at a new concoction the confectionery chef had come up with. It looked like a normal custard slice, but as she'd inspected the sugar and fat situation in the restaurant larder only last night, she doubted that there was either ingredient in the new creation he'd christened 'Victory'.

'Aren't you even going to ask what it is?' The waitress hung up her coat and tied on her apron.

'I only want to hear good news.'

'There's not much of that about,' the girl who served at the front of the shop intervened. 'Rumour has it the Germans have cut off all the escape routes for our boys. They've taken Boulogne, so the navy won't be able to get any more soldiers out.'

Suddenly finding it difficult to breathe, Tina sank down on the nearest chair. 'Does that mean the whole army is trapped in France?'

'I should think so,' the girl replied airily. It was well known that her father had engineered 'reserve occupation' positions for himself and her brothers.

Tina touched the pocket in her skirt, wanting to hear the reassuring crackle of the envelope she'd made the postman ransack his bag for early that morning when she'd met him setting out on his rounds. She'd meant to save William's letter for the quiet time, just before the eleven o'clock rush, but after hearing the news she couldn't wait any longer. Leaving her chair she took a knife from the butler's station and went to the back of the restaurant. Sitting facing the wall, she slit the envelope open.

My darling Tina,

No fears about censorship this time, or perhaps he was beginning to learn to disregard it.

France is not a bit like I expected it to be, and you needn't worry about the girls. I've been here for two days . . .

She deciphered the postmark on the envelope and discovered the letter had been posted in England. Had William handed it to someone homeward bound? The censor would certainly never have allowed the mention of France, and that might explain why they hadn't heard from Angelo and Tony, and why she hadn't received anything from William since their meeting except a brief postcard to let her know he was in transit. She checked the date on the envelope against the one he had written. It had taken nearly three weeks to get to her. Had he received any of her recent letters? She picked up the precious page again.

. . . and I've yet to see a girl as beautiful as you. The good news is that Eddie's still with us, and he's promised to show us all the ropes. He's already taken us to the shop where he bought the silk underwear he gave Jenny when he was home, and you wrote to me about. As he bought a whole lot more, it looks as though he and Jenny have really made it up. I tried to ask him what was going on between them, but you know Eddie, he always has played everything close to his chest.

We were given a pass to go into the village last night so I've seen the French at close quarters. Their inns aren't as cosy as our pubs, and their beer isn't up to much, even Eddie's taken to drinking wine and cognac, but I can't see any of us asking for a glass of wine in the Graig Hotel when we're home next.

It seems a long time since I've had any letters from you, but as no one in the unit has received anything for five days we're putting it down to a hold up somewhere along the line. I keep your last letter in my battledress pocket and think about the Tally Ho all the time. Just knowing you love me as much as I love you keeps me going, and just like you, my darling, I can't wait until we are married.

I'm sorry this letter is a bit rambling and rushed, but they only told us two hours ago that we're staying here, and I wanted to let you know that I am settled. I'm sending this back with a mate going out on a sick transport. I promise I'll write a longer letter tomorrow, but for now I want you to know where I am, what I'm doing, and that I miss you more than words can say.

I wish there had been an embarkation leave and a wedding. Wish is the wrong word, I get angry every time I think of what we've been cheated out of, but we had the next best thing thanks to you, and look on the bright side. Imagine the homecoming when I finally make it.

I love and adore you,
your ever loving Will
P.S. Eddie wasn't the only one to buy silk underclothes in that shop. I'll
expect a full fashion show when I come home.

Tina sat staring at the three week old letter. There was no mention of fighting, war or invading Germans. How long would it be before she'd get another letter, or find out what was really happening to Will and her brothers?

It was raining in Cardiff: a fine drizzle that coated the windows of the Lyons tea shop, hazing the street and distorting the faces of the people scurrying for shelter. Diana leaned back in her seat, making room for the waitress to set down the coffee and teacakes they'd ordered. She smiled at Wyn as he pushed aside the bag containing the books they'd bought as presents for her mother, Myrtle and his father.

'Will there be anything else, madam, sir?'

'Nothing thank you,' Diana answered glancing down at her wedding ring. Being called 'madam' was taking some getting used to, unlike living with Wyn. In only two days they had slipped into an easygoing, friendly familiarity. It was almost like spending time with a quieter, more thoughtful brother than Will had ever been. She picked up the coffee pot, 'Strong or weak?'

'Strong, no water.' Wyn glanced at his wristwatch. 'We've still got half an hour to kill before the next valley train comes in.'

'It was a good idea of yours to leave the station and do some shopping.'

'The longer you live with me, the more you'll realise I'm full of good ideas.'

'Was Myrtle very surprised when you telephoned to say we were coming home?'

'Not when I told her you were worried about your mother and William. From what I gathered, your mother's been putting a brave face on it, but that doesn't stop her jumping sky high every time the doorbell rings.'

'There's a newsboy coming down the street now.' Diana moved from her seat, but Wyn left the table before her.

'I'll go.'

Wyn was self-conscious about his crutches and the awkward movements he made with his artificial leg, which sat painfully on his barely healed stump, but as Diana watched him go up to the newsboy, she sensed that he was making an extra effort for her. Over the past few days there had been no trace of the self-pity he had fallen prey to in the hospital, and as she looked back she realised there hadn't been since she'd agreed to marry him.

He rushed clumsily back into the tea shop, scanning the headlines as he sat down.

'Have the Germans . . .'

'They're still advancing, but look – ' he pushed the paper towards her. 'The first British troops have been evacuated at a place called Dunkirk.'

'You think they could be the Guards?'

'There's no way of telling yet, love.'

'But they'll get them all out?' she asked anxiously.

He reached across and took her hand in his. 'Let's hope so.' He kept the thought, 'if they're still alive' to himself.

At the beginning of the war the Ronconis had installed a wireless in their Tumble café, but it had hardly been used until the German advance threatened the British positions in France. That night, the trouble with Dai Station was forgotten as a crowd of people who couldn't afford to buy their own wireless sets assembled in the back room to glean what information they could from the news broadcasts.

The town was awash with rumours. One of the tram conductors had assured Tina that a passenger had already received a telegram from the War Office telling her of her husband's death, and he was 'pretty sure' her husband was in the Guards. A driver argued with him, telling Tina that he'd heard from a mate who worked in the chainworks who had a brother in the Guards that the Welsh Guards had already left France. Mrs Evans from Station Terrace insisted that a woman in her street had received a telegram from her husband to say that he'd landed, was safe and well and would soon be home, but when Tina pressed her Mrs Evans couldn't say what regiment the man was in, or what number in the street the woman lived.

It was the same whenever Tina or Gina tried to pinpoint the origin of a rumour. Neither of them succeeded in fingering a specific person or address. The only news they could be certain of were the items read out on the wireless, and they weren't good: German bombs falling on the Rhône Valley and Marseilles; Germans on the march, advancing ever closer to Paris; the hair-raising evacuation at Dunkirk among falling bombs and bullets – and with every bulletin the faces of the men and women in Pontypridd who had relatives 'somewhere in France' grew more and more tight-lipped, and strained.

★

'I wish I could do something to help your sister,' Luke whispered to Gina as they followed Alexander and Tina up the hill after the girls had closed the café for the night.

'It's bad enough having to worry about Angelo, Tony and Trevor without having to worry about a boyfriend as well.' Gina wove her fingers into Luke's and squeezed tight to let him know how glad she was that he was with her, and not in France. 'If only we knew where they were it would be something. Sometimes I think it's the not knowing that's wearing Tina and Mama and Papa down.'

'The Guards are a crack regiment, aren't they?'

'The best.'

'Then it stands to reason they'll be one of the first regiments they'll bring back.'

'You think so? Judy thought they'd leave them to last, because they're such good fighters.'

'Evan says that they'll try to bring all the troops back and regroup them ready to invade Europe again.'

'If the Nazis don't invade us first,' she said gloomily. 'Luke, what will happen to the ones they can't bring back?'

'They'll be taken prisoner I suppose, but the Germans have to look after prisoners.'

'They won't kill them?'

'Not if they surrender.'

'I hope you're right.' She walked slowly towards the white cross painted on the wall. Alexander had already said goodnight to Tina and was waiting for Luke on the corner.

'See you tomorrow.' Luke waited until he heard Tina going into the house before kissing Gina on the cheek. Even under the cover of blackout he hadn't felt easy about showing affection to Gina since the night he had lost his head in the café. She stood on tiptoe and kissed him back before following Tina inside. Luke waited until he heard the door close, then walked away.

'You ever regret not signing up?' Alexander asked abruptly as he joined him.

'I try not to think about it.' Luke pushed his hands into his pockets as they turned the corner.

'I wish I could stop thinking about it.'

'You changing your mind about being a conscientious objector?' Luke asked in surprise.

'There's not much point in standing on your principles when you're looking down the barrel of a Nazi gun.'

'You really think they'll invade?'

'Once France has fallen, which it may well have done by now, what's to stop them?'

'Our troops.'

'In case it's escaped your notice they're being hammered in France.'

'Then there'll be nothing to stop the Germans taking over this country too?'

'If I was Hitler I wouldn't be unduly worried about a few Home Guard battalions.' Alexander dug in his pocket for his cigarettes and matches. Too many envious glances at his lighter had led him to pack it away for the duration like so many other things; including, he decided cynically, his hard-thought-out principles.

'Then you're going to join up?'

'Once France falls. They're going to need every man they can lay their hands on when the Germans cross the Channel. What about you?'

'I'll write to my father and ask him what he thinks.'

'Luke,' Alexander drew heavily on his cigarette in exasperation. 'You're doing a man and a half's job, you're living in lodgings, you've got a girl prepared to follow you to the ends of the earth. Don't you think it's time you started thinking for yourself?'

'If I volunteer it would go against everything I've ever been taught, everything my family believes in.'

'Looks like you're going to have to give up your beliefs one way or the other. If not to carry a gun, then to accept and adopt Hitler's philosophy. I'm not sure what the man thinks of Quakers, but I'd lay a pound to a penny it's not good. It's decision time for all of us, boyo,' he said, unconsciously aping the Welsh slang, 'and something tells me that every one of us is going to be mourning the passing of at least one principle before the year is out. Let's just hope that none of us are mourning our friends and neighbours along with our integrity.'

Tina gazed wistfully through the window of the café at the bright spring sunshine. The air looked warm and inviting; inside the restaurant the atmosphere was close and humid, with a stickiness that threatened to stale the cakes and curdle the cream substitutes the confectionery chef had invented to decorate and fill his creations.

She checked the tables. It was late afternoon and already the place was half empty. Another half-hour and she could close up and move on to the Tumble café to help Gina. The thought wasn't an appealing one. Pouring herself a coffee she sat at the table closest to the till. She'd taken to putting a 'Reserved' sign on it. Although Laura and her father did most of the accounts at home there was still a certain amount of book-keeping that had to be done in the cafés, and most of it had fallen on her shoulders since Tony had left.

She had just settled down with the purchase ledger when the cook burst through the door that led down to the main kitchen.

'I've just heard. It's terrible. What are you going to do about it?' he demanded excitedly.

'Do about what?' she asked irritably, expecting yet another wild rumour about parachuting Germans.

'Mussolini has declared war on France and Britain from midnight tonight. You know what that means? Italy's in the war!'

She turned around. Expelling her breath slowly she looked him coolly in the eye. 'Where did you hear that lot of nonsense?'

'It's not nonsense. Judy just heard it in Frank Clayton's radio shop.'

Tina looked across the road at Frank Clayton's electrical and record shop. He always had a radio blaring inside. Without stopping to take off her apron or overall, she left the restaurant and ran across the road.

'It's true.' Frank was standing on his doorstep, Alma Rashchenko next to him.

'Mussolini really has joined forces with Hitler?'

Alma nodded gravely. 'But no one's going to think any the worse of you or your family, Tina. Not with the boys in France. Look at Charlie, he was registered as an alien . . .'

Tina didn't wait to hear any more. She glanced back at the restaurant. There weren't many customers at the tables and there was hardly anything left to sell on the shelves. The ladies of the crache who comprised most of the restaurant's clientele were on their way home to supervise their maids and cooks in the preparation of the evening meal; but then the restaurant's customers always had been far more 'select' than those who patronised the Tumble café.

'Do me a favour, Alma, ask the cook to lock up the restaurant for me?'

'Of course, but where are you going?'

'The Tumble.' Tina ran full speed up Taff Street. Where the pavements were crowded she ran into the road, dodging trams and vans. She bowled into an elderly woman, knocking her shopping bags from her hands. Without stopping to apologise she dashed on, barely registering the indignant cries behind her.

She heard the noise first. An ominous rumble like the heavy rolling sound of thunder before a storm breaks; then she saw the crowd, mainly men, fists raised, faces and voices contorted with anger. Gina must have bolted and barred the doors of the café, because half a dozen men were hammering on them. Just as she drew level with the gathering, she heard the sound of breaking glass.

Without thinking what might happen if someone recognised her, she tried to push her way through the throng. An elbow thudded into her chest and sent her flying backwards over the step of the White Hart. Still fighting her way forward, she looked up and saw Wyn Rees leaning on his crutches with his back to the door of the café, Diana at his side as he faced the ugly mob head on. She continued to battle her way towards them, but it was hopeless: an impenetrable wall of noisy, sweating, male flesh blocked her path. She tried elbowing and kicking, to no avail.

'Kill the bastards!' a voice screamed. 'The whole family are bloody Fascists . . .'

'They're no more Fascists than you or me!' Wyn shouted, struggling to make himself heard above the noise. His voice was loud and steady, but Tina could see a nervous pulse throbbing at his temple.

'Joined the Fascists have you then, queer!' The gibe was followed by a second brick that hurtled through the air and shattered the splintered remains of the plate-glass window in front of the café.

'If the Ronconis are Nazis why are Tony and Angelo fighting in France alongside my brother and cousin? I don't see any of you beating your way to the recruiting office.'

A murmur went up from the crowd and Diana knew her point had struck home. She lifted her chin and stared defiantly at the mass of men, nodding slightly as she caught sight of Tina out of the corner of her eye. A few people moved away from the outer edges of the crowd. Tina turned and saw a tide of blue-coated policemen walking up from the town, Huw Davies in the lead. She ran up to him.

'It'll be all right, love. No one's going to do anything to you, or your family. You have my word on it.' He caught her and put her behind him. He stopped outside the White Hart and addressed the assembly.

'I'm telling you to disperse quietly. I'm only giving one warning and this is it. You have two minutes before we wade in with our truncheons. Just one thing before you go. If one of you would like to tell me who broke that –' he pointed to the window – 'and you'd like to have a whip-round to replace it, we'll say no more about the damage. If no money's forthcoming, I'll be getting out my little black book. What's it to be, boys?'

Like a rapidly ebbing tide the body of men fragmented and dispersed, down Broadway, the old tram road, Taff Street and beneath the railway bridge. Before one minute of Huw's two minutes had ticked past, the Tumble was deserted. Huw lifted his helmet and scratched his head. He'd succeeded in scattering the mob but no one had volunteered the name of the brick thrower or offered to set up a collection to replace the broken window. Yet another headache to add to his list of problems.

Wyn turned and knocked on the door behind him. He had to knock three times before a tearful Gina finally opened it. A tram crew stood behind her, armed with frying pans and ladles from the kitchen.

'We wouldn't have let anyone hurt her,' the leader of the group boasted.

Gina saw Tina and ran to her. She looked up at Wyn and Diana.

'I don't know how we're ever going to thank you.'

'There's nothing to thank us for. You would have done the same for us.' Diana turned to view the damaged window.

'We heard them come across from station yard. It's just war fever,' Wyn said dismissively. 'It will soon be forgotten.'

'We hope.' Huw pulled out his notebook. 'I'll send one of the boys for a carpenter; the sooner you get that window boarded up the better. I reckon you were a whisker away from being looted here. And if I were you I wouldn't bother to open up tonight.'

'We won't,' Tina replied. 'I'll give Gina a hand to clear up and then we'll go home.'

'Can I do anything?' Diana asked.

'Be a darling, go down to the restaurant and make sure the cook's closed up for me.' Tina handed over her keys. 'Tell the staff to clear the place. If anyone makes a fuss, give them their money back. I know it's half an hour early, but I think we've all had enough for one day.'

'You know what to do, constable?' the sergeant asked Huw Davies.

'I know, but that doesn't mean I have to like it.'

'Take half a dozen men, the Black Maria and a driver.'

'And I'm in charge?'

'Handle it any way you want, just try to avoid trouble at all costs. Here's the list.' Unable to look Huw in the eye the sergeant walked through the door that led down to the cells. He'd given Huw a foul job, but the way he viewed it, he had little choice in the matter. Huw was the oldest, steadiest and most level-headed of the constables on the Pontypridd force, and consequently the one most often landed with the worst tasks. Unfair on Huw, but it made for fewer choices for him.

Grim faced, Huw pushed his helmet on to his head and left the station. Six constables and a driver were standing alongside the black police van in the car park.

'I'll need four of you.' Huw looked at the men. Handel Jones, a young constable who'd only joined the force three months ago, was the least threatening. 'You,' Huw pointed at him. 'Sit alongside the driver in the front of the van, the rest of you in the back with me. And none of you as much as breathe without my permission. You two –' he turned to the men he'd rejected – 'I want you patrolling Taff Street with the beat coppers. One of you to be within hailing distance of every Italian café in town at all times.' He looked back at the clock on St Catherine's church tower. The sergeant had waited until dusk before striking, deciding that operations like the one they were about to embark on were preferably done under the cover of night, but it was still light enough to see the hands on the clock face. Nine o'clock. There was a lot to do before dawn.

'Where to first?' the driver asked as he opened the door.

Huw checked the list. 'Graig Street.'

'There's no one on that list who lives in Graig Street.'

'I know, that's why I want you to go there.'

'It seems funny to be out in the evening like this.' Gina picked a sprig of purple heather from the clump beside her and wound it around her finger.

'Did you tell your father you were meeting me?' Luke asked.

'On top of everything else that's happened? He would have had a heart attack. Fortunately he doesn't know you exist, otherwise he would never have let me go down the Powells when I said I wanted to see Bethan's baby.'

'I'm glad you came.' Luke dared to move a little closer to her. They were sitting on the side of the Graig mountain on a rug Gina had brought from her house. Below them shadows were lapping around the town, immersing it slowly but surely in darkness as twilight fell. They'd been enjoying the panoramic view as well as the beautiful late spring evening, but Luke was conscious that in order to admire the vista spread out before them, they'd put themselves on display, and could be seen by anyone who cared to look up at the mountain. 'It would be marvellous if we could do this every night,' he murmured softly.

'You miss the countryside?'

'More than ever after a day spent underground.'

'Then we'll have to find you a different job when the war is over.'

'Do you ever wonder what it will be like for us then?'

'All the time.'

'I know it's sinful, but I wish I could see into the future.'

'It's funny, here I am up to my neck in work in the café, and you working every day as a miner, and whenever I picture us married we're living on a farm.'

'You never said you wanted to live on a farm.'

'I didn't until you told me about Cornwall. I've come to like the idea.'

'It's hard work.'

'Neither of us are afraid of that.'

'No,' he smiled.

'It's dark enough for you to kiss me,' she prompted.

He leaned over and grazed her cheek with his lips. 'If we don't make a move your father will be pounding on the Powells' door.'

'I suppose so.' She rose to her feet, lifted the blanket and shook it free from grass and heather. 'Thank you for taking me for a walk tonight. The house was horrible. All they wanted to talk about was the mob outside the café. Mama ended up crying, Papa shouting, Tina and Laura arguing and the little ones were all being insufferable, as usual.'

'You can't blame them for being upset.'

'Who's blaming them? I had a right to be more upset than any of them. I was the one trapped inside.'

'I'm just glad you're in one piece.' He put his arm around her, and guided her down the hill.

'Papa's devastated. After living here for nearly thirty years, he never thought anything like this would happen.'

'Your brothers will be home soon, and when everyone sees them walking around town in uniform this will be forgotten.'

'By the town perhaps,' Gina said drily, 'but not by Papa or Mama. After the way Papa talked today I doubt he'll ever forget it.'

Huw Davies knocked at Laura Lewis's door for five minutes before a neighbour emerged to tell him he'd find her at her mother's. He was glad. He'd always found Laura to be the steadiest of the Ronconis after Ronnie, and the last thing he wanted to do was go into her parents' house without her there to calm everyone down.

Climbing back into the Black Maria he directed the driver to Evan's house in Graig Avenue. Bethan's car was parked outside. Ordering the driver to turn around at the end of the street, he left the constables in the van and mounted the steps to the front door. Knocking once, he opened it and walked inside.

Bethan and Phyllis started and Megan dropped the plate she was drying when he walked into the kitchen.

'It's not Will or the boys.' He removed his helmet and put it on the table. 'And if there was any news about them I doubt that I'd be bringing it. You'd get a telegram.'

Hearing voices, Evan and Alexander came in from the garden where they'd been fencing off a chicken run.

'It's not the boys,' Huw said swiftly before they asked. 'It's the Ronconis.'

'Don't tell me they've had more trouble after that mob today?'

'No.' Huw looked at Evan, and Bethan. 'I was hoping you two would come up to Danycoedcae Road with me. I've got to arrest Mr Ronconi.'

'Arrest him?' Megan stared at her brother as though he'd taken leave of his senses. 'In God's name why?'

'Round-up of enemy aliens.'

Evan reached for his jacket which he'd left hanging behind the wash-house door.

'You'll take care of Rachel for me?' Bethan handed her baby to her aunt without waiting for an answer.

Alexander unrolled his shirt sleeves and buttoned them at the cuff. 'Luke and Gina went for a walk over the mountain earlier, constable. Would it help if I found them?'

'It would.' Huw recognised the need for everyone to feel that they were contributing in some way. 'Get him to take Gina straight home, otherwise she might not be in time to say goodbye to her father.'

'What about Laura?' Bethan asked.

'I called in Graig Street on the way here. A neighbour told me she's already up Danycoedcae Road.'

'You sure you're up to this, love?' Evan asked.

'Laura and Trevor are our best friends, and Laura's got her hands full right now with the baby without any of this. I'm up to it, Dad.'

Huw gave the police driver the address of the Ronconis' house and told him to drive around via the main road and wait until he arrived. While Alexander went through the garden to the back lane and the mountain, he walked up Iltyd Street with Bethan and Evan. They saw Luke, Gina and Alexander at the end of Danycoedcae Road. Gina waved to them, and although they were too far away to read the expression on her face, it was obvious by the wave that she wasn't worried.

'Doesn't look like Alexander's told her what this is about,' Huw commented.

'Would you?' Evan asked.

'Probably not.' The Black Maria was waiting in front of the house. The driver stepped out. 'I'm not going to need you just yet,' Huw addressed the men in the van. 'But when I do, I expect you to do your job quietly and tactfully. That means putting everything back exactly where you find it. Provided you behave yourselves there won't be any trouble, not in this house.'

'It's not one of the boys, is it, Constable Davies?' Gina asked breathlessly as she ran up to him, Luke still holding on to her hand.

'No, love, it's nothing to do with the boys.'

Sensing trouble and not knowing what, Gina clung to Luke.

'I think we'd all better go inside.' Bethan had noticed curtains twitching in several front windows at the sound of the van. She knocked on the Ronconis' door and walked in.

Mr Ronconi opened the kitchen door. He saw Bethan in the passage and his face broke into an enormous smile. 'It's so long since you've come to see us, it's wonderful to have you here. Come in, come in. You too, Evan.' His face paled as Evan stepped forward and he saw Huw Davies behind him.

'It's the boys!' Mrs Ronconi's hand flew to her mouth as a sob caught in her throat.

'I don't know anything about the boys, Mrs Ronconi,' Huw assured her quickly.

'Then why are you here?'

Huw looked at Mr Ronconi. In all his years of policing he'd never felt as ashamed of having to do his duty as he did now. The only thing that stopped him walking out through the door was the thought that the next man who came to arrest Mr Ronconi might not have the same respect for the family that he did. 'I've come to take you into custody, Mr Ronconi.'

An incredulous silence settled over the passage. The five younger children crowded behind their parents. Tina followed them, opening the door wider. To Huw's amazement it was Mrs Ronconi who regained her composure first.

'Please come in, constable, Bethan, Mr Powell.' She stepped back into the kitchen, where Laura was already halfway through making tea. 'You five, into the parlour,' she ordered the younger children sharply.

'But Mama . . .' Alfredo whined.

'Now! And if you need something to do you can learn your catechism.'

Laura's baby whimpered; she picked him up and put him on her shoulder as Alfredo led the solemn column of children past the visitors in the passage.

'Is this something to do with what happened outside the Tumble café today?'

'No.' Huw took a deep breath, realising that Mrs Ronconi hadn't understood the meaning of the word 'custody'. 'After Mussolini's declaration of war on the Allies today, all Italian nationals have been given the status of enemy aliens. I've come to take Mr Ronconi to an internment camp.'

'Internment . . . you mean arrest?' As comprehension dawned, Mrs Ronconi clung instinctively to her husband. 'But why? We live here. This has been my home for over twenty years, and my husband's even longer. We are not enemy aliens.'

'I know that, Mrs Ronconi,' Huw agreed. 'And if it were up to me, I'd wring the neck of whoever gave the order. But the fact remains that Mr Ronconi's name was on a list that came into the station this afternoon from the Ministry. You never took out British citizenship?'

'I never saw any reason to,' Mr Ronconi acknowledged. 'I am Italian. I was proud to be until Mussolini came along.'

'But they can't intern him,' Mrs Ronconi pleaded. 'Not with two of our boys in the Guards, fighting in France. Please, let him stay with us,' she begged, refusing to relinquish her hold on her husband's arm.

'I can't,' Huw apologised wretchedly. 'The fact remains Mussolini came down on the wrong side today and a lot of innocent people are going to suffer. There's nothing I can do except take Mr Ronconi in, and plead his case as far as I can. I'm sorry, sir. Believe me I'm sorry. It's not just you. There's someone from almost every Italian family in Pontypridd and the Rhondda on the list we've been given. We're arresting old friends . . .'

'I understand.' Mr Ronconi straightened his back. 'Have I time to get my coat?' he asked with immense dignity.

'And pack a few things. Winter things as well. No one knows where they'll be sending you.'

'I'll pack your bag, Papa.' Laura handed her baby to Bethan and left the room.

'No!' Mrs Ronconi clung to her husband as he tried to follow Laura. 'You're not taking him. You can't. It's not right. Our sons fight for your army and you take him . . .'

'Not *your* army, Mama,' her husband corrected. 'It's "our". We're all fighting the Fascists. And Constable Davies has no choice but to do his duty.' He led his wife to one of the easy chairs. She crumpled into it and began to cry, softly, quietly. Huw could have borne it easier if she'd continued to rant and rave.

'I'm sorry Mr Ronconi, Mrs Ronconi but there are officers outside who have to search the house.'

'Now you look for spies here!' Mrs Ronconi sobbed.

'On the sheet we had from London it said that you belong to a Fascist organisation.'

'We don't belong to any organisations,' she protested.

'The Italian club?' Huw prompted.

'We meet, we talk about the old country, we drink some wine,' Mr Ronconi explained in a flat voice.

'Alexander, Luke?' Evan looked to where his lodgers were standing in the doorway. 'Nip down to the house and tell Megan and Phyllis that Mrs Ronconi and the children are joining us for supper.'

'No . . .'

'It's better that the children are out of the way when the house is searched, Mrs Ronconi,' Bethan interposed as Luke and Alexander left. 'If you don't want to leave while they're here, Laura and I will stay with you.'

'Where are you taking my Giacomo?' Mrs Ronconi demanded of Huw.

'He'll be put in a camp. There are a lot of them. I'm not sure which one he'll be sent to, but he'll be able to write to you in a day or two.'

Mrs Ronconi rose from her chair. Despite her diminutive size and the weight she was carrying she looked positively regal.

'Where my husband goes, I go.'

'Mrs Ronconi, I'm sorry, that's just not possible.'

'I go!' She glared at Huw.

'Who is going to look after the children if you come with me, Mama?'

'They can come with us.'

'Please can I have a few moments alone with my family?'

'Of course.' Huw stepped aside. He glanced at Evan and Bethan and motioned with his head to the wash-house. Tina and Gina trailed awkwardly behind them. They stood in the small back yard trying to ignore the heated Italian words flowing out of the kitchen.

'I'm glad you two are here,' Huw addressed Gina and Tina. 'I've no choice, I have to call the men in to search the house in a few minutes, and then there'll be no peace for any of us. What I'm going to say to you now could lose me my job, but I know you're both sensible girls. Get the businesses out of your father and mother's names as quickly as possible; tomorrow if it can be arranged. Sell them to British nationals.'

'Sell them?' Tina repeated hollowly.

'In name only,' he explained hastily. 'Put them in Laura's name, or better still Trevor's, and prepare your mother. The next step is resettlement of the families of enemy aliens into inland areas away from the sea. Rumour has it you're all going to be moved to the Midlands next week. Probably Birmingham.'

'But we don't know anyone in Birmingham,' Gina protested.

'You'll be allowed to stay together. Laura won't have to go, she's married to a British national.'

'But Laura will never be able to manage all three cafés by herself.' Tina suddenly realised the implications of what Huw was saying. 'Even if Mama goes, Gina and I will be needed to work . . .'

'I've told you all that I can. You haven't much time. Begin looking around for people you can trust right now.'

'People we can trust, or marry?' Tina questioned astutely.

'I know if Will was here he'd marry you, and then you'd be able to stay, which is why I want to do all I can to help. That boy is the closest to a son I'm ever likely to have.'

Tina frowned at her sister. 'I don't suppose Luke would consider marrying both of us to get us out of this mess?'

'How can you joke at a time like this?' Gina countered indignantly.

'You want me to cry like Mama?' Tina asked hotly, trying to close her ears to her mother's wailings.

'No, it's just that . . .'

'Come on, Gina.' Tina caught her by the hand and dragged her back into the house. 'We have to say goodbye to Papa.'

Chapter Twenty-One

THE morning after Mr Ronconi's arrest was the first since the German invasion of France that Bethan failed to listen to the news on the wireless. Rising early, she drove down to her father's house. Leaving Rachel with Megan and Phyllis, she carried on through the town and up the road that led to the Common.

She found her mother and father-in-law in their dining room that overlooked the garden. Her mother-in-law was monitoring the progress the elderly gardener was making in planting out seedlings, in between supervising the maid who was serving breakfast.

'Bethan, how kind of you to call, and so early.' Andrew's mother never failed to make Bethan feel like a grubby, charity case who should be grateful for whatever largesse the lady of the house saw fit to bestow. 'There's nothing wrong, is there? Andrew hasn't been – '

'I haven't heard anything from Andrew in over two weeks.'

'Dear me, no one seems to have heard anything lately. There appears to be quite a hold-up in the military mail.'

'It's called a retreat in the face of overwhelming odds, dear,' her husband informed her baldly.

'Come in and sit down, Bethan.' Ignoring her husband, she pulled a chair out from the table. 'Would you like tea or coffee?' she asked her daughter-in-law. Remembering working-class preferences, she picked up the teapot.

'I'd prefer coffee, please,' Bethan said, being deliberately contrary. 'I came to see if you can do anything for the Ronconis, Dr John?' she asked without further preliminaries.

'I heard that he was arrested last night along with just about every other Italian café owner in Pontypridd.'

'Arrested?' his wife echoed. 'You never told me anything about this.'

'That's because you were asleep when I came in. The Vittoris sent for me in the early hours. Old Mrs Vittori became hysterical after the police ransacked their house and took her son away.'

'I wondered if you could possibly speak for Mr Ronconi?' Bethan pleaded. 'After all, you're head of the practice, and Trevor is Mr Ronconi's son-in-law.'

'I've already tried,' he said shortly as his wife poured coffee from a silver pot into a porcelain cup for Bethan. 'Huw Davies was still at the Vittoris' when I got there. He told me that Mr Ronconi had been arrested so I went down to the station from the Vittoris' house. There's nothing I can do. It's a War Office, not local, directive. They've rounded up every Italian who hasn't taken out British citizenship, and those they think are members of Fascist organisations. I pointed out that the entire Italian club could be classified as Fascist by that definition, as Mussolini has put every society in Italy and all affiliated organisations under government control, but it was to no avail. And before you say anything about Tony or Angelo, practically every man arrested has at least one son or brother serving in the armed forces.'

Bethan took the coffee her mother-in-law handed her. 'It was just a thought. Thank you for trying.'

'You do know the next step is the rounding up of all the wives and children? They're going to be sent to inland areas well away from the sea.'

'I heard a rumour,' she answered vaguely, not wanting to get Huw into any trouble.

'It's not just a rumour. A couple of Italian families in the Rhondda have already sold their cafés to their friends. Get Mrs Ronconi to put everything in Laura's name, if she hasn't had the sense to do so already.'

'The problem isn't one of simply hanging on to the cafés. It's running them. The Ronconis need the money to live on, but Laura can't possibly manage all three cafés on her own, not with a baby to look after, and even if I took the baby off her hands she could only look after one place.'

'Who's managing them now?'

'Tina, Gina, and until yesterday Mr Ronconi.'

'Tina is the one engaged to your cousin William, isn't she?'

'Yes.'

'I'll see the sergeant this morning and tell him she's needed to look after Laura for six months to help her to recover from childbirth. He might not believe me, but he doesn't like what's happening to the Italians any more than the rest of us, so I think he'll go along with it. I'm sorry, Bethan, it's not much, but it's the best I can do.' Crumpling his starched linen napkin he threw it over the debris of haddock skin and bones on his plate. 'This is the unacceptable face of war, the side

I'd almost forgotten about. People you've known, liked and lived among for years being dubbed enemies and traitors overnight. In the last show it was the poor pork butchers and German bands.' He rose from his chair and brushed his lips over his wife's cheek. 'I would like to stay and talk, but unfortunately I have a surgery starting in ten minutes.'

'But you'll see the sergeant about Tina?'

'As soon as surgery's over.'

Andrew's father was as brusque with her as he'd always been, but for the first time Bethan saw a resemblance between him and his son as he stopped to straighten his tie in the hall mirror. There was the same tension in the jawline that denoted an unspoken, tight-lipped anger. Neither he nor Andrew was accustomed to expressing emotions, but she sensed that Dr John was as enraged by the high-handed round-up of the town's Italian café owners as she was, and even more furious that his hard-won respect and standing in the town was insufficient to put a stop to the senseless persecution.

Bethan stopped off at the Ronconis' Taff Street restaurant on the way back, to find Alma and Diana trying to console an irritable and highly sensitive Gina. If anything, the place was busier than usual, and when she looked around she realised that what Will and Eddie referred to as the crache 'be-hatted brigade' of middle-aged women were out in force sampling teas, coffees and what passed for cakes under wartime rationing conditions. It was good to know that the Italians who had served the community faithfully for so many years weren't entirely without friends.

'Tina wouldn't let me go back to the Tumble after yesterday, she's running the place herself,' Gina complained as Bethan joined them.

'What about the High Street café?'

'We haven't opened it this morning. Laura's gone down the police station with Mama to see if they can find out where they've taken Papa. Bethan, what's going to happen to us?' For all her outward confidence and air of sophistication, Gina looked very young and very frightened at that moment.

'I don't know, Gina.' Bethan tried to find words that would reassure, but it was difficult without resorting to meaningless platitudes. 'I wish I did. I've asked Andrew's father to do what he can. As soon as he finds out anything, I'll let you know. I promise.'

'If you have trouble finding someone to run the High Street café, I can take over for a few days,' Diana offered.

'You've got Wyn's shop to run,' Gina protested.

'Wyn and I talked it over this morning. The sweet shop never gets that busy until the early evening cinema rush, and I'll be able to help him with that if I go straight to the shop after I've closed the café. And when Wyn has to go to the hospital for check-ups, Myrtle can take over our shop. Mrs Edwards is always prepared to keep an eye on Wyn's father for an hour or two.'

'If you're serious, we may well take you up on that offer.'

'We're serious,' Diana assured her.

'I just don't know how we'd manage without all of you helping us . . .' Tears ran down Gina's cheeks.

'You won't need help for long.' Alma put her arm around Gina's shoulders. 'The War Office will soon realise it's made a mistake and release your father and the others. Look at Charlie – they imposed a curfew on him before taking him into the army, and now they've promoted him to sergeant . . . oh no!' Alma put her hand over her mouth. 'I shouldn't have said that. He warned me not to tell anyone.'

'Typical Charlie,' Diana smiled fondly, remembering his reserve when he had lodged with her mother. 'Trying to keep everything to himself, as if we wouldn't see the stripes on his uniform when he comes home on leave.'

'Gina, cook's gone doolally tap again!' one of the waitresses shouted up from the basement kitchen.

'Is he threatening to walk out?'

'Not yet, but you've a better chance of calming him down if you get to him before he reaches that stage.'

'Tina's much better at handling him than me. I wish she'd left me in the Tumble café,' Gina grumbled as she left the table.

'You'll cope,' Bethan called after her as she dived down the stairs.

'She'll cope because she has to, like the rest of us.' Alma arranged the cups the waitress had brought to their table and picked up the coffee pot.

'And because people like you two are rallying round. Nice relaxing honeymoon you and Wyn are having,' Bethan said as she handed Diana the milk jug.

'It seems wrong to take a honeymoon with a war on, besides,' Diana smiled, 'Wyn and I are happier keeping busy with the shop.'

'What it is to be young, in love, and happy,' Bethan teased gently, winking at Alma.

'It's early days, but so far we haven't thrown anything at each other. The only problem is, Wyn's too placid to have a really good row with. I'm beginning to find out I can stand anything except being agreed with.'

'Not much danger of that continuing when William and Eddie get home,' Bethan warned.

'Wyn sounds a bit like Charlie. If he doesn't like something he retreats into silence instead of complaining. It's infuriating.'

'I'm not sure that's such a bad thing, Alma,' Bethan contributed. 'Andrew and I have both said things in the heat of the moment we wanted to take back later, but couldn't.'

'You and Andrew always seem so happy,' Diana protested.

'Not always.' Seeing a wistful look in Alma's eyes Bethan decided the conversation was getting too serious. 'You should have seen his reaction when I starched his underpants the first week we were married.'

'Did you do it deliberately?' Alma asked as Diana burst out laughing.

'Just got carried away when I did the weekly wash. Apparently he spent so much time scratching and wriggling in work, a rumour went round the hospital that he'd picked up body lice.'

'I think even Charlie would shout if I did that to him.'

'Have you heard from him recently?'

'I had a letter today. He says he's well. I'd rather see for myself, but there doesn't appear to be any hope of leave, not soon anyway.'

'I'm sorry, it must be hard.'

'It's hard on all of us,' Alma said resignedly.

'Harder on you with a business to run.'

'Not really; the boy I've taken on pulls his weight. He's not as good as William or Eddie of course,' Alma qualified. 'Who would be? But he's willing, and I'm taking on a girl from the workhouse next week in the hope of boosting the brawn and pie production to somewhere near the level it was before Charlie left.'

'I take my hat off to you for trying.'

'It keeps me busy. I'm even thinking of expanding.'

'Expanding!' Bethan stared at Alma in amazement.

'Into Wyn's High Street shop,' Diana explained. 'We had to close it because of lack of stock, but if Alma can supply us with brawn, pasties and pies, we'll reopen it.'

'You make me feel idle and inadequate.'

'Idle, with a baby and a house that size to run!' Alma left her seat and looked across the road at the queue that was forming outside her shop. The ten-minute break was the longest she'd taken in a working day since Charlie had left. 'Remind Gina I'm only across the road.'

'We will.'

'And if there's anything I can do . . .'

'You'll be the first one we call on,' Bethan promised.

Tina was sitting at the counter of the Tumble café, a newspaper spread out in front of her and a thunderous look on her face. She glanced up as Bethan walked through the door.

'Have you seen this?' Without waiting for Bethan to reply she pushed the copy of the *Daily Mirror* she'd been reading towards her.

NOW EVERY ITALIAN COLONY IN BRITAIN AND AMERICA IS A SEETH-
ING CAULDRON OF SMOKING ITALIAN POLITICS AND BLACK FASCISM
HOT AS HELL.

EVEN THE PEACEFUL LAW-ABIDING PROPRIETOR OF A BACK STREET
COFFEE SHOP BOUNCES INTO A FINE PATRIOTIC FRENZY AT THE
SOUND OF MUSSOLINI'S NAME.

WE ARE NICELY HONEYCOMBED WITH LITTLE CELLS OF POTENTIAL
BETRAYAL, A STORM IS BREWING IN THE MEDITERRANEAN AND WE IN
OUR DRONING, SILLY TOLERANCE ARE HELPING IT TO GATHER
FORCE.

'Don't tell me you've been reading this load of drivel?' Bethan pushed the paper aside in disgust.

'And not just me by the look of it. Now I know why this place was attacked, our windows smashed, Papa arrested, my mother – '

'Ssh,' Bethan warned, as she looked around. Fortunately no one was sitting in the front room of the café.

' . . . and why we need a policeman on our doorstep,' Tina continued to rant.

'I've been to see my father-in-law. I asked him if there was anything he could do to make your family's situation any easier.'

'Why should he want to help us?'

'Because Laura's married to one of his junior partners. Have you given any thought as to how you're going to manage the cafés now your father's left and your mother's about to be sent away?'

'We haven't really had time to talk about it.'

'You're going to have to make time.'

'I know. Laura tried warning Mama that she may have to move last night.'

'It's not just your mother, it's nearly all the Italian families in Pontypridd. Dr John said the same as Huw Davies: you have to put the cafés into Laura's name as quickly as possible.'

'What's the point when there's no one to run them?'

'I can help.'

'You've got a baby.'

'So's Laura, and looking after two babies is no more work than seeing to one. I can take John any time Laura needs to leave him, and if an extra pair of hands are needed, we'll leave both babies with Megan and Phyllis.'

'You'd do that for us?'

'Aren't you forgetting Maud's a Ronconi? That makes us practically sisters, and besides, your family has a lot of friends and customers in Pontypridd. You can't just close your cafés on them.'

'So it would appear.' Tina smiled for the first time since Bethan had walked through the door.

'If you're prepared to allow your mother to go wherever they send her with just the younger children, Dr John said he'd go to the police station and tell them Laura needs you to look after her and the baby for six months. It's not much, but we thought it might help Laura if you were around, and hopefully William will be home before the six months are up. Then you two can get married, and as the wife of a serving soldier no one will be able to order you to go anywhere you don't want to. Between Laura, you, me and Diana, if Wyn can spare her, we may be able to keep all three cafés open.'

'You really think so?'

'I think so,' Bethan reiterated. 'After all, we can't have the boys coming home to closed cafés at the end of the war, now can we?'

By the time the day shift had ended in the pit, Huw's secret whisper to Tina and Gina had spread from one end of town to the other, and multiplied. The first thing Luke heard after the cage doors opened at the top, was that the Ronconis were being shipped out of Pontypridd within the hour. Refusing to be dissuaded by Evan or Alexander, who wanted him to wait until he'd bathed and changed out of his working clothes, he ran down the hill to the Tumble café. He flung open the door to find Tina, not Gina, standing behind the counter.

'We don't serve miners in working clothes,' she snapped tartly, looking no further than the coating of coal dust.

'It's me.'

Recognising the Cornish accent, she peered into his face. 'Well seeing as how it's you, I suppose I'd better let you in. Just stay there,' she pointed to the doormat, 'and don't touch a thing.'

'Is it true?'

'Is what true?' she asked irritably.

'That your whole family is leaving Pontypridd for the Midlands immediately?'

'Not in the next five minutes.' She relented when she saw the anguished expression on his face. 'But we've been warned we'll have to go soon, probably next week. The families of all enemy aliens are going to be resettled away from coastal areas, and although you might not credit it, for war purposes Pontypridd has been designated a coastal area.'

'Do you know what day you're going?'

'Not yet.'

'Where's Gina?'

'The restaurant, she should be here any minute.'

'I'm really sorry about your father, Tina. Everyone up at the pit has been saying it's rotten luck. No one believes he's a Fascist.'

'Except the government.'

A tram driver opened the door and tried to edge around Luke without touching him.

Pointing to a spot behind the door, Tina said, 'If you stand in that corner there's no danger of anyone brushing against you, and I'll give you a cup of tea while you wait for Gina.'

He shook his head. 'I'm making a terrible mess. I only wanted to make sure Gina hadn't already been sent anywhere. Now I know she's still in Pontypridd, I'll be back down later to see her.'

'Speak of the devil and she arrives.' Tina watched Gina walk past the window. 'But looking the way you do, I doubt she'll want to see you. Even love isn't that blind.'

Gina opened the door, recognised Luke beneath the layer of coal dust, and flung herself into his arms.

'God, you two really have got it bad, and you're hopeless, Gina. Now you're going to have to go home and change, which means I'm not going to get a break for hours,' Tina complained angrily. 'Go on, off with you, and take that filthy thing with you.'

Ignoring Tina's moans and Luke's state, Gina grabbed his hand and pulled him out through the door.

'I'm sorry about your father,' he murmured as they began to walk up the hill. 'Do you know what will happen to him?'

'Mama and Laura came into the restaurant after they'd been to the police station. The sergeant seemed to think they're going to put all the Italians in an internment camp in the country, somewhere remote like North Wales, or Scotland. The last thing Papa said to us before he was taken away, was to look after each other and the business, but now Mama is going as well . . .' She tried and failed to control her tears. Balancing his snap tin under his arm, Luke held her tight, wishing he was clean.

'I'm sorry, I'm behaving like a fool, and I'm keeping you from your tea.'

'Phyllis will probably put it in the oven, and if she hasn't, I'll buy something in the café. You don't really have to go away with your family, do you?' he asked anxiously.

'I have no choice. They won't let me stay. Laura tried arguing with the sergeant before she and Mama went to see some of the other families. Most of them aren't as lucky as us. As Laura's married to Trevor she will be allowed to remain in Pontypridd, so at least we'll have one member of the family here to keep an eye on the business for us.'

'But who's going to run the cafés? Laura can't possibly manage all three places on her own.'

'We know, and that's what's worrying Mama, because if the cafés close we'll have no money to live on. And Mama's going to have the added expense of paying rent wherever we're sent . . .'

'Laura can stay because she's married to Trevor, right?' he broke in urgently.

'Yes.'

'Then if we get married you'll be allowed to stay and carry on running the café?'

'You been talking to Tina about this?'

'No. What's the matter, don't you want to marry me?'

'Of course I want to marry you, but whenever we've talked about getting married it was always years from now.'

'If it's down to a choice between losing you, and marrying you now, there's no decision to be made. I'd hate to live here if you were somewhere else.'

'But we're both under twenty-one. Papa isn't even here to say no, which I know he would. Mama will never give us permission, and aside from my family, what about your father? You said yourself he wouldn't want a Catholic daughter-in-law.'

'I'll write to him tonight,' he interrupted, keeping quiet about the sure and certain knowledge that his father would sooner cast his eldest son out of the family than give his blessing to a union between him and a Catholic. And that was without bringing the question of age into the equation. His father had always advocated marriage at twenty-five for women and thirty for men. Twenty-one would have been diffi- cult, eighteen an impossibility.

'Even if you manage to convince your father, there's still Mama. We'll never persuade her to give her permission.'

'Wait for me in the Powells' while I wash and change, then I'll go home with you and we'll find out whether she can be persuaded or not.'

★

Evan and Alexander were just sitting down to their meal when Luke walked in with Gina. As Megan had already brought down his evening clothes he dived straight into the wash-house to bathe and change, leaving Gina with the family.

'You heard anything from your brothers today, Gina?' Megan asked after offering her a place at the table.

Gina shook her head. 'We can't understand it. The first troops came back from Dunkirk ten days ago.'

'The Guards could have been stationed much further inland.' Bethan busied herself with Rachel. The last thing she wanted to listen to was any further speculation as to where Andrew or the boys could be, because wondering in her experience inevitably ended in all too vivid imaginings of them lying dead on a forlorn battlefield, or in a ditch at the side of the road being strafed by machine-gun fire.

'You sure you don't want a plate of stew, Gina?' Phyllis asked. 'You're more than welcome.' She cut more bread to stretch the pot in case Gina accepted.

'No thank you. I have to go up the house and change so I can get back down the café. Tina will need help with the early evening rush.'

'Don't forget to tell your mother if there's anything we can do to help her pack, she only has to ask,' Megan reminded her.

'Doesn't he clean up well?' Bethan joked to Gina as Luke emerged pink and scrubbed from the wash-house. He was dressed in his second-hand suit, a collar buttoned on to his best shirt. He was even wearing a red and white striped tie he'd filched from Alexander's peg on the wash-house wall.

'He'll do.' Gina smiled despite her misery at her family's predicament.

'I'll dish out your stew, Luke.' Phyllis picked up the ladle.

'If you don't mind, Mrs Powell, I'll skip tea tonight. I'd like to go and see Gina's mother.'

'I'll walk up with you.' After Tina's comments yesterday, Bethan had guessed what was coming, and thought she might be needed.

'Tell your mother if she wants a van to take her boxes down to the station I'll have a word with Fred Davies for her. He owes me a favour or two from some carting jobs I did for him.'

'I'll tell her, Mr Powell.'

'Here, give me that little darling.' Megan held out her arms and took Rachel from Bethan. 'Don't forget to give Mrs Ronconi and the children our love.'

'I won't,' Bethan answered, as she followed Luke and Gina down the passage.

★

Mrs Ronconi was presiding at the family table when Bethan, Gina and Luke walked into the kitchen. Everyone had finished eating, and Mrs Ronconi was sitting drinking coffee with Laura. Eleven-year-old Theresa had assumed authority, and was standing in the wash-house doorway supervising her younger brother and sisters as they cleared the table and washed the dishes.

'Gina!' Mrs Ronconi frowned at her daughter after greeting Bethan and giving Luke a suspicious look. 'Your dress is black. Are those handprints I see?'

'Just smudges, Mama,' Gina prevaricated as she examined the marks Luke had made when he'd embraced her on the hill. 'That's why I came home to change.'

'And how exactly did you get into this state?' Mrs Ronconi demanded, staring hard at Luke.

'Someone came into the café in working clothes and made a bit of a mess,' Gina replied, not entirely untruthfully. 'Mama, this is Luke.'

'Pleased to meet you, Mrs Ronconi.' Luke stepped forward, hand outstretched, but Gina's mother pretended not to see it. 'You were here last night. You're one of the conscientious objectors who lodge with the Powells?'

'That's right, Mrs Ronconi.'

'I came up to see if anyone in our family can help with anything.' Bethan braved the awkward silence that fell as soon as Gina left the room to change.

'Laura and I have discussed what needs doing.' Mrs Ronconi couldn't have been more different from the hysterical woman who'd had to be physically torn from her husband's arms the night before. Calm and collected she'd clearly assumed her husband's mantle of head of the family, and appeared to have adopted his personality along with the role. 'We have decided that the best thing we can do is put all the businesses in Laura's name as she is the only one who will be allowed to remain in Pontypridd for the duration. Thanks to your father-in-law, Bethan, Tina will be able to stay with her for six months. Between them they will have to do the best they can with the cafés. We'll have to close one of them, and we decided that as High Street is the smallest – '

'I don't see why I can't stay to run that,' Alfredo broke in sulkily.

'Because you're twelve years old and too young to leave school, and because if you stay there and work hard you might make something of your life,' Laura retorted.

'Ronnie was working in the cafés at my age.'

'Ronnie worked, because we had no choice in the matter. There were too many mouths to feed and not enough hands to help in the early days,' his mother informed him. 'And I've already explained why you have to come with me. I need a man to help me with the little ones, the heavy lifting, all the work of the move, and the decisions that will have to be made when we get there. You're going to have to take your Papa's place until he is allowed to live with us again.'

'There is one way you can keep all three cafés open, Mrs Ronconi,' Luke proposed courageously. 'If Gina marries me, she can stay in Pontypridd with Laura and Tina.'

Gina chose that moment to walk through the door. Although she hadn't heard a word Luke had said, the fact that he was screwing his cap into a ball told her that he'd spoken to her mother, and was waiting for a reply.

Expecting an outburst, Laura handed her baby to Bethan and went to the wash-house, closing the door to shut out the younger members of the family.

Mrs Ronconi looked from Luke to Gina, not saying anything for what seemed like an eternity. When she did finally speak, it was in a quiet, controlled tone that neither Luke nor Gina had expected to hear.

'How long have you known my daughter, Mr . . .?'

'Luke, Luke Grenville. The time doesn't matter, Mrs Ronconi. I love her. Very much,' he added resolutely.

'How old are you?'

'Eighteen, but . . .'

'Both of you are very young. You may change your mind about one another in a year or two.'

'I'll never change my mind, or my feelings about Gina, Mrs Ronconi,' he asserted forcefully.

'I know nothing about you, Mr Grenville apart from the fact that you're a conscientious objector. And I don't mind telling you that isn't something in your favour, particularly when I think of my Tony and Angelo.'

'I'm . . . my whole family are Quakers, Mrs Ronconi. We don't believe in taking life, but we're all prepared to work for the war effort, which is why I'm in the pit.'

'A Quaker. Ronnie marries a Baptist and you find a Quaker! An eighteen-year-old Quaker!' Mrs Ronconi railed at Gina, momentarily forgetting that the Baptist her son Ronnie had married was Bethan's sister.

'We're exactly the same age you and Papa were when you married,'

Gina pointed out, concentrating on what she felt was the lesser of Luke's two faults in her mother's eyes.

'I know, which is why I haven't said no – yet. But I'm your mother, Gina. Do you know what that means? It means that I love and care for you, and it's my duty to ensure that when you make an important decision, like who and when to marry, it will be for the right not the wrong reasons. And with this terrible war forcing us into situations we can't control, it's not always easy to see the right reasons any more.' She faltered for a moment, tears gathering at the corners of her eyes, but she struggled to compose herself. Darting a quick glance at Luke, she asked, 'What will your family say to this?'

'When I explain the situation to my father I'm sure he'll give us his blessing and permission to marry. I intend to write to him tonight. I know I'm only getting a butty's wages at the moment – ' the Welsh term rolled oddly off Luke's Cornish tongue – 'but there's always the chance that I'll get promoted to miner, and you can be sure that I'll do everything in my power to look after Gina, Mrs Ronconi.'

'Gina, what do you say to this?'

'I love Luke, Mama. We planned to marry when he was twenty-one and I was nineteen anyway. This just brings it forward by a few years.'

'Three years are a long time in a young girl's life. You'll be spending, some would say wasting, your youth as a married woman. There'll be no more dances or parties, only housework and drudgery.'

'It won't be drudgery if Luke and I are together.'

'Laura?' Mrs Ronconi looked to her eldest daughter. 'You must have something to say about this?'

'Only that they're young, but it seems to me that everyone is having to grow up quickly these days, and,' she smiled wryly, 'to look on the practical side, miner or not, Luke has an extra pair of hands to help out in the cafés at the weekend.'

'Of course I'd be glad to.' Luke seized his chance to prove willing.

'And you'll talk to Father O'Donnelly about converting to the one true faith?'

'I'll talk to him, but I can't promise anything, Mrs Ronconi,' Luke replied, ignoring the pressure of Gina's fingers on his arm.

'At least you're honest, Luke. I'll give you that. I wish things were different, but as they're not, I'll tell you what I'll do. Presumably your father knows you better than anyone here. If he gives his permission, I'll allow you to marry Gina.' Mrs Ronconi turned to her daughter. 'I'll write and tell Papa about it tonight. I know it isn't what he hoped for you, Gina, but it seems to me the best thing you girls can do is marry British nationals, and the sooner the better.'

'It might be just as well if you and Gina live here after Mama and the children go, Luke,' said Laura. 'Tina had better move in with me as she's supposed to be looking after me and the baby, and that way both houses will be occupied.'

'That sounds like a good idea.' Mrs Ronconi looked to Gina for approval.

'I haven't even got enough money saved for an engagement ring,' Luke confessed.

'Seems to me you don't need one.' Bethan handed Laura's baby back to her. 'And wedding rings, especially wartime nine-carat-gold patriotic ones, are somewhat cheaper than diamonds.'

'As long as I marry Luke I don't care if I have a curtain ring,' Gina smiled, starry-eyed up at Luke.

'Spoken like a true romantic,' Laura said gravely. 'Cling to it, little sister. Something tells me the Ronconis, along with all the other Italians in this country, are going to need every bit of romance and happiness they can get in the coming months.'

Chapter Twenty-Two

BETHAN, Diana, and the three elder Ronconi girls scarcely had a minute to themselves during the next few days. In between helping Mrs Ronconi decide what should be shipped to the Midlands and what should be left behind, and the best and safest way to pack her cherished belongings for storage in her own, or Laura's house or transit, they ran the cafés and restaurant, took turns in caring for the babies with Phyllis and Megan, registered to take evacuees from the bombing that was expected to start any day on London and the Home Counties, and arranged Gina's wedding.

Despite all the bustle and activity, there was a peculiar atmosphere in the town. As though everyone was marking time, holding their breath, waiting for something huge and momentous to happen. Pontypridd had never been busier, the streets were packed throughout the day, and in the evenings it seemed as though the entire population of the surrounding valleys turned out to queue at the entrances to one or the other of the picture houses. The films were incidental: half the time no one registered what was showing, but everyone wanted to see the latest newsreels from Dunkirk in the desperate hope that they'd recognise a face amongst the thousands of men dug in on the shell-torn, bomb and bullet-swept beaches, or patiently wading out into the sea in orderly files; rifles held high above their heads as they waited up to their chests in water in the hope of finding a corner in one of the rescue boats. Occasionally there was a cry of recognition, and one or two lucky families left at the end of the evening, smiling, ecstatic in the knowledge that their husband, father, brother or son was safe and well – or at least had been when the newsreel was filmed. But there was still no official news of the whereabouts of the Welsh Guards, only rumours that escalated into the wilder realms of fantasy and fiction with every passing day.

Gina and Luke arranged their wedding for two o'clock on Thursday afternoon, early closing day in Pontypridd, so there'd be no problem with Wyn, Diana or Alma attending, and exactly one hour before

Mrs Ronconi and the younger children were due to leave Pontypridd railway station on a special train bound for Birmingham.

Fred Davies had already been entrusted with the packing cases of clothes, and bare essentials of cutlery, crockery, cooking utensils, bedlinen and towels, which were all that Mrs Ronconi could bring herself to take to equip herself for her new life as the wife of an enemy alien.

She spent the last two days wandering from room to room in her home, picking up ornaments and putting them down again, taking photographs from frames and adding them to the growing bundle in the cardboard case in her handbag – and waiting for a letter from her husband that didn't come.

'We have to go,' Laura urged impatiently as she stood in the kitchen doorway watching her mother pace uneasily between the letterbox and the parlour.

'I have to say goodbye to the house. There'll be no time to come back afterwards.'

'I know, Mama, but everyone's waiting. The taxi's outside, and so is Bethan. We only have ten minutes to get to the Registry Office. You do want to see Gina get married, don't you?'

'Not this way. A girl's wedding day is important. It should be one she'll be proud to remember for the rest of her life, the church decked with flowers, a proper white dress that she can fold away for her own daughters, bridesmaids in long frocks, and her papa to give her away.' Mrs Ronconi opened her handbag and rummaged in its depths for a handkerchief.

'We would have all liked that, Mama, but it can't be helped. There's nothing we can do now except give Gina the best wedding we can under the circumstances.'

'I suppose so.' Mrs Ronconi called to the younger children. Laura had already lined them up in the kitchen for the inspection she knew her mother would want to give them. They were dressed in their best clothes, not just for the wedding, but also for the journey afterwards. Mrs Ronconi walked slowly in front of them, smoothing down their hair, tucking in shirts and blouses, wiping spots she insisted were jam off Alfredo's face with her handkerchief, much to his disgust.

'Right, you lot.' Tina shepherded them to the door as soon as her mother reached the last in line. 'Into the taxi and behave yourselves.'

'It's unlucky to get married on the thirteenth and a Thursday,' Mrs Ronconi began for the tenth time that morning.

'Don't worry, Mama. In wartime everyone makes their own luck.

Gina and Luke are in love, they'll be happy together and that's what's important.' Laura crossed her fingers beneath John's shawl.

'I hope so. If only I could be sure that I'm doing the right thing in letting Gina get married. She's so young. Your papa would have known what to do. I wish I could have spoken with him . . .'

'Mama, we really do have to go.'

'Where's Gina?' Mrs Ronconi looked around for the bride.

'Here, Mama.' Gina walked down the stairs in a red costume she had bought in Leslie's Stores. Apart from the shoes it was the only new thing she was wearing. She'd borrowed Laura's best navy blue hat, blouse, handbag and gloves.

The sight of her daughter in her wedding finery jolted Mrs Ronconi out of her uncertainty. Whatever the outcome, the events of the next hour were inevitable. 'You look very nice. Just make sure you take care of yourself when I'm not here to watch over you. Air your underclothes properly and eat plenty of – '

'I'll be fine, Mama. You're not to worry about me. I'll have Luke to look after me from now on. Are you sure you can manage without us in Birmingham?'

'With Alfredo to do all the work, there'll be nothing for me to do except turn into idle crache.' Mrs Ronconi squared her ample shoulders and faced the door. 'Come on, it's time we went. Bethan is waiting for us outside in her car.'

Laura gave Gina a knowing wink before following her mother down the steps.

Luke sat nervously in the ante-room of the Registry Office sandwiched between Alexander and Evan, who'd had a devil of a time persuading the pit management to give them all a half a day off in the middle of the week. In Luke's hands was the envelope that had arrived in the post yesterday morning. He had tried to forget the letter it carried, a vitriolic, angry letter absolutely and expressly forbidding him to marry an enemy alien and a Catholic to boot. He had torn it up as soon as he had read it, flushing the pieces down the ty bach, before replacing it with another letter in his own hand giving him full permission to marry Miss Gina Ronconi, and wishing them both well. Suppressing his qualms, he had signed it with his father's name.

Logic told him there was no way anyone in Pontypridd could possibly know the difference between his own rather immature, rounded script and his father's more spidery hand, but at that moment logic had lost the battle against nervousness. He felt as though forgery was a sin every bit as unpardonably dreadful as murder. Then he turned and saw Gina walking through the door in her new red costume, clutching her bible which had been decorated with an early rose one of the girls had scavenged, and all his doubts faded. What if he had told one small lie? It was nothing set against Gina's happiness, and there were a lot of miles between the valleys and Cornwall. Miles no one would be travelling until after the war was over.

For the first time he found himself wishing that the war would last until he was twenty-one. His father could say or do whatever he liked after 1943; once he was a man in law, words wouldn't be able to hurt him or Gina. Just three more years. Then he considered just how many soldiers might die in that time and he was ashamed of himself.

Rising to his feet he took Gina's hand, tentatively returned her smile, and led her through the open door.

'You'll write, Mama?'

'I'll write.' Mrs Ronconi's bottom lip trembled. 'You three girls look after one another; and you —' she kissed her new son-in-law on the cheek — 'you take care of my girls. You're the only man in the family able to do so now.'

'I'll take care of everything,' he assured her solemnly.

'Goodbye, Mama!'

The whistle blew and Laura, who couldn't wait for the leavetaking to be over, slammed the carriage door on her mother and brothers and sisters. Ordering Alfredo to keep everyone in the carriage, she stepped back.

Up and down the platform goodbyes were being shouted in a mixture of Italian, Welsh and English as other families leaned out of the windows of the train to catch a last glimpse of Pontypridd station. Some were trying to put a brave face on their deportation, but most of the women were in tears, and Laura burned with a white hot fury at the injustice of it all and her own impotence in the face of this mindless, heartless bureaucracy.

'What's Mrs Ronconi going to do in Birmingham?' Alexander asked Evan as they leaned against the wall of the waiting room out of the way of the Ronconis' farewells.

'Survive for the duration, the same as the rest of us.'

'I'm going to find it difficult to think of Luke as a married man. He should be still in school, not keeping a wife.' Alexander watched Luke put his arm around Gina's waist as the train chugged slowly down the tracks and around the bend that led towards Treforest and Cardiff.

'He's grown up fast in the last few weeks, and Gina's the same age Maud was when she got married.'

'Your youngest daughter?'

Evan nodded. 'God alone knows what's happening to her and her husband now Italy's joined the Fascist cause. I can't see Ronnie Ronconi fighting in the Italian army.'

'Damn this bloody war.'

'Well said, Alexander.' Laura clutched John as she watched the last vestiges of smoke from the engine blow over the track.

'What happens now?' Alexander asked as he stood up and brushed the soot from the shoulders of his jacket.

'We all go to the restaurant and eat,' Laura said firmly. 'I've ordered a lunch to be served in the upstairs function room. This might be a wartime wedding, but I won't allow it to be a hole in the corner affair.'

Laura had done her best. There were flowers on the table, the linen was spotless, the chicken dinner was excellent and the waitresses cheerful as they congratulated the happy couple. Alexander tried to sustain the party mood. At his most expansive and entertaining, he insisted on adding to the bottles of wine Wyn had provided in the hope that a little alcohol would lubricate the party, but every time a newsboy cried in the street someone left the table to see if the headlines were new.

Alma was beset by a peculiar mixture of gratefulness for the letter she had received from Charlie that morning, and guilt because her own husband was safe when the Powells and Ronconi girls didn't even know where Eddie, William and the Ronconi boys were, so she concentrated all her attention on trying to cheer up Megan, Bethan, Jenny, Laura and Tina, but neither her own nor Wyn's and Alexander's well-intentioned efforts succeeded in driving the anxious look from the women's eyes.

'I should go and check the Tumble café,' Tina said as soon as the plates had been cleared. It wasn't the thought of the work that needed doing that motivated her to make a move, but an acute longing for William that worsened every time she saw Wyn put his arm around Diana, or Gina and Luke gaze into one another's eyes.

'The cook can manage for another half-hour.' Laura signalled the departing waitress to bring the cake. A cake for which she had allowed the cook to squander half a week's ration of butter and eggs.

'What about the High Street café?' Diana asked.

'That's staying closed today. I'll take it over tomorrow. But for now let's forget about the cafés and celebrate. Mr Powell, would you fill everyone's glasses for the toast please?'

Evan picked up the bottle and walked around the table. A year ago he'd never have imagined Gina and Tina, who'd rarely had a thought before the war other than what film to see or what scent to buy, running the Ronconis' cafés. So much had changed, and so many sacrifices were being made.

Laura and Bethan pulling together without the support of their husbands, trying to keep one café open between them by sharing the workload and the care of their babies. Tina running the Tumble café, which had always been the roughest, by herself. Gina taking over the restaurant, and a married woman at sixteen. Alma keeping Charlie's shop open with only a couple of young boys and an untrained workhouse girl to help her. Jenny living alone and managing Griffiths's shop while her father languished in the asylum, making no discernible progress for all the doctors' confident predictions that the depression that had clouded his brain would lift within a year.

'That's the cake,' Laura announced as she heard a step on the stairs. 'Now who wants coffee and who wants tea after the toast?'

'I don't know about you,' Alexander whispered to Wyn, 'but I wouldn't mind raiding the wine cellar to see if there's any bottles left.'

Laura cleared a place on the table for the cake. She turned her head to look for the waitress. Somehow John ended up alongside Rachel on Bethan's lap as she ran headlong to the top of the stairs. Trevor stood there, hollow eyed, exhausted, his uniform creased and filthy.

Laura flung herself into his arms, half crying, half laughing. The others looked on awkwardly. They would have left the room if Laura and Trevor hadn't been blocking the only exit. Megan reached out and lifted one of the babies from Bethan's lap, taking the opportunity to grip Bethan's hand as she sat, white-faced, trying not to think the worst as she watched Laura and Trevor.

Wrapping his arm around Laura's shoulders, Trevor stepped forward. 'They told me downstairs that congratulations are in order.' He managed a weary smile for Gina, as he held on to Laura's hand on his arm. 'You going to introduce me to this new brother-in-law of mine?'

'Trevor, this is Luke.'

'Pleased to meet you.' Trevor extended his free hand. 'We must have a talk some time. I can give you hints on how to handle the Ronconi women.'

Bethan couldn't wait another moment. 'Have you see Andrew and the boys?' she begged.

'Let the poor man get his breath. Sit down, Trevor.' Evan pulled out a chair and took the wineglass Bethan hadn't used. He tipped the last of the wine into it and handed it to Trevor.

Trevor looked to Bethan first. 'I have a letter for you from Andrew. Don't worry, he's fine. Overworked maybe, but perfectly well.'

'What's it like over there?' Tina asked.

'Difficult.' Trevor closed his eyes against images that would haunt him to the end of his days. Images he had no right to inflict on anyone who hadn't been through the hell he had. 'We're retreating on every front.' His words were short, clipped as he made an effort to produce a sanitised view of the war for his audience. 'It's orderly enough but we're having to fight every step of the way. The Germans don't let up for a minute. They're hot on our heels however fast or far we run.'

'And Eddie – ' Jenny's question was interrupted by Tina and Megan.

'And Will . . .'

'And Tony and Angelo?' Gina pleaded.

'I heard before I left that the Welsh Guards are being used to fight the rearguard. But Tony will be home in a few days, he'll tell you more. He's been wounded.'

'Is it serious?' Laura asked anxiously.

Trevor shook his head. 'I dug a bullet out of his shoulder. It's not bad, but it was enough to get him a place on the medical transport I came home on. All the boys were fine when he left them. They gave Tony some letters.' He pulled a small bundle of papers from his pocket and distributed them among Evan, Megan and Jenny. 'And these are for you – ' he passed two battered and stained envelopes to Tina and one to Gina. 'I'm sorry they've been through the mire.'

'Like you, by the look of you.' Laura couldn't stop staring at her husband as though she found it difficult to accept that he was really home. He held out his hands to his son.

'Oh no you don't.' Megan whisked John out of his reach. 'Not until you've washed.'

'I suppose you're right.' He settled for tickling John under the chin.

'If the Guards are fighting the rearguard action, they'll be the last off the beaches,' Evan said slowly, as he absorbed the full implications of Trevor's revelation.

Trevor picked up his wineglass. 'That's if they get off at all.' He looked around the table. 'I'm sorry, but it might be as well if you all prepare yourselves for the possibility.'

The party broke up as soon as the cake and coffee had been served.

Evan, Phyllis, Brian and Megan went across the road to Alma's after first extracting a promise from Bethan to join them later. Clutching her letters, Tina made her way up Taff Street to the café. Jenny, Gina and Luke walked with her as far as the Tumble on their way up the Graig. Luke still had to move his few belongings from Evan's house to Danycoedcae Road. Wyn and Diana left to open the theatre shop. Finally only Bethan remained.

'I'll give you two a lift home,' she said as she buttoned on Rachel's cardigan.

'I'd appreciate that, Bethan, I'm whacked.' Trevor's eyes met hers and Bethan knew that he hadn't told her all the news of Andrew, not yet.

'I'll make us some tea.' Laura opened the car door and went into the house. As the front door swung wide Trevor saw the packing cases Mrs Ronconi had asked Fred Davies to deliver to Laura for safe keeping. Laura's mother had insisted on splitting her 'best' china and linen between Laura's house and her own in case of bombing, in the confident, if misplaced, belief that a device falling on Danycoedcae Road would leave Graig Street totally unscathed.

'We're moving?' Trevor asked Bethan.

'It's a long story, Laura'll tell you about it.'

'You're coming in, Bethan?' Laura asked as she returned to the car to fetch John.

Bethan shook her head. 'I have to pick up my father and the others and take them home. But if you're willing, I'll borrow your husband for five minutes.'

'Ten if you like, as long as I can have him all to myself afterwards. But you'll come tomorrow?'

'I'll telephone. I'll manage the High Street café while Trevor's on leave.'

'I haven't even asked how long you've got?' Laura looked at Trevor.

'Twenty-four hours. It's all they could spare. They need every doctor they can get. The wounded haven't stopped flooding in, and won't for a while.'

'I bet you're hungry.'

'And tired. I intend to spend every minute of my leave in bed. Sleeping,' he added, reading the amused expression on Bethan's and Laura's faces.

'I'm sorry,' he apologised after Laura had taken John into the house. 'I'm in such a state I've messed up your car. And unlike me, Andrew is always so particular . . .'

'He's staying, isn't he?' Bethan broke in abruptly.

'We drew lots. He was caught with the short straw. One of the bachelors offered to take his place, but he wouldn't hear of it.'

'He wouldn't have.' There was bitterness as well as resignation in her voice.

'I'm sorry, Beth, but none of us felt we could just abandon the wounded. Someone had to stay in Dunkirk . . .'

'And it had to be Andrew.'

'Here,' he pulled a creased scrap of paper out of his pocket and pressed it into her hand. 'I wish you'd come in.'

'You want me to eat into your precious leave minutes? If it was Andrew who was home I'd be telling Laura to get lost.'

'Beth . . .'

'Leave me in peace to read my husband's letter, and remind Laura not to set foot in the café until you've gone.'

Bethan laid the letter on the front seat after Trevor left the car. She turned her head to check that Rachel was still sleeping peacefully in the cot on the back seat. Driving slowly and steadily she made her way back through Taff Street and up on to the Common. She didn't go straight to Andrew's parents' house but parked on the bluff overlooking the town. It was only after she'd checked on Rachel a second time that she unfolded the scrap of paper Trevor had given her. There was no envelope.

Darling Beth,

I'm sorry this is so short, but Trevor's convoy moves out in five minutes.

I love you and Rachel, and always will. One day we'll be together again. I have to believe that, it's all I have to live for. I'll write the very first minute I can.

Don't worry about me, even the Germans need doctors.

Your loving husband Andrew

She crouched over the steering wheel, clinging to the note as though it were a lifeline. He was alive, and hopefully he'd stay that way. She tried not to think how long it would be before she'd see him again, or what the Germans would do when they overran the medical post he was working in.

He was alive!

She laid her hands over her abdomen. One day they'd be together again – all four of them – and it was her job to look after their children, and wait for that day to come.

★

'I thought I'd feel completely different once we were married, but I feel the same as I did yesterday. Don't you?' Gina asked Luke as she shut the door on the bedroom she'd shared with her sisters and walked down the landing to the box room.

'I don't feel married after that Registry Office ceremony, if that's what you mean. I'm sorry, it was all a bit impersonal. I know you would have liked a white wedding with all the trimmings.'

'I couldn't have had that and a Quaker for a bridegroom, and as I didn't want anyone else, I realised from the start that it would have to be a Registry Office or living in sin. But I'm still amazed after what you told me about your father that he gave you permission to marry me.'

'It was the letter I wrote.' He stepped past her and examined the tiny box room. Anything other than meet her steady gaze. He never had been very good at lying. She retraced her steps along the landing and opened another door.

'And this is my parents' bedroom.' She glanced down the stairs. Luke's case was still standing where he'd dropped it, by the front door. They'd been in the house two hours, and as yet they hadn't even decided which bedroom they were going to occupy.

'I don't think it would be right for us to sleep in here,' he said, as he looked at the stripped mattress and dark heavy furniture.

'I agree, I'd never feel comfortable in Mama and Papa's room, but you saw the room I shared with my sisters. There's precious little space between the two double beds.'

'That leaves your brothers' room and the box room.' He moved clumsily backwards, stepping down from her parents' bedroom on to the landing. 'If you like, I could sleep in the box room until you get used to the idea of being married,' he offered nervously, remembering her reaction the time he had lost his head in the High Street café.

'Don't be silly.' Feeling as apprehensive as she sensed he was, she opened the door to her brothers' bedroom. 'The decision's made, then. I'll make up this bed.' She went to the wardrobe. 'If you carry your case up I'll hang your clothes away, and I'll move mine in here too. At least they left the room clean and tidy.'

'Do you want some help?'

'No, but I'd love a cup of tea afterwards, and if you feel like spoiling me you could make some toast.'

He went downstairs, trying to remind himself that this was his home now, and would be until he and Gina could afford a place of their own. Taking his marriage certificate from the inside pocket of his suit jacket, he read it again in an effort to convince himself it was real.

★

'Do me a favour Alexander?'

'For you, Tina, anything.' After the traumatic day, Alexander's lighthearted comment fell flat.

'Drop a note into Laura's house on your way up the hill.'

'I thought you'd moved in there?'

'I'm exhausted. If I don't sleep here tonight I'll never get up for the early-shift tram crews in the morning.'

'This has nothing to do with Dr Lewis arriving home unexpectedly?' he asked perceptively.

'Nothing,' she bit back sharply. Trevor's arrival had intensified her longing for William into an acute yearning that bordered on pain, but she had no intention of admitting or discussing her heartache with Alexander.

'What about your things? I could go up there and bring them down for you?'

'No, I'll go up tomorrow morning after the cook comes in. In fact, thinking about it, it would make sense for me to move in here rather than with Laura. Sooner or later John's going to reach that horrible crying, teething stage. At least here I can be sure of getting some rest in between opening hours.'

'There's a flat upstairs?'

'A couple of rooms. They're a bit shabby. I don't suppose you're any good at decorating?'

'I've never tried, but I'm willing to give it a go. How hard can it be?'

'Alexander?' Ieuan, the miner who worked with Evan, called out from the back room. 'Fancy a game of cards?'

'Why not?' Alexander raised his eyebrows in surprise as he picked up his tea.

'Watch it, you're in danger of becoming accepted around here,' Tina mocked.

'I can just see the headlines in next week's Pontypridd *Observer*: 'Conchie makes inroads into town's society'.'

She forced a smile as she turned to the kitchen and shouted to the cook to take over for ten minutes. Lighting a candle she walked upstairs. She pulled the blackout and examined the two cheerless rooms. There was no electricity in the upstairs of the building, but she could manage without. The walls were damp, the paint peeling, the floors filthy, but wallpaper and paint could still be bought on Ponty market, and she wasn't afraid of hard work. What furniture there was, she'd probably have to pay to have carted away, but there were plenty of pieces in Danycoedcae Road that wouldn't be missed. She could bring down one of the double beds to replace the creaking, single, iron bedstead; a dressing table and a toilet set for washing, the small wardrobe from Ronnie's room, a rug – she and Laura had found three rolled up in the attic. Ones that her mother had re-placed but never thrown out because she'd thought them 'too good' so had consigned them to cold and damp as a way of preserving them.

She walked along the dusty landing and opened the door to the second room. At the beginning of the war it had been filled with tins and boxes, but rationing had put paid to stockpiling. A couple of easy chairs from the middle room at home, another rug, a table, and perhaps an electric fire for the winter and she'd be self-sufficient, reasonably comfortable, and out of Laura's way whenever Trevor came home on leave. The only wonder was she hadn't thought of furnishing the rooms before.

Trying not to think how happy she and William could be here once she'd effected the transformation – if he ever came home again – she returned to the room with the bed, sat on the mattress and pulled the envelope Trevor had given her out of her pocket. The writing on the outside wasn't Will's. Someone, probably Trevor, had put the pieces of paper Tony had given him into envelopes. It was no more than a scrap, a single page torn from a notebook and scribbled in pencil:

I'll be home even if I have to swim the Channel. Wait for me. Love you always, Will.

The two rooms weren't much, but she was determined to turn them into a home of sorts. Was it tempting fate to hope that some day she and William would be together again?

'Please God, let it be soon,' she whispered as she pressed her hand down on the damp mattress.

'If we're going to get up in the morning it's time we went to bed.' Gina had washed the cups Luke had used to make cocoa, and tidied the kitchen and the larder. Luke had banked down the fire, swept the hearth and clipped the fireguard on to the grate. There wasn't any-thing left for either of them do, yet both of them were lingering, waiting for the other to make the first move.

'I suppose it is.' Luke averted his head lest she see his blushes as he rose from the chair where he'd been pretending to read last week's *Sunday Pictorial*.

'It feels as though nothing will ever be the same again in this house.'

Gina looked around the room, checking for the last time that she'd left nothing undone.

'It will be when your parents come home again, you'll see,' he reassured her clumsily.

'But when will that be?'

'I wish I could tell you.'

'And I wish we didn't have to get up early tomorrow.' She gave him a wry smile. 'Some honeymoon.'

'Why don't you go up first? I'll follow in a little while,' he suggested, in an attempt to avoid further embarrassment.

'No.' She reached out and took his hand in hers. 'I don't like rattling around in this big house by myself. Let's go up together.' She led the way. While she pulled the blackout in all the bedrooms, he opened the drawer she had stowed his clothes away in and removed his pyjamas.

He went downstairs to the wash-house and took his time over undressing and washing, but eventually he knew that if he delayed any longer she'd come down looking for him. Carrying his best clothes over his arm he slowly mounted the stairs.

She was lying in the middle of the double bed. He sat on the edge, and kicked off his slippers. Folding back the blankets she switched off the light. He lay beside her, keeping his arms to his side lest he accidentally touch, and startle her.

'It's customary for the groom to kiss the bride,' Gina murmured into the darkness.

'You must be tired.'

'Not that tired.' She turned to face him. Wrapping her arms around his chest she dragged him into the middle of the bed.

'I'm sorry, this just doesn't feel right.'

'If you kissed me it would be a start down the right road.'

He reached out hesitantly. Holding her face in his hands, he kissed her on the lips.

'You're shivering, come here.' She drew even closer to him. 'Are you cold?'

'I don't think so.'

He felt her fingers moving over the front of his pyjama jacket, slipping the buttons from their loops, baring his chest.

'I could take off my nightdress.'

'Not just yet . . .'

She wrapped her arms around his neck and whispered in his ear. 'There's only one thing I'm really frightened of.'

'I told you I can sleep in the box room.'

'That would only postpone things and make them worse because I'd have more time to worry. I'm absolutely terrified of doing something wrong. You will give me another chance, if I make a complete hash of this, won't you?'

He hesitated for a moment, then laughed out of sheer relief as he took her into his arms and kissed her again. Then suddenly neither of them was nervous or shivering, not even when her nightdress joined his pyjamas on the floor beside the bed.

Chapter Twenty-Three

'I'M beginning to understand the saying that you can get used to anything given time. It's true even of café work,' Bethan said to Megan as she slumped into a chair in her father's kitchen. It was the end of a long, busy day in the High Street café, and for once she was only too glad to take her aunt and Phyllis up on their offer of tea and sympathy.

'No matter what, I'll never get used to this business of not knowing what's happening to my own son.' Megan handed Rachel over to Bethan and picked up the tea caddy. 'Do you think they would have told us by now if the boys had been on the *Lancastria*?'

'According to the papers all relatives of casualties have been informed.'

'They also said there were twenty-seven thousand people on the ship.' Megan tried, and failed, to visualise that many bodies, alive or dead.

'I still think we would have heard if they'd been on board. Dad has to be right. The boys must have been taken prisoner.'

'Almost everyone seems to have heard something except the relatives of the boys in the Guards. They keep saying POW lists are going to be posted soon. When is "soon", that's what I'd like to know?'

'Soon is when the War Office decides.' Bethan's thoughts were with the casualty station in Dunkirk which must have been overrun by now.

'I wish you'd move in with us, love,' Evan said as he walked in from the wash-house and lifted down the chess set from a shelf in the alcove next to the stove. He and Alexander had fallen into the habit of playing a game every night after tea. 'The place seems empty with Diana and Luke gone. You could have your old room back.'

'I've put my name down to take evacuees, Dad. They'll be arriving any day now.'

'I suppose they will.' He started as the key turned in the lock. They all looked expectantly to the door. Megan's fingers were crossed, her eyes closed and her lips moving as if in prayer.

'Luke!' Evan greeted him in surprise. 'We weren't expecting you. Come in, sit down. How's married life treating you?'

'I came to see if Mrs Powell could go to the house.'

'Something wrong?' Alexander asked, glancing up from the chessboard he was setting out.

'We've had a telegram. Mr Ronconi's dead. Gina's taken it hard. I said I'd go down and tell Laura and Tina. I don't think Gina should be left alone while I'm gone.'

'What on earth happened?' Bethan asked, her blood running cold at the thought of Mr Ronconi dead, and Laura's mother left alone with the unruly brood of young children.

'A constable visited us, one I hadn't seen before. He said they put all the internees on a ship called the *Arandora Star*. They intended to send them to Canada for the duration. The ship went down. Torpedoed somewhere off the coast of Ireland.'

Megan put her head in her hands. 'That poor, poor woman, and the girls. How much more can they take?'

'Whatever's sent,' Evan said grimly, 'because they've no choice but to take it. Bethan?'

'I'll drive you to Laura's and we'll go from there to pick up Tina.'

'Phyllis and I will sit with Gina until you get back.' Megan took the baby from Bethan.

'Come on, Luke.' Evan abandoned the chess game and rose to his feet. 'You get back to your wife. She'll need you now, more than ever. Bethan and I will tell the girls.'

'That's it?' Laura stared disbelievingly at Huw Davies. 'My father's dead. We don't get a body, there'll be no funeral, no nothing?'

'I can't begin to tell you how sorry I am, Mrs Lewis,' Huw murmured sympathetically. 'The sergeant is arranging travel passes for all of you to visit your mother.'

'I don't want a travel pass. I want my father!'

'Tina, talk like that isn't going to help.' Father O'Donnelly rebuked her mildly. 'You have to be strong, for your sisters, your mama, the little ones – '

'Strong!' She glared at him, eyes blazing. 'That's easy for you to say. How do you think I feel with Angelo and Mama God knows where, and Laura, Gina and I left to run everything by ourselves? And now Papa won't even be coming home . . .'

'Were there any others from Pontypridd on the ship?' Laura asked.

Huw nodded. 'We were sent a list.'

'The same one you used to arrest them?'

303

'Tina, it's not Constable Davies's fault,' Father O'Donnelly intervened again. He was bone weary, sick, tired, and despairing. This was the sixth house he'd visited to offer condolences and professional services, there were twelve more waiting, and he'd seen the same anger and bitterness in every one. A stony-hearted, arid bitterness that he had so far failed to ease for all his faith and prayers.

'Four hundred and eighty-six Italians and a hundred and seventy-five Germans went down with the ship.' Huw repeated the statistics bleakly in the hope that Laura, Tina and Gina would understand just how impossible it would be to locate one body amongst so many.

'When will we be able to go and see Mama?' Laura asked.

'Tomorrow,' Huw promised.

'Tell them to keep their travel warrants,' Tina countered angrily. 'We want nothing from a country that can kill our father, wound one brother and lose another.'

'I think it's more important you see your mama, Tina, than give way to sinful pride,' Father O'Donnelly reproached.

Huw stared at the ceiling, hoping that the girls wouldn't find out that it wasn't the government that was paying for the travel warrants, but the town's businessmen who were wretchedly ashamed of the way the Italians had been treated.

'What's going to happen to the cafés if we all go to Birmingham?' Gina asked, tearfully.

'We'll close them,' Tina decided abruptly. 'Let people get their tea elsewhere for a change.'

'I doubt there'll be a single café open in town or the Rhondda tomorrow,' Father O'Donnelly said. 'I just hope, and pray that all the Italian families can find it in their hearts to forgive those responsible for sinking the *Arandora Star*.'

'I don't know about that, Father,' Laura said evenly. 'It's a lot to forgive, and I don't just mean the Germans.'

'Well I, for one, didn't expect them to come back and carry on as though nothing had happened.'

'What did you expect Laura, Tina and Gina to do then, Mrs Jones?' Jenny added details of the small pile of items on the counter to Dai Station's wife's tab.

'I don't know, but it's peculiar to think Mr Ronconi's gone, just like that. One minute he's here, the next he's taken away, and –'

'It's three weeks since the *Arandora Star* went down, Mrs Jones,' Huw Davies addressed Dai Station's wife as he walked into Griffiths's shop. 'I think it would be better for everyone concerned if we tried to stop talking about the tragedy. When all's said and done, there's nothing any of us can do to right a terrible wrong.'

'You're probably right, constable. If we stop talking about it, they might forget . . .'

'Oh I don't think they're going to forget, Mrs Jones. Not in a million years.' Huw slapped two shillings down on to the counter and nodded towards the cigarette shelf. Jenny took the money and handed him a packet of Players.

'I noticed Tony Ronconi didn't come back from Birmingham with the girls.'

'Probably because he wanted to spend whatever leave he has with his mother.'

'Say what you like,' Mrs Richards chipped in, 'those Italians know how to look after themselves. Tony Ronconi's the only Welsh Guardsman to find his way back to Pontypridd.'

'Because he was shot, Mrs Richards,' Huw pointed out forcefully.

'I don't see our Glan home, or your Will if it comes to that.'

'Or Tony's brother Angelo?'

The bell clanged and Bert Browne walked through the door. Jenny glanced up at the clock. 'Second post is early today.'

'I'm sorry, Jenny.' He held out a small yellow envelope. Jenny stared at it, but made no move to take it from him.

'Look after the shop,' Huw ordered Bert. Opening the door that connected with the living quarters he took the envelope from Bert, placed his strong hand on Jenny's arm and led her out of the shop and up the stairs.

'It's Eddie, I know it's Eddie.' She touched the telegram in his hand.

'You won't know until you open it, girl, and the last thing you should do is read it in front of that audience.' He walked her to the sofa in the living room and pushed her gently down on to the seat, laying the telegram in her lap.

'Please, stay with me.'

He stood and watched as she picked up the envelope and turned it over. She clung to a wild irrational thought that as long as the envelope remained closed, Eddie would be alive. She sat staring at it while seconds ticked past on the grandmother clock in the corner.

'Do you want me to open it for you?'

Without looking at Huw she pushed her thumb into the flap and tore at the paper.

She stared down at the words, reading and rereading them without comprehension. Huw stepped forward and looked over her shoulder.

DEEPLY REGRET TO INFORM YOU GUARDSMAN EDWARD JAMES PO-
WELL HAS BEEN KILLED IN ACTION. ARMY COUNCIL DESIRE TO OFFER
YOU THEIR SINCERE SYMPATHY (.) = UNDER SECRETARY OF STATE
FOR WAR

'I'm sorry, Huw.' Huw turned to see Bert standing in the doorway.
'I've sent the customers away and closed the shop. I have to be on my
way.'

'Of course, I'll see you out.'

'I'm really sorry,' the postman apologised again as Huw walked him
down the stairs. He held up a second telegram.

'Will?' Huw asked, his chest tight with grief.

The postman nodded.

'Anyone else I should know about?'

'Not yet, but they're still coming in. The first POW lists have been
posted. Dr John's on them, Angelo Ronconi and Glan Richards too.'

Huw knew he should have given thanks for small mercies, but he
couldn't, not with Jenny sitting upstairs and his sister waiting in Graig
Avenue for the bombshell that was going to shatter her life.

For weeks after the POW lists had been posted and the trickle of men
from Dunkirk had dried up, Huw Davies timed his beat so he would
be within hailing distance of the railway station every time a train
chugged into Pontypridd; especially the early morning milk and late
evening trains.

Everyone in the police station knew what Huw was doing, but the
sergeant refrained from passing comment. There was no point in
telling Huw it was over when it was common knowledge that the war
in Europe was finished. The men who weren't dead, and hadn't been
lucky enough to climb aboard a rescue boat, were all heading for
prison camps under German armed guard.

The whole civilian population of Britain was making an all-out
effort to put the tragedy of Dunkirk behind them and prepare for the
invasion that was expected any day. Everyone that is except those like
Huw, and the Powell and Ronconi families, who couldn't bring
themselves to look to the future because the pull of the past and their
grief was too strong.

Instead of immersing himself in sandbags and ARP duty, Huw
continued to haunt the railway station, and the sergeant couldn't find
it in his heart to blame him. Not when he saw the wretched, anguished expression in Evan, Megan and Diana Powell's eyes, and the
swift disintegration of Jenny Powell's and Tina Ronconi's youth and

beauty, or the long-suffering look on the faces of women like Bethan Powell who had been doubly hit, by the death of a brother and the loss of a husband she had no idea when, if ever, she'd see again.

What was cruellest of all, was the way in which the families the sergeant had known and lived among for so many years had lost their men. One day they'd marched away to war, then came letters and finally a small yellow envelope, then nothing. No body – no funeral – no mourning – no absolute, conclusive certainty; only vague rumours of men who had served in the last war and been pronounced dead to reappear months, sometimes years later. Rumours the women repeated and tried to believe, because that was all they had left.

But when Megan dared to say to her brother that she didn't believe William was dead, Huw told her sternly that mistakes didn't happen; not in this war when communications were so much more advanced than they had been the last time round and identification disks were made of sterner stuff than the pressed, varnished cardboard he had worn in the trenches.

But for all the lectures Huw delivered to his sister, and the long, mutually supportive conversations he had with Wyn Rees who was doing his best to comfort his wife and mother-in-law, Huw's step still turned towards the Tumble whenever he heard a train rattling into town.

Somewhere deep inside him lay the same small germ of futile hope that kept the Powell family going through bleak days and sleepless nights. A desperate belief that, one day, his nephew and Eddie would return.

It was darkest between the hours of three and four in the morning: the time Huw reserved for checking under the railway bridge that marked the beginning of the Graig hill so he could listen to the engine of the milk train rattle in on the tracks overhead.

It had been over three weeks since the telegrams had arrived with news of William's and Eddie's deaths, and Huw still couldn't stop himself from thinking about the boys every waking moment. The second he opened his eyes in the morning, he remembered, and grief, like a lump of stone, dogged every step he took during the days that followed. And for all his protestations to the contrary, deep down he knew he was no nearer to accepting the news than his sister, Diana and Tina, or Evan, Jenny and Bethan were to accepting the idea that Eddie and William had gone.

Huw wanted to make them understand that they would never see the boys again, but it was an impossible task when he himself expected to see Eddie and William's faces around every corner in the town.

He left the shelter of the short tunnel and glanced to the left. A shadow moved out from the black hole that concealed the wide, stone flight of steps that led to the platforms. A tall figure moved out of the gloom into station yard, the inevitable khaki battledress picked out in the moonlight.

Huw moved closer, expecting to see one of the wounded survivors from Dunkirk home on a twenty-four-hour pass. Then he stood and stared, and stared again.

'Will . . . Is it really you, boy?' he whispered, half expecting the apparition to fade like a ghost.

'Can't keep a bad penny from turning up, Uncle Huw, thought you would have learned that by now.'

The voice was William's but there was none of the jauntiness he remembered. 'Good God, boy, where have you been?'

'Hell and back.' William pulled a packet of cigarettes out of his pocket and offered them to his uncle before lighting one.

'I can believe it, by the look of you. Come here, sit on the wall for a minute. I can't imagine what your mother and Diana are going to say to this.'

'Eddie's dead,' Will said briefly.

'We had telegrams telling us you were both dead. Trevor said the Guards were fighting the rearguard.'

'We were. Captain gave us orders to surrender. We laid down our arms, the buggers collected them, rounded us up and shot us where we stood. Bloody SS unit, we didn't stand a chance. They opened fire without warning. Eddie fell right next to me. I couldn't believe it . . .' He closed his eyes and gripped his cigarette so hard it broke in two. 'Sometimes I still think the whole bloody massacre was a nightmare. All I have to do is wake up and they'll be alive. But I'll never see Eddie or the others again, Uncle Huw. None of us will. Eddie was standing right next to me and all I could do was watch him die . . .'

The clouds shifted and moonlight fell full on William's face. It was then Huw saw the bandage on his head.

'You were shot?'

'We all were. The only difference is I'm alive, and they're dead.'

'How did you escape?'

'The Germans left us where we lay. They ordered the French villagers to bury us. When they realised I wasn't dead they hid me, then got me to the coast. I waited a couple of weeks before begging a ride on a trawler.' William dropped the remains of his cigarette and ground it into dust with the toe of his boot. He opened his cigarette packet again with a shaking hand only to discover it was empty.

'Here, have a Player,' Huw offered.

'When are you going to start smoking a brand I like?'

'These are better?' Huw looked at the packet in William's hand.

'Someone gave them to me when I reported to a police station in Devon this morning. You know I haven't even been debriefed properly. They tried to do it, but I screamed and shouted until they gave me a twenty-four-hour pass. I have to report to base camp tomorrow.'

'Tell you what,' Huw squinted at his watch. 'By my reckoning it's somewhere close to three. How about I go up the Graig when I finish my shift at six and prepare your mam by telling her you're still in one piece. I'll get Diana and Wyn to go up there too, then, when the taxis start running at seven or so, you can go home and see them for yourself.'

'Everyone really thought I was dead?'

'Yes.'

'Everyone? Di, Tina . . .'

'Everyone.'

'Oh God what a mess.'

'You need some sleep, boy, and across the road there's a young lady who might give you a hot drink, some comfort and a bed for a couple of hours.'

'Tina's in the café?'

'She's living there now.'

'But how . . .'

'This is no time for explanations, boy. Go on, off with you.'

'You'll see Mam and Diana?'

'I promise.'

William rose to his feet, straightened his dirty jacket and ruefully rubbed the stubble on his chin as he crossed the square. When he reached the café he knocked lightly on the door.

'You're going to have to bang louder than that, boy,' Huw advised as he turned his steps towards the town.

William knocked again. A sleepy voice shouted, 'Whoever you are, we're not open, so go away.'

'I've got a present to deliver.'

The blackout blind lifted, a head appeared in the window and Tina looked down, blinking at the moonlight. Her lips moved, but William didn't hear a sound. She disappeared. Seconds later bolts grated back and the door opened.

'It's you,' she whispered hoarsely. 'It's really you?'

'It's really me. Please, love, stop crying. I told you I'd be back.'

She dragged him inside and switched on the light, for once forgetting all about the blackout regulations.

'You're filthy, you look as though you haven't washed in a month . . .'

'It's probably nearer two,' he confessed wryly.

'They said you were dead . . .'

'Pinch me. I promise I'm not a ghost.'

'. . . and you promised me a present.' She was too shocked to realise what she was saying.

'So I did.' He put his hand inside his battledress and pulled out a handful of cream silk edged with lace. 'You're lucky to have them, there were times when I was so bloody cold I nearly put them on myself.'

She flung her arms around his neck, burying her head in his shoulder so he wouldn't see her tears.

'In return, I asked you to give me a fashion show, remember?'

'Not down here. Oh damn, the blackout.'

'You've learned to swear.'

'And a whole lot more besides. Oh God, Will,' she pulled the curtain across the door and leaned against it, staring at him. 'I thought I'd lost you.'

'Me? Never!' He smiled, and the sensation felt strange, as though he hadn't had anything to smile about in years.

'Come upstairs.' She took him by the hand.

'I need to hold you.' He wrapped his arms around her, as though he never intended to let go. 'Just for a little while.'

'And then?'

'And then I'll love you, for ever.' He looked down into her dark tear-stained eyes, 'and ever.'

Author's Notes

THE characters in *Such Sweet Sorrow* are creations of my imagination. The traumatic events they lived through are not. The round-up of innocent Italian-born businessmen in Wales is just one of the infinite number of tragedies and injustices of the Second World War. Prior to the internment of Italian nationals, there were several incidents of looting and affray in Italian-owned cafés across Wales.

The Pontypridd *Observer* of 20 January 1940 recounts just such an incident when a haulier tipped furniture over in Marenghi's Bridge Street Café in Pontypridd. (How we miss it, and its jukebox since it was demolished to make way for the Taff Street precinct development in the sixties.)

Forty-nine men born in and around Bardi and the Ceno Valley in Italy (the area from which the majority of Welsh café owners came) died on the *Arandora Star*. Nearly all of them were arrested in Wales. No one who knew them would believe for an instant that they were Fascist sympathisers. Most had sons and brothers fighting in the British army, or with the Italian Resistance. The Italian home of at least one man was marked as a safe haven on a map (without his permission or knowledge) given to RAF personnel prior to flying missions over Italy.

It says a great deal for the spirit of the families of the Italians who were interned or killed on the *Arandora Star*, that practically all of them returned to Wales either during, or after the war. They continued to run their cafes, picked up the threads of their lives, and were gratefully accepted back into the community. I have yet to find a single Italian/Welsh family that bears a grudge or harbours bitterness for what they endured during those difficult years.

Several families forcibly moved from their Welsh homes at a moment's notice were forced to hand over their businesses to friends and neighbours. At the end of the war those same friends and neighbours handed the restaurants and cafés back, complete with accurate accounts, and weekly banking sheets.

There is eyewitness evidence that Welsh Guardsmen, men of the

2nd Norfolk Battalion and other British units were massacred in separate incidents during the retreat from France in May/June 1940 after surrendering their weapons to invading soldiers of the SS Regiments of the army of the Third Reich.

Only one SS officer, Oberstürmfuhrer Fritz Knoechlein of the 4th Company, 2nd Totenkopf Infantry Regiment of the SS, was tried and found guilty of committing the war crime of massacring unarmed, surrendering British troops-(principally on the evidence of French civilian eyewitnesses who saw the incident at Paradis, Pas-de-Calais, France on or about 27 May 1940).

He was subsequently hanged at Hamburg in 1948. Knoechlein was involved in the killing of about ninety disarmed POWs, members of the 2nd Battalion the Royal Norfolk Regiment, and other British units. Despite eyewitness evidence and a television documentary which named him, as well as detailing his crimes, the SS officer commanding the troops who massacred the disarmed Welsh Guards during the retreat from France in 1940 has never been brought to trial. He lives in comfortable retirement in Germany to this day.